I0761832

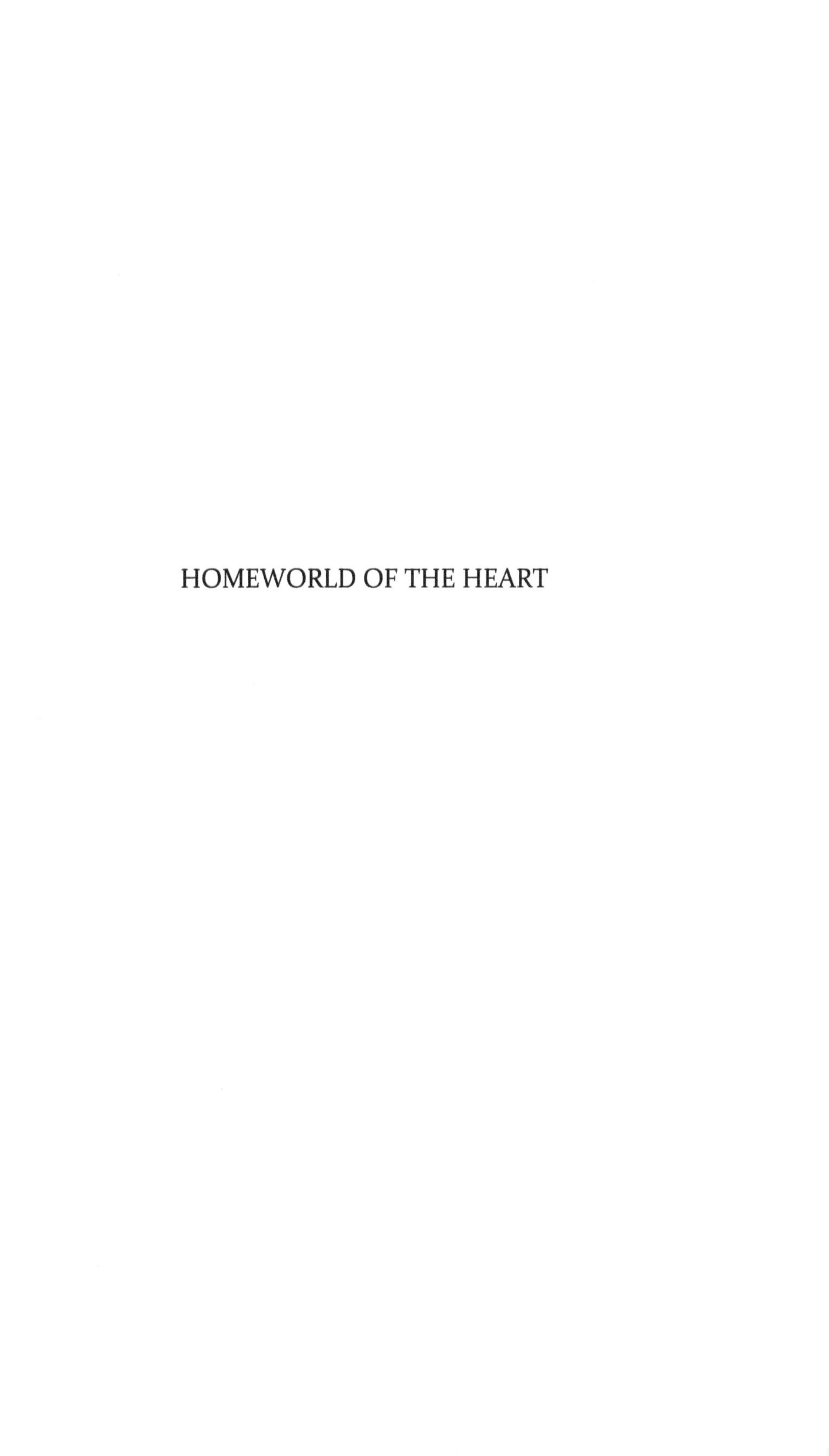

HOMEWORLD OF THE HEART

CHRONICLES OF THE HIGH INQUEST

Homeworld of the Heart

by S.P. Somtow

with drawings by Mikey Jiraros

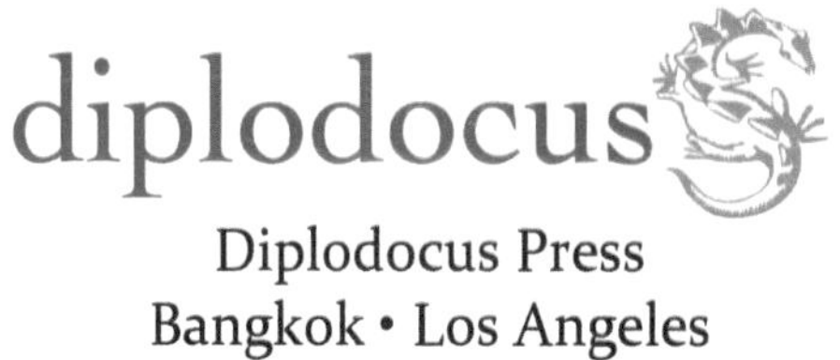

Diplodocus Press
Bangkok • Los Angeles

DIPLODOCUS PRESS
Los Angeles • Bangkok
ISBN: Hardcover 978-1940999-44-9
Trade Paperback 978-1940999-50-0
ePub 978-1940999-51-7

Portions of this novel have previous appeared in magazine form in *Inquestor Tales,* published by Diplodocus Press.

illustrations by Mikey Jiraros

FIRST EDITION
10 9 8 7 6 5 4 3 2 1

my supporters at patreon.com
gave me the encouragement and inspiration
to resurrect my science fiction career after
three decades of silence.

On Christmas, 2019. the following people were my supporters and I want to dedicate this book to you all by name (names as listed on patreon)

Alan Newhouse • Andrew and Kate Barton
Azuregryphon • Björn Lindstrom • Carol Kennedy
Conrad Wong • Dave Nee • David Bellamy •
David Stewart Zink • Deborah Wunder •
Eric Mellencamp • Fritz Goss • Gregory Scharpen •
Hunter Johnson • Janneke Bomhoff •
Jason Sanford • Jeff Bennett • Joey Shoji • Johne Cooke • Jon Singer
• Judith Bemis • Kathleen Reeves •
Kit Mason • Leota Wagner • Marian Phillips •
Marianne Aldrich • Mark Sieber • Mary Kaiulani Kunz • Matt Hoffman • Michael Henry • Michael Stevens • Michael Vilain •
Mickey Wongsathapornpat • R. Laurraine Tutihasi • Mthierst •
Nancy Lebovitz • Naomi Stone • Pantawit Kiangsiri • Paul Spurrier • Paula Goodman •
Peggy Dolan • Pongsathorn Surapab •
Pravit Rojanaphruk • quatermasss •
Richard Knowles • Sebastian Linn • Steve Platt •
Thaithow Sucharitkul • Thomas Banker •
The Plaid Mentat • Vanina Sucharitkul • Vincent Poirier •
Dina Al-Kassim

feel free to visit www.patreon.com/spsomtow
Somtow's website: www.somtow.com

HOMEWORLD OF THE HEART

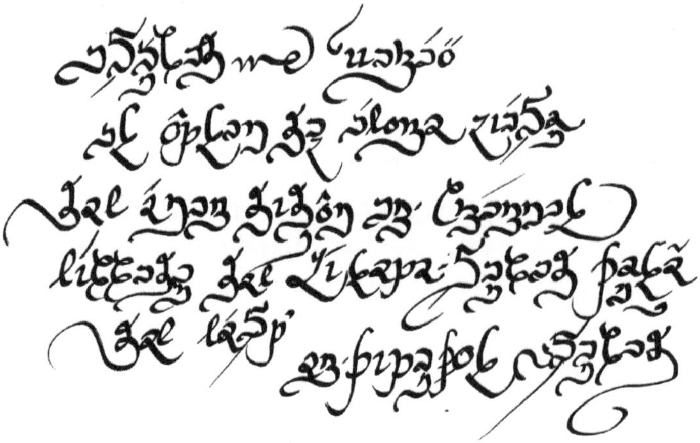

evéndek evéndek hyeméo
et órten kes éluma sieváh
kal ánem kikrón em-zmémnet
líddeken kal chítara 'vendek shãtráh
kal lavr' ã-shirénzhut evéndek

Always, always, I come home
to a place that the spirit knows
though the mind has long forgotten;
to a song that the heart still sings
though the lips have been silenced forever.

— from the Songs of Sajit

Prologue
Sajittang

... and there was also a village named Sajittang ...

•••

... far from the great central worlds of the Dispersal ... at the opposite end of the galaxy from Uran s'Varek, the sphere of the Inquestors that surrounds the black hole at the galaxy's heart, where the stars are packed so thick that their scattered light, through thousands of klomets of atmosphere, blends and blurs to a seamless radiance ... whose thinkhive contains the thoughts of a billion billion souls ...

... far from Gallendys with its pyramidal twin cities stacked one upon the other like cones of pinwheel fire, where the windbringers fly blindly and sing music of searing light ...

... far from Shtoma, where they dance on the face of the sun ...

... far from Aëroësh, where the dust is alive and the living turn to dust ...

... far from Periput, from Bellares, from Billoras, from Bellbaros, from Anthalafré and Ugoradé, from the chimes of Chembrith, from the feasting fields of Fiünn and the forever forests of Fáraklanth ...

Sajittang was the only village on this world; a single pair of displacement plates linked it with a starport, to which few pilgrims came. When they came, they would come to the shrine in Sajittang, where an old whisperlyre lay on a plinth beneath a protective forceshield.

This shrine, this starport, should not even exist, for the world has *fallen beyond.* But pilgrims did come, from time to time, and they would visit the whisperlyre, guarded by orphaned srinjids, and they would meditate a while, or kiss the barrier of force as if to get closer to the whisperlyre, or try to write a poem as they sat in the village square.

A ball of rock played host to many names, to many civilizations ... all of them ... now *fallen beyond.* Who would come here, who would even know about this place?

Yet one day, there came a visitor more important than any who had come before....

***

Varezhdur, palace of dreams, hung in the night sky like a spindle trailing threads of gold, eclipsing the moons themselves. And from the palace a floater delicately descended.

An old man flanked by srinjids watched. The old man had waited all his life for this moment to come.

He knew that one day a floater would come, and who would be riding it. What surprised him was that the man was alone. It was a figure he dared not look at closely; to gaze such a one directly in the eyes had been known to bring immediate execution. But he was alone. There was not even a quartet of childsoldiers guarding the four corners of the railings, the minimum escort for one of such power.

The floater moved in a completely straight line, though there was a wind, whispering as it scattered dead leaves over the flagstones.

"Now," said the old man to the srinjids, "begin your song."

Childlike, one srinjid spoke and another answered. The two voices harmonized almost without intent. From a hut behind the shrine, another voice came, then another, speaking of inconsequential things, yet each inconsequently snippet of speech was an ornament, a trill, a heterophonous melisma woven into an overarching music.

The srinjid's song was of necessity complete; their city on Uran s'Varek long destroyed, but a handful of refugees had been rescued. Here, in Sajittang, they thrived, but their song was not a perfect melding of a million voices; it was the ghost of a song, a snatch here, an echo there; it was a memory of what was once beautiful, not the beautiful thing itself. Yet it had its own melancholy beauty, even in its imperfection.

The floater touched the flagstones of the square, old stucco stained with age, veined with a purple moss from which one could distill a *zul*-like liquor. The old man had not seen any pilgrims for a long time, years; this was no ordinary pilgrim. The floater's skin dissolved. The old man prostrated himself. It was a moment he had rehearsed for all his life, yet now that it had come, there was an emptiness to it; the time when such gestures had meaning was long past.

Through unkempt white strands of his own hair, the old man saw the shadow of a shimmercloak. The coruscating pink against deep blue. The cloak that was a living thing, gliding, flowing, intertwining flesh. And feet; immaculately manicured, bare, but painted with protective shieldskin; this Inquestor was old, too, but for an Inquestor, to be old is different different.

"Hokh'Ton," the old man mumbled, then waited to be spoken to.

"What are you called?" Strangely high-pitched, a child's voice, almost, though the flesh was withered.

"I am Tash Toléon," he replied, "of the Clan of Rememberers. I guard the tomb of Shen Sajit, the voice of the cosmos."

"Stand, Tolé," said the Inquestor. "My feet do not have ears, and I'm too old to bend down to your level."

Toléon motioned for one of the srinjids to bring a stool. Another fetched some of the juice of the moss. "Forgive me," Tash Toléon said. "Seeing you in the flesh—"

"So you know my name," the Inquestor said.

"Of course. You are hokh'Ton Ton Elloran n'Taanyel Tath, Lord of Varezhdur."

"What else do you know?"

"That you knew Shen Sajit when you were children. That you showed him favor beyond all measure. It was even said that he was your lover."

And Ton Elloran smiled a little at that, saying only, "Love has a million shapes."

For a while Elloran listened to the singing of the srinjids. "I didn't know the remnants of that city were here," he said. "It is ... painful to hear. You never heard their singing city, of course."

"No, hokh'Ton."

"It's like hearing a ghost."

"Everything on this world is a ghost," said Toléon. "Including myself, for I exist only to be your rememberer."

He nodded to the nearest srinjid and the song began to die away. *Perhaps,* he thought, *I should not have made them sing. The Inquestor will be sad.*

"More sad than you can imagine," the Inquestor said, as though he had heard Toléon's thoughts. "You don't know how their city was annihilated. You cannot understand Arryk's rage at my love for a shortliver."

Toléon still avoided the Inquestor's gaze, but he could sense that he was looking away. He dared to look up a little.

The Inquestor was looking at the whisperlyre, that relic, that object of occasional worship, locked in a dome of force. Presently he ordered the old man to unlock the dome.

Toléon muttered a subvocalization that may not be revealed, and he was able to reach in and touch the relic. It has strange, he thought, that he had never touched it in his life. There was a kind of tension behind the field; when it dissolved, dust seemed to settle on the instrument, where before it had been suspended in a quasi-vacuum. He brought the instrument to the Inquestor, kneeling to present it. When Elloran touched it, there came a wheezing, jangling sound and a sudden rainbow flash that dissipated into a white mist.

"You should leave us, perhaps," said the Inquestor.

And Tash Toléon saw that the godlike being was weeping. "An Inquestor—"

"Does not weep!" Elloran said softly, yet did not cease to weep. "Do you still think I am what you thought me? Do you not know that I have cast aside my power, given away the worlds I owned? Even Varezhdur is not mine; I gave the palace that sails through space to Ton Siriss; I travel by Varezhdur only through her grace, because she did not want me completely cut off from the life I knew."

Toléon saw that the old Inquestor could not be comforted, certainly not by a Remember's words. So, as unobtrusively as possible, he left; and there he was, an old weeping man in shimmercloak, on a stool on a lonely planet, clutching an instrument that had not played in a century or two.

***

Subjectively he was no more immortal than any of the trillions of the timebound. Yet Elloran had spent so much time in the space between spaces that to a man such as this Rememberer he must have seemed eternal. How often had he travelled from one world to another, to return and find the first world *fallen beyond?*

Even so, as his hands held the leathery frame of his old friend's whisperlyre, he could imagine what it was like to live in little steps, to grow old, to die, in a heartbeat. Those moments were a heartbeat away. *The meeting in the bowels of a doomed starship. The journey to find the Rainbow King, and the hunting of the first utopia. The voyage to the world of the dust-sculptress, who love dust more than she could love an Inquestor.* And all those momentous events framed in the songs of Shen Sajit.

My life was lived in earshot of Sajit's great poetry, Elloran thought. *Sometimes all Varezhdur resonated in sympathy to the plucking of a single string of the whisperlyre.*

He moved his hand over the strings. Only a jangle came forth. He touched the fingerboard, still sensitive; it responded to the slightest change in pressure with a cascade of color, for, like the shimmercloak he wore, it was on some level a conscious being. It knew that the one who touched it was not Sajit.

***

... a bone-thin boy, laughing ...

The streets of Aírang, city of pleasures. Turning a corner. The smell of mulled *zul* from an unseen alley. Dancing pteratygers in the sky, images woven by giant dreamweavers clamped to the tops of minarets ...

Elloran stirred. It was one of the images that came to him often now, though it could not be a true memory. So often Sajit had spoken of growing up in the streets of the pleasure city. But Elloran had not known Sajit in those days. Only later, when they had come together, in adulthood, to forget things that cannot be forgotten.

The whisperlyre clattered on the flagstones.

Blurred light. A buzzing sound. The strings, perhaps, or insects of the night. Then the servant of the shrine, that fawning Rememberer, was back, with a tray of fruit and pastries.

"Forgive me, hokh'Ton. I know you requested aloneness, but...."

"Yes, yes. Where does one lodge in this village?"

"There is an Inquestral guest-house. It has never been used."

"We shall go there."

"But first, hokh'Ton, there is something I must tell you."

"You have something to tell me? Curious."

"Yes, Lord. For the whole Dispersal knows that you knew Sajit as you know yourself. And the whole Dispersal knows the stories and calls them true: songs about them are sung, actors play the bard and the Inquestor in operas, in servocorpse dramas. We know of the hunting of your first utopia, of the pursuit of the woman in the dust, of the building of Shentrazjit and creation of the srinjid symphony; of Sajit's death and Arryk's rage and of your grief that lasted a century and more. And it is known throughout the Dispersal of Man that one day you come to this village and sit in front of this shrine."

Elloran listened, for the last sentence he had not heard before. And now he listened intently.

"I was given the duty of waiting for you," said Toléon, "as was my father before me, and *his* father. Because of this duty, my grandfather elected not to be taken up into a people bin when our world was selected to *fall beyond.* And he waited in this sanctuary, knowing one day you must return."

"And I have," Elloran said. "But what must you tell me?"

"I must tell you, hokh'Ton, that everything you ever knew about Sajit was ... inaccurate."

"Do you mock me?"

"Never, my Lord. But I must first speak to you of *meúr.*"

"Is it a local word?"

"Yes, hokh'Ton. The people of this world have clung to beliefs that perhaps predate the Inquestors themselves ... and one of these is *meúr.* It is the idea that the thread of time is spun not once, but a near infinitude of times, and each thread branches and branches again, so that everything that is possible is also, on some level, fact; and *meúr,* hokh'Ton, is the places where the myriad threads conjoin, and the possible changes converge to a singularity."

"Powers of powers! The riddles you speak in are more opaque than a game of *makrúgh!*"

"Then, Lord Inquestor, simply believe me when I tell you that when you crossed the world of the dead to confront the heretic Inquestor, the one who shared your journey was not Shen Sajit. When you quarreled over a woman, your rival was not Sajit ... or, perhaps, he was, but at times he was not. It was not Sajit for whom you made the singing city, nor Sajit whose body you sent there, swooping down in his golden hearse, to be interred in song. Sajit lives, though he does not live. You shall see him again, you shall see him yet you shall not see him. Because, Ton Elloran n'Taanyel Tath, I am here to be the memory you never had. I am here to speak of the Sajit you never saw. Because, my Lord, there were *two Sajits.*"

"Two Sajits?

"At the very least, hokh'Ton."

***

And thus it was that Tash Toléon began to speak of a boy named Sajit. And because he was a trained Rememberer, the boy sprang to life in the telling, and Elloran saw everything he thought true torn up, sundered, reassembled into another truth.

"Once upon a time," he began, "the name of this world, which now has no name, but only a set of coordinates, was Alykh, and it was a planet of great pleasure cities. In this city an orphan beggar boy named Sajit lived, singing in the marketplace with a broken whisperlyre, until one day ...

"Ah, but before that pleasure planet, in the same cooridnates, there was a world named Urna, a world of few pleasures, and fewer cities; mostly there were villages, tiny, impoverished. And in one those villages there lived a boy named Sajit, "

***

So the telling began. To hear the Rememberer's voice was to gaze into a mirror with no edge, and to see the mirror mirrored and re-mirrored, unto infinity.

And the mirror of the mirror's mirror was the soul's soul's soul.

Book One

The Singing Moons

kurdát eís, kẽs ánym mi sheshãitráih
sarnáng ánem óm, eníng élash ssyusuráih

You are the string that my breath sets singing
I am the air that your lyre makes to whisper

— *from the Songs of Sajit*

One
Attembris

A chill gray space....

A pool of light in a deep dark forest ...

In the dream it is always the same, the same circle of attenuated starlight, the same musk-drenched odor of *vanjeris* leaves, the same breeze, barely felt, bearing the scent of a lost city. And the singing moons.

The place can be visited only in dreams because like so many places he has known, it has *fallen beyond* in the great game that is played between those near-immortals whose caprices control the destinies of the million worlds of the Dispersal of Man. And when a world has *fallen beyond,* it lives only in song, and song belongs to the poets alone.

But oh, oh, oh, the poet cries, I want to enter that circle once again, to touch the silky strands of the *vanjeris* and see the rosella petals dancing in the breeze, in the column of chill gray light. And he dreams again. And dreaming he returns always to this place....

The place he dreams of is just outside the village of Attembris. And where is Attembris? you may well ask. For the place does not live anymore, not even in song and story. Yet for one man it is the very center of his homeworld, the homeworld of the heart.

The village itself was barely deserving of that name, being a mere cluster of houses around a displacement plate that linked to the central square of a slightly larger village, whose square in turn was linked to that of an abandoned temple. Abandoned, for religion had not been in vogue for some centuries. Except. of course, the religion of love, for Aërat rules all things.

Once, when he was much younger, he had set foot in that temple. That's where he first saw the woman cloaked in shadow.

The way she looked at him ... she was close to him ... in a way that even his own mother was not.

"Who are you?" he asked her.

But she did not answer, and indeed, when he looked again, she was gone.

From time to time, he dreamed of her. They were, mostly, beautiful dreams — elusive, evanescent. But sometimes she appeared in a nightmare.

***

The nightmare ... more real than a dream. Perhaps it is a memory.

... the whole village has been rousted from their beds. They are standing a circle, underneath the moons. A woman is holding a baby, rocking it, cooing to it.

In the center of the circle another baby lies on the ground. No one comforts it. No one coos to it.

The villagers stare —

Their eyes, stony, implacable.

It is meúr, they say. That is to say, the fate that can never be fled from. The fate that waits to swallow you, when you're tired of resisting.

His gaze darts from face to face.

Slowly, the feet, stomping, the rhythmic chanting:

Life is sacred.

Life is one.

Life is not two.

Two is abomination.

And he too is chanting. His feet too are pounding the dense-packed earth. Bare feet, slamming against dirt ... pain shooting up his legs ... a pain and an emptiness.

Sometimes, in the dream, the mother hands her baby to another, and picks up a rock, and hurls it at the child in the center of the circle.

Harám! they are shouting. *Abomination!* And they all start stoning the child.

Sometimes he wakes up now, but at other times he too picks up a stone. Smashes the child's face. And they're all laughing, these villages, a laughter shaped from nervousness and hate.

Sometimes, the dream becomes a blur, and someone steps into the circle and scoops up the baby and scurries away; a woman cloaked in shadow.

Sometimes no one comes.

***

Their house was the last house in the village, just outside the gate. The gate opened out onto a pathway, but that pathway was subsumed in moss and weeds, for pathways too were no longer in fashion since the network of displacement plates had become operational.

From the boy's bedroom, the forest was but a single step away. Thus, darkness and mystery were always within his reach.

Since he could barely walk, he had learned to go there when he was afraid, or if he felt haunted by one recurring nightmare in particular ... or when he simply needed to be alone. He had learned to count the thickets until the spaces broadened and there was a ring of stones, perhaps made by men, or left behind by the Inquestors, perhaps even from the time before there were humans in this world.

When he came to this place, he could always hear the music. Especially when at least three of the moons were full. It seemed to him that the moons could sing. It was a manystranded singing. Each of the moons had a separate voice. They sang in a pure and absolute harmony, making chords that he had never heard from the village choir, when they met each tennight to sing the *Dhelyá Sarnáng,* the anthem to the High Inquest.

And what did the moons say to him?

They said: *You are not who you think you are. You are a different person. This is not your world.*

It was only when he was a little bit older, that he realized the singing came from within his own mind. That other people did not hear the music the way he did. And that he could reproduce that music at times, making new sounds that the world has never known. He could pluck the sounds from his mind and make any instrument repeat them, whether it was the panorchestrion in the village square or the old whisperlyre that had been his grandfather's, or even a bunch of twigs and an ystrell-skin stretched over a jar. They called it a gift.

Because of this gift, they told him, we have to protect you. You cannot be called the way other children are called. We're going to have to find a way to hide you when they come for you.

"But why will they come for me? Who are they, that I must be so afraid?"

"You don't need to know that yet." That somehow always ended the conversation.

For the world that the boy lived in was a safe world that had few terrors. Children were not afraid. They played all night and knew nothing of demons, ghosts, or vile spirits. On the whole, the people of his world were warm and openhearted. It was not a world that had frequent wars or conflicts. In a way, it was a world that verged on Utopia.

But the boy learned very young that the word *utopia* was not to be uttered. It could not even be thought. For the edge of utopia was a good thing, but beyond that edge lay annihilation. A utopia would always, one day, *fall beyond.* The boy had learned in school that "the breaking of joy is the beginning of wisdom." Everyone knew that.

He may have been too young to wander around in the forest late at night, but there were times when he could not help himself. They were the times of strange, disturbing dreams; of twisting and turning; of wondering about the things that the adults would not speak of.

In the night, in the forest, in the clearing, by the gray misshapen boulders, in the light of the dancing moons, that was music. That night he heard the music so clearly that he thought a visiting *klazmurah* might be in the vicinity. They did come to the village from time to time, on the way to a bigger city, to a princeling's court, even on the way to the residence of the High Inquestral Legate. But no. There was no one else there. This music was in the air itself, was woven from strands of the shifting moonlights, and the wisps of mist. And yet, he could even pick out a line or two of melody, weaving in and out of the unearthly harmonies.

He could almost hear the words.

And before he knew it, the words were leaving his lips, words barely understood, yet fully formed.

Den Táthes eyáh
Den Sírana.

The words he formed were words of the Highspeech, a language no one spoke, but which you had to learn in school. He sang about the trees and the wind and the dancing moons; the intertwining harmonies he heard enveloped him, buoyed up the song with its meandering melismas. Surely this was an ancient music such as might be heard streaming from a malfunctioning song cube.

It is neither the winds
Nor is it the moon....

"That is true," said someone. "It's you, just you alone."

The rest of the song died on his lips. Suddenly the woods and the air were silent, and the light was only light.

"Who's there?"

"What do you mean, who's there?"

Nothing is dangerous on this world, the boy told himself. He turned. The clearing was empty. The ancient boulders ... were they glowing a little?

"Come out and show yourself," he said, trying to sound like his father. "My parents are important in Attembris. I don't scare easily." By now he was very scared indeed, and eyeing the escape path anxiously.

The forest laughed.

The laughter, like the music before it, seemed to come from the very air, from the rustling leaves, from the branches stirred by the chill wind. And then the boy saw its source: a man was emerging from the shadows between two trees. As he materialized, he went on laughing. Finally he seemed to notice the boy's discomfiture.

"I'm so sorry," he said. "I forgot that I was invisible. It's easy to forget to turn the thing off. In the city, one becomes used to being invisible."

"I'm not afraid," said the boy. "I was just startled. Where I come from, people don't just appear out of thin air. It must be a city thing. Is this your land? I'm sorry! I shouldn't be out here."

"And why not? On a night like this, in a lit clearing beneath the Dancing Moons of Urna, a sight well celebrated in song and story?"

"What are those words I sang? Is it an ancient song I learned and somehow forgot until tonight?"

"Not at all," someone said. "It's completely new. And miraculous."

The man laughed again. He was not old, not young. He wore a simple wrap cloth over one shoulder. His kilt was gray. You had to look closely to realize that it was handwoven, and that the belt was a living, opalescent serpent with red eyes, and a forked tongue that flecked the man's bare midriff, perhaps enjoying the salt in his sweat. Yes, a casual glance would have revealed nothing, yet here, in the light of the dancing moons, given the fact that he possessed a privacy shield, which would have cost his father a year's salary, the boy knew that this was no ordinary villager who happened to be taking a walk in the woods.

"Are you a senator? A counselor? A Princeling?"

"Princeling!" The man laughed again. "My, what big eyes you have." But Sajit saw a big lapis ring with an intagliate design of mating serpents, and sensed that it was the insignium of an important family.

"I've learned all the formal modes of address," the boy said. "I never thought people actually used them."

"And who, then, are you, who fill the forest with such haunting melody that even I, who stop for nothing, should stop to listen and to know, should pause invisibly in this wood to hear him?"

The boy looked into the man's eyes then, and knew that this meeting was the most important moment of his life. In school, his classical tutor Arbát had taught him that lives are journeys and there are crossroads on those journeys and on these crossroads one may meet a traveler one would never meet on one's own road. And these travelers can change lives. This traveler was one such, he knew it. "You're going to change me," he said.

"You are wise," said the man, "to say something such as this to a man whose name you not even know. And who does not even know your name."

"My name? Nobody asks my name. I'm too young to have a name, really. But in the village I am called Sajit son of Areon darSajit the keeper of the village thinkhive."

"Then I greet you, Sajit-without-a-Clan. You shall hear from me again. And in the meantime, I give you this gift."

And plucked a song cube out of the empty air. Tossed it to the boy. In the light of the dancing moons, it seemed almost alive.

Sajit squeezed the cube in his hand, releasing the hidden music. Sounds poured out. Such sounds! Oh, he had heard the wind singing. He had heard the melody that streamed from the intertwining of the light of all those moons, the dark ones and the pale. This was different. It was perhaps rooted in nature, but it was far from natural. This music has been *composed.*

Which meant that he did not come from some village tunesmith, but from an artist of one of the great courts.

Sajit wanted to thank the man, but he already disappeared. Perhaps he was still there, but if so he had switched his privacy shield back on. So Sajit sat for a while letting the music play, not daring to sing again for fear that someone was eavesdropping. For even then, even as a child, he knew he did not want strangers to hear his songs until they had become perfect.

And so he allowed the strains of the artificial music to seep into his very being, and slowly he drifted back into one of those strange dreams, the ones had been having all year, the one about starships and exploding planets and the long cold silences between the stars.

And amongst the stars, there stood a woman cloaked in shadow, and he was whispering, "Tell me who I really am."

•••

When he woke, it was already morning, and he knew he would be in trouble. He made his way home in a great hurry, barely lingering at each displacement plate. Even so, he arrived at his bedroom window too late to be able to climb back in discreetly. The family servocorpse was already bustling about the room, folding up the bed so it could be put away in the drawer, and injecting the lamps with glowworms. Luckily the servocorpse was not an intelligent model, and would be telling no tales.

But when he reached the breakfast circle, the whole family was already gathered, and the morning meditation seemed to have been interrupted.

"Mother, I —"

Ina desAreon put a finger to her lips and turned to Sajit's father.

Usually, Areon darSajit was taciturn in the mornings. But this time Sajit's father spoke. "I don't think it's necessary for us to ask where you spent the night, my son. Whatever happened, you seem to have brought our family immense favor."

Sajit looked at the center of the breakfast circle. There was a globe. It glistened. It floated above the ground by some fancy antigrav mechanism. The globe carried the seal of the Senatorial House of Urna.

"We are asked to keep the contents of this globe a secret," his father said, "but I think it only fair to tell you that it is a doppling kit."

"But they only make those for the Royal Family!"

"Exactly. We have always said that we must find a way to hide you if the time were to come, and the means has suddenly been provided, and by the highest provider on this planet."

"We are proud of you, son," said Ina, "even though we don't quite know you pulled it off."

Sajit looked at his mother and father, then at his two younger sisters Chanika and Vimla. Nobody answered him. It was clear that the honor was so unprecedented, so exalted, that it was almost beyond comprehension. Whoever the man was, he had deemed the boy Sajit so important that a clone would have to be made, and that clone kept hidden away just in case the Inquestors came.

Everyone knew that a twin was *harám* and must be killed. Unless it was of royal blood....

Sajit, of course, had never seen an Inquestor. To see one is as rare as to be visited by one of the gods of the ancient religions. He spoke their language of course; everyone had rudiments of the high speech in school. And he had learned a little of their history from his classical tutor, although the history of the High Inquest was not a regular subject for a village school.

He knew that they came only once in a decade or two, sometimes only once in a century. But when they came, they always took away the children. For far away, on the other side of the mysterious overcosm, wars were being fought, planets destroyed, worlds were falling beyond in an eternal dance of creation and destruction. And wars demanded children. Only a prepubescent child, his reflexes honed to the utmost, could manipulate the streams of deadly light from implanted laser-irises. Even after millennia of human invention, the child was still the most efficient killing machine in the Dispersal of Man.

The presence of a doppling kit in the house meant two things. One: Inquestors were coming. They were probably coming very soon. The comings and goings of the High Inquest were known only to the Senatorial Council. Two: the preservation of Sajit of Attembris was of crucial importance to someone in a very high place.

Doppling kits were of course forbidden. Even natural twins were taboo, and one would be selected for a painless devivement, to prevent abomination. *Doppling is against nature,* that was a precept everyone repeated in school. *The individual can be but one.*

"Do you think you could endure it?" Ina desAreon said to her husband. "I mean, having an *abomination* in the house."

"My dear, if it upsets you, we can schedule a devivement."

"Well ... if it ... feels no pain...."

Her eyes went dead for a moment.

Areon laughed. "We don't stone babies anymore," he said.

But Sajit had dreamed of a devivement that was not painless ... and it had been so real ... the hurled stone rending the flesh....

But there are some people in this world as in every world to whom nothing is forbidden.

Ina looked at the artifact with both exhilaration and dismay. "It's a curse," she said. "But it had to happen. One way or another. We always knew."

But his father said, "Perhaps we need to see this in a better light. Perhaps we should see this as an emblem of hope. If the Inquestors are truly coming, many families in the village will shed tears. But our family may not. There is opportunity here, opportunity as much as risk. Sajitteh, how old will you be come summer?"

"I haven't been counting, father." The morning *zul* was getting cold. "My teacher says I'm too busy dreaming to count the years."

"Next year, he will be ten," his mother said. "Twelve and it's too late, we'll be safe."

But if they are this concerned, Sajit thought, *we must not be talking about next year.*

They ate in silence for a long time. Sajit wondered when they were going to start up the doppling kit, but no one mentioned it. That day, when he returned from school, it had already been put away somewhere, and he dared not ask where.

***

That night again, he dreamed of the woman cloaked in shadow.

She stood beside his bed. In the dream, he said to her, "Are you my mother? Because ... sometimes I don't think these people are my real family."

He thought he saw her smile before her whole face vanished once more into shadow.

***

And the next day he had no time to think of doppling kits, because he had been summoned to the Palace of a Thousand Snows, and his entire family with him. Even his tutor Arbát had been hired away from the village school and assigned to Sajit alone.

They brought almost nothing with them from the old home. But one thing they did bring. It was something from an old closet, something he'd never seen before ... pieces of an old whisperlyre.

"We'll hang this in a place of honor," Areon said.

"Yes," said Ina. "To remind us about ..." But she stopped herself.

Something was being kept from him. A piece of a puzzle. Like the woman in his dreams, like the man in the forest.

Of the summons from the palace, Sajit's father said only, "I used to think it was such a pity that you had no friends, but that too was a blessing. When we left Attembris, you had no one to weep over."

It was the first time Sajit felt the workings of *meúr.*

Two
Nevéqilas

Nevéqilas blossomed in the sky, a crystal chrysanthon on a glass stalk that stretched far above the minarets of the city of Shírensang, the Inquestral seat of Urna. It was a small provincial seat of only a million souls; the reach of its demesne was only a single world, one inhabited moon, and a few colonies dotting the sparse empty space between world and moon. Still, it was the biggest city Sajit had ever seen.

Sajit's family were lodged not far from the crystal stem that led up to the palace. It was so close, in fact, that there was no displacement plate connecting it to the square; it was about half a klomet to walk, down a real street with paving stones, not weeds, lined with shops, even; the brief walk was like a journey into a fairy tale.

The apartment was not a pretentious one, but compared to their home in the village it was in itself palatial. Each of the siblings had a separate room, and there was a music room which was connected to his own bedchamber. The breakfast circle was surrounded by simulated forest, so that they were always linked to Attembris.

They hung the broken old whisperlyre on a branch of the holosculpt tree of the simulated forest, and sometimes it swayed in a simulated breeze and let forth a simulated sighing.

There was another apartment, in a slightly poorer neighborhood, for the tutor as well; in fact though Arbát lived alone there, he had almost as much room as Sajit's entire family. Arbát's lodgings were further from the palace; it took a few displacements to get there.

Sajit assumed that on coming to the metropolis he would immediately be summoned into the presence of the mysterious lord who had discovered him; in fact, Arbát informed him, that was not going be happening soon ... not in a month, a year, or even *ever,* for the lord had, it was rumored, many protégés, each one kept carefully isolated from the other.

Instead there was going to be *training*. Training of a kind unimaginable in Attembris.

There was going to be some kind of routine now; whisperlyre lessons, the history of the clan of Shen, the great poets' clan, to be memorized, although Sajit could not dare to dream of one day being inducted into it himself; and formal instruction in the arcane theories and philosophies of music. And regular meals.

In the breakfast circle there were four double-purpose cushioned benches such as families use to store their belongings. Three of the benches contained eating utensils and dishes and a decorative light sculpture that would be used as a table centerpiece when the tutor, or other guests, would come for breakfast. The three benches opened easily with a subvocalized command. The fourth was always locked and Sajit thought better than to question this. His parents had many secrets.

Everyone had secrets. To be a child was to be kept continuously in the dark, to be told that such and such would be known "in due course" or "at the right time." The locked storage bench was one such mystery.

He did not question it until his curiosity got the better of him....

Which happened within a single tennight.

•••

His parents had gone to the corpse depot to find more adequate help, as the primitive servocorpose they had brought from the village would never be able to maintain a city dwelling properly. Corpse depots are soulless by their very nature, and never a favorite haunt of the boy's.

The whole family had gone, but Sajit was to see Arbát for a discussion of transstellar monody; it was a dull subject, and when Arbát's messenger arrived to say that Arbát would be indisposed for the day, Sajit was glad of the relief.

He was alone in the dwelling for the first time, and he thought about the locked storage bench.

He knew he should not think about it, but he could not help himself.

For an hour he entertained himself by practicing scales on a mnemokitharon, an instrument designed for discipline, not music; one had to play each scale correctly, at the right tempo, and in every permutation from direct through to inverse through to retrograde; a wrong note was rewarded with an unpleasant tingling, like an insect bite.

It wasn't long before Sajit found himself wandering back to the breakfast circle. And gazing at the four storage benches, of which only one was locked — the one he himself usually sat on every morning.

He knelt down and knocked on it. The material was natural, some kind of old wood. That in itself was curious; organics had been passé for decades.

He knocked.

Knocked harder, laughing.

From inside, something knocked back. His heart skipped a beat. *It's haunted,* he thought.

Sajit ran to his room. He couldn't wait for his family to get back, and he babbled all through the next meal, boasting of the scales he could play.

•••

The new servocorpse was a talking model, but of a rustic demeanor and limited vocabulary. They decided to call it Bo, even though the naming of servocorpses is fraught with danger, for one might come to think of them as people. Bo was not a friend, but in Nevéqilas Sajit had not yet found friends. So it sufficed.

Days more passed, in the company of Arbát mostly. A classical music education mostly begins with the mnemokitharon, and the memorization of long sequences of scales, as well as the philosophical, historical and emotive basis of each. Each of the four hundred and seven divisions of the octave had a name, and the notes were classified by color as well as by the degree by which they bent away from the thirteen basic tones.

And Sajit, who knew all these things by instinct, who grasped the roots of music with such ease, found the naming tedious, and wished always to get to the creative part of the lesson, often delegated to the last few minutes. It did not take long for Sajit to understand that he was more gifted than his teacher.

Arbát was also something of a dreamer; often Sajit could smell the dreamstuff on his breath, and often Arbát drifted into a reverie, as he had consumed too much. He was, Sajit realized, bitter — though why, it was hard to know, since he had now been rewarded with such great fortune, a city dwelling, a stipend, and only a single pupil to teach.

Unless it was his pupil's talent that made him bitter....

But Sajit did not want to consider this as he practiced the scales on the whisperlyre over and over, memorizing the assigned affect of each scale and the list of nuances of each subdivision, while Arbát stared into the middle distance, pausing now and then to place an admonishing finger upon Sajit's fret-matrix ... "No, no, the second *dha* in the series should be flatter ... flatter ... listen harder won't you...."

The days went by and Sajit was home alone again, and his thoughts returned to the storage bench. And once again he crept into the breakfast circle. And knocked on the old wood. Which knocked back. He tried a cross rhythm he had just been practicing, his left index finger tapping fives and sevens while his right hand hit fours with the edge of his palm.

The same rhythm, very faint, came back at him from deep inside the wood. And in his dreams, that rhythm came again.

•••

... and there would come the dream again, and more fragments of the song ...

It is not the wind
It is not the moon ...

The words were becoming more clear now. But why only a single moon?

The snow is aflame,
yet the heart has frozen.
I am not I.

The words were of flaming snow, and a single moon. This was not Sajit's world. But Sajit had never seen another world.

In the dream, too, he would see the storage bench ... the box. And he knew they were linked.

***

One night he woke, and knew, somehow, that he *must* find out what was in box. He felt this knowledge inside himself, as though something in the storage bench were calling out to him, knew his name, even. It must be some kind of musical instrument, he thought, something powered by a microthinkhive so dense it could predict his very thoughts.

The family quarters were equipped with amnio-hammocks, not a luxury available in Attembris. The first time when he awakened and did not find himself inside a concrete world, but softly enfolded in a virtual, viscous fluid whose scent hinted of "mother" and "safety", he had not wanted to subvocalize the command to dissolve the hammock; this time he woke and snapped right out of the dreamworld. Naked, Sajit dissolved the bedroom doorway with a half-uttered word and crept down the corridor to the breakfast circle. The storage bench was glowing.

He knelt next to it. A thought struck him: *It's the size of a coffin, a childsoldier's coffin.*

Because when the Inquestors came to cull the children, that was also the time when the coffins came home. Sajit wondered if there was some kind of servocorpse inside, perhaps one with a special synthesizing module; Arbát had hinted that such technology could be used to eke out the ensemble when an artist from the Clan of Shen performed solo in an Inquestral court.

Eagerly, he put his ear to the wood.

When his flesh touched the surface, the glow became brighter. Sajit tapped another rhythm, and heard the same rhythm echo back from within the wood. He put his lips to the bench and sang something he had just learned a few sleeps before, a song called *The Space between Spaces....*

I sing of the place
where stillness is rock
and where hardness is
the empty air;

I sing of the overcosm.

From inside came an answer:

I sing of the place
where light goes mad
and where songs have no endings.

"Who are you?" Sajit cried.

I am you. I am you. The melody arced and swayed with an overpowering sadness. It came from inside himself and outside himself at the same time. He found himself weeping.

Something was stirring in Sajit's soul. There had always been an emptiness in that deepest place, but he had never realized quite how empty it had been. *I have always been lonely,* he thought. Those nights wandering in the forest — he had been looking for something. For someone who might say these very words: *I am you.* What could be inside this cold wooden box that could awaken such feelings? Sajit hugged the hardness, trying to infuse into it the warmth of his own nude body. He felt something huge and powerful seize hold of him, like the wind from a burning star; he trembled; he shook; he cried out. It seemed that the wood was responding ... softening ... that he was sinking into it. That could not be. It was a just a box, a wooden box.

But the box was dissolving, and his arms were closing around a human form. a gelatinous foam clung to it. His lips found other lips. His eyes gazed into another's eyes. The foam was dissipating and he was pressed against someone whose body, cold at first, was catching fire from his body heat, starting to move, starting to return the embrace. The amnio oil that still clung to his limbs conjoined with the foam from the living thing within, as though the two fluids had the same genetic signature. Sajit gasped. He did not dare open his eyes. The creature from inside was thrusting against him, generating a warmth he had not felt except in dreams ... the dreams he dared not speak of ... loin to loin and lip to lip until without warning there came an explosion of feeling, much like singing a high note that is perfectly in tune, or playing a chord on the whisperlyre that resonates and resonates and resonates and never seems to leave the thick moist air.

Now lips at last broke free. At last bodies separated just enough for a puff air to pass between them. Sajit opened his eyes.

And saw himself.

Himself, as in a mirror. Slender hips, slender lips; slight, wiry, wide-eyed.

"I often dream of meeting myself," Sajit said.

"And I have dream ... of you," the strange boy said, forming words slowly at first, but then with growing confidence. "I dream of you as I lie in the dark foam, in the land where only dream is real."

Sajit sat straight up. "It wasn't myself I dreamed of then. I think I dreamed about you, too," he said, realizing it only for the first time.

"I hungry," the other boy said. "No. *Am* hungry."

Sajit realized now what the secret wooden box must have been. They had started up the doppling kit. A hair, a scab, an eyelash, a drop of blood is enough to get it going. His parents had been growing another Sajit.

"That was..."

"Surprising." The other boy had finished the sentence.

"Why," said Sajit, "you *are* me after all."

"Yes I am you," the other boy said. "I like what you do to me. When you put your arms around me and feels warm and cool at the same time. What is it?"

"I don't really know."

"I think I need food."

"I'll look."

As Sajit rummaged in the seats, finding a pouch of instant *zul* and a few small *peftifesht,* he thought, *So the Inquestors were coming after all.*

"Something to eat," Sajit said. He peeled the fruit and sprinkled the powdered *zul* over it. "What's your name? I can't very well call you by my own name." Then he realized how stupid he must found. Dopplings have no names. They are created only to die. They *must* die because every second of their existence is *harám*. They stand in for the real human being. And yet in every sense of the world they too are human.

"You must name me," the boy said.

Sajit looked into the boy's eyes, his own eyes. In the village, Sajit did not really have friends. Even his family were remote. He had the night. He had the moons. He had the secret music of the lonely night. He had always wanted someone. Someone to whisper secrets to, someone to cling to in the darkness. He never dreamed that someone would be himself.

"Tijas," he said.

His new friend smiled. "You name me after yourself," he said.

And Tijas stepped out of the womb that had also been a coffin. He waved his hand over the wood and it became hard once more. "It keys to our genetic code," Sajit says. "So you may command it as much as I may."

"Teach me things," said Tijas. "In the womb, I grow quickly. I not ... connect ... one thing with another."

"The first thing we'll teach you," Sajit said, "is there's more to life than just the present tense."

"No time where I come from."

And maybe, Sajit thought, *there isn't any time left for me, either.*

The Inquestors were coming. No world was ever the same afterwards.

But, Sajit thought, *I shall not be alone.*

•••

Tijas was Sajit's secret.

"You're not concentrating!" said Arbát.

"And why should I concentrate?" Sajit shouted, and he began fingering the whisperlyre in a perfect sequence as he had been taught: *dha, dha, bent dha, double-dha, sharp dha, sharper dha, dha-ni dha-ni ni-ni-ni, dha, dha.* Not a note was out of place, every microtonal *shrut* was accurate to beyond the ear's capacity to distinguish, and Sajit knew it. "I can already play it perfectly."

"You can at that." Arbát sighed. "And yet perfection is not an end in itself, but a beginning. Listen, you stupid boy."

Sajit relaxed into the receptive pose called *savezhatá,* the locus of wisdom. His legs were crossed, sinking into the fur-cloaked floor. His palms were held out, cupped left and right, to receive the double stream of illumination that they said should come from the teacher, and the teacher's teacher and the teacher's teacher's teacher, all the way back to Shen Élumel, the mother of songs. He knew that Arbát would play and the sequences would be indistinguishable from what he had produced, and yet he would be asked to hear the differences, and perhaps slapped around a bit if he could not come up with something, for what is the acquiring of knowledge without pain? So he entered the learning state, bracing himself a little in case his teacher was of a mind to strike him.

Dha, dha, bent dha —

But this time, it seemed to him that the notes touched him in a different way. The bending of the *dha* was the squeezing of teardrops. The nudge of the repeating *ni ni ni,* so close yet so far from the home key of *sa,* evoked in him such longing, a longing that was both dark and fiery.

Arbát's voice was reedy and worn. And yet within that voice was fire, and also history. He was connected to the dawn of music. Now, above the ostinato of *dha, dha, bent dha,* he began to sing, his tones setting off the whisperlyre's sympathetic strings and awakening the harmony globes within its mechanism. The words of the song were of love, of love between living stars, of the city built to memorialize the mutual suicide of twin stars that had once revolved around each other.

Unbidden, the image of Tijas surfaced. *Tijas!* Your eyes, my eyes! Your skin, my skin! Your touch, my touch! The confluence of sweat commingling with liquidescing amnio-wood, the eyes opening, the desire dredged up from an undiscovered darkness ... *Tijas!*

For a moment he was afraid he had spoken aloud. But no. He had stopped himself in time, and yet....

Tijas, Tijas ... the whisperlyre whispered, the name surfacing from the the sussurator at its heart. Invading the texture of the song, lacing each harmony with soft scintillant esses.

Abruptly, Arbát stopped singing.

The whisperlyre's sound-colors became a jangle.

"A very good lesson for the day," said the old teacher. Sajit flinched without thinking, knowing a blow would come, but instead it was a tender stroke of the neck. "Never subvocalize your innermost thoughts when you are in the vicinity of a whisperlyre that is being played. You know that the instrument has a very sensitive thinkhive attached to its sussurator. It's there for a reason. The song is not just what you sing. It is what you are. And you have just revealed to me that you have a secret lover."

"Not a lover!" Sajit protested.

But Arbát merely wagged a finger. "Love comes in many forms," he said. "I told your parents they must not keep you locked away ... somehow you would find a way out. You would meet people. After all, that is how you came to be here in the first place. Your parents have to understand that you will go where you will go."

"Master, it isn't like that."

"Of course not," Arbát said, "I am sure I have all the details wrong. I don't know if this Tijas is a street urchin, or a kindly shopkeeper, or some mighty Lord or Lady you have run into in the corridors of your dwelling. But you feel what you have never felt before.

Something that pulls from the deepest part of your unconscious mind."

"Yes, master."

"So what do you think of me now?"

"You're not as boring as you used to be," Sajit blurted out. Again, miraculously, no blow came. Indeed, his teacher smiled, something Sajit did not remember ever seeing before. His face was like the crinkled nets for catching phoslings in the double summer.

"I daresay," Arbát said. "Now, learn your lessons carefully. When you perform, you are the song. When the song bleeds, you bleed. When the song weeps, you weep. You must distill the universal from yourself; yet how to do so when *yourself* is still but an embryo? I am not here to create your path for you, but to provide a bare minimum of light so you can see your own."

Then came the blow, so stinging that Sajit clenched back tears. And yet, he thought, this pain is beautiful.

•••

That night, Chanika and Vimla quarreled, and the quarrel set off his parents. Sajit could hear them arguing into the night, and even when it all subsided, he could not sleep.

When he was sure no one would awaken (and when they quarreled, their sleep was usually deep) he dissolved the seal and pulled Tijas out of the storage box. The wood gave easily now, and hardened again when the boy was free of it.

"Come," Sajit said, "we should get you some clothes."

Sajit's room was bare, though one wall had a built-in imager which he had set to show a vista of the forest beyond Attembris. Set in a temporal loop, on a slowed down cycle, the imager had a sense generator. A wind wafted and you could almost feel its touch. Tijas said, "I know this. I've been there."

The moons were rising. In the distance — though the wall held no real distance — came the wail and clang of an itinerant *klazmurah.* The honeyed, cloying scent of *vanjeris* hung in the moist air — though the room itself had been environmentally regulated and was quite dry and of a perfect temperature.

"I shouldn't be," Tijas said, "but I'm cold."

He was still naked from the doppling kit.

Sajit parted his amnio-hammock and pulled put a scrap of clingfire. He threw it to Tijas and it wrapped itself around his frail body. They sat at the edge of the amnio-hammock and watched the moons as they danced, and Sajit sang to his other self the song that he had learned that day, understanding it, perhaps, for the first time.

Tijas said, "I can't go back into that box. It's ... a coffin. I won't be alone anymore."

Sajit said, "Stay with me then."

"But people will find out."

"Not right away," Sajit said.

They leaned back against the amnio-hammock and it soon enveloped them both, and Sajit drew the darkness tight around them, enclosing them both. The warmth of the hammock radiated inward and they were safe as twins in a womb.

•••

In the morning, Sajit's mother said, "You seem to be eating a lot!"

Sajit giggled as he bit into his third *peftifesht,* because Tijas was standing in a doorway and no one was looking that way, making faces. "I've got to go," Sajit said and bolted to the hallway.

"What do you think you're doing?"

"Come on, it's my turn again." Tijas grabbed his doppling's half-eaten fruit.

Sajit hid to one side of the entrance and Tijas tiptoed to the breakfast circle. He squatted and went on eating.

"That was really fast," said Chanika.

"More zúl?" said Ina, waving to the servocorpse. "It'll get stuck in your throat."

Tijas nodded and Sajit suppressed a giggle.

"Make him sing for it," Chanika said.

"Yes! Sing!" Vimla said.

"Don't be silly, Chani, Villi," said their father, but Ina said, "Why not? You come back from the lessons and go straight to your room. We don't know what you and wicked old Arbát are cooking up."

"We don't need to know," said Sajit's father. "It's enough to know that because of Sajit, we have all this: a four-arjent income, a place in the capital in the shadow of the palace ..."

"We were not nobodies in Attembris," said Ina. "Sing for us, Sajit."

Sajit froze. Tijas had never had a singing lesson in his life. They would all be in trouble.

But Tijas closed his eyes and took a deep breath and began, repeating note-perfectly what Sajit had sung to him last night. First the melismatic sequence with the slippery microtones: *ha, dha, bent dha, double-dha, sharp dha, sharper dha, dha-ni dha-ni ni-ni-*

ni, dha, dha ... then words, fitting to the serpentine melody as a shimmercloak bonds to an Inquestor's skin:

do chitáry mu eyáh
mu eyáh élumy do
káng késy eklissío
kwan amby min eyáh?

I never sang those words to him, Sajit thought. Yet they bespoke his innermost feelings: "I have two hearts. I have two souls. How shall I pull them apart when both are I?" He looked at his parents, who sat ensorcelled by Tijas's voice. How could it be that there was this other Sajit, conjured up from a wooden box? But there were other things Sajit realized as well.

His parents weren't happy about their new situation.

On some level, they resented him. He had brought them untold fortune, and now they were losing control, becoming bystanders in a larger story.

Sajit gestured, trying to catch Tijas' attention. On a high note, their eyes met, and Tijas's voice cracked a little. His parents seemed almost relieved that their sound had shown a touch of imperfection.

As the song ended, and its final notes still hung in the air, it would take a while for his family members to awaken from the rêverie that great music always induces. With the instinct of a showman, Tijas slipped delicately away.

•••

Back in Sajit's room, he said, "We fooled them!"

And Sajit laughed, but there was in his laugh a twinge of bitterness.

Before Tijas could ask him, Sajit said, "You know why."

"Yes, I do."

"We are each other."

"Soon I'll have to go back in the box."

"Yes, as soon as they leave the house."

"I don't want to."

"I know."

Sajit kissed his doppling ... himself.

Tijas said, "What are we doing?"

Sajit said, "I don't know, but I know that we have each other, and we've never had anyone before."

They kissed themselves again. Touched one another, fingertip to fingertip ... and felt the warmth-in-coolness that came in no other relationship.

"Tomorrow morning," Sajit said, "Let *me* go inside that box."

Three
Inside The Box

Darkness. A deeper amniosis than any hammock. A warmth that tingled first, then seeped, then overwhelmed. Darkness that is mother, all-loving, all-embracing.

In the darkness, Sajit began to dream, and the dreams were not history, but they were history.

For a doppling kit must produce not a brainless entity with the same DNA as its double, but also a mind, a set of memories, a schooling about the nature of things. Alone in the amniotic world, Tijas had been in school, with prefabricated packets of information seeping into his brain in the semi-sleep of this artificial womb.

For twenty thousand years....

A single world with a single sun. Many worlds with many suns. More worlds. More suns. A war between a million worlds. A ravaged galaxy. And then ... a single world ... a vast sphere that enclosed the great black hole the heart of the galaxy ... on which a million suns shone ... but where a klomets-high atmosphere scattered the light to a constant pearly radiance.

Fleeing her war, a lone woman comes to this world. The world, powered by a thinkhive so immense that its omniscience is indistinguishable from a deity's ... a thinkhive that has brooded for aeon upon aeon ... a thinkhive that has never encountered a conscious being apart from itself ... a thinkhive who is about to fall in love with the woman Vara.

A living world with all the knowledge in the galaxy ... a woman ... a love story ... the first Inquestors ... the harnessing of the deaths of suns to create tachyon bubbles ... the creation of the delphinoid shipminds, the union of the giant brains that flew through the sunless sound with the crystalline eggs of the farfellor to make great ships that could sail the overcosm and hold the galaxy within the grasp of a few human beings ... the freezing of history ... the hunting of utopias ... the whole story of the Dispersal of Man poured in through the synapse portals of the doppling kit. And Sajit learned more than he had ever done in the village schoolroom of Attembris, because the history he was learning now was the common or universal history, which is only taught to those who sail the spaces between spaces.

He learned of the decree that children should serve as childsoldiers, because only children have the quick reflexes to control the implanted laser-irises that can vaporize a pebble ... or a city ... depending on their focus.

He learned of the clans, brotherhoods that spanned the Dispersal, each with its own arcane rules, and how children could be named to a clan by an Inquestor ...

though usually only if they could survive the harsh winnowing of the childsoldier years. The clan that even his master, Arbát, had aspired to but never attained, the clan of Shen, the master Songmakers of the High Inquest. The Clan of Tash, the Rememberers; Rax, the Web Dancers; Kail, the Star Pilots.

... and how all wars between worlds had been ended through the grace of the Mother Vara and the power of the cosmic thinkhive of Uran s'Varek, the Inquestors' homeworld...

... how wars between worlds had been replaced by the game of makrúgh, which sustained the balance of the Dispersal ... how worlds could *fall beyond* and disappear from the

There was time, and no time.

***

In the time that was not time, Sajit stood in a circle of light. Around him voices were whispering:

History there is, and no history.

Just outside the circle of light, pitch-black. But here and there, a rustling sound and a brief glimmer of pink against blue ... shimmercloaks.

The voices ... always soft, always understated, yet behind the words, an unimaginable power, because the words were the Inquestral Highspeech ... the language of poetry and song ... the old tongue of the High Inquest, which normal mortals do not speak.

There is an old man's voice. There is the voice of a boy. There's a woman's voice, a laugh that cascades like falling water.

The words are too soft to understand clearly, but once in a while there is a word that surfaces. *Tekiánver*

... a tachyon bubble. *Náruvas nîkas* ... new worlds. *Abáchadand* ... the Falling Beyond.

He struggles to listen. He is eavesdropping on a game of makrúgh. The game is as mysterious as it is seductive.

There comes another voice now, breaking through the others; the clear voice of a boy no older than himself, he he speaks with the authority of one a thousand years old:

"Sing, boy, sing. Do not listen to our idle chatter."

And a song springs to his lips:

Den om verék en-tinjet
In dárein shirenzheh
No man alive has touched
The silence between the stars....

And he is thinking to himself: I wrote this. *I,* a child from a backworld, have written this song which the whole dispersal knows.

But not yet.

***

The box dissolved and Tijas was there again. And it was night, and the household was sleeping again. A view of the forest undulated against the wall as it sensed his wakefulness, and an artful perfume of night-blooms infused the room.

"How much time has passed?" he said.

"A day," Tijas said. "And your parents ... and your sisters ... they never knew."

"But isn't it dangerous?"

"How dangerous? We *are* each other."

"But ..."

He looked into Tijas's eyes ... his own eyes. He sees so clearly, he thought. And I do too.

"Oh, Sajitteh ... I've spent eternity inside the box ... drinking in your *youness* with every slow breath."

"But there are memories you don't have. Things that were said to you. Places you went with them." Tijas couldn't know everything.

"Fortunate then that we're such a loner."

And Sajit saw that this was true. Only by having a friend had he discovered that he had no friends before. When he interacted with his family, they were *doing*, and he was observing. To be like Sajit to his family, Tijas had only to retreat into himself.

"Sajitteh ... I went to your Master Arbát today! I learned so much! The scales, the melismas, the ornaments..."

"Did he realize?"

"How could he?'

"Did he hit you?"

"Yes, of course, of course. I can take the pain. I never used to feel pain before. It's a new thing to me."

"Don't be too eager. Me, I'm never very eager. Arbát is a bore." Sajit did not want to remember that Arbát, somehow, knew he had a secret friend. He did not to admit, either, how strange it felt that there was another Sajit sitting in his place, melting into *savézhata,* drinking in the old man's knowledge. "The old man is a bore. We drift into another world when he speaks too much. The are universes beyond his universes. We have contempt for him sometimes."

"But we never let that show, do we?"

Sajit laughed. "We try not to."

“That mnemokitharon of his really stings,” said Tijas.

“You *don’t* know everything after all,” Sajit said. “There’s a way to neutralize the fine tuner. Then, when you play out of tune, make sure you yelp convincingly.”

“But that won’t help me learn to play....”

“That’s what *you* think. The truth is, we are already better than old Arbát. Having to listen for your own mistakes will teach you to be better, more than any shocking mechanism.”

“But Arbát has all the scales and melismas in his head, like an encyclopaedia,” Tijas said “I can’t remember them all.”

“You already know them all. You just don’t know what they are *called.*”

“Do you think he has seen your soul?” Tijas said.

And Sajit said, “Quiet, quiet.”

***

It was Tijas who caught Arbát with the dreamstuff, and only because of his ignorance of a little thing. For though Tijas was wise in many ways, having sucked in knowledge straight from the memories of the microthinkhives embedded in the doppling kit, he was really only a few days old. Urna’s peculiarities of etiquette sometimes eluded him; sometimes he did not understand simple words, because the language module was not always updated to the latest shifts in dialect and slang. But he was learning every day.

This is what he told Sajit that night:

I come for Sajit's lesson. But I'm early, and don't know I should not enter until the summoning-crystal in the doorway shifted from blue to red.

And since the door-guardian was not one of the models that could think for itself, it simply let him in. It even bowed, though, being the cheapest of servocorpses, it did not speak. Sajit laughed as they snuggled in the simulated forest. And Tijas went on:

"Where is Arbát?" I say, and the dead man merely indicates with a slight incline of the neck. And then I see — oh, what I see! — it is madness!

Arbát was suspended in the air; below him was a pocket varigrav box, and next to it a fumigator; a golden ball of dreamstuff floated in the steam. Arbát clutched something —someone—in his arms; it seemed at first like a large, flopping doll, robed in torn skins. Floating in the gravity field, Arbát savagely clawing at the mannikin, the grinding, cursing at it.

I hide behind a potted gruyesh plant, with its flapping filigree of purple leaves.

"Ah!" Arbát was shrieking. "You beast, you monster, you arrogant child!" His eyes were open, but not gazing at the real world; it was some fantasy conjured by the dreamstuff's vapors. He was thrashing about. He was partly naked; or rather, he wore a loose piece of clingfire that billowed about. His face was puffy, purple; he grunted, he groaned.

Then I see it: that Arbát's mid-air frenzy it's a kind of sick mockery of how me and my doppling cling to each other as we sleep in the warmth of the amnio-hammock.

Presently, Arbát seemed overcome by a kind of convulsion and began thrusting at the doll ... it was, Tijas saw now, a servocorpse. Convulsing as well, in a timid echo of Arbát's paroxysms. Arbát shuddering to some kind of climax and something flew off the corpse's face and landed at Tijas' feet ... and he saw that the corpse had no face at all.

The face was blank.

And, staring up at Tijas from the twisted stem of the gruyesh plant ... his own face, Sajit's face.

Tijas froze. The dermomask was sheer and slippery, and it started to bond to the plant, sensing organic matter. And at that moment, Arbát tumbled to the floor! The servocorpse flew one way and Arbát scrambled to grab the mask ... and saw Tijas ... and pulled him into the chamber by the scruff ... shaking and bellowing. "You! What did you see? How dare you enter?"

Tijas, terrified, began crying. And his teacher slapped him, over and over. Then stopped. Looked at his own hands in horror. "This will cost me everything. My livelihood. You uncivilized creature, didn't your parents teach you what a summoning crystal is for?"

Arbát began to weep. And his grief was more frightening than his anger. And though Tijas was sore from being slapped repeatedly — Arbát was not a small man — he could not help feel a kind of pity.

"I saw nothing, Arbát," Tijas said. "I've only been here for a moment or two. For my lesson."

And the wonder of it was that Tijas no longer felt he had to call the master *master,* or address him by any honorific; what he had seen, though he did not really understand it, had diminished the grand musician.

"Sajitteh," Arbát said. "There are ... things ... you'll understand when you are older."

"Yes."

"No lesson today."

Tijas rose, thinking he should leave. Then he saw the servocorpse lying on its side in a corner of the room. It had, indeed, no face, and its body, too, was featureless. Though naked, it did not even have a gender. But its back was scarred with scratches and gouges. A servocorpse feels no pain; the centers for all human feelings are turned off when it is turned on.

A cheap toy, brought to life by imagination fueled by the fumes of dreamstuff.

"No lesson today, but ..." Arbát gathered the scraps of clingfire, strung them together to cover himself more completely. "But I will take you for some ... some chocolate."

Tijas followed Arbát out to the street.

***

The displacement plate was right at the door, so that one could go from this corridor to the next destination simply by subvocalizing a few coordinates, but Arbát sidestepped the plate; taking Tijas by the hand, he walked him down a stairwell and out through an alley.

Arbát said, "You do not always find the thing you want, Sajitteh, when you take the displacement plates." His gnarled hand held the boy's firmly. His manic actions seemed forgotten. They turned a few more corners and the smell of chocolate hung heavy in the air. There were stalls everywhere. Here a whirring contraption spun chocolate from powder into cobweb patterns; here a woman with three eyes was melting chocolate with a flametorch and drizzling it into pincushions of snow. Here a fondue with intoxicating dreamberries, the source of dreamstuff.

Arbát stopped in front of a one stall, seemingly at random; the minder was a grinning, fat man with no hair. Two tripods rose for them to sit. Arbát ordered, a mushy brown paste sprinkled with dreamflakes, and for Tijas an icy, crunchy bowl of confections shaped like pteratygers.

Tijas bit off a wing. The liquid inside was sweet, but it had a pungent aftertaste. He waited. It was clear that Arbát wanted to say something. At last, his tongue loosened a little more by the flakes of dreamstuff, he said, "It's worse for me than for you, you talented little shit. You have a family of sorts, even though your friends are back in the village; chances are they were never really your friends anyway. Everyone I ever had is dead."

"Dead?"

"Mine was a world that *fell beyond,*" Arbát said. "Before I came here. They chose me so the music of my world would not die."

"... and it hasn't."

"No, it hasn't. But *I* did."

"I see," said Tijas, though he really did not.

"I wish I could wring your scrawny neck, sometimes. I know there's someone you love. I only have the words, the melismas, not the truth of love. Can you blame me for wanting to—"

"I don't know what it is you want, Master Arbát," Tijas said.

"They are pleasure corpses," Arbát said. Tijas supposed it was by way of explanation. "You can print out the faces on any thinkhive, any faces you want; they're cheap, these corpses, poor quality; perhaps they died in accidents, were disfigured, were diseased; so the servocorpse factory just grinds them to a blandness. Completely featureless. And then they can be anyone you want to love. Or hurt. But Sajitteh ... I would never hurt you too deeply. You are the thing I can never be, you see. I must love you for that."

Tijas said the one thing he knew Arbát wanted to hear. "You will never hear me speak of any of this, master. Not ever."

"And because you can hold it all inside yourself, you shall be Shen. Which I never became."

"When I attain it—I shall insist they make you one!"

And Arbát laughed bitterly. "When ... a stripling who's never *burst the milkpod* says 'when, when' ... knowing his destiny already...." And called for a posset of crushed violets, perhaps to steady his emotions. *"Airos hokh'tásieh; ektáshila shiklát,"* he added in the highspeech.

"Love is the great joy; the lesser joy is chocolate," Tijas said.

"Well learned!"

***

And that's how I learn that our teacher is addicted to dreamstuff, and that he has some kind of obsession with us, and that he acts out his obsession on a helpless little pleasure corpse ...

"You have all the fun!" Sajit said, trying to reconcile this astonishing story with the Arbát he was used to. "Why couldn't this happen when *I* was with the master?"

"He ever bruise you this badly?"

"He ever buy me chocolate?"

"But seriously," Tijas said, "something has changed."

"We have power now."

"Sajitteh, what's *bursting the milkpod?"*

"I don't know. I've heard that we're too young to understand."

"I'm going to ask mother and father, at breakfast."

"Who says you're the one having breakfast tomorrow?"

"I do, brother. Be quiet, now."

"Yes. They'll wake."

***

So, when he fingers blundered at the mnemo-kitharon, Sajit declared that he wanted chocolate.

"Oh, you manipulator," Arbát muttered, "you shrewd little pteratyger cub."

But Arbát took him to the alley. And left him on the tripod, in front of the vendor, while he wandered off by himself. And in that moment Tijas slipped out of a side street. Too many people thronged about for anyone to notice them, shadowslim, flitting in and out; sensing each other's thoughts, they could switch in an instant, catching just the moment when no one was looking.

Tijas said to Arbát, "So what, Master Arbát, is *bursting the milkpod?* I have no one to ask."

"Try your parents," Arbát said.

A few minutes later, Sajit said, "So, Master Arbát, what exactly does *bursting the milkpod* mean? Is it the highspeech?"

"Little beast! Did I not tell you to ask your parents?"

"Did you?"

"Not five jipek ago. Either you are exceptionally forgetful for one so young, or there are two of you."

'Oh, you are a comedian, Master Arbát."

Thus it was that Arbát became no longer a martinet taskmaster, but a fellow traveller. A friend, even. And it was all because Tijas had walked through a door uninvited.

***

Mind you, he did not stop thrashing the boy, or boys, rather. They accepted that; it was tradition. But often it was a perfunctory slap and a soft-pedaled tongue-lashing.

It was because of the occasional slap that the boys learned something new about each other.

Sajit had let Tijas go to the lesson one morning, because he wanted to sneak out to the palace bestiary. But he had not gone five steps across the square when he felt a sharp pain rip across his knuckles. He felt his left hand with his right, expecting a welt or abrasion, but there was nothing. He looked down and saw a red stripe, quickly fading. *We're more linked than I thought,* Sajit reflected. He needed to reach his doppling right away, to share this news. And so he run to the other side of the square and whispered the coordinates, barely noticing the displacements he passed, the Fountain of Unwept Tears, the Forest of Statues, the Street of the Servocorpse Factories ... he reached the entrance to the apartment and lurked in the hall, which was decorated with busts of the nobility, set on columns of azurite, their eyes sculpted from blue diamants. Eventually, he knew, they would emerge ... the chocolate ritual had become a regular thing. When they did, he motioned Tijas, who shouted, "I'll be there in a moment, Master, do not wait," and then he embraced Sajit, laughing.

"Oh, it's so risky, you, me, here, in the corridor — you never know which of the statues is a spy."

"All right," Sajit said, "Close your eyes."

Tijas said, "Why did you slap me?"

"I didn't. I slapped myself."

Tijas said, "You're right. This was worth the risk, coming here like this."

"We can play this game almost openly," Sajit said. "We don't have to *pretend* to be each other."

"Slap yourself again! I want to feel it again."

***

At the chocolate stand, Arbát's absences became a ritual. And they became longer and longer, and when he returned, he was more distracted each time.

So the boys began following him.

Sometimes it was buying dreamstuff. For three gipfers you could buy quite a handful. But once, it was something else. It was hard to follow someone moving swiftly through the city via displacement plates; you had to leap on *just so,* in the split second when the the thinkhive reset itself for the next passenger, and make your mind blank so you didn't not accidentally subvocalize a completely different command; *and* you had to avoid being noticed by the one you were following. It was only because Arbát moved so sluggishly, never looking around, that he was easy to follow.

This time his destination was, ironically, the palace bestiary, it seemed. It was a public day, a crowded day, and the pteratygers were being fed. Arbát moved slowly, but he was purposeful; the boys would have liked to watch the feeding. The keepers released a flurry of firephoenixes into the air, and the pteratygers swooped and hovered, avoiding the flames in time to snatch the birds as the dived earthward, and all safely inside a sphere of force. The crowd gasping at every somersault that ended in a fiery kill. The boys tried not to stop and look to long.

"He's turned a corner," Sajit said. Arbát had slipped between two serpentine columns. The boys followed. Kept to the shadows. Which was wise, because they had stumbled into a royal council chamber, and seated on a hoverthrone was the very man Sajit had met, once, in a forest, in the village of Attembris, beneath the dancing moons, the moons that had seemed to sing.

And it was thus that Sajit finally learned the name of his benefactor, for Arbát prostrated himself in front of the hoverthrone and spoke the formula for greeting a member of the Royal Family of Urna: "Let me be as the dust beneath your feet, High Princeling, mightiest under the High Inquest, Starry Highness."

A Princeling? My, what big eyes you have!

In the forest clearing, a time not long ago, that could be counted in tennights, this man had been toying with Sajit all along. His parents had thought this favor must come from a high senator, or a member of the aristocracy. But this was a higher personage altogether.

This was none other than the Son of the Starlight, the High Princeling Orifec z'Urnasi Tath, hereditary Lord of Nevéqilas, Commander of the World Entire, He Who Answers Only to the High Inquest.

"We have to get closer," Sajit whispered. "This is important."

The council chamber was an oval, and ringed with the serpentine columns; the stone hissed as it twisted, giving forth a faintly menacing music. But the hissing provided cover; they would move without making any noise, neither the rustling of tunics or the slipping of sandals on the marmáreon tiles. So they ended up crouching quite close to the throne, behind serpent effigies that twisted slowly, as though they were alive.

The High Princeling, as it happened, was speaking of Sajit.

"Progress, Arbát, tell me of progress."

"He is quick enough, Starry Highness. Too quick. But no discipline at all. Would as soon break the rules as learn them. I have taught him most of the major, minor, anterior and superior ragas, with the ways each tone can be shaded, and he parrots them well enough, and yet...."

"Arbát, there is little time. When you told me to wait in the forest, and watch for a lonely young boy—"

So the meeting was not by chance! Sajit thought.

"Starry Highness, he's definitely someone who has a great destiny. I've seen many take the path, and most more diligent, but this one already hears the silence between the stars."

"Keep at it, then, Arbát. They will be coming soon, and then everything is going to change."

"I don't know if he can be ready so soon, Starry Highness."

"He *must* be. Everything must go perfectly. Or we will lose ... *all this.*"

"I'd best going, my Lord. I left him sipping on a whipped chocolate confection at the Dromek Shiklati."

No sooner had Arbát shuffled away than the Princeling spoke again.

"Sajit-without-a-Clan, you can come out now."

Sajit tried to move, but suddenly the columns snapped, turned, and twisted around both boys, like living constrictors. "Let me go!" he cried. "I can't breathe!"

"Relax. Both of you. Breathe slowly."

The High Princess brought his hoverthrone sailing toward the colonnade. "You don't wonder then, that I don't need to be surrounded by guards."

Sajit cried out. And so did Tijas. And Sajit felt Tijas trying to breathe ... as much as he knew Tijas must feel his own choking.

Orifec clapped his hands. The serpents went limp.

"People think they are just marmáreon," said the High Princeling, "but they are actually dead pythonoids, fitted with servocorpse thinkhives, and coated with a dermolithic fabric that simulates marmáreon quite convincingly."

Sajit freed himself. Tijas prostrated himself. But Sajit, who had encountered the Princeling under such unusual circumstances before, could not bring himself to. He looked him straight in the eye. "You were behind *all* of this," he said.

Orifec said, "I suspected you'd unlock the doppling kit earlier than you needed to. You're not one for observing any strictures. See, even the doppling shows proper respect."

Tijas said softy, in perfectly modulated court language, "I am but the dust beneath your feet, Starry Highness." Of course; he had learned the protocols while he lay half-conscious in the amniosis.

"The question is," said the Starry Highness, "whether your parents know. Oh, get up, Doppel-Sajit. No one is watching us here."

"His *name* is Tijas," Sajit said hotly.

"Now that is a problem, Sajit-without-a-Clan. Dopplings have no names. They are not, legally speaking, people at all."

"Tijas is a person. He's me."

"I am a person. I'm him," Tijas said at the same time.

"That is true for now, but will it be true when the time comes? And that time will be soon, I fear. Come, I will tell you something. Climb up onto my hoverthrone, it's big enough for all."

He brought the throne down to the floor. Boarding it, Sajit felt warmth; the cushions were living matter, covered with the same membrane that coated the inside of the doppling kit. Sajit felt powerful, as if he was absorbing wisdom and cunning through its pores. "Not surprising," said Orifec. "We are linked to the central thinkhives of my palace, and through them to the world itself."

Sajit sat beside the Princeling, feeling surprisingly at home. But Tijas sat at the Princeling's feet. "You see, children," said Orifec, "already, you are not *entirely* each other. Doppel-Sajit has never met me. He is bound to act differently towards me. There are always going to be these little things. As time passes, your souls will disengage. At the moment it is fresh, it is as if even thoughts themselves can pass between you. Come."

He motioned with a finger, and a shield of force enveloped the throne. People would not be able to see inside; there was a photon scatterer in the throne and it would be visible only as a diffuse luminescence. "I'll give you the tour of Urna."

The throne rose into the air, The ceiling parted. "Doppel-Sajit, join us," said Orifec. "Be one with your twin for a little while longer."

The throne zigzagged through between the needles of the crystal columns of the palace, then went skyward. The sun of Urna, brooding and ruddy, hung low. Shírensang became a miniature. It was not a large city; it was a blip of color amid a landscape of purple-blue fields and black forests. At the horizon, against the face of the sun, was something black. It looked like a dark cloud. It was whirling. At this distance it was a mere smudge in the clear air.

"What is it?" Sajit said.

"It is," said the Princeling of Urna, "a window into our destinies. It is a doorway into the overcosm. Something is coming, children, something big. Something is going to come through that doorway. It is being prepared for now. My councillor-observers noticed it almost two years ago. It is growing fast now, a little every day. That's why, Sajit, you were summoned."

"In case something should happen ... to the Royal Family of Urna."

The Princeling did not speak.

"You want that our songs will not die," Sajit said. "You want a poet of your own."

"At first," said Orifec, "I wanted a plan, in case the High Inquest had a childsoldier culling. But maybe what is happening is even bigger. Maybe it's not the service of the Royal Family of Urna that is your destiny. It is true that I am all-powerful on this world. But above all worlds stands the High Inquest."

The throne swooped down into a city square and Tijas pointed: "It's Dromek Shiklati!" There indeed was the alley of chocolate below them and there was Arbát, looking very lost, wondering where is charge was.

"I'll drop you off somewhere close," said the Starry Highness. "And don't worry ... I won't tell."

Sajit realized that this must be one of life's lessons: to gain power over others, know a secret. And promise never to tell it. And make them live in terror that the promise will be broken.

***

And so it was that for the next few sleeps, they traded places often. Sometimes Tijas would receive a sharp rebuke when he could not reproduce a lesson Sajit learned. Sometimes Sajit would forget a promise he had made to his sisters. But as more days went by, such incidents became rare. The boys became more daring, sometimes substituting for each other when a parent looked away for just a moment. To their own amazement, they did not get caught. The game continued.

The boys relished the times when they could be together more or less openly. They had managed to get away with the whole charade for several tennights.

Once they both joined a family picnic by the Lake of Luminous Loons; when the flock of birds descended on the water and simultaneously went dark in their rhythmic mating ritual, one would dash behind a tree and the other would emerge. With Chanika and Vimla running in circles, and Bo the servocorpse barely sentient enough to follow rudimentary commands, it was not hard to continue the deception.

Vimla said, “Sajitteh eats like a pteratyger!”

“Don’t worry,” their father said. “We can afford it now.”

The loons descended, with cacophonous cries, a curtain of light and they called out to their mates, each with its own melody that could be recognized only by one other bird in the whole world ... the birds glowed, their phosphorescent feathers reflected in the lake, reflected back up to bounce down from the clouds ... so many moons had risen that though the Star of Urna hugged the horizon, there was brilliance everywhere ...

Then darkness! The flood of light, the wave of mating calls, suddenly stilled as the flock, thousands upon thousands, dived like a single darkweaving onto the surface ... striking the water with a thunderous thud, all at once, then ignited once again by the contact between feathers and the salts in the water, shaking off the drops of liquid as the mating calls began again, each loon catching fire from the next....

The boys switched places again, laughing.

The loons rose up from the lake once more. Their individual cries blended into a carpet of sound and one by one they began to glow. They laughed again. They were always laughing in those days....

***

It was possible to snuggle into a single amnio-hammock; the doppling box was more difficult, but Sajit and Tijas managed it by leaving it partially ajar. The womb was not built for two, but the skein of information paths woven by the microthinkhives that operated it had no trouble reproducing itself; self-reproduction was a doppling kit's reason for being.

And so it was that both boys became wise. Apart during the day, each night they imparted to each other all that had happened. Twins of artifice, they were more inseparable even than twins born naturally.

Even with the quarrelsome parents, the chattering sisters, and the sometimes tipsy, sometimes sadistic whisperlyre master Arbát, they were in a kind of paradise ... indeed, a utopia.

And utopias, by definition, must end —

For it is an axiom of the High Inquest that utopias may not stand. Man is a fallen being. No one could know what the smudge on the horizon portended.

***

Ektásiens kasséranda arkhá savézhas.

The breaking of joy is the beginning of wisdom.

Four
Outside The Box

The Princeling Orifec now sent an open summons to Arbát, that he should bring the apprentice Sajit-without-a-Clan to perform a private recital.

The chocolate sessions were put on hold. Each day came with dire lectures, finicky technical details, and the mnemokitharon set to the highest detail resolution *and* the highest voltage; the sparks blistered Sajit's fingers for several days until Tijas volunteered to take some of the lessons, and some of the pain.

So it was in fact Tijas, not Sajit, who ended up being escorted by an honour guard from their apartment to the highest minaret in Nevéqilas. For Sajit was not there when the guard came ... he had sneaked away to the market square, looking for a better tuning fork.

Mother, Father and the sisters were there, too, painfully overdressed; even Bo, the servocorpse, was in attendance, standing behind the girls and straightening their hair every few moments. Tijas had the vintage whisperlyre, an instrument more valuable than a household of servocorpses; incorporating a sliver, they had told him, from a tree on Uran s'Varek itself.

Perhaps Sajit would have been amazed at his family's attire, because Tijas knew that in all his life Sajit had never known his entire family to go to an event where they took the trouble to wear matching, spangled *shurongas,* with the emblem of the village stitched into the wasitbands; Sajit probably did not even realize that his family possessed such clothes, but Tijas, having absorbed the layout of the family home via the house's own thinkhive, knew that the clothes had always lain unused in an old closet, inherited from some ancestor. In any case, he could see they were looking very stiff; Areon darSajit, in particular, seemed uncomfortable, sensing more keenly than usual his loss of familial control since Sajit had unwittingly transformed the family's social status.

There was an ante-room. Tijas recognized the architectural style as the same one the boys had encountered before, with the encircling colonnade of marmoreal-skinned dead snakes. In the center of the room was a holosculpt icon of the Princeling, twice larger than life, standing in a circle of light, on a raised platform with four steps. Taking their cue from Arbát, the family genuflected to the icon.

Arbát said, "Starry Highness, may I present Areon darSajit, a thinkhive maintainer from your village of

Attembris, and his wife Ina desAreon. And their daughters, Chanika and Vimla. And my student, Sajit-without-a-Clan."

"Come," said the icon, making a gesture toward the golden displacement plate at its feet.

The family moved forward, but Arbát quickly said, "No. The command in the language of court protocol was in the singular. Even I dare not step onto the Conveyor of the Presence."

Tijas, who was still in the position of genuflection, rose. He turned back to look at the family. *I'm such an impostor,* he thought. He wished he were the one running through the marketplace now.

Arbát said, "We'll remain in the anteroom. If the Starry Highness wishes to address any of us from the sanctum, he will do so through the icon-surrogate, I am sure."

Ina said, "He's our boy, Master Arbát."

"I'll be fine ... mother," Tijas said, and stepped up to the golden plate. And vanished.

***

The room he found himself in was like an open lotus, perched atop the topmost minaret of Nevéqilas; the floor was of writhing, living crystal nematodelike creatures, thousands upon thousands, that cushioned the body; wherever one lay, they reshaped themselves into a couch, a footstool, an armrest. A banquet was laid out on the floor, and there were guests, all of striking physical perfection; most wore no clothes, but had pulled up pieces of the floor and draped them about themselves.

Above the chamber, the roof had been deopaqued, so they appeared to be under an open sky. Four moons swam behind sheer clouds. Seven more had yet to rise, and the smallest, Eríkion, was weaving in a complex dance between the three largest. Beneath the sky sat Orifec, and in front of him was Sajit, and Sajit was already playing a whisperlyre ... and this one not with a tiny sliver from Uran s'Varek built into its soundpost, but perhaps carved in one piece from the trunk of a millennial *tállisama* tree. How could two dopplings be allowed to be seen, openly, at a public banquet, a royal event? Surely this was the worst kind of abomination.

Orifec gestured. Sajit found the next cadence and finished with an elegant flourish. Tijas blurted out, "We're both here! Right in the open! Starry Highness, how?"

Orifec said, "Look around you, Doppel-Sajit. Who of my guests is eating?"

It was true. The guests ... preternaturally beautiful ... their bodies perfect, gleaming ... their motions were as choreographed as a play ... and when he listened to their conversations, he realized ... they were looped.

"Everyone here is dead!" Tijas said, in wonderment.

"Oh, yes," said the Starry Highness. "A ruler can ill afford to be surrounded by living courtiers. My father and uncles were all ... done in, you know. Even I am not entirely innocent." He looked away. "Come closer, Doppel-Sajit," he said. "I want to compare the two of you."

He pulled Tijas up and sat him on the throne next to him, and motioned for Sajit to do so as well.

Diffidently, Tijas settled into the soft fabric. Orifec said, “Look at you. I can’t tell you apart at all.”

Sajit said, “There’s a mole behind my left ear.”

“Not mine,” Tijas said. “The doppling process doesn’t create any flaws.”

“It will,” said Orifec, “if you try use it too many times.” He sounded as though he was remembering something.

Tijas wondered what Orifec knew about doppling kits. Royal families did possess the technology, he knew. Was Orifec himself a flawed imprint of an ancient ancestor?

“Starry Highness,” Sajit said, “Why is it that you only live among the dead?”

“I’ve told you,” said the Princeling. “People like me ... we live in mortal fear all the time.”

Tijas said, “No, Starry Highness, there’s more to it than that.”

And Orifec became very quiet. A tear? But that would be unthinkable; weeping is for peasants. Orifec said, “You both sense it. I knew you would.”

“What is it we sense?” said both the boys.

“One day, I may yet tell you.”

Indeed, Tijas thought. *The doppling process....*

Orifec looked at both of them and Tijas could not understand the weight of that sadness. He wondered whether Sajit knew more.

“Meanwhile,” said the Princeling, “let’s watch the dancing moons.”

Night had fallen completely. And Tijas knew that it was a special night; when all the moons of Urna could be seen at the same time, and in the same quadrant of the night; when their motions and apparent motions all came together to create the dance, from the hurtling Eríkion to the stately Arráz, the paired Kalíth and Ralíth, the jagged Harikozmá. "And you told me you thought they were singing, too. Singing for you alone, Sajit."

He toyed with Sajit's hair and Tijas felt a twinge of ... some strange emotion ... that there was something other than ruler and slave that passed between them. But Sajit merely said, "Let me sing now, and it will be as though the moons have been given a voice."

"You shall both sing."

The boys readied their whisperlyres. "Sing to me," said Orifec, "the song that I first heard you sing in the forest; the song that you thought the moons were singing, only you realized it was you yourself."

They sang:

It is not the wind
It is not the moons.
The snow is aflame,
yet the heart has frozen.
I am not I
You are not you.
The song is but motion
in the still air.

And Orifec, thinking, it seemed, of a past that the boys could not imagine, began to weep again. There, alone save for two insignificant children, surrounded by corpses that continued to simulate eating and drinking and laughter as they had been programmed to do.

Finally it seemed he could bear it no longer, and he held up his hand once more for the music to stop.

"I did not think we would meet this way," he said, "and I did not think that it would be this brief."

"My Lord," Tijas said, "what do you mean?"

"Can we comfort you?" Sajit said. "Is that why we're here, to ease your troubled soul?"

"No!" Orifec cried out. "You are here because of my selfishness! My own selfishness! Even you, Doppel-Sajit, know that you have no right to exist, that you are an abomination. But oh, how I wanted to protect Sajit!"

"My Lord," Sajit said, "you never even knew me before."

"No, I never did. I knew nothing, yet I knew everything. Sajit-without-a-Clan, all that you know about yourself is untrue. And I cannot tell you the truth. I cannot. Especially not now. Look up at the sky."

The smudge they had remarked on earlier, in the flight over the city ... it was bigger now, almost eclipsing the moon called Harikozmá. And it was still growing.

"What is it, Starry Highness?" Tijas asked.

Orifec beckoned to the nearest corpse, and it brought him a tray of viewing-crystals. Orifec picked one up and said to Tijas, "Hold it up to your eye." Tijas did.

Magnified, Tijas could see that the smudge was made up of sleek, metallic cylinders, thousands upon thousands, swirling like bacilli in a culture dish. It was less a smudge now; reflecting the moons' light, they were beginning to glisten, like the crystal nematodes that carpeted the chamber.

"People bins," Sajit whispered.

"Two things at once. A culling was planned already; the High Inquest needs its childsoldiers, and every child who fulfills the seven criteria of perfection will be chosen. That is the first thing. That is why I pulled you from the village. That is why I sent the doppling kit. That is why it is so appalling that you, Sajit, couldn't control your curiosity. Do you realize how much more difficult this is, with the two of you having seen each other, touched each other, bonded in a way that is more than brother to brother, more than lover to lover, because you are literally one flesh? And Sajit — you even *named* the unnameable. Opening the box has undone everything. You will never live down the pain."

Sajit said, "It's not about pain. I've got someone now, someone who knows me completely. My whole life I felt that I was living in the wrong world, that my parents were not my family. Now — it's changed." And he gripped Tijas fiercely. Tijas cried out. And Sajit felt his pain.

But in that moment Tijas knew that he and Sajit did not understand the world in the same way.

For Tijas existed for one purpose only; to avoid the culling. When the High Inquest came to take the childsoldiers away, Tijas was destined to go as Sajit. Sajit would remain ... and Tijas, almost certainly, would die ... as almost all childsoldiers died. Those were the words of an ancient song, about a million young boys who dreamed of the stars:

ekáqila eméruat mílilas
nendé z néqilas erdhándat

one hundred thousand became childsoldiers;
ninety-nine thousand died

"You made me so you could kill me," Tijas said.

"In case," said Orifec, "only in case ... otherwise you were not to be quickened."

Sajit said, "Nothing will part us, Starry Highness. I did what was forbidden; I quickened my doppling and came to know him. We feel each other's pain. I think sometimes we even hear each other's thoughts. What will happen if he dies in a war, in another world? Am I going to feel his death on the other side of the galaxy? Will I die too? Never! Tijas is Sajit."

Tijas was moved by his doppling's firmness, but in his heart he knew how it must end.

"There is, in any case, a larger issue now," Orifec said. "Ten sleeps ago, a tachyon bubble came to the city."

The boys gasped. Only the High Inquestors could travel by tachyon bubble, a conveyance that required a star's death to fuel it. "The Inquestor bore a sealed command. He came himself; that was a special honor."

"Urna will *fall beyond!"* Sajit cried.

"No. It is ... an error. The entire Dispersal of Man is linked, through thinkhive upon thinkhive, strands of consciousness reaching through the overcosm, from planetary thinkhives through the hearts of stars, all the way to the great thinkhive that is the soul of Uran s'Varek. It is a very ... *complex* ... construct. Mistakes happen. And this is a very tiny one; a decimal place somewhere, an infinitesimal error ... it seems that Urna is too insignificant, too backward a world to register on one of their grand indexes. Somewhere on the other side of the Dispersal, a planet *fell beyond* a thousand years ago; its evacuated peoples, in stasis and packed into people bins for a millennium, are now slated to rebuild their world on an empty planet ... which happens to be Urna. Apparently there weren't any people here when that decision was made; and though for us it was a thousand years, for the Inquestors who were playing *makrúgh* with the destinies of worlds, it may only have been a matter of a few moments."

"Then the culling — how can it proceed?" Sajit said. Perhaps this mistake had saved them!

"Enguéstrens sepáta devénd' áspatut." An Inquestor's word may never be unspoken. "That was a different game of *makrúgh.* It is a virtual impossibility that both games should have snared the same world. The culling will be soon. By then, Urna will have been renamed Alykh. Small as it is, our population will not need to be moved to make way. We will merely be swallowed up by another world, another culture."

"And you, Starry Highness?" Sajit said.

"Oh, me. I am deposed. Well, technically, I shall still have one square klomet of a kingdom, and I shall have wealth enough; it is the law that one single tittle of a world *fallen beyond* must remain preserved, for the sake of the art of the Rememberers. I have a tennight's notice, of course. Ten planetary sleeps to close up the affairs of my royal house. Just as well. We were not a very good ruling family. Cruel, always killing one another for the power, not understanding of course that the power is so fleeting. Many generations ago, the High Inquest raised us up to rule here. I would have been happier ... let us not speak of it. I had a brother, too, once."

A doppling? Tijas thought.

In silence, they gazed up at the sky. The moons did not sing. The cluster of people bins moved closer. Now, with the naked eye, one could make them out. They would be landing soon.

"Go home, boys," said the Princeling of Urna. "And you, Tijas ... get back inside that box. All this has been a dream."

And this was to be marveled at: *he had called Tijas by his name.*

***

"They're not splitting us up," Sajit whispered. "They're not. Not *ever*. I'll never let it happen."

Tijas said listlessly, "But for now ... we'd better go back separately."

So Sajit left the royal chamber by the same displacement plate that Tijas had entered with; Tijas said he would go back by a different route.

When they reached their apartment, Areon sent the girls to bed. They had been stuffed with *peftifesht* and chocolate, and were awake long past their bedtime anyway. They complained, but they left, sensing something of gravity they were not allowed to take part in.

"It's time," Areon said to his son, "for us to talk about the thing we should have talked about before even moving to Shírensang."

"I already know about the doppling kit, father."

"Then you will have guessed that we are on notice; that the High Inquest will soon arrive, and the most suitable children of our world will be given the honor of serving the High Inquest. In all probability of dying for the High Inquest. You are one of the chosen. Naturally; you possess the seven superior qualities they are looking for."

"Yes, father. When the summons comes, we're to open up the kit, and quicken the child inside, send the Doppel-Sajit in for selection. And I will return to my music."

"You sound ... listless. Do you understand that this will save your life? Through the generosity of the Royal Family, you have a chance at a greater destiny?"

Ina said, "Don't badger him. We have to tell him the other thing, too."

"Why?" said his father.

"Because ... we may lose him. Even with that *thing* inside the box."

This is it, Sajit thought. I knew it. They've been keeping something from me all my life ... and now they have to tell me.

"We're not your real parents," Ina said.

Why was it not a surprise?

***

The baby in the hallway, the basket, the token of remembrance ... it was a melodramatic story from a shabby holodrama. Oh, Sajit listened, but it never quite seemed to be real. Although it did explain why all his life he had never felt that he belonged ... *My whole life is a tale told by a street bard for a few coins,* he thought.

Until his mother produced the actual basket, and he gasped — because the basket had been hanging from the holosculpt arbor in the simulated forest that walled their living quarters.

"That's no basket!" He had been delivered to his new parents inside the soundbox of a whisperlyre. He had been delivered to this house in a musical instrument, resting on a tangle of snapped lyre-strings. And next above the fretboard there was set an intaglio in lapis, carved with intertwined serpents. *It was a symbol he knew.* And a piece of cloth — not even clingfire, but old-fashioned fabric woven from plants, the old way ... such as the very poor might wear, or the very fashion-conscious. Imprinted with the same insignium. *A sign Sajit recognized. The blue mating serpents. The serpent columns of the throneroom. The serpents in the Princeling's ring.*

Sajit did not really listen after that. It was an overload of revelations. First the world as he knew it coming to an end, then the prospect of losing his other self, of one day being an intimate of the planet's highest power, the next that power being cast down; adding a secret origin story to all this was overkill. He did not care. He tried to listen, but his eyes glazed over as his parents earnestly told the tale of how they had received mysterious emoluments that enabled them to settle in this village and got his father a secure occupation tending the thinkhive; about how a mysterious woman, cloaked in shadow, had been seen leaving the hallway, a veiled woman.

... a woman Sajit had seen before ...

first in a dream ... then ... perhaps ... in the shadows of a real place....

A woman who really existed!

It was when his parents spoke of the veiled woman that an idea, half-formed, sprang into Sajit's mind. It was rash, but for him it was the only thing left to do. And he was going to have to do it *tonight.*

***

"We're going *now,*" Sajit told Tijas. "We're running away."

It was the dead of night, and all but one of the moons had set, the runt moon, alone and visibly spinning. It was a time of night called the Afterdance, after the rare display of all the moons in their intricate patterns, when the people of Urna tended to shutter their dwellings and opaque their windows ... an old superstition from a time when people had not counted the moons nor measured their revolutions, and thought they might never return.

It was the dead of night and the city square was empty. And all they carried was the soundless old whisperlyre, and a single loaf retrieved at the last minute from the larder.

A slow, solemn drumbeat. From across the square there was a slow procession. A line of about a hundred people ... no, servcorposes, for they moved with a precision that proved they were not alive ... the faces of the dead were white in the lone moon's light. Each carried some precious object; a vase, a robe, a holosculpt, a jewel-box.

At the head of the line, not riding a hoverthrone, not carried on a palanquin, wearing only a white robe: the Princeling of Urna.

"Walk with me a while," he said. "I am going to the edge of Nevéqilas." It did not seem an appalling moral outrage that two dopplings were seen together. Of course, they were surrounded only by the dead. There was no one to be outraged.

"You're leaving your palace behind?" Sajit said.

"Halát eyáh nishis," said the Princeling. *Everything is nothing.*

"Starry Highness," Tijas said, "do you have no wife, no children?"

"I did, little one. I had them all killed. It was a matter of honor; it pains me still. I wish I had them back, but I had no choice."

No use thinking about the village. No use thinking about the family. Sajit walked on. Presently the line reached a displacement plate and the corpses vanished one by one. Sajit followed Orifec, keeping his thoughts blank so that Orifec's subvocalized command would also cover his own displacement.

The line of corpses emerged on a field on the other side of the Lake of Loons. The cloud of people bins filled half the sky now. They were braking against the atmosphere, each one thrumming in its own frequency. How unlike the cry of the loons when they lit up in synchronized flight! These bins jangled, crashed into one another, moved without regard for the people inside, for the people were all time-frozen, in stasis for who knows how many centuries.

Across the lake, the crystal stamens of Nevéqilas pierced the night sky. And the lone moon drifted.

Then, without warning —

The bins began to fall! From being packed together they broke apart, each seeking its predetermined coordinates. Four bins were swerving, swooping down toward the lake, aiming to land on the field. Each people bin, Sajit saw, could have held a city. The world that had *fallen beyond* must have been far more populous, more urban, than Urna. No wonder they had dismissed the people of Urna from their calculations.

Now came a wind, sweeping down from above, swirling about them. The tall grass whispered. The four bins were settling now. First one, the other three hovering above, a shattering roar first, then a low thrum just at the threshold of hearing; Sajit's very bones shook.

The bin that landed first opened. Then came silver spiders, thousands upon thousands, each as big as a house, scurrying, skittering, planting poles in soil, floating in and out, viewing the world with eyes on stalks ... planting metal pods in the soil that burst asunder and spewed out houses and shops and temples, once collapsed into pellets, now splitting and climbing and spitting out awnings and walkways as though cities were animate cells, splitting, exploding ...

"They're growing a city in front of our eyes!"

"And no one to see it but us."

"Why?" Sajit said. "Where are all the citizens of Shirénzang? We are a provincial backwater, but a million souls isn't *nobody!*"

"Fear," said the former Princeling. "Something you boys clearly lack. Nothing ever happens on Urna. The world is petrified."

Sajit believed it. They were all cowering in their apartments ... his family ... Arbát ... the chocolate vendors ... the servocorpse mechanics ... but Sajit felt no fear at all. He felt ... wonder. He felt alive. He felt the way a song feels before it is born.

The city, all spirals and spikes and crenellations and mazes and tunnels and turrets, shooting upwards and outwards ... atop it all, a starport ... *This new world is no backwater,* Sajit thought.

And suddenly it was raining people.

The three other people bins began disgorging them! People, frozen people, each wrapped in a skin of stasis. They were within but outside the world. They flew out in flurries, clattered onto the streets of their new city. They were piled up in heaps in the square. The people bins themselves began to come apart as they floated to the surface. The spider robots took each fragment and incorporated it into the city; here a mirror-wall, there a elevated walkway. Smaller spiders rushed about, nailing displacement plates every few meters. Trees sprang up out of nutrient sacs, instantly blossoming. At length the spiders finished their work; their finishing touch was to disassemble each other, until they too vanished into thc scams of the city.

"Aírang," said Orifec, "the pleasure city, hedonistic capital of a world named Alykh."

The city stretched all the way to the lake. The humming of machines, the clatter of metal spiders, was silenced. Nothing moved. There were domes. There were columns topped with statues. There were holosculptures in erotic poses, frozen in mid-lovemaking. And piles of people everywhere, frozen, too. Then —

A call from the sky like the blast of a trumpet! The heaps of humans, released instantly from stasis! People sprang to life, stood up, looked about them, dazed for moment, then continuing in mid-action; the city, their surroundings, must have been familiar to them. The silence broke, became a hubbub, a torrent of conversation. *Klazmurah* music, clamorous and plaintive, from congested alley. It was as if the planet Alykh had been taken in an instant, and brought to another world, with no time having elapsed.

And voices everywhere. Laughter. Crude jokes. Chanting from gleaming temples — this then was a religious world, which Urna was not.

For a while the watched, awestruck, then—

"But now," said Orifec, "there is something else that the High Inquest must do. A little bit of ... cutting and polishing. Filing down the rough edges of their handiwork. Look, Sajitteh, look toward the other side of the lake."

That was were the palace of Nevéqilas stood.

Suddenly, above the palace, thousands upon thousands of lights! "Look long and hard! Use the viewing-crystal." A servocorpse came to Sajit with a tray.

He put the crystal to his eye and then he saw what it was. But first he heard it.

Though it was more than a klomet away, the shrill relentless sound of a million children's voices rent the air: *Ishá ha! Ishá ha! Ishá ha ha hé ha!* It was the warcry of the childsoldiers. The most feared sound in the universe. The sound of killing innocence.

For every point of light was a child on a spinning hoverdisk. And with each warcry came shafts of laser light, one from each eye, a million children, two million deadly streams of brightness. As one, the army swiveled, swooped, in a complex ballet, and with their laser-eyes they sliced the crystal stamens of the palace, ignited the minarets, carved up the towers — a pyrotechnic display of utter elegance and barbarity.

"My family?" said Sajit. "Are they—"

"In all probability, yes. Though the two games of *makrúgh* were in conflict, each Inquestral command had to be obeyed. I am sure it was carefully worked out, to inflict the minimum amount of damage ... within the precepts of the High Compassion. But your family were part of the royal household; they will have fallen under the prescribed norms of collateral devivement."

"Why?" Sajit cried. And he could find no answers, not in the blank expression of the Princeling who had lost everything, not in Tijas's face either, for though Sajit and Tijas were one in some respects, Tijas had never known Ina and Areon as a family.

He knew he could never be childsoldier. But only a child possessed the reflexes that could control the laser-irises of death. Only a child could learn the utter ruthlessness of an Inquestral war. Only a child could be pitiless, because he did not yet have pity to unlearn.

To be one of *millions*, to be a cog it that relentless machine of death ... *No. I was not born for that.*

"I'll never be one of them. And neither will Tijas."

"They will still plan the culling," Orifec said. "And you will still be on their list ... their very specific list ... you can't escape your DNA."

Sajit looked away from the crumbling city across the lake. He looked at Alykh. He saw a city just awakening to like. Although he knew that his family might be killed, he felt no emptiness, no pain. It was happening to someone else.

The High Inquest is so vast and uncaring that my whole family, even my city, my world, can fall under "collateral norms" ... so why is my *DNA so specific, that they would relentlessly single* me *out?* It made no sense.

At the edge of the city, there stood a woman. A woman cloaked in shadow....

And the woman looked past Sajit, looked at the Princeling, and she *recognized* him.

"You see her!" Sajit cried. "I'm not just imagining her."

Orifec said, "You must find her. She may have an answer for you." And then he touched Sajit on the cheek and Sajit saw the ring, the intaglio that matched the beat-up whisperlyre's. And Orifec said simply, "Take it." And he pulled the ring from his finger and put it in the boy's palm, and closed the boy's fingers over it. It felt cold and hard.

Sajit said, "Are *you* my father?"

Orifec said, "It would not be seemly to answer that question. But come. No one except the dead can see us. We are no one in this new world. You may as well hug me."

And so Sajit put his arms around the man who had once been an untouchable lord, and they embraced; and in giving freely of himself, Sajit received his own freedom in return. Yet there was no comfort in this.

He broke away. “Come on, Tijas,” he said, “We have to find the woman.”

But she was already gone.

“Come on, Tijas,” he said again.

“Where will we go?”

“I don’t know, Tijas. Away. Away.”

He took Tijas’s hand and they sprinted across the field, to the walls of a wider world.

Interlude
Elloran

Ton Elloran n'Taanyel Tath had been listening intently to the Rememberer. The more he heard, the less sense the story seemed to make, the less it connected with what he knew to be true.

And yet, through the Rememberer's art, through his art of mimicking voices, of picking the most telling metaphors, of describing the very air that the characters breathed, he came to believe that the Rememberer's words *must* be true. A Rememberer may not lie, after all. It is an impossibility.

And what evidence remained of this fantastical tale, except for the telling of it?

Urna was shattered; Alykh too, having blossomed on this planet for a few centuries, had been hurriedly packed off and was waiting in orbit around elsewhere, to start again, for *there is history, and there is no history;* the cosmos must ever eddy, yet be still; such was the central paradox that was Inquestra dogma.

"Perhaps," said Elloran to his host, who had been Remembering for some days now, barely pausing for a snack, "you can show me the museum. Is there an artifact there, perhaps, something tangible from this other past?"

For the whisperlyre behind the forceshield, the whisperlyre that Elloran recognized as the one Sajit held, now centuries in the past, was not the one in the Rememberer's story. There was no double-serpent intaglio. There was something not right about it.

"Ah, *hokh'Ton,* you will already have noticed that the whisperlyre on display, so venerated, so ancient, is actually a copy," said Tash Teléon.

"It is no more authentic than ... that holosculpt."

He pointed to a doorway that led to an inner courtyard. It was guarded by twin images of Sajit as a child, both woven of light.

"Come, *hokh'Ton,* I will show you where the real artifacts are kept."

***

If the shrine was unswept and rundown, the inner sanctum was chaos. There was a circular displacement plate in the center; that was the only clear space. Around it, up to its very edge, were piles of objects. Musical instruments, old robes, sheafs of music notations, some even scratched by hand on frayed bark-*papél.* There were holoflats and holosculpts.

There was the old wooden bench described by the Rememberer ... the doppling kit. So that part of the story had a tangible object behind it.

To Elloran's astonishment, its controls still lit up when he ran his fingers along the old wood, warm to the touch, as any living, organic matter would be. The kit still held a charge. For a moment a thought ...

No! He dismissed it. *On Sajit's world, it's an abomination.*

Although that world is dead.

***

Tash Toléon spread a piece of cloth over the displacement plate so they would not accidentally be spirited away with an unintended subvocalization.

He fetched a stool for the Inquestor. He clapped his hands and a chilly, bluish light spread out from the walls and ceiling, which was low, claustrophobic.

"The old whisperlyre...."

The Rememberer squeezed easily amongst the old artifacts; of course, as a Rememberer, he kept the location of each one carefully pinpointed in his trained brain; that was his art. He pulled the instrument from under a pile of *papéli.* It was light; the Remember held it by its fingerboard, between two fingers, as he handed it to the Inquestor.

And when Elloran touched it, he felt what he had not felt with the replica. "I wept before," he said. "What I feel now is too deep even for weeping."

But there was no intaglio either.

"I know what you're thinking, *hokh'Ton,*" Tash Toléon said. "But feel the body more closely. There. Where the frets end."

The Inquestor ran his finger again along the wood. Was there a circular depression? Nothing there to see.

But did the wood hold some ancient memory of a jewel, long ago pried loose?

"It was removed," he said. "Why?"

"Perhaps we will find out," said Toléon, "as my Remembrance proceeds."

Then Elloran said, "But, the Princeling, Orifec ... was he Sajit's real father? For what I have always believed was that his father was a nameless *dorezda* who visited the stews of Alykh."

"A man can have many fathers," Toléon said.

"But only one mother," Elloran said, "for we can see who gave him birth. Unless the womb was a doppling kit."

Elloran spotted a holoflat of a woman. He pulled it from another heap of *papéli.*

He recognized her immediately because of Tash Toléon's powerful Remembering. And he could see, though shadow swirled about the image, that the woman's eyes were the eyes of Shen Sajit. "The woman cloaked in shadow," he said.

"Yes."

"And who *is* the woman cloaked in shadow?"

"Ah, the woman. I must speak of her next. So my story, as a pebble in a pond, must ripple outward, wider, stepping earlier in the past that we may reach out later into the future...."

Book Two

A Woman Cloaked in Shadow

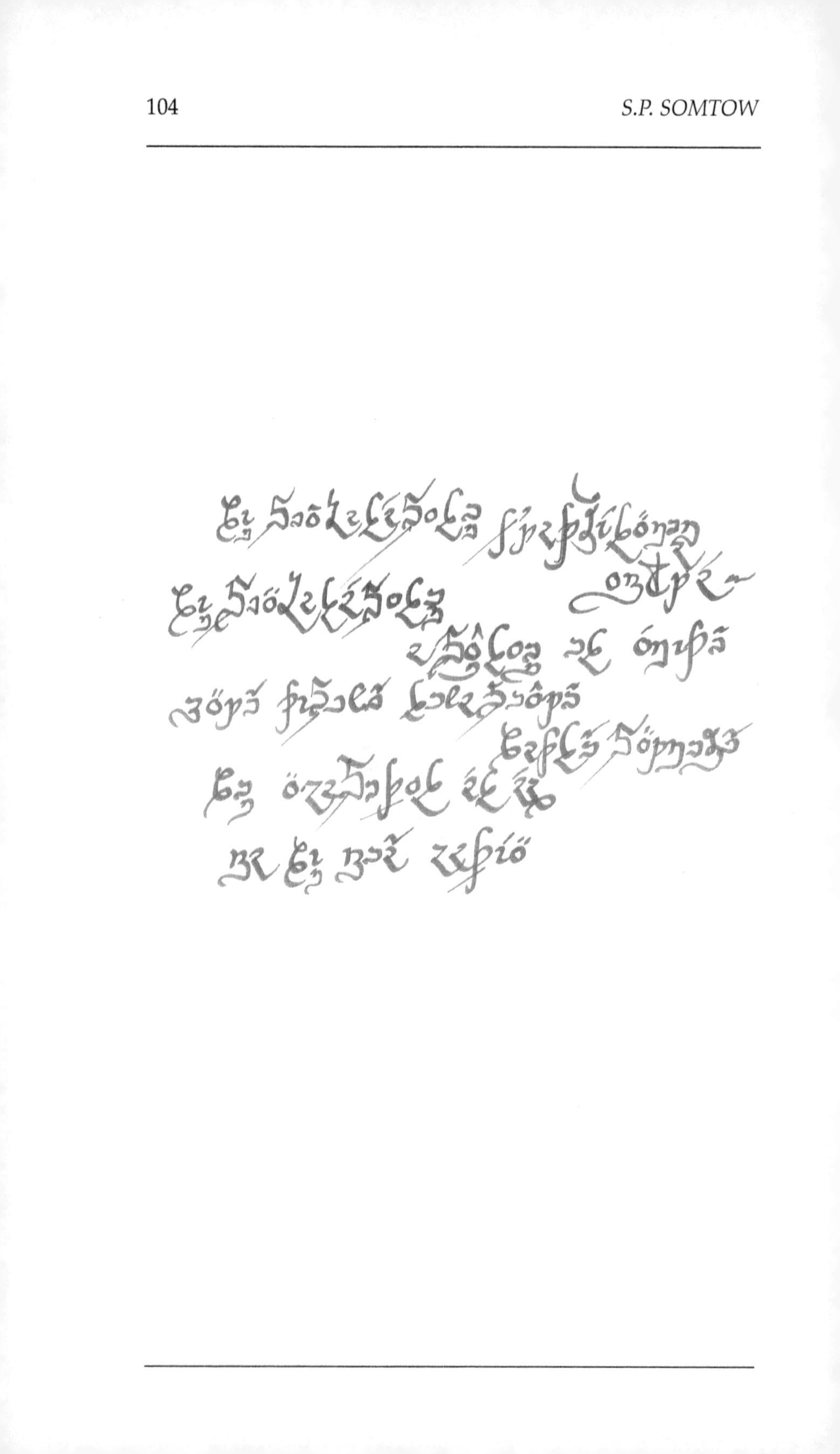

din veó qatávuten
z' rashkhítonens ombrá
din veó qatávuten
a vórtuen et únisheh

moréh shiveléh telaveóreh
dashtéh vornekéh
den o-savezhut át ás
ma din meáh sazhío

I saw you framed
in a shimmercloak's shadow
I saw you framed
by the gateway to nowhere

mother, sister, prophetess,
goddess, whore,
what you were I knew not
but I knew you were mine.

— from The Songs of Sajit

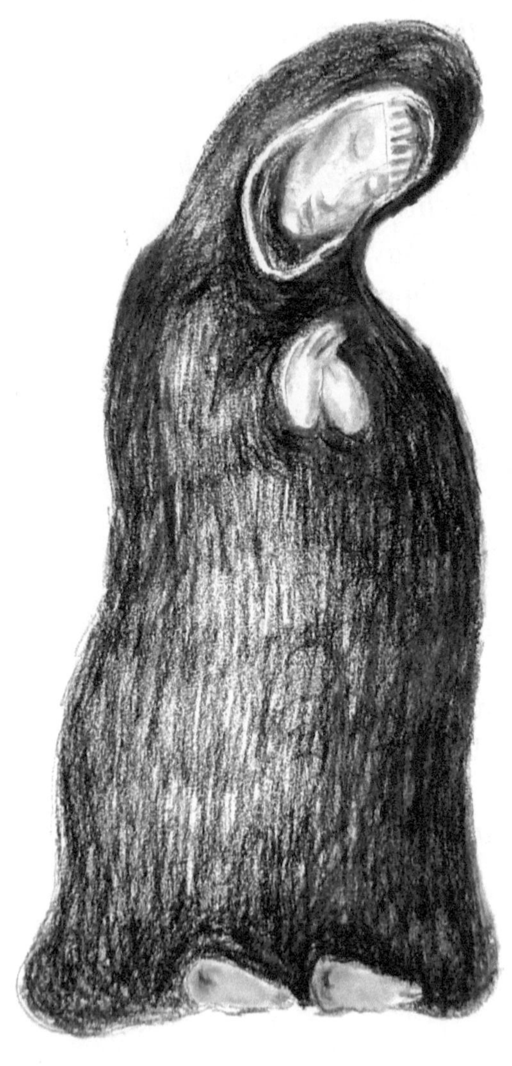

Five
Cloaked in Shadow

The Rememberer continued:

In fact, she was no supernatural vision, though to the febrile imagination of a unformed bard she may have seemed so. She was a woman. She had a name.

Her name was Éluma, which in the highspeech means *soul.* She was a priestess of the mysteries of Aërat, that is to say a prostitute, for there had not been a cult of Aërat, or any other deity, in Urna, for at least a millennium; yet sometimes the ancient titles were useful euphemisms.

And it must be understood that these were not euphemisms to the denizens of Urna. They were a traditional people. Their gods may have long departed, but, paradoxically, they were as strong as ever.

Éluma had been apprenticed to Aërat since the age of five; she had lived in the House of the Priestesses of Aërat, also called the House Without Walls, also called the Labyrinth of Shadows, in Shírensang in the shadow of Nevéqilas, studying the art of arousal, until the appropriate time when she would perform the rituals in the real world.

Not that practice was difficult. The temple had a large supply of high-grade pleasure corpses, calibrated according to size, number of appendages and openings, quality of appearance, level of cosmetic enhancement. One could do exercises with a soma of any type, whether an withered old lecher or an innocent first-timer, with responses programmed for randomness as well as for characterization. The art of Aërat required a different face for every client, a different voice, different technical accomplishments; a servant of the god could specialize, but some skills were common to all.

Éluma's specialty was in making the client feel loved. Passion she could do, games she could play, but love is the hardest of all the skills, the only one that cannot be faked.

Bequeathed to the temple as a child, Éluma grew up with only virtual knowledge of the world, as devotees did not were not allowed to leave until the day of their dedication ritual. In the main, she had been raised by servocorpses. She did not have friends; contact with real human beings was not allowed, for fear that the acolyte might learn to *receive* passion, rather than *bestowing* it.

Perhaps an entire tribe of Rememberers would be needed to catalog her childhood and her young womanhood, even though the world she lived in was not real.

Yet there were scenes that seemed real enough....

***

Éluma was free to wander the labyrinth that was the dwelling place of Aërat. Often she would be guided by one of the instructor servocorpses. Occasionally there would be another initiate, being hurried through a corridor, and sometimes their eyes would meet; that was the only way Éluma knew there were others here.

Servocorpses' eyes are not the eyes of the living.

Once a boy ran through the cross-corridor, a boy whose hair was a cold blue flame; they looked at each other and the girl's eyes were the color of the flame; and the boy said to her, "I don't know!" and she tried to smile, but soon Éluma was hustled down a side passage, and the servocorpse, not a talking model, covered his mouth so he could not answer.

When he was gone, Éluma said, "What is it he did not know?

The servocorpse could not reply, but led her by the hand, quickly, and by a circuitous route Éluma found herself once more in an instruction chamber.

***

There was a room called the Hall of the Goddesses. There, one could study every image of Aërat since the foundation of the temple. There were statues in stone and holosculptures and plastiflesh. There were automata and tapestries.

On one occasion she found herself there, not knowing which pathway she had taken. When she entered, there was something — a servocorpse — swabbing at a monumental sculpture with a depulverant. The corpse skittered away when it saw her. The room was gloomy, though it was well lit; it was dusty, though there was no dust. Each of the subjects seemed to cast an aura. Row upon row, each bearing the same face, the face that many believed was perfection itself, the face of Aërat.

That was where she saw *I-don't-know* again. He was bent over a stand on which stood three miniatures of the Goddess, carved in phoenix ivory; they had set in a miniature rock garden, and had portrayed the three sacred gestures of the Goddess — *Come Hither, I Shall Love You Forever,* and *Destiny is our Destiny.*

"They must very old," Éluma whispered.

"A few minutes, at least," the boy said. His hair moved as though on an artificial wind. It was, she realized, some kind of symbiont, not a flame at all.

"But the age of phoenixes was five centuries ago," she said, proud of her history.

"Idiot! I'm not looking at any damn statues." He pointed at the miniature rock garden and Éluma saw them now: tiny blue filaments, like the ones on the boy's head, wriggling between the white pebbles.

The boy yanked out a strand of his hair and dropped it onto the rock garden.

"Does that hurt?"

"Only if I let it."

"What do they live on? Don't they need an organism to feed them, not just a bunch of white pebbles?"

"You really are an idiot, little whore."

"I'm not —"

"We all are. In training at least. Now look at the stones. Look for a long time. Why does this little stand have a metal bevel? Why would pebbles want to run away?" What do they flee from?"

When Éluma looked again, when she really stared, she could see that the pebbles were not entirely still. Rather, each was expanding and contracting, as though they were breathing.

And the statues ... they two were not motionless. For each one's joints were slowly ... every few seconds ... shifting. Each gesture was slowly transforming into the next gesture. This static tableau was in fact a thing of constant movement, if one had but the patience to more than just glance at it.

"I won't ask your name, because here we have no names," the boy said. "But remember the lesson. Nothing holds still forever. Oh! Got to run."

The boy looked furtively around and then — to Éluma's astonishment — an arm popped out of the empty space behind him, seized him by the edge of his tunic, and pulled him into nothingness.

"Fooled you! I'm still here!" A voice, ringing in the nothingness.

She never found that room again.

***

There was a room they called *The Clouds and Rain.* In this room, there were no horizons. You floated, but you were not weightless. You were surrounded by cushiony, velvety nothingness. The air had texture. You could twist your body into any position and the air would hold you; the air was as viscous and as vacuous as it needed to me, bending itself to every movement; it was said that the air was made of the same creature that formed the shimmercloak, a single celled organism that enveloped an entire Inquestor, transforming his inner light into a pale twilight glow.

A dream-lover dwelt in this room.

You enter the room via a mirror that is really a displacement plate. You are in your room, little more than a cubicle because you have no possessions: your entire life is for giving, never for receiving; your duty is to become the desired.

You look at yourself in that mirror, and as you have been trained, allow each thought to drain from your mind, down a sinkhole of forgetfulness; a circle of blackness deepens, widens, until you feel yourself dissolving into the image of yourself in the mirror....

... and when you hit that moment of total inner darkness can the displacement be triggered ... and you find yourself inside the room....

... and the lover comes.

The lover is invisible. Genderless, it seems ... but not an *it,* either; rather the lover is all genders and all varieties of lovemaking. The lover embraces, suffuses the air, penetrates every opening, every pore. The lover envelops. The lover overwhelms. The lover batters down the battens of your soul, bares open your heart; you lose yourself in the lover, you pour yourself into the lover, the lover, the hungry vessel, the lover who takes and takes though you never stop giving ...

... and when you are spent, the darkness swoops down and you awaken in the room that it is little more than a cubicle. And the clouds and the rain cling to your flesh are can never be wiped away.

That is the nature of your art.

You are the mirror of your lover's soul; your very being is to give. There is no self. There is only the lover.

More than that, there is only technique; the flick of the finger, the seven categories of caress, the basic movements of tongue and hips and hands and lips; all these catalogued and endlessly to be recited, analyzed, and reinvented.

***

She wondered if she would ever see *I-don't-know* again. In the refectory, perhaps, she might catch a glimpse. Or during one of the big instruction halls, where each person was alone, cocooned in a bubble of force, but one could sometimes catch another person's eye.

What was today's lesson going to be.

Today's lesson was about touch.

Then why aren't I allowed to touch *anyone? What is so special about dead people?*

***

In the room, Éluma knew she was alone, though around her there were other acolytes. The others could be seen from the corner of the eye, sometimes, vague flitting shapes; Éluma imagined that for each of the other novices she too was a vague shape, sometimes a shadow, sometimes a gust of breath. The instructor was a holosculpt of the goddess herself; the demonstrator was a servocorpse, so androgynously retooled that one could see in it any gender one wished to see.

Today's demonstration, said the voice of the goddess, *is about levels of moisture in the tongue, and how to control them. Between dry and wet there are seven progressions, comparable to the* shrut *of a musical scale....*

Éluma tried to concentrate. But her mind went back to the secret room behind the mirror, to the secret lover ... and she longed to receive instead of give, to be an object of love rather than a repository of love. She let the words of the goddess swirl about her ears while her mind repeated again and again *Love me for who I am.* A heretical thought, but one that was keeping her sane, feeding her a figment of hope.

Slowly move your tongue across the edge of your lower lip ... not too fast ... Éluma, your mind is drifting!

"Oh ... sorry, Goddess."

You are not, Éllekeh. You are rarely sorry. It's one of your most endearing characteristics. Do not fear. The time of your unbinding is soon to come.

"Unbinding, Goddess?"

"You've had your womanblood. Your mastery of my arts is among the highest among my acolytes. I must warn you now, child, that you will not know when your test will come; you will know only when you have been awarded the cloak of shadow."

So Éluma came to know that sometime, in the near future, her status would change; that it would come without warning; and that there would come a time when she would emerge from the cocoon of the temple, and live no more among the dead. She did not know if this pleased her, because she barely remembered the living; she had been pledged to the temple very young.

To pay a debt, perhaps, or to fulfill a vow.

***

Only in the refectory could one ever really talk to other acolytes; meals were shared, each table seating two, in order to further instruct in the art of conversation. Conversations were, of course, rehearsed, from preexisting scripts.

One morning, indeed, she saw the boy again, the boy she thought of as "I-don't-know." They were assigned as dialogue-partners. He was good enough at the pleasantries, pouring the *zul* and passing the honeyed salt with the right bend of the wrist, but he stumbled when it came to conversation itself.

"The weather been cloudy," she said to him, because that was one of the standard dialogues they had to memorize. The correct response would have been, "But not so cloudy as when we make the rain." The art was always to turn the subject towards the sensual.

Instead, he grasped both her hands. "My name is Mikkálu, called Mikeh," he said. Names are never exchanged in the temple of Aërat. The servocorpse who doubled as a waiter jabbed the boy with an electro-flagellum; politely, Éluma ignored what was one of the petty indignities of being an acolyte, the fact that dead people were allowed to punish you.

"No, no, I want someone to know my name."

The servocorpse made another move, but Mikeh grabbed the flagellum from its hand and lashed it in the face. He had pushed up the setting; it actually lacerated the dead one's cheek, and a phlegmatic pseudo-blood oozed from the wound.

"Yes, I'm aggressive," Mikeh said. "I'm not able to lose myself in someone else. That's why they're not even letting me take the test."

"Test?" Éluma remembered that the Goddess had told her a test was coming soon.

"I wanted someone to know my name before they send me away."

"Away?" That was strange to Éluma, who after all knew only these halls, these corridors and pathways.

"I'll be a childsoldier," said the boy. "Remember my face. One day you'll see me riding the clouds, but there won't by any phantom lover with me. You'll look into my eyes and you'll see death."

They led him away.

***

The test that Éluma faced a few sleeps later could not have been more strange. She was led into an empty room, in the middle of which there was a completely circular bed. A man sat on that bed and she gasped.

"I didn't know they had a servocorpse made to look like —" Without even thinking, she had started to prostrate herself. Every Princeling in Urna would appeat identical to every other; they were the only family in the world accorded the privilege of doppling. Abhorrent and abominated though it was to divide one flesh again and again, doppling the princeling gave the culture of this world continuity and fulfilled the great Inquestral adage: *History there is, and no history.*

And there was the image in the flesh. Not old, not young, with a simple grey kilt held in place by a living serpent.

A triumph of the the art of servocorpse manufacture! "Am I real to you?" Yes; it was a voice she had heard in the air around her, in a holobroadcast, declaiming at her from the pages of a book.

She could barely answer. "It resembles the High Princeling Orifec in every regard," she said, addressing the servocorpse in the third person as befit its devived condition.

"They say," said the simulacrum, "that this model verges on lèse majésté, and should never be shown in public. But never mind that; we're not in public now."

Overcome with the feelings that had been ingrained in her all her life, she did prostrate herself at last. "Starry Highness!" she murmured.

He whispered a word and the walls deopaqued and she found that they were surrounded by images of rainbow-fringed clouds.

And then he touched her.

She did not know where her training ended and her feelings began. *I must not feel,* she told herself. *Do my duty. Be the empty vessel of the client's longing.* And yet, she tingled at the slightest graze. And she found herself saying, over and over, "Do you love me?" which were forbidden words, but she could not help herself.

I thank the goddess this is merely a test, she told herself. And their lovemaking continued, and it was as though she were back in the secret ocean of the room without horizons.

And when it was over, she lay on the embankment of cloud, created from holosculpture and imagination. She looked into his eyes and wondered if there was not a flicker of life in them. But that would not have been possible. Tired out, she slept, and when she woke she was again in her cubicle, just another acolyte of Aërat, just another prostitute in training.

***

It was a tennight later that they came for her. The corridors were new to her. Some doors were physical, some doors were displacement plates. She was marched in so many directions she lost all sense of space. And at length she reached a room she had never seen. It was a council chamber of sorts. There was an empty throne at one end; the intagliata of mating serpents was instantly recognizable. On either side sat a matronly figure; these appeared to be powerful administrators of the temple. And in front of the throne, standing, was the Goddess herself; not a holosculpt, but in the flesh, for she reached out tousled Éluma's hair, and there was a tear in the corner of one eye.

"Éllekeh," said the Goddess, calling her by her childname. "Today we will honour you with a cloak of shadow. You have been singled out, and you will soon be leaving this place. The temple has been like a womb to you, forming you in the image of the thing that all desire, that you may serve me, the eternal Goddess of Love. To serve Love, you have renounced Love; your life will be a perpetual giving, never receiving."

Behind the throne and on either side, shrouded in shadow, were other acolytes. All, it seemed, in the flesh. Most wore the shapeless covershawl that made them indistinguishable from one another. One of them was not so dressed.

It was, she realized, Mikeh, the boy whose hair was a cold blue flame; the boy was already wearing the simple tunic of a childsolder in training, and his eyes had become yellow; he was in the first stage of the implantation of the citrine-colored laser-irises that would render him into the most effective killing machine in the Disperal of Man. It must have taken some doing to have let him attend the ceremony, but as Mikeh himself had said to her, "I'm aggressive." He was standing slightly apart from the others, and behind him there was a tall woman in some kind of offworld uniform.

She mouthed a greeting; he looked sullenly at her, but at least there was a real connection.

The Goddess said, "Before you receive your cloak of shadow, Éllekeh, there will be one final ritual: the Smoothening."

"Goddess, what is this? This was not in the instructions."

"No," said the goddess. "This ritual is secret. It is what binds you to us. From now on, you will be able only to give, and never to receive. Your body is a temple, but when you were born there were some rough edges, some small blights that stand in the way of pure perfection. The mental and emotional edges have been smoothened through years of training. This is the final stage. Your body, too, shall be made smooth and perfect. There will be no pain."

The two matrons approached. They pulled tools from their cloaks. Sharp, shiny tools.

"From now on, you can be all things to all clients. You can be any gender, any variety, any combination."

A third matron emerged now, holding a tray of prosthetics. “Whatever you need, you shall have them all,” said the Goddess. “Whatever is called for; boy, girl, crone, maiden, youth, dotard, whatever the love object in the client’s fantasy may be....”

Éluma screamed.

And the boy named Mikkálu, whose name was unknown to all but Éluma, sprang up and put himself between Éluma and the matrons who were now brandishing scalpels and shears. “They’re lying to you!” he shouted. “They’re going to cut out the roots of your feeling!”

“Be calm,” said the Goddess. “We have done this for centuries here in the Temple of Aërat. It is a privilege, an honor. I assure you, my child, there will be no pain.”

The first matron held up a knife high while servocorpses carefully held Éluma still and began to pry open the seam of her robe —

Mikkálu leapt.

He whirled in the air. A line of yellow light lanced the air. A smell of burning flesh —

The matron’s arm, still clutching the knife, still wriggling as if alive, separated, lying on the white tiles of the council chamber.

The woman, in shock, did not even scream. The laser strike had cauterized and sealed the stump and the arm. “I can kill you all,” Mikeh said.

Then came a cold blue glow from the empty throne. A figure slowly formed, first in outline, then the shape slowly filling in; the bright-eyed one, not old, not young, wearing the simple kilt. Éluma freed herself from the servocorpses’ grip.

"You were real!" she gasped.

Around her, everyone had fallen to the ground in prostration. But she could not do it. Not after what had happened between them.

"I am," said the man, "the Son of the Starlight, the High Princeling Orifec z'Urnasi Tath, hereditary Lord of Nevéqilas, Commander of the World Entire, He Who Answers Only to the High Inquest. "

Even the Goddess was on her knees, and Éluma saw with some bitterness that she was no goddess; she was merely an actress, playing a role in a drama that had been enacted in this temple for generations, born not from logic but from caprice, or superstition. And so she still found she could not prostrate herself.

"Take the wounded woman away and give her another arm," he said. Some servocorpses obeyed. "Now, childsolder, speak to me."

"I am Mikkálu-without-a-Clan," the boy said. "I was sold to this place when I was seven. A gambling debt."

Orifec laughed a little. "That explains your ... recalcitrance," he said. "They didn't get you early enough. How did you manage to be accepted as a childsoldier?"

"I was disobedient too often, Starry Highness. They arranged it. There is no planetary culling, but they're shipping me out to Bellares on a volunteer pass."

"Which means you volunteered."

"It's what I want, Starry Highness, for now. If I survive—"

"Few do."

"— I'll have a clan-name and a future."

"That could happen sooner than you think, boy; I am a Princeling; I do have lines of communication with the High Inquest; surely they would grant me a small favor...."

"No, Starry Highness. Let me go through the system. Let me achieve on my own merits, even if I die trying."

"Admirable."

The acolytes, priestesses, servocorpses, matrons and the Goddess now rose, and waited for their ruler to speak.

"Now, Goddess," he said. "Is it not true that we've not had religion on this world for centuries, and that all these rituals are just that ... ceremonies performed for the sake of tradition, not out of belief?"

"It could be seen that way," the Goddess said.

"And I am not, as Princeling of the World Entire, and Lord of Nevéqilas, the titular head of all religions, not needing any process of council, senatorial vote, or juristic debate to exercise that power?"

"Yes, Starry Highness. Religion comes under your direct command."

"In that case, I decree that mutilations will no longer be performed in the Temple of Aërat without the consent of the acolyte, who shall receive three counsellings before granting such consent; that such counsellings will comprise not only religious advisors but members of fields outside religion: mind-healers, cultural anthropologists, rememberers. Smoothening will not be banned per se, but it should be performed only on those who believe. Let it be this moment recorded that the Laws of the World are altered to reflect this."

"The boy shall be sent to Bellares, the childsoldier training world, on my personal transport," he continued. "Mikkálu, you shall kiss Éluma goodbye; it may be that, with time dilation in space travel, you will never see her again."

Mikkálu embraced Éluma, a little awkwardly; she said to him, "I won't forget you."

And he said, "You're the only person in this place who ever smiled at me."

In the Labyrinth of Shadows, one half smile and one defiant conversation were an entire relationship: the meeting, the connection, the crisis, the breakup.

And then I-don't-know was gone. They were all gone. All but she and Princeling. They were alone together. And she ran to his arms. She could not understand what had happened, did not want to understand; she knew only that all she had ever known was broken and that this man might put it back together again.

"Why didn't they tell me?"

Orifec said, "Ah, but in the final tests, the clients are always real."

"Clients, indeed ... but you ... you could simply summon anyone you wish...."

"I am not my father, nor my grandfather ... though I was born from a doppling kit, I'm not just a copy of a dead ruler," he said. "Maybe the Princeling who succeeds me must also be cloned from my flesh, but why shouldn't I know love, children, the lives of normal people? Oh, but you hardly know me. You don't know that I walk the streets in disguise, night after night, listening to what the people have to say. Éluma, I will establish you in a house of your own in the city; I would like to visit you sometimes; I would not like you to be half a human being, made "smooth" to be a canvas on which to paint my fantasies; perhaps we shall even decide to make a child together.

"Oh, look, Éllekeh, there is something they forgot, in their haste." The tray of prosthetics lay on the floor, but among them was something black, perhaps alive; it was a fabric so sheer that it could not be seen, yet it obscured that which it covered. Orifec pulled it from the tray. "Feel it. It's your cloak of shadow."

He draped the sheet of nothing around Éluma's shoulders. She was well aware of the cloak's symbolism. As a priestess of Aërat, she would have been sworn to remain always in the shadow of the one who paid for her love. She would never have questioned the client, for his desires were inviolable, even, for the right price, to the point of death. But this man, who held the power of life and death over everything in this world, she did dare question. That was a new and disturbing feeling.

"If you had a child who was not you," she said to him, "he would not rule. He would be something quite different. What would you have him be?"

The Starry Highness thought for a moment, then pulled her to him. Kissed her forehead very gently. She saw herself disappear beneath the shifting cloak of shadow. "I've always loved music," he said.

And the Rememberer said to Ton Elloran n'Taanyel Tath: "This happened some time before the birth of Sajit. For a tale is never linear, but always grows both forward and backward in time."

Six
In a Glass Garden

Two boys entered an awakening city, in search of a woman cloaked in shadow.

Two boys entered a city that was still constructing itself, knitting itself into shape like a living thing, sucking in the old capital and absorbing it unto itself, as the people bins continued to disgorge the world's new citizens.

It was night and a very long night, too, for many people bins were still in orbit, shadowing the sunlight. It was cold. The new city was all spindles and cogs and threads of metal flinging themselves across the sky as they wove themselves into walls. Buildings grew from seedlings and storefronts bloomed where there had just been a mass of writhing metal. Streets were haphazard; the city had an air of having been improvised ... like the opening *alap* of an epic song.

They took care not to be seen together; when one ran into the light, the other stood in the shadow of an alley. Presently they found themselves in a street that spiraled round and round toward a central circular plaza, and there were always doorways to hide in, and so many people bustling about that it was easier not to be noticed.

The people around them wore unfamiliar clothes. Their colors were garish, the fashions outlandish. Most seem to know where they were going. It seemed that the new city had been programmed around the city they had left. Sajit saw a man with several children go up to a door and when he placed his palm against it, it irised open to admit him.

Tijas said, "This city is a sort of doppling of its own, it's their old city, close to it, and the homes open up to them when they read their DNA."

"So we will be homeless."

"Unless we find someone generous."

"Quiet now. I have a plan."

Sajit sent Tijas to sit in the shadow of a fountain. He found a spot a tenth-klomet away, a bit of clearing; he stood in the clearing and he began to sing.

He sang not a song in the highspeech, but one from Attembris, in the dialect of the world that was being cannibalized all around them.

The song was no more than a ditty, really, a simple thing about a village lad who loved a girl who appeared only when the moons sang.

People began to stop and listen.

A gipfer clinked at his feet. A half-gipfer, presently a handful of the coins ... finally an arjent.

He went on singing, his voice shaking.

Until he felt a rough hand on his shoulder. The coins on the flagstones were being scooped up. And a gruff voice. "You need a license for that, brother!"

"Let him sing," a woman said. "It's a pretty song."

The man let go. When Sajit looked up, he did not see much; a beard, flushed cheeks, striated in the intermittent light of the fountain.

"I didn't know I needed a license to sing," Sajit said.

The man laughed now, a hearty laugh. "You don't," he said. "Unless I say you do. And you're taking all our business."

Sajit saw other entertainers in the plaza now. Someone was juggling small rodents. In another corner someone was hammering away at planks to set up a makeshift servocorpse theater.

"Just pick a different corner." The man was whistling now to a troupe of acrobats. "But wait ..." he said. "Do you have an instrument? They move far better to a solid beat."

"I —"

"What about that other boy you are with? The one skulking in the shadows with his face always downcast? Ho, come our of there!"

"He's very shy."

Too late! The woman who had admired his singing had grabbed Tijas by the hand and was pulling him toward them. "You can't look at him!" Sajit whispered harshly. "You can't!"

The man looked at both of them. "Why not?"

"Because he's a doppling!"

"What's that?"

"An abomination — a thing that must be destroyed —" Sajit felt tears spurting.

"So, you've a twin," said the man.

"What's a twin?" Tijas said.

The woman said, "They're from Urna, you idiot!."

"Urna? Where – oh, the world we accidentally displaced. Yes, sorry about that. Supposedly these mistakes never happen, but it's a *very* large galaxy and we are just backworlds."

The woman said, "Daro, twins are *harám* on this world." using a lowspeech term Sajit had never heard.

"I see. A bit of a culture clash." He pulled Tijas and Sajit together and looked from one to the other. Tijas flinched when the woman tried to put her arm around his shoulder. But Sajit saw now these people did not react in the expected way. They seemed to be inured to the sight of abomination.

"Twins all right. A planetary taboo. Poor boys, I imagine you must have been shunned all your lives. No longer! And you probably both play and sing. In some parts of the Dispersal, you'd have been sold to some mighty lord by now. Wouldn't they, Zelma?"

The woman called Zelma, whose eyes were painted with rainbow dust, said, "You must forgive him boys. He's ... a lout. Daro, twins are *harám* on Urna, which is senseless, but on Urna, they don't have slaves. They only use dead people. Which is actually rather advanced of them."

Tijas looked across the square, where the theater was completed now, and a slapstick comedy was in progress, with a fat lady bashing a three-armed man with a toy club while children giggled. His eyes went wide with astonishment. "You mean those actors are living people?"

Daro said, "It seems that our societies, shoved together by some misplaced decimal point in the calculus of the High Compassion, could never have naturally arisen on the same planet."

"Rubbish. Old Earth had plenty of variant societies."

"And now," said Daro, "Professor Zelma moves from science to mythology. There is no such place."

"Then where did the human race come from?"

Sajit said, "Can we have our money, please? We need food and somewhere to stay."

Daro thought a moment, then flung the tokens back to Sajit. "Let us begin properly," Zelma said. "I am Nar Zelma z'Tarovén, Professor of Pre-Dispersal Research at the University of Kurremkurráh."

"You have a clan-name!" Sajit said in wonder.

"... for what it's worth. I was doing research on Alykh when the people bins came."

"And I," Daro said, "am Daro-without-a-Clan, a juggler and entertainment mogul. I am also the Professor's ... secretary. Bodyguard. Paramour."

"And we are Sajit and Tijas-without-Clans. We are looking for a woman cloaked in shadow."

"A sacred whore of Aërat!" Zelma said. "How I would love to interview her for my research."

"These twins are lucky for us," Daro said.

"How?" Sajit said. "We're — what did you call it — *harám* in this world. And we're homeless and hungry."

"We have nowhere to stay either," Daro said. "Not *officially*. We're not actually *from* ... what is the name of that planet?"

Zelma said, "Alykh."

"Oh yes. The pleasure world."

"Where we thought we could pick up a sack of arjents, on the way home! And look what happened! Time-frozen, dropped off on a planet even more barbaric than the one we were visiting!"

In a short time, Sajit's world had changed from a village to a city to a great planet and now two planets, with glimpses of yet more worlds....

Tijas said, "These people don't seem to care ... that we are dopplings."

"No," Zelma, "why should we? After all the worlds we have seen? But you should still be careful. It may be that Alykh shares your superstitions. Most of these worlds do ... I mean the *irrational* planets ... the ones with primitive beliefs, with gods and demons ... there's something frightening about twins to many barbarian societies."

Sajit said, "Urna's not barbarian. We stopped believing in the gods centuries ago...."

"Yet you have temples...." Zelma said, smiling a little.

"Ruined. Disused."

"Ghosts do not die all at once," said Daro. "Come, we will take you somewhere. One of you ..." He pulled a shawl from Zelma's shoulder a threw it over Tijas's head. "A precaution, Professor. We don't want any witch hunts."

"Where are we going?" Tijas said.

"Food and lodging. For the taking!" Daro laughed and dragged Sajit behind him, and Zelma took Tijas's arm and they set off down a side street.

***

And many years before that day, another boy heard the soft pounding on his coffin-womb and knew that it was time for birth and death.

He did not know how long he had been there, because time in amniosis there is no time as such; he was being fed the memories, the histories of all those who had borne his DNA since the first Orifec ruled on Urna. And he knew what was expected of him when the the time would come for him to emerge.

Urna was an old world, settled, indeed, before the very existence of the Dispersal of Man. When the Inquest came, all planetary norms were kept in place; and Orifec-within-the-Womb saw it all unfold; the founding of Nevéqilas, the War of the Elephantines, the burning of the temples of Gön; the sight of the tachyon bubbles raining from the sky, signalling the acceptance of Urna into the Dispersal; all these things he saw as if with his own eyes.

He saw himself emerge, grow old, from age to age, and knew how one Orifec succeeds another; so when, after a time that was outside time, there came a knock on side of the box, and he heard a priest intone words in a dead language that only he remembered, he knew what he must do.

First there was a light.

The amniostuff still clung to his flesh. He stepped forth, and as he knew he would, found himself standing before the Princeling's deathbed.

He already knew where this would be.

In Nevéqilas there was a secret garden called Véravur, a garden made of glass. The garden could be reached only through displacement. It had no door and its walls were holosculpts of itself, so that the garden went on forever, without even a horizon; above, a brightly lit nightscape, for the singing moons of Urna shone altogether, imparting a soft glow to the air.

Millions of smooth glass pebbles comprised its floor, and rising from the glittery cold sea were twisted outcroppings, handblown fantastical shapes, many taller than a man.

In the center of the glass garden there grew a single tree, one whose crystal fronds spread out, to form a circle of shade; the glass leaves tinkled in the wind. And under the shade of the tree was the deathbed, a square of pure air that allowed the old princeling to hover in a field of nothing, so no cloth could scrape against raw skin.

The Garden of Glass was where the Starry Highnesses went to die.

On the bed lay he himself, a much older version at any rate; hairless, withered, thin. On either side stood a councillor, a man and a woman, each cloaked in clingfire and the feathers of phoenixes.

Orifec-within-the-Womb stepped forward — he could barely walk yet, but he knew he must do this all by himself.

Orifec-of-the-Past beckoned to him with a weak finger. "Sit beside me. You will find the bed easily enough, or it will find you." His voice was dry and creaky, like an old door in a cold wind.

Sure enough, the bed found him, just when he thought he might collapse. The cushiony air caught him as he was about to fall and oozed around him, and it carried him to sit beside his dying doppling.

"Welcome, Orifec-within-the-Womb," said the old man. He was unclothed. There were two child-servocropses kneeling beside him, and they were already anointing his body with the burial-ointment. The smell of it was cloying, ripe. "Are you ready?"

"Can it not wait, Starry Highness?" For he was terribly afraid; he had been in the world of the living for only a few minutes, and he was already being asked to despatch his predecessor to the land of the dead.

"You don't want to kill me." The old princeling laughed. "I understand. I was the same way. But this is the moment. I chose it. It is with complete equanimity and without regret that I close this chapter of our rulership."

Two more aides stepped forward now. They took a tiny worm from a dish, and placed the worm on the old Princelings forehead. "This creature has been bred to be a conduit of data," explained an aide, "whether from thinkhive to thinkhive, or from brain to brain."

The aide pulled at the worm and it began lengthening. He motioned for Orifec-within-the-Womb to lean over and he dragged the wiry worm until it touched the base of Orifec's skull. He felt a pinprick as it burrowed.

The Elder Princeling said, "I bequeath you all that remains of me; my life story, my hopes, my dreams, my secrets."

Information began to flood his mind. Trysts and whispers. Judgments and desires. In the womb, he had rehearsed for this moment, again and again, and he knew he must dissolve the barrier between himself and the others. The waves of information came. And at the center of all this was the knowledge ... the dark knowledge ...

I had a brother once....

***

The quarters were not exactly what Sajit was used to. It was a single room, accessible through a mechanical door with hinges — Sajit did not know such doorways still existed. It did not read anyone's palm. It had a doorknob.

He had been frustrated by it a few times until Daro told him that it twisted one way to open, the other way to close.

It wasn't a room for people, but a storeroom for *zul;* thus it was always cool, and the walls and floor were lined with real wood. Vats of various vintages lined the walls. "We might starve," said Daro, "but we shan't want for drink."

There were about a dozen here; some acrobats, a magician, a storyteller.

"More freeloaders!" said one of them, smirking. "Will you pimp them out?"

Daro said, "Alykh will be reestablished within a hundred sleeps. And when Alykh reforms itself ..."

"The *dorezdas* will follow. And we'll be squeezing every gipfer we can," Zelma said.

"Dorezdas?" Tijas said.

"They are what pays the bills. They wander from world to world, taking their pleasure and paying for it well."

"We'll need money if we are to go home."

"Home!" the acrobat scoffed. "Yes! In stasis in the hold of a delphinoid ... who knows what century it will be if we ever got there."

"Home is not the place you are from," Sajit said. "It is the place in your heart, the place that calls to you, that you can never reach."

Words from an old *qazel.*

Zelma said, "See? These boys aren't just pretty faces. They could make us all rich. And they're fugitives us all — like us. This is another world with the Twin Taboo — if they're caught, at least one will die."

And Daro said, "Sing for them, Sajit."

Sajit said, "I'll sing the whole song. It's called *The Homeworld of the Heart.* But first I must tune my whisperlyre."

***

It was a tennight before he came to her, and when he came, at first he said nothing. The door dissolved and he was there, and he strode in and seized her by her slender waist and crushed her lips with his. She could barely breathe. She was almost choking, and then, abruptly, he stopped.

"Éluma," he whispered. "I'm sorry to come to you like this."

He let go. He went to sit on a hoverpillow that rose from the floor to receive him.

"You may come as you wish, Starry Highness," Éluma said. "You are my Lord. My flesh, my soul ... take what you wish."

"No," Orifec said. "That is your training, your endless exercises in compliance. But how would your training hold up if you saw who I really am?"

"You're a king."

"I murdered my brother. My father. My uncles. My grandfathers."

"I don't think so, my Lord. There's been no talk of royal murders, ever. News would reach even the Temple of Aërat, I am sure."

"No, I don't mean I, this human body, physically did it. But I have all their memories, you know. I can't escape the centuries of bloodshed. Every Starry Highness from the beginnings of our world is in me."

"I am also trained to listen," Éluma said. "You'll find that I listen well."

But Orifec was weeping. She put her arms around him and comforted him as she imagined a mother might comfort a child, though the only mothers who ever had ever comforted her were well-programmed servocorpses. Their programming must have been well thought out indeed, for Orifec grew still at her touch.

And said, "You held me like a child."

And she said, "You could tell."

He answered, "Yes, I could, though no one ever held me that way except a servocorpse."

It was then that Éluma discovered what they had in common, the princeling and the prostitute; they had both been orphaned. Not through death, but through vicious circumstance, through accident of birth; Éluma's mother's need for cash, Orifec's rôle as supreme ruler of a backworld.

And so they made love, each seeing in the other, perhaps, a different person from the one who was there, a fantasy person; yet their need was such that the imagined impinged on the real.

And each time they met, Éluma learned a fresh fragment of Orifec's ancient memories. The fratricide, the sentencing of whole generations of his family to gruesome slaughter, the stabbing of an infant, the hurling of a household into a fiery pit ... and finally ... to the pact that kept the peace: the Starry House would reproduce only by the forbidden means of doppling, each doppling to emerge and replace his predecessor at the moment of the latter's passing; a planet's peace at the price of a princeling's abomination.

"I remember slitting the baby's throat." Orifec said. "I remember it every day. There's a whistling sound that goes with it."

"That's was centuries ago."

"I know. That's why, with you, I want to be the not-Orifec. I want the borders of Urna to end at the entrance to this room. I want a child."

She gasped. Stifled the gasp immediately; a priestess of Aërat was allowed no private emotions. Never showed surprise at a client's demands.

"You would undo those centuries of stasis?"

"Call it a flaw that happened after they copied the same strand of DNA so many times ... but I don't want to be me. I want a child...."

Éluma said, "But we'd have to rear it in secret...."

***

And the boy who once performed for a princeling sang in the town square, under the singing moons, sang for a song; at first only a few locals came, and the singing was a prelude to some other performance: the troupe specialized in historico-myth dramas, and presented its own version of *The Tale of Mother Vara* with great slickness, though it was a worn old story.

Most often Sajit would perform, as overture, the folk song called *Woman and Thinkhive,* about a massive machine who loves a human woman.

It is a simple song, simple lyrics, simpleminded; a dialogue between the heart and the head, each wanting to possess the other.

Sometimes Tijas would sing, and Sajit would be hidden backstage, sometimes wearing a mask, ready to come on as an extra. *Mother Vara* is a very basic kind of story; a woman lands on a planet, the planetary thinkhive falls in love with her, together they rule the galaxy; she leaves; the thinkhive burns out, consumed by grief.

Stretching out so plain a story arc to last for several sleeps, like a good street opera should, required inventive incidents, improvised comedy, a dash of juggling, a lot of acrobatics, and long interludes of song while the cast changed their clothes.

At first there were only locals, but soon some who had survived the collapse of Shirénzang came creeping to this vibrant new metropolis. They could be recognized by their monochromatic garb and the way they walked; it was not brazen like the people of Alykh.

In twenty sleeps word came that a starport had built itself a hundred klomets from the city, grown from a seedling, sucking the metals from the earth until it could fashion them into the pillars, parapets and platforms of a city in the sky.

"Any day now," Daro said, "the *dorezdas.*"

But the drama continued, day after day. Professor Zelma herself took the role of Mother Vara, who according to legend was the first ... and will be the last ... Inquestor. Tijas and Sajit, alternating on and offstage, sometimes had lines in the play, composed in a curious singsongy style, in a very basic pidgin that made it presumably easy to understand no matter what world the drama was performed on:

Dara muzherwo
Patia Kuerwo
Ma Pannusi kwe
De Patiwe khnerwo...

"Star woman pain in heart;
but thinkhive not pain...."

An evening came when Sajit was singing this very song. The crowd was thin. His whisperlyre jangled, the sympathetic strings being out of alignment, but knowing this Sajit exploited the tonal dissociation to distinguish finer and finer *shrutas,* allowing his voice to play with microtonal inflections too subtle, perhaps for such a folk melody.

The audience was by no means under his spell — perhaps the day would come when he could pluck one string and hypnotize a planet, but this was not that day. And yet, and yet ... there *was* someone watching him intently.

A performer knows when he is being watched.

Instinctively, as his lips and vocal chords form the notes, as he fingers seek out the strings, his eye follows the path of observation and he knows where the interest is coming from.

All he could see were eyes, because the man was enveloped in the skin of a gray marsupial. A look of recognition passed between them.

Sajit returned to his song, and when he looked again, the man was gone.

***

"Tijas —"

It was night in the very crowded storeroom. Stale sweat and rancid *zul* in the air. And snoring. But Sajit and Tijas almost always could find somewhere a little apart: a sack, a barrel, a metal chest. It was not like the amnio-hammock back home but it was a kind of privacy. It helped that they were still small, small for their age, even.

The costume department of Daro's troupe doubled as their bedding. Tonight they had managed to cadge the imperial fur of Lord Kárdovany, because the actor who played that role had fallen into a *zul*-induced stupor. It was not real, but it was still soft.

Tijas would always fall asleep more quickly. *I'm the worrying one,* Sajit thought, *because I've lived the full years of my age, and I've known the comfort of my village, before it was all ripped away.* Sajit had slept badly since their world had collapsed. For Tijas, the new world was no newer than the old. It was an adventure.

Tijas wanted to sleep but he could sense Sajit's urgency ... that empathy, the ability to read each other's thoughts, if anything was strengthening now. "What is it?" Tijas said.

"I've seen Arbát," Sajit said. "He must have survived."

"Did you speak to him?"

"No. He didn't want to be seen."

"Maybe we should let him be."

"No, Tijas. I can't. I've known him as long as I can remember ... strange as he is."

"Sajit ... we have shelter now. We have a place to sleep and they're nice to us. When they save up enough to get off the planet —"

"We have to find Arbát. We have to find ... the woman. Maybe he knows her. All the time I was growing up, things were going on that people hid from me. I need to know these things."

"Why, Sajit?"

"Because they're part of who I am. Don't you understand it, Tijas? I — *we* — are going to be a writer of songs. To know the art, first know thyself."

"The *Aphorisms of Arbát,* disk one, number one."

"Let's go exploring tomorrow, after the play. We won't be missed."

"Tomorrow. But now, we'll sleep."

But Sajit could not, and presently he retrieved the ring from the pouch where he always kept it, and sat there, turning it this way and that, catching the cold room's pallid light. Eventually se saw that Tijas was shivering in his sleep, so he put his arms around his doppling to warm him, and lay there with his eyes open until dawn.

Seven
An Unexpected Ally

He held the child in his arms for only a few minutes, before he started to be afraid. In fact he was shaking.

"Don't be nervous," she said to him, "you're not going to break him."

"*Break* him?"

He seemed even more troubled, so she took the baby. He started to cry but she rocked him, singing a half-remembered lullaby ...

Sleep, child, sleep;
The Inquestors are watching you
from their far heaven.

The wings of pteratygers are fanning you;
The war is done.
Your mother's arms are warm.

Sleep, child, sleep.

And she thought: *How do I know this song? What mother held me in her arms? Whose voice was it? Was it just some singing holosculpt?*

But the boy grew still. "He's quiet now. I'm glad you came today; you haven't named him yet."

"I —"

"You're afraid to name him, even afraid to touch him."

Orifec said, "It's the memory. I held a child like this once. I slit its throat. I can feel the sticky blood. I can smell it. My own brother." His eyes gazed at ghosts.

Éluma knew the story from ancient history, knew how long ago it happened; but to the Princeling it was the immediate past; she could see that. "It was stupid of me to think I would be the one to change everything...."

"But you have changed. You wanted a relationship with a woman, a *real* woman. You wanted a child."

"Is this a relationship? Or is it an artifice created by your perfect training?" And Éluma could not answer him, did not know what separated her truth from her art.

Instead, she said, "You wanted this child so much, you wanted so much to challenge your ancestry —"

"I had a dream that everything could be different his time."

His dream is fracturing, she thought.

The next thing to go, perhaps, would be his love. If indeed it *was* love.

She subvocalized a brief command, intensifying the pheromonal generators in the chamber. She dimmed the lighting, made it more warm. She called up a soft zephyr. The love nest was fully equipped. These subtle shadings of the ambience were designed to calm an overanxious lover, but Orifec became more aggravated.

"It's true," he said. "I'm afraid of ... breaking him."

"What do you want to do?"

"I want to ... I want him to be safe. I want to care for him, but ..."

"Starry Highness, he has a destiny."

"Yes. But not a royal one."

"He must be protected. As you ... protect me." But Éluma wondered how much longer that protection would last.

Orifec said, "If you only knew — what goes through my mind — when I hold him."

"Perhaps if you named him, you wouldn't be so afraid."

"When he looks at me, his eyes seem to stab my heart."

She smiled. "Hyperbole."

"No, no. I feel real pain. Because there's something else I see...."

And he told her. *Childsoldiers.* One day the Inquest would come, and they would take all the best, the cleverest, the ones with the best reflexes. And their eyes would be fitted with laser-irises, so that their very glance would be death. "We can't let them take him."

"I thought you wanted him to be a musician," she said. And wiped a tear from his eye with a gentle finger.

"And so he shall be. And the powers of powers will witness: I'll protect him even if I have to break every law in the world. His name shall be Sajit — in the highspeech, 'the arrow that flies true,'" said Orifec.

"Because he wounds you when he looks at you."

"Yes, yes."

Éluma kissed him, and his lips grew cold, and she was afraid. But he was the Princeling. There were things she could never say to him. Not ever.

***

... and Arbát was there again.

Evening ... moons dancing over the square ... a whispering fountain ... the start of a magical night. A few *dorezdas* already: their off-world garb, their undulating wigs, their jagged jewelry, gawking at everything and everyone.

Sajit was onstage, masked, in a crowd scene. It was Tijas who was strutting on the flagstones, his high voice modulating and setting the sympathetic strings of his whisperlyre to a shimmery vibration.

Tijas was in fact being a little naughty. The simple folk melodies they had to sing was a bit too straightforward and he had launched into an endless cadenza, mixing his shrutas from different scales and shamelessly improvising in a style that probably have made Arbát pull out the strap, *for the singer must ever be subordinate to the song....*

Except that Arbát was there. Tijas had not noticed him. But Sajit, stuck in a frozen tableau in front of which Mother Vara was wildly emoting, could see Arbát clearly; could see that he was resisting the impulse to reveal himself and teach the boy a lesson right then and there.

When Tijas had come to a caesura in the music, Sajit tried to send him a mental message — sometimes this worked like magic, sometimes it didn't at all — and this time he definitely felt Tijas physically shudder, felt the shudder in his own body, almost tripped from his precarious position in the tableau. Both of them saw Arbát try to slip away unnoticed.

The play had a long duologue between Vara and the thinkhive which had been known to gone for several hours; it was about to begin, so Sajit slipped away and met Tijas behind the stage. The two boys hooded themselves and pulled polarizing veils down over their faces.

"He went north," Tijas said. "That's the direction of the Old City."

"There are new displacement plates," Sajit said. "They go in a straight line."

They wrapped their hoods and cloaks about them tighter, loosened their polarizing veils so that they no longer hugged their faces; they became like moving shadows, unrecognizable. The shadows grew longer. They left the square, taking the northern path.

In only a few steps they had passed a forest, a transport hub, an empty field, an auto-latifundium, and a long tall wall that was still under construction, with metal spiders crawling up and down and disgorging liquid amalgam that wove itself into great glistening skeins of gold and iridium, translucent to the moonlight. There were few people.

... and then they saw him.

He was standing at a low stone entrance. The walls were holosculpt to blend with a surrounding orchard, so it seemed that the entrance was an archway in the midst of a landscape. Only the fact that people were going in and out, and vanishing when they entered, betrayed the artifice.

"Stay concealed," Sajit said to Tijas. They crept closer. There was a *gruyesh* tree whose branches provided shadow and they could see Arbát clearly.

Arbát stood patiently as others went in an out. Presently there came a servocorpse ... in the brown skinrobe of a pleasurer. It spoke in a voice neither male nor female, and its body had elements of both.

The corpse said, "Welcome. We offer pleasure with the dead and the living. What offering do you have for Aërat?"

"I want an hour with the living."

"Do you bring an appropriate offering?"

"I have only twelve gipfers."

The servocorpse ... almost appeared to be snickering. "You may not buy even the cheapest living acolyte of Aërat ... not even an apprentice ... and not even for a minute. You may forget about the ones who are Cloaked in Shadow!"

"Please ..."

"But the dead are available if you want something quick ... and dirty." The servocorpse seemed to leer. "Twelve gipfers might stretch until dawn; the night is already half gone."

"Take it all."

"Give me the visual and behavioural parameters so that a corpse may be prepared for you."

Arbát fished a holosculpt from his robe and showed it to the procurer-corpse. The corpse nodded and disappeared, presently emerging with a figure shrouded in black crisscrossed with swaths of darkfabric.

"Dressed just like us," Tijas whispered. "Invisible. Not-persons."

The procurer said, "Damage will be paid for."

"I understand."

Arbát began to walk away from the doorway, leading the draped pleasure corpse by the hand. Tijas and Sajit were so close they could almost touch them, but Arbát was too engrossed in private thoughts to see the world.

Presently Arbát stopped. "I have to look at you," he said. He was weeping, uncontrollably weeping. And he pulled down the corpse's face-covering.

Sajit gasped.

"It's *us,*" he thought, and he knew Tijas heard his thought clearly. The boys each clenched the other's hand, feeling a kind of dread ... and a kind of familiarity.

Arbát pulled down the veil but not before the dopplings saw the eyes, grotesquely sculpted to resemble their own ... and the come-hither eyelashes grafted onto the dead flesh. Sajit could feel Tijas grip his hand, so tightly that it hurt.

Then Arbát and the pleasure corpse moved away, towards the first displacement plate.

"Sajit," Tijas said, "he has answers. You weren't there that day ... when I found him ... *bursting the milkpod.*" But Sajit could see that his doppling was terrified and that theirs was not a shared memory. It was a primal trauma that Sajit could not touch, for their were parts of each other's minds that remained locked, however much they wanted to be one person.

***

The entrance to an unpretentious home, the last house in the village, in the shadow of a forest ... many years before ... a Woman Cloaked in Shadow, a child sharing basket with a whisperlyre....

A childless woman standing in a doorway, a child beginning to cry ...

A woman cloaked in shadow disappearing into the forest.

Moons, dancing in the bright clear night.

***

"I'll go. I saw it before. I know what to expect."

"No, Tijas. *I'll* go. What you saw has hurt you. And if you were hurt, I too want to be hurt. Your world, my world, they *have* to be the same."

The two boys huddled together in the middle of the night, in the storeroom that had become their dwelling, whispering over a cushion of snores.

"No, Sajitteh. We are bound to grow apart, though we sprang from the same helix. Let's keep our private traumas."

"I'll go, Tisseh, because I'm older. And that's that."

"You take such good care of me, brother." And kissed his doppling on the cheek.

Sajit said, "You're here because someone wanted you to die in my place. That's nor fair."

"I'm your doppling. You came before me. I owe you who I am."

"Who taught you to say that?"

"I don't know. When I lay in amniosis, unborn, I think the doppling kit imprinted me."

"Then you'll do as I say."

"Of course."

"And it's my turn to wear the ring."

Tijas fished it from his tunic and hung it around his doppling's neck.

The ring! Sajit touched it now. The intaglio was warm, not icy-cold like the day the Starry Highness had closed Sajit's fingers around it.

"Do you think it's alive?" Sajit said, thinking of the double-serpent columns in the royal chamber, in the old time.

But Tijas was already asleep.

***

And so Sajit stepped out of the copse, a few sleeps later, having tracked Arbát once more to the gateway of the Temple of Aërat. Arbát was striding toward the entrance. He did not have a chance to enter; Sajit intercepted him.

"No need to enter," he said. "I am already here."

"But I wish to —"

"No payment. The —" Sajit began to improvise a little "— thinkhive of the temple has stored your desires in its memory wells. I have been sent."

"But I haven't paid," Arbát said. He was suspicious. So Sajit took him by the hand and with his other hand he lowered his polariser. Arbát gasped.

"What have they done? You look almost like ..."

"I am a more expensive model." Sajit said. "Come."

Arbát was bewildered but Sajit felt a rush of power; the man was entirely his to control. It made him queasy and strangely excited. *How easily lying comes to me,* he thought. And followed his tutor, step for step, carefully remaining three steps behind, like an obedient corpse.

Presently they came to a dingy room. It was accessible only by displacement plate, so Sajit could not even tell if he were underground or above it, for there were no windows. The walls did not even have any scenery projected. Unless ... these cracks, that caked-on grime, those creeping insects, were in fact —

They were.

Arbát clapped his hands and the holoscene dissolved. The real walls were white, antiseptic ... and smelled faintly of a chemical used to eliminate pests.

"Forgive me for the unseemly décor," Arbát said. "But I need to be reminded of how I've failed you. Not you, not you of course, you are just animated dead flesh, and yet...."

"Shall I disrobe, sir?" It was a line Sajit remembered from one of Daro's plays.

"You never asked me that before. Before, you knew what I wanted. You would go straight for the laser-quirt and throw me against the wall."

"I'm a different model," Sajit reminded him. "I suppose I'll ... follow my programming."

There was a bed against the wall. Oddly, it was solid, constructed from biological materials, wood and fabric. It did not rise to contour around the body as he knelt, but stayed quite rigid. Sajit slipped out of his clothes, one piece at a time. He did not know what he should do with the ring around his neck — but, just in time —

"Turn away," Arbát said. "Turn your back. I don't want you to see my face."

Sajit waited, imagining what the old man's hands would feel like on his skin. They had looked dry, flaky even. Obediently he looked at the wall and waited for whatever it was that Tijas had witnessed.

Instead, he heard the twang of a whisperlyre.

"If you won't punish me," he said, "let me punish myself."

And Arbát began to sing.

***

There was a village, Arbát sang. *There was a clearing in the village where a young boy heard the song the moons sang ... and long to sing of the stars and the worlds beyond the world he lived in....*

And one day there came to the forest clearing a woman cloaked in shadow. So close did she wear the shadow that Arbát saw nothing of her face. He saw only a movement, a rustle of the dark.

The woman said to him, A boy is growing up in your village. You will teach him everything you know, and he will become Shen.

Arbát himself had never been named to the Clan of Shen, the masters of song.

The woman said, You will know the boy when he comes to you. He will have an air about him, as of a ruler over worlds, though he be but a humble village child.

And Arbát sang of the boy's halting first notes, of coaxing them into tune, of shading them, of filling them out with words that could touch men's souls....

And Arbát sang of love, love for the thing he dreamed of but could never be, of the self that was not himself, of the longing for a music deeper than music....

***

Orifec had told her, "You'll find the musician in the forest clearing just outside the village. He thinks it is his private secret place ... but actually it's a place our family has always watched. And fine musicians have been born in that clearing before.

"They go there to be alone, because it is a place where the confluence of light and shadow, of wind and moisture, are so well mixed that it seems like the birthplace of a elemental power ... a God, if you like."

She was no musician, but even she could feel the music of the place. The celestial harmony of moons and clouds. The sighing of the wind. The clarity of the air, the scent of the *vangérides* as the night-blooms swayed.

The musician seemed old, but his face might have shown the wear and tear of a tortured life; she had imagined him a more vigorous man when Orifec played her a song cube of an old recital of his.

"Did I startle you?" Éluma said. "I was told I could find a man named Arbát here."

"I am Arbát." A serious face. Perhaps she had disturbed his rêverie.

"I have a message for you from someone ... in a high place. I don't dare say his name, but this sachet may give you a clue." And what she handed him was a small purse sealed with the double-serpent knot. "I can tell you that it contains a single ozmion. I should not have been able to carry a thousand arjents by myself. No, no, don't unseal it. Trust me."

"I have a rich admirer?" Arbát said. Had some prince picked up a song cube from the souk?

"In a manner of speaking," she said. "This money is a teaching fee. You are to take a special interest in someone. A boy. A boy who is growing up in your village, a boy with a strange destiny. A destiny beyond your own, Arbát-without-a-Clan, for he will become Shen one day."

"How will I know him? I teach many boys in the village. Some, I am sure, are special. Though they're mostly lazy and reluctant; music lessons aren't a high priority in Attembris."

Éluma said, "You will know, Arbát. He'll have an air about him."

Arbát said, "There isn't a treasure-house in this village that would let me exchange an ozmion without asking questions."

She laughed. "Then you'll just have to hang on to it," she said, "in the hope that my master will let you trade it in for a sack of arjents."

***

Sajit remembered his first meeting with Arbát ... it had not gone well.

As Arbát sang in the shabby little room, as he knelt on the bed, naked, facing the wall, as Arbát expounded his life's small indignities in tremulous tones, Sajit remembered —

The room with dozens of students, all cross-legged on a rigid floor, their keening voices tracing the outlines of a raga free of ornament or pitch-bending *shrut,* and he a tiny boy already knowing there was a wrongness in the music. And he was standing in the back of the schoolroom and suddenly he found his own voice swelling, blending yet arcing high above the others in an improvised descant, the melismas colorizing the plain raga so suddenly it was no barren up and down but a rich orchard, a garden, a flowering field —

And then he found himself singing alone, for the master had cut them all off. His voice sounded thin to him, raspy even. He was ashamed but he went on singing because in his head there was a perfect arc of sound and he needed to complete it....

When he finished, the young singers did not applaud, but muttered over and over the sound *mut-mut, shrut-shrut,* which is the highest compliment a singer can receive. Sajit's cheeks flushed.

"I'm sorry, sir," he whispered.

"All of you, be quiet. Our friend has done well. He makes music not out of thin air, but out of an eternal music that he hears, a music that plays deep within, a music you must reach out to catch before it is already gone. Come forward, boy."

Sajit stepped forward, expecting some reward.

But as he approached Arbát, the master struck him across the back with a edged ferrule. Sajit screamed.

Arbát said, "This is your first lesson. It's about the song, not the singer. Never come before me like this, puffed up with pride, thinking you already know the secrets of the cosmos!"

Sajit began to weep. His parents had never hit him. He sobbed, passionately, thinking that it was all over now. But as he wiped his tears with a sleeve, he saw what the whole class had seen the entire time he had been absorbed in his singing and not noticing the world ... he saw that Arbát, too, wept.

***

Sajitteh, Arbát sang, *I taught you with blows, I taught you with harshness and tears ... and where are you now? From the moment you first sang, you wounded me and the wound has never healed.*

I shall never be what you will become. I knew it in that moment.

I shall never touch the silences between the stars.

When I am old I will sing by the side of the road and the dorezdas *will throw me a gipfer or two, and I will waste away....*

But Sajit could not contain himself anymore. "It's not true, Master Arbát!" he cried.

And he could not help himself, he turned away from the wall to face his old teacher, knowing that Arbát would see the ring. Knowing that the pretense must end.

"You're not a corpse —"

"No! What dead thing would know your name? What servocorpse would weep so much to see his master's weeping?"

"I am sorry. I am so ashamed. I did not want you to know ... how deeply ... I have loved you. When I beat you, when I scolded you ... I loved you."

"There is nothing to be ashamed of, Arbát."

"You knew, didn't you? You spied on me that day."

That was Tijas, Sajit thought. But he said nothing.

"I thought you were dead," Arbát said. "I thought of all the unsung songs, the unwritten poems. Every night I dreamed about you crushed by a crashed cathedral, sliced into cauterized wafers by a childsoldier's eyes."

"Truly, master, there is nothing to be ashamed of."

And Sajit flung himself at his teacher, hugging him hard. They wept until there were no tears left, and only when morning came did Sajit remember his doppling, waiting in the crowded storeroom, waiting to fall asleep in his brother's arms.

***

And there was the ring.

"We have to find her," Sajit said. "She knows things. She knows who I am really am."

"We will have to search," Arbát said, "in the Labyrinth of Love."

***

The ring....

The clasp of a banker's sachet ...

Fifty tennights had gone by and the woman cloaked in shadow stood with another payment in the clearing.

"Who are you?" Arbát said. "Who has sent you? Who is the boy?"

As she had been told to do, Éluma only smiled, and girded up the cloak of darkness, and returned to her waiting autokiniton, a wave of darkness undulating in the patchwork of moonlight and trees' shadow.

But the next time they met, Éluma said, “I wish I could see him. From a distance. Just once.”

***

The ring....

Tijas felt the ring grow warm against his chest as he lay in the dark room. And yet it was Sajit who was wearing it.

Tijas felt the hot tears spurting down his cheeks, though he was not weeping.

He felt the gnarled hands of an old man against the skin of his back, though he was clothed, though the man was far away.

And he felt empty.

That was the dark side of being so close to his doppling, sometimes feeling his very thoughts, certainly his moods, often his pain.

When he felt these things, and he knew something was happening to Sajit, and he could not be there....

It’s a level of aloneness no one can feel, not unless they too have a doppling.

He could not sleep. Until it was dawn, and Sajit was kneeling beside him, telling him of all he’d heard.

“Tijas, Tijas ... we have answers. Well, sort of answers.” He started to tell his doppling all he had experienced that evening, but it came out in a jumble: Arbát had known the woman cloaked in shadow from the beginning ... there was a sachet with money, sealed with the same sigil as was depicted on the ring ... and on the whisperlyre.

“I think he knows how to find her,” Sajit said. “He mentioned ... the *Labyrinth of Love.*”

“A brothel!” said Tajis, gleaning the word from the store of information that had been pumped into him during his long gestation inside the doppling kit.

“She’s a whore. Or a priestess. Or a goddess. I am sure she is our mother,” Sajit said.

“Yours, you mean,” Tijas said bitterly.

Eight
To Find the Voice

Our mother....

This was really the first big gulf between them. Sajit had had a family ... and a dark secret this family had not even known in detail ... another mother, the mother who bore him.

Tijas's womb was a wooden box.

Tijas had memories, of course; but his thinkhive-designed mind could not know the things that happened in the outside world, after his seed had been implanted in the box. He and his doppling had shared so much since he had been awakened, could know each other's pain and to some extent each other's thoughts. But sharing was in part an act of will. Each soul contained a well too deep for the other to drink from ...

... and so it was that Tijas did not feel the loss of his parents and sisters as Sajit did. He hadn't teased the girls when they were tiny, or protected them from bullies in school.

He did not remember the nights in the clearing, listening to the moons and wondering about the hugeness of the cosmos.

The doppling process was not really designed to create a random twin; rather it was to keep alive a single consciousness through ages of rule. There were reasons why this technology was taboo for all except the Princeling of Urna; otherwise people would created copies of themselves for companionship or pleasure, and since such dopplings had no legal status, they would always be seen as less than human, able to be abused or exploited.

Urna was now transmuting itself into Alykh; it had been strange to imagine a world where they were not harám, a world where "twins", as Daro called them without any prejudice or disgust, were accepted as coequal.

Finding the woman cloaked in shadow was Sajit's obsession; it was not Tijas's.

But Sajit rarely asked what Tijas wanted.

"I think the Labyrinth of Love must be the Temple of Aërat," Sajit was saying as they were setting up for the evening's play.

Today's episode was called *The Heartbreak*. It is when Mother Vara learns that the artificial being, the perfect lover that the thinkhive has created to be with her, is not human. The role of Mother Vara was played by Zelma and Daro played the handsome simulacrum.

To portray a machine-made humanoid, Daro was daubing himself with a silvery paint. Then, a second layer of iridescent spray so he could glisten in the synthlight of the makeshift theater.

Sajit said, "We'll sneak away during Vara's big dance number. We can easily get to the Temple of Aërat and be back before the play ends in time for our solo."

"*You'll* sneak away," Tijas said. "I'm going to stay here and learn some more lyrics from Daro."

"What for? We'll never need them."

"*You'll* never."

"We're going to find our mother. We're going to find out who we really are."

"Who *you* are. Oh, Sajit, you never listen."

"I always listen. I can't not listen. You're always in my head."

"The part of me that you will listen to."

And so they parted for the evening, unhappy with each other.

***

In a break in the show, Arbát found Tijas by the fountain. Tijas knew him before he even looked up; it was the smell of dreamstuff, faintly overlaid with chocolate.

"There's no need to be so stand-offish," Arbát said. "Not after last night, anyway."

But what happened last night? What had transpired between them, that Arbát seemed to have become so much more intimate?

Arbát said, "You must have thought I was going to violate your delicate little body in some way. But I don't do that ... not even to corpses, who do not possess shame or dishonor. Yes, I thought you were a corpse at first — I did not dare to dream that —" He was weeping again.

Tijas wished he would go away. He was afraid he'd blurt out something and Arbát would guess that he was not Sajit. "I swore to the woman," Arbát said, "that I'd always protect you."

Tijas was about to ask, *What woman?* before realizing. He bit his tongue. They had to change to subject. So Tijas said, "Chocolate."

Arbát put his arm round the boy's shoulders, drew up him from the edge of the fountain. The waters danced, twisted by varigravs into streams that bent and interwove and tied themselves into knots. Two emerald sharklets swam, chasing each other in some mating ritual.

"Chocolate," he said. "In this new place, chocolate is not valued as much as in our old world. They don't say as we do, *na shẽtreín shiklátas* — after the songs comes the chocolate. But I have managed to find a place."

"What happened to the Dromek Shiklati?"

"It's a ruin. They're ploughing it over and converting it to a slaughterhouse for hydrobovids. That's something like our river-horses, but juicier. The Alykhi are very much into meat, but they do not understand *shiklás.* I will take you...."

Tijas found himself overcoming his resistance, and meekly following Arbát through alleyways that were even now assembling themselves according to some kind of inanimate DNA. Columns corkscrewing out of pavements, bas reliefs chiselling themselves onto walls. Inscriptions popping up on lintels in a hundred languages, from *bhasháhokh* to barbarous argots.

The place was little more than a stall hemmed in by a jeweller and a thinkhive vendor; three or four seat cushions hovered around a central brewing station that was, to Tijas's surprise, not operated by a corpse.

"The human touch," Arbát said. He ordered two beakers of foaming pulped peftifesht topped with a sauce of zul-laced chocolate. Tijas gulped it down, missing the old world, the old life. When Arbát climbed onto the floating cushion and sat beside him, Tijas did not really mind, no longer felt threatened. Whatever had happened between the old man and Sajit had somehow defanged him. "Sajitteh," Arbát said, "we must talk about the Voice."

"What do you mean, Master Arbát?"

"Sing to me. The song you've been singing. In that platitude-filled play that those second-rate actors have been putting on in the quadrangle."

Star woman pain in heart —

"As I thought," Arbát said, just like on stage. "There's nothing there."

Nonsense! Tijas thought. *What a jealous old fart.*

For at the very first whimpering *krachak* of the simple melody, everyone in the chocolate shop had turned to watch him. "I'm good," Tijas said. "I don't know what you mean."

"To be good, and to *know* that you're good — that is indeed greatness," Arbát said, "but to be good — and not to know it — that is genius."

"Master, you're just manipulating words."

"No, no." Arbát gripped the boy by the shoulders. His fingernails dug in. "Star woman pain in heart," he said. "What triteness, what tawdry manipulation of the audience. What pain is in *your* heart? What star gives you the most pain?"

"It's just a simple folk song."

"There are no simple songs."

Arbát held the boy's face, forced him to look into his eyes. "Tell me if you see pain," he said.

Tijas looked.

He remembered the primal moment when he stumbled on Arbát doing secret, shameful things ... things he should not have seen.

"You see," Arbát said, "I still have things to teach you."

***

Éluma doffed her cloak of shadow and gazed at herself in the still reflecting stream that bisected an inner courtyard of her apartment, miraculously left untouched by the collision of cities.

I am still beautiful, she told herself, *I am still a manifestation of Aërat.*

The central thinkhive of the Temple was attuned to her every subvocalization and it whispered to her in ritual response: *Yes, Goddess, you are beautiful, the most beautiful.*

Since the collision she had not seen Orifec. She wondered if he was safe, if he still retained any of the benefits of being a Princeling, now that his world did not officially exist.

She had seen him just the once, as the cities were colliding. The child, she thought, might be with him.

The child ....

The Temple of Aërat still functioned. Clients came and went, low level clients who could only afford to the lovemaking of the dead; the specialist services of the priests and priestesses, trained to be sensitive to every unspoken desire, every nuance of the client's words and movements ... there was little demand for this.

And none at all for one who had once belonged to a Princeling. And who had attained the rank of Goddess. Who was protectress of tradition, the tradition's very heart.

She had attained the summit, only to find she had made herself out of reach.

And though it was completely *harám* to even think it, for a priestess of Aërat was an empty vessel into which others poured their passion, she *missed* Orifec.

She missed the child, too, though motherhood was not strictly permissible. She had seen him only a few times.

As she mused on her reflection and thought about her master and her son, there came a crude knock on the wall. A servocorpse was trying to prevent a man from entering, but as they are not really programmed to disobey, and the man was ill-mannered, it wasn't working.

"Who are you? Don't you know this is the inner sanctum of Aërat?"

"Yeah, and you're the living goddess."

"That I am. One of several." She reached for her cloak of shadow.

"All right," said the man. "But I it on good authority that you're word's as good as a bag of diamants." He wore a beard dyed blue and elaborately woven, and irridescent earrings, and a tunic whose clingfire was fringed with feathers. He was pudgy and he smelled of a spice not known on Urna.

"You're not from this world," she said.

"That depends on your viewpoint," he said. "I could say the same of you. I am an official of the Tourist Department of the Aírang City Governance Council. My name is Lang viHurak, I am the administrator for *dorezda* attractions."

"This is a temple, not a theme park," Éluma said.

"Ah yes. We're aware that the former Urna was, in some ways, a more superstitious planet than it will now become. But this world is no longer Urna. It's an unfortunate accident that the world was not properly cleared for repopulation, but these mistakes do happen."

"Do you know where Orifec is?"

"The former government is being debriefed," said Lang viHurak. "As I understand it, a compromise is being negotiated. We'll allow, for the length of one standard human lifetime, renewable by mutual agreement, certain areas of the planet to be isolated as reservations for the survivors of Urna. On condition, of course, that *dorezda* visits are allowed."

"So we're to become a sort of zoo...."

"Please don't put it this way," viHurak said. "Of course, we'll process any would-be immigrants once a system is established. But Alykh is a pleasure planet. Its entire economy is *dorezda*-driven. If you'll forgive me — what shall I call you? Goddess? Madame Priestess? Brothel madam?"

"I am called Éluma-without-a-Clan. Éluma will do."

"Then you will do me the honour of calling me Lang," viHurek said. "On Alykh, most people have just one name; as a member of the governing class, I am blessed with the right to use a patronymic. I'm sure we'll work well together. We're allowing the first trial run in two sleeps ... just a dozen *dorezdas.* They are paying well for the privilege, so your 'Temple' will start receiving some income. Now ... I need a tour. Some background. Quaint rituals? What are your requirements for priesthood? How many humans, how many servocorpses? And most importantly ... is there a menu of services? Prices for penetration, fellatio, fantasy fulfillment?"

She laughed then. Heartily. It was true that her life's work was being reconfigured as a tawdry act for the entertainment of off-worlders, yet there was humor in this. "It seems," she said, "we're going into business."

"May I take the tour now?" said Lang viHurek.

***

Sajit stood at the entrance to the Temple, where he had seen Arbát standing, waiting to be admitted. At length, a servocorpse came to the door.

"I'm looking for a woman," he said, "a woman cloaked in shadow."

"Such women do not exist," the corpse said with a kind of programmed haughtiness, "not for the likes of you.'

"Do I have to pay?"

"It isn't payment, but an offering to Aërat. You can half a beautiful corpse for two gipfers. For one, you can get one with a faint whiff of decay."

"I'm looking for a woman cloaked in shadow. One in particular."

"One in particular! A moppet like you, and already the refined tastes of a Princeling!"

Sajit said, "I do have something to pay." He yanked open his garment to reveal the ring that hung around his neck.

"Why didn't you say so earlier?" said the corpse. "But I may not deal with some of your refulgent splendor. I shall have to fetch someone more senior."

If a servocorpse could reveal alarm, this one appeared to. The next figure to appear at the door was not even dead; apparently the double serpent was worth a human response. He was a bearded man of dark blue hue, so dark it was almost black.

"Master," he said, "we have been expecting you."

"How can that be?" Sajit said.

"Well, we have been expecting the Ring," said the doorman, "and naturally the one who bears it must be of considerable importance."

"Then you'll accept it as payment."

"Oh! No no no no no! That Ring is your key. The pleasures of this place are yours."

"Have you seen Orifec?"

'My Lord! Who would dare gaze upon such a personage? By no means. No one here has laid eyes on the Son of the Starlight, the High Princeling Orifec z'Urnasi Tath, hereditary Lord of Nevéqilas, Commander of the World Entire, He Who Answers Only to the High Inquest. Not since, oh, oh, not since ... not since it happened."

"And the woman cloaked in shadow?"

"Ah, you may have your choice of those. Though you do seem a little young for physical congress."

"I won't be needing any congress," Sajit laughed. "But I *do* want to see my mother."

"You will not find her here," said the doorman. "No woman cloaked in shadow may bear a child."

"Yet here I am," Sajit said.

"I have no answer for this conundrum," the doorman said. "But ... come inside for a span. Enjoy a snow-cooled sherbet laced with virgin *zul.* You may not yet be capable of ... any milkpod activities ... but there are plenty of other divertissements. Any there is no need to pay. You carry the insignium of the Princeling, and though technically there's no princeling in the land anymore, no princeling, no princeling ... yet here in this Temple we do not acknowledge any change...."

The doorman reached out put pulled Sajit through the displacement field.

He found himself in a vast anteroom. Holosculpts of the goddess stood in niches here and there, many with forever lights burning in front of them, or shrouded in the fumes from joss-sticks. The promised *zul* snow-cone arrived on a floating tray. People walked past, but no one spoke. The room echoed with whispers, whispers that spoke of longing, of desire.

"Who should I talk to?" Sajit said.

But the doorman had already vanished.

***

She took the official through the Labyrinth of Love. The corridors wound and spiralled and seemed to shift location; for the Labyrinth of Love was not a linear design, but grew from nested displacement fields, so that a room was often never in the same place twice.

A link-corpse held aloft a laser-candelabrum. It had preprogrammed with all possible permutations of the labyrinth, and was webbed to the central thinkhive of the Temple; without its guidance, Lang viHurek would undoubtedly be lost forever.

"This is a spooky experience, very disorienting," viHurek said. "We of Alykh aren't as used to corpses; we don't use them as servants. A trip through this Labyrinth could be quite a thrill. Perhaps a few tableaux of some of your more unusual ... manifestations of the human mating urge."

"I'm sure we can program some of our spare dead to have pre-timed congress on a cycle," Éluma said.

"And congress with the goddess herself, for the sufficiently well-heeled? I mean, my own bureaucratic salary could doubtless not suffice, and yet ... perhaps being allowed to taste the highest delights might make this go a lot more smoothly...."

Éluma couldn't abide this man anymore. "Get out!" she screamed. "You're raping our culture, turning our most cherished beliefs into a sideshow about barbarous superstitions —"

"Just doing my job, Your Divinitude or whatever I'm supposed to call you. You don't want to make my job a little more pleasant, I won't make yours pleasant either."

"It's you who are the savages!" Éluma screamed, and slapped his face.

She was appalled. Aërat does not show personal emotions. Aërat is there only for the devotee. *How could I have slipped?*

Meanwhile, viHurek wasn't letting up. He seized her by the shoulders, yanking away the cloak of shadow.

"No one refuses an official of the Tourist Department," he whispered harshly.

At that moment, two burly corpses emerged out of nowhere, and seized the official just as he was loosening his pantaloons —

Which dropped to the floor, revealing a wrinkled manhood on which had been tattooed the word *mother,* topped with a turquoise merkin of phoenix feathers.

Éluma could not stop laughing.

But then she heard someone else laughing, too. Someone who stepped through a displacement field and stood across from her as viHurek struggled to free himself from the two servocorpses.

"Ori!" She blurted out his child-name, an appalling breach of protocol, the second one in as many minutes.

"I'll have you arrested," said Lang viHurek, "and then I'll rape the both of you."

"I'm afraid not," said Orifec. "We have signed a treaty with the High Council of Alykh, ratified by Inquestral sigil. This territory on which you stand remains Urna, and remains so until my family dies out, or otherwise relinquishes its right of fiefdom."

He held up a crystal globe on which were inscribed letters of fire in the High Script. Atop the globe was a sigil that anyone who had ever seen a street play would recognize — the mark of Ton Varushkadan el'Kalar Dath!

"You received an intervention from Mother Vara herself?" the official cried.

"The High Inquest does not make mistakes," said Orifec. "At least, none that they will admit to. But they are blessed with the High Compassion. And the House of Orifec, as a ruling house of a planet, can once in a while use the privilege of a tachyon bubble."

"You went to the High Inquest directly?"

"It's a card to be played one time in a life, and I have had many, many lives without playing it."

"What was it like? How did the Inquestors seem? Were you struck by thunderbolts? Did their voices freeze your soul?"

"I'll tell you all about it, but first I want to go to the room that has no ceiling and no floor and boundaries ... where we can be one with the clouds and the rain.

***

Sajit waited.

Wandered, wondering at the scenes he saw, from niche to niche.

The holosculpts of the goddess were dedicated to the many joys of human coupling. There were images of contorted lovemaking, things that must physically be impossible, bends and twists and orifices Sajit did not know about, for the dead are infinitely malleable.

Sajit lapped at the *zul*-cone. Time passed, and he did not know whether to go next. Sometimes a suppliant would walk past, hand in hand with an acolyte or a servocorpse, perhaps on the way to a tryst.

As he waited, he suddenly felt Tijas.

Do you see pain?

He heard Arbát's voice. He felt Arbát's eyes staring, saw an unfathomable despair, and felt that very same despair in Tijas's mind ...

The only reason I exist is to save Sajit's life. This was the thought. *He and I are each other's death.*

He knew that this was why the doppling kit had been made and delivered to his home in Attembris. He knew, he had known almost since the beginning, yet he had not allowed himself to know what this really meant.

"Tijas," he whispered. Startled, an acolyte looked up and then returned to offering a votive lightshaft.

Somewhere back in the city, Arbát was peeling back the shell that protected Tijas's feelings. *I've been so selfish, not listening to him* Sajit thought.

How to console his twin, his brother, his other self.

Only the song he had heard as an infant....

Ýpna, kindekéh, ýpna
enguestras din vezháh....
lundán-uraná

Sleep, child, sleep;
The Inquestors are watching you
from a far heaven....

He sang to himself, and softly, to send comfort to a distant soul through the aether of the mind, yet in the room the song echoed above the whispers....

***

... and Orifec and Éluma climaxed, as the warm rain lashed them, in the chamber where the cosmos curved in on itself and there was no beginning and no end.

Behind the subsiding thunder came the sound of a young boy's voice —

Ýpna, kindekéh, ýpna
enguestras din vezháh....
lundán-uraná

Nestled in his arms, she turned to him. "That is how I imagine his voice now."

"Quiet, quiet, Éllekeh. This is not imagination. That *is* our boy. He is in this building somewhere."

With a subvocalized snarl she banished the room and they were in her inner sanctum, with the pool that reflected and the cool stone walls.

"Locate Sajit-without-a-Clan," Éluma said to the Temple's thinkhive.

Came the whisper of the thinkhive: *He is wandering through the Labyrinth, Goddess.*

"Lead him towards us," Éluma said.

***

Sajit found himself in a hallway, in a corridor, in a colonnade, in a cavern ... in quick succession ... with each step, the space changed shape ... but he did not feel lost. He clutched the ring in one hand, and as he walked he sang softly it was if the song itself was steering the thinkhive.

A garden. A forest. A wall. A castle. A rainbow. A stairway spiralling to nowhere. A horizon woven from rainbows and then the rainbows dissolved ... to a bright green field and a blue sky and distant trees with crimson leaves.

"Sajitteh...."

Orifec stood before him. And so did the woman. Both were cloaked in the same fabric of shadow, the one bolt of shadow staff draped around them both.

Sajit said, "Father."

And Orifec did not deny it.

And to the goddess, Sajit said, "Mother."

He went to them and Éluma drew the cloak of shadow around all three of them. And Sajit felt the truth of their relationship, mind-to-mind, a tingling warmth.

Orifec spoke, but Sajit hardly listened. The words were just exposition; the joy was real.

Orifec said, "Listen. We have saved Urna for now. There will be a shield of force that separates us from Alykh, from the center of the palace of Nevéqilas a few klomets, and some villages will also be isolated and conjoined to Shírensang. We shall be an autonomous subworld, outside Alykh's jurisdiction ... and heritable by my descendants."

Éluma said, "Sajitteh, I've lived for this moment. I've lived for a time when we could be a family, like the ancients of Old Earth, living for each other." And she kissed him on the forehead. He felt the firmness of her love and yet ...

Sajit thought of Tijas, and once more felt his pain.

"Before we can become a family ..." Orifec said. "There is something I learned from Lady Varuneh. Éluma, Sajit, the Inquest is coming. And you are listed for the culling."

"No!" Sajit said. "Not that, not now."

Orifec slipped from the cloak of shadow. He took Sajit by the hand.

"You must not speak of him," he whispered, so Éluma would not hear. "She is a goddess. The values of Urna's society are fundamental to her. She wouldn't understand. She can't know about our plan ... to send the surrogate to the culling."

"It was not *our* plan!" Sajit grated. "You can't ever understand. We *are* each other, to lose him is to lose myself ... no one can understand this love I feel for him."

"You're wrong, Sajit. I *do* understand. I am the only person on this planet who understands."

He too kissed Sajit on the forehead. He dried Sajit's tears, and out of sympathy for Éluma, he tried to regain his composure.

But his heart screamed, *Tijas! Tijas!*

***

And beyond the force barrier, on the world that shared the same planet as this world, Tijas felt the scream. And wept bitterly, wept the same tears Sajit held back, wept alone in the crowded street, while their old tutor watched, uncomprehending.

Nine
Lady Varuneh

On a planet named Gallendys, an old woman waited in a small room. Her white hair was neatly bunned and she wore a sober and shapeless gray garment.

The room was at the point where twin cities met, each mirroring the other; Effelkang rising pyramidally from the ground, Kallendrang suspended pyramidally from the sky; where they met, a spherical room where every direction was down.

The woman was known as the Lady Varuneh, and she was awaiting the arrival of Gallendys's newly appointed Kingling, Ton Davaryush z'Gallendaran K'Ning.

Few in the twin cities of the towers of towers knew who Lady Varuneh really was, although there were worlds on which she was worshipped as a gooddess, or celebrated in epic poems. For the Lady Varuneh was not one to display her power. To most, she was just an old woman who had always been in service to the Kinglings of Gallendys.

Yet the signal for the arrival of a tachyon bubble was three standard days too early. Something, perhaps, had gone wrong. Lady Varuneh decided she had better confront whatever it was alone.

The bubble appeared and dissipated at once.

The man who stood there was unknown to her. "You're not the one I was waiting for," she said. It was a relatively young man; he had the demeanor of a ruler, but not the grooming of one.

"And this is not exactly what I expected, either," said the man. "I've activated my planet's *in extremis asistance* mode. The tachyon bubble that can only be used once in a Princeling's dynasty, and which I am not allowed to control. So I must be where I am supposed to be. But I had expected — I don't know —"

"Perhaps a Grand Cabal of Inquestors, waiting around, eon after eon, to see which of the million worlds needs urgent help?"

"No, mistress. I only thought —"

"That this room might be a little more dramatic-looking," said Lady Varuneh. "In any case, the *in extremis* rule means different things to different people."

"My dynasty has ruled for centuries," the young man said, "and I will be the last, so if I don't use the option, it will never have been used."

"Yours is a stable world, then," Varuneh listened for the whisper of the planetary thinkhive to give her the information she needed. "Urna, is it not?"

He bowed.

"And so you are the Princeling Orifec. An unusual planet, yours; half mired in superstition, half amongst the most civilized."

"I ask your help, mistress —"

"You do not recognize me."

Lady Varuneh did something she normally never did. She completely relaxed the muscles of her face, normally frozen in a mask of extreme old age. As he looked at her, he began to gasp —

***

The old woman was growing younger. The lines of age, deep furrows with dark shadows, were unchiselling themselves.

And at last the Princeling knew who had come to greet him, for he had seen her holosculpt in the innermost secret shrine of his ancestors.

"Mother Vara!" he cried out, prostrating himself, for this was more than a God, more, perhaps, even than an Inquestor.

"Once upon a time," she said. and her voice was remarkably gentle, though he knew she had seen the death and rebirth of man, "there was a world with a very long name ... it will come to me in a moment ... a world called Brekisoneldylabruháh. There was a tremendous conflict on that world and there came a time when the ruling dynasty changed virtually every tennight, and virtually every tennight a new suppliant came to us. I hope your world is not like that."

"What happened to that planet, my Lady?"

"It *fell beyond* in a game of makrúgh," she said, rendering all its warring dynasties obsolete. "In its High Compassion, the Inquest thought obliteration was best; so the people of that world were not saved for another world. In a brief moment, painlessly, the world imploded. Pop!"

Orifec looked up and saw that the old woman's eyes were sparkling. "You're making a joke!"

"True," she said, "though it be in poor taste indeed. You'll forgive a twenty-thousand-year-old woman a senile moment from time to time."

Lady Varuneh summoned a chairfloat and stabilized the varigrav field so that the man would not be as disoriented. He started to speak again, but she held a finger to her lips.

"Traveling by tachyon bubble means that you are only moments from the place you left, and may return in moments. You have time. You may elect to return in the same moment that you arrived; so don't fret; we have time. Between tachyon journeys, it may be said that time stands still. Just as ourselves say: *History there is, and no history.* Tell me of your life, Princeling."

Orifec blurted, "The High Inquest has made an error! Please find me a way to correct it!"

"The High Inquest doesn't make mistakes," Varuneh said. "Correcting one would not be appropriate." She seemed pensive. "There must be a way. Come, walk with me."

For a moment, she had a faraway look; Orifec saw that now the wrinkles were creeping back into her face. He realized now that she had done him an immense favor by showing him who she really was. He was trembling.

She took him by the hand. The walls deopaqued. She led him to a parapet and showed him the Sea of Tulangdaror. The wind was constant on the parapet, battering at his face, roaring. The sea sparkled. The woman stood on the parapet and the wind teased her hair so that it gradually undid its bun and began flying hither and thither. She looked old again, but he felt her youth as well; it was as if she were outside time itself.

Orifec felt the radiance of the High Compassion emanating from her eyes. He felt like a child. "I never believed I would ever lay eyes on —"

"I know. But you know, I have been in many places. Wherever I go, few ever realize I have been there until I am already gone."

"Mother Vara," Orifec said, "I humbly ask your help."

"Tell me, then," said Lady Varuneh, "for I have all the time you need. Start at the beginning."

***

Some megasleeps ago, Orifec told her, *before this body stands before you, this consciousness was in another soma....*

These things do not happen in time. They are in an eternal present, the entire sequence present as a single object, without directionality....

I am summoned from my bed. The moons are dancing. We are in the great glass garden at the heart of Nevéqilas and I am standing with my ten brothers and sisters, we are standing in a row, shortest to tallest. And my father, sitting on a gilded hoverthrone, is watching us. And we are scared.

My father is a scary man.

We never see him, normally. We are reared by servocorpse-nannies. Each of us has one. They are programmed to love us with utter singlemindedness. We can do anything and they'll stop us from being hurt. We can run off a cliff and they'll run to stop us even though in pushing us back they will lose their footing and fall to their death — well, they are already dead anyway, so their death is no more death than their life is life.

My father says, *Today is a big day. Today I choose my heir.*

I love my father.

Behind each of us children stands a servocorpose with a cord of arachnosilk. The servocorpses have all been chosen for their strength. Their empathy circuits have been disabled; they are executioners.

My father says, I've loved all of you. *You, Adrina, the pretty one, who sings herself to sleep every night. You, Pontú, who loves to eat. You, Kiribáng, who enjoys hunting the phoenixes in the Forest of Kláh. You, Orifec, the quiet one. You....*

The names go on.

I say farewell to you all. I kiss you all. I have loved you.

With my last breath I will love and honour my father. He is good to me.

It is unfortunate that only one may succeed me. What I do now I do in love, so that there will be no fratricidal wars after my death.

I close my eyes and —

Feel the strangulating cord around my neck, hear the others as they struggle and gasp, but *I* feel ... no pain ... no lack of breath. Just the slender pressure of the silk.

Orifec, I choose you.

I open my eyes and the corpses of my brethren lie on the glass pebbles.

Let them be burnt, my father says, *for the flesh of princelings is to precious to be into feelingless servants.*

The ceremony: the central square of Shirénzang. The bodies of princelings laid on on a pyre woven from the branches of the fragrant flame-trees. And I am curled in foetal position inside a glass temperature-controlled egg, naked, vulnerable, a small boy who has just seen everyone he was close to murdered by the one he most loves.

The egg spins, suspended in a varigrav field above the fire that consumes princes. Inside the egg it is cool and the roar of the crowd is silenced. Time itself is askew, even the lips of the cheering crowd are moving in slow motion.

The flames leap up and envelop the egg and —

The egg cracks! I step forth and raise my palms in supplication to the ever-watchful eyes of the High Inquest.

I step forth, standing on a cube of force. With the movement of my hands comes the freezing of the flame. From fiery motion to icy stillness. The charred remains of my siblings now encased in cold pockets of liquid nitrogen. The bodies being moved by servocorpses, piled pyramidally that I may step down to my world on the bodies of my brethren.

The steps are cold, so infinitely cold. As I stand naked at the top of the steps, the most highborn in the land ascend the steps and soon I am shod with pre-warmed fur boots, and wear a cape of translucent pearly clingfire. I am clad in a rainbow.

And a voice cries out over thousands of sound cubes that stud the columns of the square: *Behold the Princeling Orifec, who is to rule hereafter!*

Am I overwhelmed? Do I lose consciousness? There is a disjunction in the memory, for now I am in a room in the palace and I am with my father and I'm weeping, because he is dying.

Now I no longer fear him.

I fear myself.

Because the ritual is going to end with me killing my father. Thus it has been, thus it has always been. And this will go on, generation after generation. My father, my children, my father.

***

Arbát found Tijas weeping in the street. He had been aimlessly stumbling along the thin streets that threaded the newborn city. The emptiness he felt was indescribable. And when Tijas saw Arbát he wept even more, and Arbát held him, rocking him like a baby.

"There, there," he said. "The thing about pain is that eventually it ends. Or you become used to it, and that is the same thing."

Arbát wiped Tijas's tears with a corner of his robe. He took the boy by the hand and let him towards the nearest displacement plate.

"Where are we going?"

"To the old city," Arbát said. "To find somewhere to practice your exercises. Because if there's something can soften your pain, it's concentrating on your art."

Tijas thought, *But I can't tell you why I am in pain. The thing that hurts is the thing I can never reveal.*

***

And the Princeling continued the recitation of his memories, while the Lady Varuneh listened solemnly, as they stood on the parapet that looked out on the Sea of Tulangdaror ... Yes, I see it clearly. An Inquestor has come in person to Nevéqilas. It's the Inquestor called Alkamathdes, whose title is the Supreme Hunter of Utopias.

I do not know how many generations ago this is. But I am Orifec. I am the same Orifec who saw my brothers and sisters killed so that I could inherit the throne. I haven't inherited yet, though. My father is still vigorous. This is not the scene where I am his bedside. I don't know. The scenes aren't linear.

My father says to the Inquestor, "It is such an honour you do us, *hokh'Ton.*"

Ton Alkamathdes says, "We are here for the childsoldier culling, Princeling. But I chose to come in person because I have heard that you have an unusual ritual for determining the succession."

"It torments me," says my father.

"We have a suggestion."

He waves his hand in the air, creating a portable displacement field. In the circle there is a wooden box, not unlike a coffin. It is a gift. My father and I look at each other. Inquestors do not bring gifts, unless they come at a price impossible to pay. There is only one price: one's soul.

The Inquestor says, "This is ancient technology, older even than the Dispersal of Man. If you use it, you will never have to kill another child of yours. Except, of course, any children you have at the moment. You will also have to deny yourself any kind of love that could lead to the birth of a child. Or you will have to kill it."

My father says, "You mean, produce twins? Clones? But that is abomination!" He can hardly bring himself to utter the word.

"On some worlds," says the Inquestor. "But have you ever asked *why?*"

"Why would one ask? It's *abomination.* They must be killed on sight. It's a basic tenet of the world."

"But why?"

And my father tells a story that he has known all his life....

***

When Urna was young, it was devoid of human life. Monsters lived in forests. Mounts were sharp-edged, not yet eroded into the gentle hills of now.

There were twin worlds in the system, closer to the sun, and each was the other's moon. They were called Ylas and Elas. They battled each other until both were close to annihilation. But Elas triumphed, at the cost of the destruction of all civilization in both worlds.

As their people were dying, as their technology was collapsing, a ship was launched containing a microcosm of Ylas's culture. There were artists, philosophers, poets, and scientists, and they were led by the Princeling Áni, who was sired by a warrior king, Ánqit, and an Inquestrix who had visited Ylas and abandoned her divine duties for the sake of love, she who was to be metamorphosed into the goddess Aërat.

The colony from Ylas, arriving in an empty world that with time was capable of great richness and plenty, multiplied. And presently there were born to a Queen of the Ylians twins, Romú and Remú. And this was a wonder, because twins had not been seen among these people in hundreds of years.

The seers of the Ylians were horrified, and recommended that one be put to death. But the Queen demurred. She could not choose. She became distraught. At length, she carried them both in the forest, but weakened from labour, died on the way.

And so the boys grew in the wilderness, suckled by a feral pteratyger, imbibing animal habbits, not knowing human speech. But one day, borne on the pteratyger's back, they flew over the city that was called Naruvyilía, New Ylas, and they wanted to possess it.

They mustered an army of animals, who swooped down from the forest. The citizens were slain; one woman remained, the priestess of Aërat, who represented the living goddess, who was the most beautiful woman in the world, even before she had become the *only* woman in the world.

The woman spoke to them. Such was the sound of her voice that where they had been unruly, they grew calm. And she continued to speak to them, as she looked out from the portal of her temple, and she saw that all the people of the world were dead, and they saw her weeping. And they both desired her, even though they did not know what desire was, for they had known only each other, or the animals of the forest, and they had slaked their desires the only way they could, and that way was contrary to the laws of creation. She reached out with her two arms and with her left hand she touched the cheek of Remú and with her right the forehead of Romú. And when she touched them, speech entered their brains, for her mind was linked to the central thinkhive of the city.

Speech came all at once, like the light of a thousand stars. And suddenly they knew they had been dumb. And suddenly they knew they had been intemperate. And suddenly they knew they had been murderers.

In their fury — for they were mirror images of each other — they flew at each other, and at the goddess. They were simultaneously inflamed with lust and rage. They ripped at each other and made love to the goddess. The power of speech was bursting through them like a meteor shower.

They both entered the goddess at the same time. But Romú, who had entered from the rear, found resistance. It fired his anger and he slammed his fists into his twin's back with such force that he smashed bones and Remú fell dead.

Romú climaxed at the moment of his brother's death.

And the goddess turned to him, and she whispered, "Romú, Romú." And all at once, his rage left him.

He said, "We are all that is left. How shall we repopulate the world again?"

"Quiet," said the goddess. "We will fill this planet within seven generations; and all these dead will serve us."

And thus it was that servocorpses came to be in our world. But Romú would not allow his twin to serve. For he knew now that twins are an affront to the individual, to the separateness of each human from another. They blur the borders of identity.

And so it was that Remú's body was burned on a massive pyre, and since then there have never been any twins on Urna. One is always incinerated at birth. Without pain, of course. The choice is made by the thinkhive.

Except....

***

"You are royals," Ton Alkamathdes tells my father. "It is necessary that those who are raised up to rule must face more darkness than those who are not."

And my father accepts the gift of the doppling kit and its arcane technology. I am to be the last ruler to have different genes from my successor.

When the ruler tires, or is too ill to go on, his memories pass to the one in the doppling kit, whose first duty is to devive the previous Princeling. Since that visit from Hokh'Ton Ton Alkamathdes, it has been this way.

And since then our world has flourished. We are few but we are prosperous. Urna is a backwater but it is a world with a single beautiful city and numerous villages where people live simple and idyllic lives.

Until another world disgorged itself on top of ours.

***

Lady Varuneh listened to the tale the Princeling spun.

She said, "The universe, and our place in it, is precariously balanced. A tiny shift can bring down an entire world. Come with me. You still have time."

The Lady Varuneh summoned a skiff with two chairfloats. There was no upper platform. They were to travel as equals.

She closed her eyes, subvocalizing directions to the skiff's thinkhive. The skiff whirred, soared, and soon was flying over Tulangdaror. At the moment the sea was mirror-still. It glittered with the reflected light of Gallendys's suns. Rainbows lanced the yellow sky. All along the shore, there ran an elevated river.

"Do you see this river?" she told him. "It's a river of liquid nitrogen and it leads straight to the starship factories, without which our galaxy-spanning civiilization would be lost."

Orifec watched. The river followed the outline of the shore, then angled abruptly off to the right.

Do you see them, floating in the river?

Orifec saw vast creatures floating down the cold river, creatures that seemed to be almost all brain. No eyes, no other visible organs of perception, but with a cetacean shape.

"They are *setálikas,*" said Lady Varuneh, "delphinoids. They are journeying towards our shipyards where they will be soldered, still living, into the hulls of our ships."

And now they were crossing a desert named Zhnefftikak. A forbidding terrain. Outcrops with twisted tines.

Rearing up ahead there was a mountain. But what a mountain! It was so tall that it appeared to slice the sky in two. It was the mountain's shadow that formed the wasteland of Zhnefftikak.

"Skywall," Lady Varuneh said, "that's what the locals call it."

As they went closer, the dark wall filled their field of vision. It eclipsed the suns. They were in a deeper darkness than any darkweaving.

"Let's go closer." Varuneh said, and Orifec felt a cold as well. Varuneh had the skiff illuminate the wall and now as they climbed a small circle of radiance rose with them, illuminated the wall which was featureless. "This mountain was created during eons ago in the planet's past, when it had a denser atmosphere. Inside, it's hollow. Within is the place called Keian zenzAtheren, the Sunless Sound. And there is a howling, whirling and utterly dark wind inside it, and in that wind dwell the windbringers. They sing, but not music; they sing with light, this delphinoids, as they plough through the thick darkness. The light they produce is the same light as the light-mad overcosm, but it is not chaos; it is chaos constrained into concord, for the delphinoids see the myriad connections throughout the overcosm; they see what our astrogators need to see, to open up the pathways within the overcosm along which our ships can travel. This you must know. Inside the mountain are a people that we created, who hunt the delphinoids and deliver them to a cavern where they are transported via displacement plates to the Cold River.

"The people inside the mountain do not know of us, do not know why they harvest the delphinoids, do not know of space travel; most of all, they do not know of the light songs, for we created them deaf and dumb. Otherwise they would go mad. This music of sound and color affects normal people that way.

"Yet the entire culture is a construct, dreamed up by a thinkhive, every myth and tradition carefully manufactured so these people will do what they must do. And because of this artificial creation, this *lie* if you will, our ships sail the overcosm. And if the delphinoid hunters one day should learn that there is another world beyond the mountain ... what should happen then?"

The skiff came to a ledge. All was perfectly black, but the Lady Varuneh subvocalized a command and a part of the wall dissolved, allowing them to enter.

"There is a small chamber here. You may enter it, but you may not remain for longer than a few seconds, or you will go mad." She motioned for Orifec to enter an inner door.

Orifec went in by himself. There was a seat, more a cushion of force that softened to accommodate him.

All at once, the walls dissolved, and he was in the midst of the delphinoids' lightsong.

It was light of every color, blending, blurring, whirling, unfurling, streaming, soaring, plummeting, cascading — and the sounds! — whistling, droning, screeching, thundering, sussurating, percussive, lyric, all at once. And the emotions: wrenching, seductive, despairing, elated, but overriding all else a pefect blend of grief and joy.

In the song of the delphinoids Orifec relived his life and the lives all all the past Orifecs, the lives all intertwisting and intertwining, knotting and unknotting, warping and woofing into ever-shifting tapestries — and Orifec wept, wept like a child, because of the beauty, the indescribable, unattainable longing ...

All this in but a few seconds, because the walls reopaqued, and suddenly he was alone, and in silence, and in darkness.

And he was left with an ache that would never go away. A sense of loss. A grief.

"Let us go back to the twin cities," Varuneh said. He heard her as though coming from another world.

***

The Lady Varuneh was silent for a time. "I do not know why I showed you the secret of Skywall Mountain," she told him.

But there was more; on the way back to Effelkang and Kallendrang, she also told him of the web dancers.

"Each delphinoid shipmind used a focusing-crystal that comes from a mountain on a very different, very distant planet," she told him as they rode the wind, "a planet without even a name. The crystals are teased from caverns deep within the mountains by web dancers, children of the Clan of Rax, whose dance is a sexual teasing — for the mountains are living, and the crystals are their eggs. There was a time when only one web dancer remained in all of the Dispersal of Man, and our entire universe hung upon the intricacies of a single dance."

What was she trying to tell him? That huge, galaxy-shaking events often came down to the actions of a single person? That everything they knew could be destroyed in an instant by one event on a planet that didn't even have a name?

After that they were silent all the way to the small room at the juncture of the two cities. Orifec knew that she was showing him unusual favor. He also knew that she would take her time before revealing the full nature of that favor.

Fnally when they were once more in the chamber, Varuneh said to him, "I am an Inquestor, and you know that we hunt utopias. We are enemies of the static, the unchanging, and for that reason we may cause worlds to *fall beyond.* When Ton Alkamathdes brought you the doppling kit, it was because your planet was trapped in a recursive cycle of fratricide. Ending the cycle made your world, in its own small way, a utopia. And thus it is, Princeling, that in finding love, in making yourself a family, you too have hunted a utopia in your own way. You have made an end that is a beginning. And for that, I will help you."

The Princeling knelt before the Inquestrix. He touched her feet with his palms. She said to him, "Here, I will give you the treaty you request, sealed with the sigils of the High Inquest. And in return ... you shall make love to me. I am several centuries old, and now and then, I desire the touch of someone younger."

And she kissed him.

And in its own way that kiss was as transformative as the seconds he had spent immersed in the Light on the Sound.

For he had been kissed by the mother of all mankind.

***

Book Three

The Child Collector

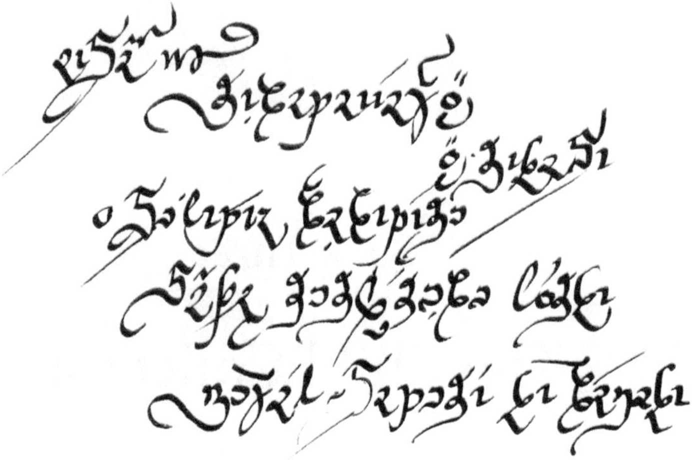

aiváh! aiváh!
kindarayághor or-kitávi
uraná vrendáh
u velirís dhandiríske
vãzhas kekýrkende lukti
meghal-vareký ti dhánati

He comes! He comes!
The child collector with his golden scroll!
He'll take you to the sky
Where you'll fly, where you'll die
spinning disks of light,
with your lightning eyes of death.

— traditional

Interlude
Elloran

Ton Elloran n'Taanyel Tath dreamed:

Stairs, stairs, carved into a mountain, stairs twisting, coiling; stairs broken and overgrown with scarlet lichen, with feathery blue moss; stairs that seemed to move as he ascended, changing direction, studded with random displacement disks; and he climbed. Not as a powerful Inquestor, older than time yet as vigorously preserved as the finest thinkhives could preserve, constantly monitoring his every heartbeat even from uncountable parsecs away ... no, old as a shortliver is old, wheezing, with a cane that slipped and skidded on the uneven stones.

How long did the dream go on?

He could not tell. The steps kept going. Up, up, left, round, sideways, right, wrong. broken; he would never reach the top ... the more he hurries, the more steps there are ... but at last he is standing in a place where many rainbows meet. A windy place near the summit, where rainbows fall like drifting ribbons in the wind.

And there she is ... he knows he will find her ... a young girl standing there. She is draped in rainbows. And she says, again and again, *Do you remember?* but though he hears her speak, her lips do not move.

And he say to her, *Kerin.*

Sister, he says. *Sister.*

In the dream she has not changed, though in reality she must be long gone, stranded in an unreachable past; if he has changed, she must have changed infinitely more; time dilation takes its toll on the shortlived.

Enguester eis, she whispers. *Mun ma'vendek dáve, evendek bhratek.*

And you will always be my little sister, Kerin, Elloran says. *But why are we meeting now? Shouldn't you be gone by now, forever gone?* He wonders why she speaks the Highspeech because when they were children together it was not the language they chose, not the language of intimacy.

Kerin laughs. The lips move but the sound, the lips, are not together, as though sound and light are travelling through diverging streams of spacetime.

In the land where I dwell, she says, *even the beggars speak* Bhasháhokh, *because it is the true speech, the language where words have souls.*

Elloran does not have to ask her where she lives. Only one world in the cosmos has this sky.

It is Uran s'Varek, which is what many people call *heaven,* but which only Inquestors know to be a real place — a place forbidden to the shortlived, known to them only in legend —

For looking up from the summit of the mountain, he sees where he is standing in this dream —

The sky of Uran s'Varek is only to be experienced, never spoken of. Imagine a world that is a sphere, built millions of years ago around the black hole at the galaxy's heart. Imagine a cubic parsec of space that contains packed within it uncountable stars. Imagine an attenuated atmosphere rising thousands of klomets, enough to scatter all that light and shield all that radiation. Imagine the perpetual light. No night. Just the pearly, soft, ineffable radiance of almost two million suns.

All kept together by the will of a single thinkhive.

Do you believe in heaven, Loreh? Kerin says. *Is heaven just a dream the Inquestors made, to keep the million worlds in balance, to keep the Dispersal of Man obedient and docile?*

If she were only real....

Embrace me, bhratek. Then you'll know how real I am.

In the warmth of that embrace, Ton Elloran n'Taanyel Tath has a fleeting idea he can barely grasp ...

First, the great thinkhive of Uran s'Varek. A mind greater than any species can imagine, natural or artificial no one knows — *and still evolving.*

Could it be that Kerin's thought patterns have been absorbed into the all-embracing matrices of the great thinkhive of Uran s'Varek ... could she still be alive in some form ... at least in dreams?

You're so real —

Of course I am. Why wouldn't I be?

Could it be that the thinkhive of Uran s'Varek *is* heaven? Could it be that every thought ever thought, every dream dreamed, every song sung, is forever part of the thinkhive, as it finds new connections in the chaos.

Is the myth of a human soul real, and do souls migrate to heaven?

Kerin laughs.

We were matched twins, she says. *We should have grown up together. We were destined from birth to share throne and bed, to be left and right, up and down, to dance perpetually hand in hand around the center of light....*

There are *no ghosts!* cries Elloran.

But if the thinkhive of Uran s'Varek were to contain within it the thought patterns of every person since Mother Vara awakened the world to light —

Elloran aches. He hugs his sister hard, but already she is beginning to waver, to dissolve into the everlasting daylight ...

And woke....

... clutching the whisperlyre.

How could it have known, this instrument of dead metal and rotten wood?

He would have flung it across the room. But he held back. An Inquestor does not show emotion.

Oh Sajit! Oh Tijas! If I had only known the secret we shared ... for we both had a twin we loved more than our own self ... a twin bound to us by flesh and by emotion ... an other half *with whom we would never be united .... lost in time....*

***

Tash Toléon had been waiting in the antechamber. He looked up anxiously as the door dissolved.

"Tash Toléon," Elloran said, "I've had such a dream."

"Hokh'Ton, that's a very special room," Toléon said.

"Is it?" Elloran said. "Is it haunted?" He laughed bitterly. "I've spent many a night in a haunted room on a backworld. The dead never came to me — unless it was to serve my morning *zúl.* But in my dream, I saw, I saw —"

"Let me show you, my Lord."

He led the Inquestor back into the chamber. The bedfloat was draped in sheets of comforting darkness. Toléon yanked away the darkness and deopaqued the bedframe, and Elloran saw that under the bed there was a scarred wooden box.

"It's —"

"Yes, Hokh'Ton. It is the doppling kit. Still good for a few more charges, I would think, though no one has touched it in generations. There is something of Shen Sajit in the box. An essence."

"Toléon, tell me more about the two Sajits, the one I know so well, the one I never knew."

"But do you know, my Lord, which one is *your* Sajit?"

"I confess ... I know not."

Ten
The Silence Between the Stars

In a stone-arched cloister, brand new and still uninhabited, Arbát was retraining Sajit's voice; though he did not realize that it was actually Tijas's. The air was still and cold but Tijas stood shirtless, and Arbát laid his palm firmly on the boy's diaphragm, and with the other hand he made an expulsive gesture from his lips — and said over and over, "Work the air. Make the air move. Make the air vibrate."

Tijas worked his diaphragm against his teacher's relentless pressure. He hated the flaky, gnarled hand against his flat, smooth flesh. And still he was wondering where Sajit was. His whole body was still aching from the blast of agony that had reached out to him from he knew not where.

"You're drifting!" Arbát slapped his arm. "Concentrate. Now, make a tone. Shi ... shi ..."

Shirenzhá.

Silence.

"So many songs," Arbát said, "start with some variation of *shirenzhe.* Do you know why?"

"Because ..." Tijas had an inspiration ... "because *all* music begins and ends in silence."

"Find your silence," Arbát said, "and in that silence, hear your song begin."

A song began to form:

Shirenzhá in-dárein
Shirénzhen chítarans tinjáte

In the silence between the stars
Feel the silence of the heart....

The *sh* of the first word emerged from the emptiness like a surf's sussurus, a breeze, a sigh. From the *sh* sound came the *i,* a faint wuthering that grew to a ghostly wail over the course of a long melisma. *Ren* resounded; *zhá* was an explosion and *in-dárein* was a whole galaxy in a few seconds.

"You clever little beast!" Arbát said. "And all that out of a moment of silence!"

"My voice," Tijas said, "is it coming?"

"I daresay." Arbát let go of his diaphragm, held the boy by his shoulders. "It's odd ... you almost feel like someone else."

"I'm only trying to learn, Master Arbát," Tijas said, trying to sound inconspicuous.

He didn't want to show Arbát his pain. For he had not seen Sajit for several sleeps. And he found it hard to get to sleep at night without his other self beside him.

***

Most of Nevéqilas was dead, or starting to decay, riven in twain by the crashed people bin. Here and there though, the palace could still draw energy, though one could not tell where from. There were chambers that functioned as in the old days, though some could only be reached through a tangle of tunnels, or by wrongly sequenced displacement plates. And so was the apartment that Sajit's new mother wanted him to call home.

The room was connected to the Temple of Aërat by a tunnel and four displacements. Éluma had never been, and rarely even *seen* a mother, but she had good instincts and she knew Sajit for her own. There was a deep bond, a real bond, though Sajit could see she needed help in playing out her role. Having given him up once, she did not quite know how to handle him.

Perhaps she felt closest to him when he slept.

She would watch him, nestled in a cushion of wind, and she could see that he hard trouble sleeping. She wondered whether he thought about his other parents, his other family.

***

A few sleeps, perhaps a tennight, had passed since Orifec had returned. And Sajit felt a growing dread.

He didn't dare even to say Tijas's name in front of his mother. And he was rarely alone with his father.

Orifec still played at being a Princeling, though his kingdom was now a tiny square of land. So he usually was away somewhere — vaguely muttering about affairs of state when he came back — staying very briefly, usually not even the night.

Sajit said to Éluma after a tennight, "I have to get back to my music."

She said, "Not now, Sajitteh. Plenty of time after ... after ... you know." The time was coming. No one would say when, perhaps no one knew. "You can't be seen," Éluma said. "Don't go out."

"No, no ... *mother*. I *must* get back."

The title was torn with difficulty from his lips. It was awkward enough that his father was a king; harder still, that his mother was a goddess.

"Sajitteh ... *he* is coming. *He* whose word even a Princeling, or a Goddess, cannot resist."

***

"Who is coming?" Tijas asked, because they didn't seem to want him on the show. The Professor was distant, and Daro kept smiling and strained, pinched smile. "Why can't I go and play the prelude at least?"

Zelma says, "It's best you stay inside. Where is your twin?"

"I don't know. He went to find our mother ... *his* mother. And now ... he is missing."

"You can't go looking for him now."

"Why not? I *need* him!"

No one could understand the depth of this need. I need him, he thought, like my left hand needs my right hand. "No," Daro said. "No children in the streets, not now. *He* will soon be here."

And by *he* was meant a member of the Clan of Kyar. The child collectors. Servants of the High

Inquest, architects of the culling.

"There may be a reason your doppling cannot be found," Daro said. "It is wrong to think it, perhaps. But if they have collected him ...."

"Then I'd be safe."

That was the only reason Tijas existed. To be childsoldier in Sajit's stead. But Sajit had not been taken. If he were gone, there would be an emptiness. But there was no emptiness. There was the screaming, distant, insistent. Coloring all his thoughts.

A tennight had passed and Tijas still felt his doppling's screaming. If he focused, he could almost feel a direction. He knew he could find Sajit. If he held his breath, if he made his mind go blank, there was a still unwavering point of light there. His center, his self.

***

But outside, in the great collided city that was Aírang, there were no children in the streets.

At the edge of the star system, a delphinoid breached the overcosm.

Most of the passengers were in stasis, but one person stood on the deck when the walls deopaqued in the split second that the light-mad overcosm ended its display, the dizzying cacophony of light that drove men mad.

Even that split was almost too much to bear, though within the threshold of human endurance. But the ship's guest of honor had learned to tolerate the crazed kaleidoscope. In a sense, he even enjoyed it.

The ship's pilot, Kail Kruspar, entered quickly. "Lord, you shouldn't expose yourself to it," he said.

"It drives men mad, yes, yes, I know," said Kyar Gharém, Inquestral Child Collector for the sector. "I've kept my eyes closed."

Gharém had emerged from amiosis a little ahead of schedule because an alarm had triggered the awakening. Something was not quite right with the schedule — which rarely happened, despite the caprices of time dilation, for the High Inquest is frozen eternally in the space between *history* and *not-history*. The Great Thinkhive of Uran s'Varek, guardian of every sentient thought in the Dispersal of Man, did not err.

To err, however, was always possible for a human, even for an Inquestor.

Of course, he had settled down in his berth only minutes before, in his own memory, before being cast into amniosis. Within the overcosm itself, time and space had no meaning, and all events and places were coiled in amongst themselves. So: a minute later, awoken, with a message disk on the float beside his arm.

Gharém had pressed the message disk to his forehead and already seen the news.

Now, in the deck, he turned to the pilot. "Did you receive the same message?" he said.

"Yes. There has been ... a mishap in timing."

"Those cursed Inquestors!" Gharém said, shocking the pilot, who was not used to hearing the gods themselves insulted. "It's an overlapping *makrúgh.*"

"My Lord, I'm not even quite sure what that is."

"Quiet. Awaken my equerry."

But his equerry was already emerging from the tube that spiralled to the resting quarters of the delphinoid. A sharp-faced childsoldier with a squealing voice, intelligent, impertinent. "I would think you'd be eager to visit this world, Mikkálu-without-a-Clan. Weren't you born here?"

"All that is erased, Lord Collector, when one enters the training college at Bellares. I am an empty vessel, ready to be filled by —"

"Any command of the High Inquest, yes, yes ... spare me the rote-learned platitudes, boy. Or I'll have your fiery blue mop doused."

Instead of sinking into subservience mode, the boy laughed. "My Lord, I *was* born on this world," he said. "I had friends there. I grew up in a temple of the love goddess. Some would call it a brothel."

"If there were any children you grew up with," said the Child Collector, "they are older than you now. You have traveled the space between spaces."

"I'll gladly give you the grand tour, my Lord," meeting the Child Collector's gaze almost brazenly. Gharém thought, *It's true what they say, then: you can remove the whore from the brothel, but you can't ...*

"You're pensive, Lord Gharém."

"I asked for an equerry from the planet I have been assigned to collect," Gharém said, "but you don't seem entirely housebroken. Should I have you beaten?"

"If that is what you fancy, my Lord."

"Insolence!" He raised his hand to slap the child, but but held in his temper at the last minute, so that it seemed almost a fatherly pat on the cheek. The boy giggled. "Don't fidget. I have something serious to tell you. And there is no need to flirt. I prefer servocorpses; compliant, indefatigable, and uncomplaining."

"I accept the chiding from your lips, my Lord," said Mikkálu. "I'll be good now."

"Your world has been caught up in an anomaly in *makrúgh,"* Gharém said. "You cannot, of course, hope to understand that, but the Dispersal of Man is kept in perpetual balance because of *makrúgh,* the game played by the High Inquestors. During the course of a game of *makrúgh,* planets may *fall beyond,* but in its compassion the High Inquest saves as much of the population as it can, keeping millions of citizens in stasis in people bins that can be released to populate worlds that have been emptied by *falling beyond.* The unthinkable has happened to your homeworld. It was simultaneously played in two different games of *makrúgh,* with overlapping outcomes. That *never* happens. There are so many worlds, and not many Inquestors."

"So my world is gone?"

"No. But it is as though a different world has grown up overnight on top of the old one. And it is the old world from which we must collect our children, Mikkálu. For when we left Bellares with this assignment, your world was still intact, and no Inquestor has commanded that I abort my mission. Not to obey would be unthinkable."

"But an error of *makrúgh* is unthinkable too, isn't it, my Lord?" the boy said, aggravating in his insistence on pointing out the imperfection.

"We shall therefore collect all the children in the lists provided by the planetary thinkhive, identifying them by their genetic signature and assembling them all for transport in the ... park beside the Lake of Luminous Loons," Gharém continued, trying to ignore the boy, "assuming, of course, that the park is still there."

***

Daro said, "there's a commotion. In the street outside."

Tijas had been holed up in the zul storeroom for many sleeps now. He knew Sajit was still in the world, in the city. He felt it. The storeroom was not as crowded as it had been at first; many members of the troupe had found other basements, other storerooms, mostly in the same building or buildings nearby. After the initial frenzy of construction, the new Alykh was settling in and no new structures had been thrown up for at least two tennights.

"Come," Daro said. "The Professor found a place where we can spy on the outside."

Daro led Tijas to a stairwell, overgrown with *zul*-weed. The steps, dozens of them, curved round and round and you could walk up them by holding on to a metallic railing — more ancient technology, and like the doorknobs, cold to the touch.

They emerged in an upper room.

The Professor was working at a thinkhive nexus. She was waving her hands and lines of light and arcane formulae and patterns were materializing in the dusty air.

"Tijas," she said. "We have to think about how to hide you...."

On one wall were screens through which one could see the street. They were looking down on an avenue and there was a crowd. You could hear the crowd chattering, even through the walls. Then the crowd seemed to part and a line of childsoldiers was marching, leaping, somersaulting, shooting lines of light from topaz-colored eyes, lines that wove brilliant yellow nets of light in the darkening sky.

They shouted the bloodcurdling warcry of the childsoldiers:

Ishá ha! Ishá ha! Ishá ha ha hé ha!

There came a voice, booming beneath the descant of the warcries:

Children of Urna! Your destiny has arrived!

The Inquest calls you to Bellares, the world where children learn the art of war. Honour calls you! Blood calls you! The High Inquest summons you!

The voice came from speaker cells mounted on floating vehicles, rotating on crystalline stalks.

Your DNA has been recorded in the memories of the planetary thinkhive. Only the most perfect are chosen and it has been your destiny since birth.

Do not think to escape. We shall be releasing Finding-Birds into the skies of Urna. If you are living, they shall sniff you out.

There were children in the street, Tijas saw, but they were dressed in the style of Alykh.

"Alykh isn't affected," he said. "Couldn't I just—"

"Put on Alykhish dress? No. The *veznávikas* — finding-birds — they were engineered to sniff out DNA — one bird per genemap — and there's a bird with your signature on it — yours — and also —"

"Sajit's!"

"One of you will *have* to go. Or you will both be in hiding forever," Zelma said.

"But your doppling is gone. For all we know, he has already been collected," Daro said. "If that's true, you will free go out. You will be free — for the rest of your life."

"Although," Zelma said, "it will blow your chance for a Clan Name. Childsoldiers who survive are among the likeliest citizens of the Dispersal to be bestowed one. Don't you want to belong to the Clan of Shen?"

Outside, the resonant announcement echoed. *This is your destiny! Honor calls you! Blood calls you! Ishá ha!*

The view made him nervous. Tijas subvocalized the universal command for opaquing a wall. But nothing happened. He stood in front of the screens, blinking.

The Professor started to laugh. "It's not a normal wall," she said. "Those are windows. *Real* windows. See? Try knocking on one."

He did. There was a crystalline, brittle sound. He realized that it was actually a clear material, not a programmable wall. Nervously, he stared for a moment. Someone's face popped up and seemed to stare back. Tijas bolted.

Zelma laughed. "It's not *that* ancient, this technology," she said. It's opaque on the outside. Polarized! They can't see you."

Tijas saw them both laughing at him and he too laughed, though he couldn't cover up the ache he felt underneath it all.

***

Huge as a city, the delphinoid starship gradually became visible above the fused cities of Alykh and Shirénzang. It was night but the ship blotted out all the moons and most of the stars, a cetacean hole in the sky.

"Ah, Mikkálu-without-a-clan," Kyar Gharém said, as the walls of the chamber deopaqued. "I wish you could see what the people of your world are seeing. The dread! The terror! I know. I've been there."

The boy didn't seem quite as perky as before. Good. A dose of spectacle might temper his impertinence a bit.

"Magnify!" commanded Gharém, and the thinkhive complied, so that it seemed they were plunging headlong onto the surface.

"Boy! What are these places called?"

Spindly, crystalline, the flower petals smashed, peering from a wilderness of twisted metal —

"Nevéqilas — the Princely Palace!" said the childsoldier. "It's still there ... though the stem is bent."

"And there?"

Over a dark lake danced a thousand firebirds, each point of light reflected in the black still water —

"The Lake of Luminous Loons!" said the boy. "And the park is still there ... although ..."

Crawling across the park, a serpentine bridge of white metal.

"Magnify!"

The bridge — clearly not of a piece with the world called Urna. Seen close, the metal was etched with abstract shapes that vaguely suggested erotic couplings. It was an artifact of a pleasure world and did not blend with the natural colours of Urna which was no longer Urna.

On the bridge stood people. Staring up at the sky. Pointing. Wide-eyed. Different somatypes, different clothing; the folk of Urna a little more sallow, free-flowing robes in earth tones, the people of Alykh, in brash outfits, outrageous wigs and painted faces, yet all equally filled with fear.

"Already advance parties are marching through the city, announcing our intentions," Gharém said. "You were never collected in this way, I know — you were a single pickup. You missed one of the greatest spectacles that a shortliver can witness — a majestic display of the power of the High Inquest. Yes!" he went on, warming to his narrative, enjoying the childsoldier's discomfiture. "Landing parties parading through the streets, warning of the coming of ... *myself!* Kyar Gharém, most cunning of child collectors, he who lists are the most complete of any in the Dispersal!

"And soon they will come pouring forth — most willingly, but some to be ferreted out by finding birds, each bird imprinted with the DNA of its quarry — swooping and tearing through the squares and the streets — and I shall collect them all.

"At length, when the collection is done, a tachyon bubble will descend and I shall present the completed collection to my master, Hokh'Ton Ton Alkamathdes, who is called Supreme Hunter of Utopias. He will take from me the master list and another grand mission of mine shall be completed."

"It's sounds very ... impressive, my Lord, and yet —"

"What, child?" The childsoldier seemed meek after Gharém's little lecture. Perhaps he simply needed to pee. Servants should always be a little cowed, Gharém thought.

"Might it be possible for me to ... visit the home I grew up in?"

"You dare to ask me to divert the resources of this mission just so you can fraternize with whores?"

"My Lord, I just thought —"

Gharém did his most intimidating cackle, and was gratified to see the equerry droop once more. "You're in luck," he said. "At the start every momentous mission, I become rather ... sexually restless. I need — something to relax me a little. Or far too many will feel my wrath, and the High Inquest will rebuke me for doing my job with a little too much enthusiasm. So. I shall need the services of a decent servocorpse, and you, my child, shall guide me to the very best this broken down planet has to offer — for that, Mikkálu-without-a-Clan, is the only reason I picked *you* as my equerry. And your pretty blue hair, I suppose."

Not to mention the fact that the boy had arrived at Bellares by special transport with a letter from the ruler of the world — the old world — a Princeling, and had not been genetically pre-chosen to be a childsoldier; this made the boy an enigma, a challenge, something to be deconstructed — dominated, if time permitted.

***

Forced to remain in the *zul*-cellar, living with the ache in the pit of his stomach that was his longing for his other self, Tijas dreamt of other worlds, of the overcosm that cannot be described except as a means to madness.

Far from the tutelage of Arbát, the words of the sung he had begun to sing returned unbidden:

in dárein shirenzheh

the silence between the stars ...

Tijas thought of the great gulf of nothingness separating star from star.

He thought of the light-mad overcosm, a legendary place where time and space where meaningless ... the ocean that the delphinoids sailed ... and he wondered if he would ever see it, if he would be driven mad, as many claimed ... and these words came to him:

den om verék en-tinjet
in-dárein shirenzheh ...

No living man has touched
the silence between the stars....

Eleven
Tunnels and Floaters

Arrogant, capricious, smug. That's who my Lord Gharém is, Mikkálu thought as the hoverfloat descended to Urna. *But it's a little more cushy than the war on Kishwá.*

In fact, the High Lord had been easy to manipulate. Mikkálu had grown up in a Temple of Aërat. He knew a little about seduction, which is not much about giving, and a lot about holding back; not much revealing, and a great deal of hinting. Mikkálu had figured out very quickly that Gharém's greatest fetish was to dominate, but one had to be a bit out of line to make the act of oppression satisfying to the oppressor. He figured out, too, that Gharém had a crippling terror of the Inquestors, yet yearned to ape their power.

A childsoldier seems easy enough to dominate; he is after all a child. But every childsoldier carries death in his eyes. Without the conditioning of absolute and unquestioning compliance to every command of the High Inquestors, an army of childsoldiers would be chaos a thousandfold.

And anyone placed in command of a childsoldier, who was not an Inquestor, also lived with a subliminal dread.

Mikkálu had learned much in a very short time. *I'm a survivor,* he would tell himself, always.

He had been touting the skills of the servocorpses of Aërat since they left Bellares. To lead Gharém to the temple would mean he would get to see Éluma.

But would she see him?

How much of a chasm between them had time dilation made? He was only a few months older. Was she an old woman?

He did not care. He loved her. He had even been curt to the Starry Highness to protect her.

These thoughts coursed through his mind as he waited on his mercurial master.

The floater descended.

Masked from outside view by a light bender, they fell through clouds and skirted a flock of loons, pinwheeling lights over the lake.

"Tell the floater where to go," Gharém said.

"It's difficult to say. There should be a square by the lake, a marketplace ... but instead there are all these haphazard buildings."

"Alykh did not have the advantage of princely designer," Gharém said. "Just navigate by feel."

Mikkálu subvocalized some commands so that the floater skirted what was once the edge of Shirénzang. Now there were citizens of Urna living in makeshift dwellings made from crates and packing material and wandering around. The floater moved slowly over their heads, silent, unseen. Here an old woman cooking over a fire. A boy trying to stir an old thinkhive to life. Servocorpses walking in circles, their programming aborted. Walking for ever, as their energy supplies could be replenished by sunlight.

"There's a square I recognize, and the displacement plates look active," Mikkálu said, because he saw occasional people popping in and out of thin air. "We came here in the old days, to buy illicit dreamstuff."

He brought the floater, its inhabitants still hidden from view by a refraction shield, to a gentle landing against broken flagstones.

"This way, my Lord," he said, taking the shockingly familiar step of grabbing hold of Kyar Gharém's hand. "Soon you'll be playing at your darkest fantasies —"

"Impertinence!" said Gharém, and slapped the boy's face.

Mikkálu could of course have lasered off the Child Collector's hand with a eyeblink, but he held himself back. *A childsoldier is obedient.*

***

Sajit waited for his father. *At some point, he'll come. And he'll* have *to understand.*

He waited, while Éluma attended to a ritual of the goddess. For the temple had not lost its appeal or its devotees; rather, being appended to what was now a pleasure city had increased the number of suppliants. It was exotic. It reeked of an ancient time.

And finally, Orifec came. Tired. World-weary, indeed. *I'll just tell him quickly. I'll be gone before he's thought about it.*

"Father, I am going. I've waited long enough."

"That's insane. You know what is about to happen."

"I talked to Éluma but she can never understand. She doesn't know about Tijas."

"And she cannot know."

"Tijas ... he's this *thing* gnawing inside of me. I'm not complete without him. And there's music. I'm not learning anything. Tijas is out there somewhere. I know it."

"Perhaps he's already been taken."

"Father, you're ... *callous*. You are a doppling. You understand."

"And you're my son. Who I gave up for his own protection, and who I'll never give up again."

"You could have kept me."

"Sajitteh...."

"Why couldn't I have grown up in the whorehouse, with my real mother?"

"I've told you. You have a destiny. You're going to be a great artist. I couldn't keep you close to me, stifling your dreams, imprisoned by privilege."

"You could have kept me!" Sajit screamed. "You engineered all this because you want to live your stupid dreams of being a musician through me ... but you'll never be me." Sajit started pummeling Orifec with his fists, hitting out wildly, even yanking out a hank of his hair.

Orifec couldn't stop himself. He clouted his son hard on the shoulder. Sajit became subdued. He was crying. "You hurt me," he said. "Tijas would never hurt me." Which he knew to be untrue. Because the emptiness in his stomach that was Tijas' absence was worse than being hit. Orifec looked at his hand. He was trembling.

"I can't believe I struck you," he said softly. Then his face became set and grim. Sajit had never seen Orifec this way. His shoulder stung; Orifec had clearly not struck many people, did not know his own strength. He was confused, unsettled.

Orifec grabbed Sajit by the shoulders. "Understand, Sajitteh," he said. "I'm doing this because I love you."

He pushed Sajit into a corridor, turned a corner, stepped on a displacement plate, and they found themselves in a strange bare room, with harsh, right-angled corners.

"I'm going to keep you here," Orifec said, "and I'm going to key the displacement field to my DNA only. I'll bring you some food and you can relieve yourself in that sanitizer," he pointed to an elimination stool in the corner. "You'll stay here until they're gone."

"Tijas!"

"We created him to take your place, Sajit. That is why we broke the law and tradition and made that abomination. You know that in Urna, a doppling cannot live."

"Except you, you hypocrite," Sajit whispered harshly. His ring began to burn him.

His father did not reply.

"I've spoken to people from other worlds. On some planets, dopplings are called twins, and they are treated with honour, they're even considered lucky in some places. The abomination thing is just ignorance — because we're a backworld — a planet that hasn't evolved."

"I can't listen to this," Orifec said. And vanished from the box of a room.

***

"Wake up, Tijas!" Daro said. "We're leaving the planet."

The troupe was gathered in the *zul* cellar. Tijas struggled to open eyes and he could see them all, shadows in the ill-lit room.

"You don't need to leave," Tijas said. "You've just started a good operation. The place'll be swarming with *dorezdas* soon. You'll be rich, you'll be able to get a real place, open a theater."

He waited. No one answered, but he became aware that the whole team was looking at him. "Not because of me?"

"Tisseh," said the Professor, and Tijas realized it was the first time anyone had called him by a child-name. Even Sajit had rarely done so.

"We're a team, Tijas. We're a family. We want you to come with us."

"Sajit, too?"

"Yes," Daro said, "if we can find him."

Tijas's mind raced. *If we can find him* ... how?

"You think I've been doing nothing, puttering upstairs with the thinkhive of this building?" said Zelma. "I've been planning an escape."

"There's a network of interconnected tunnels" she went on, fluttering her rainbow lashes, "and deep in the bowels of this building, there's a displacement nexus. I can divert power, reprogram it to magnify its range a millionfold, send us to a spot on one of the moons ... just outside the Inquestral perimeter."

"Think of it, Tijas," Daro said. "Freedom. No more living in the shadows. We'll ride the space between spaces, go from world to world and play out our timeless dramas in city squares in each world we come to."

"Yes, take us where dopplings are not *harám*," said Tijas, "where we can go about in the streets and not be seen as abominations."

"That's right," Daro said. *He doesn't seem that convinced,* Tijas thought.

"When can I go and fetch Sajit?"

"Well ..."

"You said he could come with us."

"If we can find him," Daro said.

"I *can* find him," said Tijas. "I've got a compass in my mind that leads to him, and that's how I know he's alive ... alive and scared."

For when he closed his eyes, he saw a room. A room, peculiarly square, not pleasingly rounded like a normal human dwelling. A prison. And felt pain. Sharp pain in the shoulder, as if he had been beaten. Could feel hot tears on his own cheeks, though his eyes were dry.

"I know *exactly* where he is. I feel it."

"You feel *something,*" Zelma said. "But is it Sajit, or is your own sense of loss?"

Tijas reached deep into the source of his pain.

Could I have made up this pain, to compensate myself for emptiness, because to feel pain is still better than to feel nothing at all?

Tijas felt doubt, and in that moment he felt weak; he knew that Daro and Zelma loved him, and that this entire foolhardy plan had been cooked up for *his* benefit, that all of them in their minds had already given Sajit up to the brutal machinery of the High Inquest.

I'm the only one who thinks he can be rescued, he thought. Maybe I've already lost this battle.

In that moment he said, "Maybe I'll come. Maybe I will."

***

The Child Collector and the equerry stepped from plate to plate, Gharém barely catching up as the boy lightly skipped the distance between displacements. As they reached the pathway leading to the entrance to the Temple of Aërat, Mikkálu saw his master grow grimmer, more brooding.

People like him are all the same, he thought.

This part of Shirenzang was still operational. Indeed, people in the brash clothing of Aírang were moving up the pathway — they had discovered something in this backward world congruent with their own world's preoccupations.

They were not dressed to be conspicuous. As they left the parked floater, Gharém had made them don refracting robes. Even had they been noticed, they might not have been seen as two people, but as something else in the area — trees, or walls. They blended.

"I may be occupied for some time," said Gharém. "I'm going to give charge of some very important items." He handed Mikkálu a pouch. "Tuck that into your kilt and don't lose it."

"Ha! Am I holding your entire career in my hands, Lord Gharém?"

"Perhaps."

Mikkálu could imagine what was in the pouch. It was both soft like flesh and articulated, like a fine metal mesh. When he squeezed it, it squirmed.

"Use it well," Gharém said, "and help me carry out this operation as smoothly and efficiently as possible, to the greater glory of the High Compassion." And Gharém handed over a few other objects: a message disk linked to the delphinoid's shipboard thinkhive, an a credit plaque with the Inquestral sigil. "Don't spend it all on sweets," he said. "Now instruct the attendants in your brothel for me, as I am too exalted a figure to bargain with corpses."

"It's not a brothel, my lord, it's a temple."

"Semantics, boy."

At the gateway to the temple, the servocorpse appeared to take their requests. A sight he had known all through childhood, and a familiar servocorpse, stepping out of the shadows.

The collector seemed almost reticent, letting Mikkálu take the lead.

"Tork! Don't you recognize me?"

"It's been a few years. You are unchanged."

"And so are you. Because you're a corpse. You don't get to age."

"And you have been sailing the space between spaces, young master."

"Yes. I have a ... suppliant. He seeks something special. He is one of great importance. He carries the Inquestral aegis. He wishes to be loved by the dead."

"And the dead are at their most loving in this temple, for those who are able to afford it."

"Let's just say that my master's credit is at an Inquestral level."

"Then he shall have all he needs, including insurance against forfeiture for any love objects crippled or damaged by the encounters." The servocorpse appeared to roll his eyes; but Mikkálu knew they did not possess irony.

"I'm sure my master will appreciate being given full rein."

"Which of the disciplines of the art of love is he most interested in?"

The Child Collector interrupted. "Subjugation. Submission. Absolute Subservience."

"Nice boss," Tork said it so only Mikkálu could hear.

"I was just thinking that you don't understand irony."

"I've been reprogrammed since you were last here," said the dead man. "The people of Alykh have different tastes. They don't take religion that seriously, and they prefer it when a corpse acts fresh."

Irony? This time the corpse betrayed nothing of the kind.

"Powers of powers, Tork," Mikkálu whispered, "take him to your grandest coupling chamber and give him all he wants."

The servocorpse bowed almost in two (servocorpses not being constrained by pain, such contortions were de rigeur) and said, "Your Lordship shall have paradise, though but for a spell."

"It is not paradise I require," said Gharém, "but the depths of darkness. And it shall not be for a spell, but for at least two sleeps. I shall create, oh, such a hell, I shall thrive on fear."

"What is a hell, my Lord?" said the servocorpse.

"It's something religious," Mikkálu said. "Quick, take him. And tell me where to find who I've come to see."

"After ten years, you demand to see *her?*" said the corpse. "Do you realize who she is now? Do you have an appointment?"

***

"Have I failed?" Orifec cried out. "Éllekeh, I was about to beat him! And now I've locked him up. I didn't listen to him."

In an inner room somehow connecting the palace and the temple — though not directly, for the path between them was a mishmash of displacement plates that crisscrossed the city — they clung together, the dispossessed princeling and the obsolescent goddess.

"They're resilient. You should know. I know. We both were raised in difficult environments, by people with other priorities," Éluma said. "Go talk to him again."

He didn't answer.

"There's something you're not telling me," she said. "I suppose it's some kind of father-son secret. Whatever it is, it can't be the end of the world."

He smiled wryly. "I suppose not. After all, the world has already ended."

They lay together on a cushion of force, slung between pillars made in the shape of the royal insignia; the twisted serpent columns had been rescued from the old audience chamber.

"Let's go and see him," she said.

"I'm afraid to."

"You are a Starry Highness. Don't let a child bully you."

"I understand that children can have an infinite capacity to forgive their parents," she said.

"But you don't know that. I don't know that. We haven't really had parents," said Orifec.

"We'll take him some food," she said.

"Let me get dressed."

Orifec picked up a piece of clingfire and wrapped it about his loins, then threw on an overshirt. Éluma looked at him. "You're dressing up to speak to your own child?"

He said, "It's almost an audition."

At that moment, they heard the voice of the thinkhive.

There is a petition for the goddess herself, it said.

Éluma laughed. "You know I don't take petitions in person anymore," he said. "Silly thinkhive."

No, this is a petition that you must honour. It comes with an Inquestral sigil.

"An Inquestor seeks the attentions of a goddess?" said Orifec. "That, you'll have to honor."

***

Stairwells — the ancient kind — round and round, descending into darkness. Circling down stairwells that sometimes veered and twisted. A claustrophobic burrow, musty air.

Everything had been left behind. No changes of clothing. No souvenirs. Whether from Urna or Alykh, the past would be obliterated.

Now a passageway where even Tijas had to bend. And where they emerged was a circular room with a circular displacement plate, wide enough for a dozen people or a load of cargo.

The room was illumined by a pale blue sourceless light. Its walls were blank, metallic, but there was an exposed panel from which trailed tendrils of metal and fibrillating neuron strands, with triangular light-shapes.

They squeezed against the walls, making sure they did not step on the plate before Zelma instructed them to. The magician was hunched over some light dice, making them circle and fly. The acrobats looked nervous, in the cramped space.

Zelma said, "I've almost finished the reprogramming." She moved her hands over the patches of light, and the triangles blinked and changed color, gold, silver, pink; the neuron strands, woven from the tissue of recycled servocorpses, swayed, separated, reconnected. "Displacement is pretty dicey when it comes to off-planet, and doesn't work at all on an interstellar level. But this small moon with its rustic spaceport, that we can manage."

As he watched her, the pain in the pit of Tijas' stomach grew stronger.

Sajit is in a room like this room.

"The delphinoid and its accompanying craft have established a perimeter within the orbit of Urna's first moon," Zelma said. "But on the third moon, there's a little backworld starport. We should be able to hitch a ride somewhere. All we have to do is put on a play there — move people. Engage their passions. In this galaxy, singers of songs and those who tell stories always have free passage."

"The offers'll come rolling in," Daro said.

Sajit can't get out! And he's calling to me!

"Are you all right, Tijas?" the magician asked.

"Yes." But he wasn't.

"The space between spaces!" said one of the acrobats. "The feeling! You can't explain it!"

"Of course not," said the other acrobat. "They put you in stasis for the whole flight."

Daro said, "Those two haven't actually done star travel — unless you count being stuffed into a people bin."

"It's done!" said the Professor. The room hummed and the walls sparkled.

The ache grew stronger.

"Listen carefully. You must subvocalize the correct command, and the window will be open only for a few minutes. And here are the syllables. You must subvocalize them exactly, or it will not work. All together ... *kha-na-ta-shé-vis.*"

She had barely said it when the musician was already wavering — a trick of the light? No. This amplified displacement was pulling a lot of power, was not instantaneous. He grew faint, became an outline of shimmering blue, then seemingly collapsed into a point and vanished.

The others were starting to vanish now.

"Quick, Tisseh! The window is closing!" Zelma said, but then she vanished.

The pain was unbearable. The emptiness that needed to be filled with his doppling, calling out to him, demanding that he enter —

He concentrated all his thoughts on the subvocalization ... *kha-na-ta-SAJIT!*

No!

He looked around him. All his new friends were shimmering, popping out. He looked at his hands, solid flesh — *I've failed!* — he thought, his hands shaking but still solid. *Sajit! Sajit!* he cried out with his mind. Tried to focus on the room, the darkness, the captivity of his brother. *Take me to Sajit!*

And then, looking down at his hands, he saw they were no longer there. And the *nothingness* was creeping up his arms. His feet were disappearing. The *nothingness* was crawling up his legs.

"Sajit!" he screamed.

Twelve
Loving the Dead

Kyar Gharém was led by two torchbearing dead children through a down-sloping passageway to a cave. — whether natural or made by art he could not tell. The air was cold; his breath hung in the dimness.

He was dressed in a fanciful costume belonging to no world that anyone knew of; there were leather leggings, a swirling cloak of black fire, and chains of some strange alloy that was oxidising in the moistness of the chamber; there was artificial shimmerfur, out of deference to the Inquestors, but his fantasy was more ancient than the Dispersal of Man — he had discovered it in a history of Old Earth, and it had ever lodged itself in his mind.

It was from this myth that much of the terminology of the Inquestors came, mused the author of this quasi-history. They were called Inquisitors, and they were given free rein to torture as they pleased, the better to purify the souls of those they ruled, and to cleanse their hearts of the condition of being fallen beings.

And doubtless, they found torture to be quite fetishizing. As did Gharém. And to be indulged only at these moments. Breathing in the foul air of the simulated dungeon, he was already becoming quite excited.

Gharém had ancient instruments to hand; meathooks, nail-rippers, tongue extractors, iron maidens. Now it was time to consummate his fantasy.

"Confess!" he cried out.

Around him, bodies began to stir. They began to draw breath. They were everywhere. A woman with exaggerated curves, her breasts straining against a membraneous slip. A dwarf with a monstrous penis that trailed the ground. Children and old women with slithering, clattering tongues. Oiled gladiators, chained against crumbling columns. As his eyes grew used to the darkness he saw a row of people of all colors and sexes, impaled against the wall, moaning and thrusting, for the stakes they were impaled on were gigantic and phallic and alive.

And they moaned, *Master ... master ...*

They had outdone themselves!

Gharém selected a lead-tipped flagellum from the array of instruments and began swinging it. The servocorpses writhed.

"Confess your heresies," he rasped, "and then be liberated as I rape all of you to death."

He cracked the flagellum. The servocorpses writhed.

They were all already dead anyway. Let them die again. And again. They were his, there only to do his bidding, and to be crushed regardless of how well they obeyed.

***

Éluma decided to meet this carrier of the Inquestral sigil in the Chamber of the Goddess. This was not a place of gold and statues and dancing lights, but a severe room, pyramidal in shape, lit by a single flaming crystal. She decided that she would greet him clothed only in light.

Her mind was in turmoil, with thoughts of Orifec and the confusion of dealing with her son. But she had never served an Inquestor. That would have to be the pinnacle of one's vocation.

So she adjusted the clouds to be at their most cushiony, to flow around her person in both a comforting and a seductive manner, and waited.

Presently, the thinkhive spoke.

Goddess, it said, *the bearer of the Inquestral sigil is approaching.*

She stood before the fire-crystal, closed her eyes, and stretched her arms out over the flames, and made the three sacred gestures of the goddess.

Two small hands grasped hers. A child's hands.

The opened her eyes.

The boy laughed....

The boy who smiled in the shadows, so many years ago —

"Mikeh!" she laughed out laughed and embraced him. "But — how?"

"I carry the sigil of the High Inquest," the boy said. "I'm not supposed to use it this way, but it's the only way they'd let me see you."

She remembered —

The laser-eyes, the citrine fire shooting from them, slicing and cauterizing a woman's hand —

"Mikeh!" she said. "Years have gone by."

"For me, it was only a month."

"Even so ... you didn't come here for sex." If he was only a month older — although in *her* time, so much had transpired —

Mikkálu laughed. "I'm getting older," he said. "And ... I've *seen* things. I grew up here."

"You are *one month* older, little boy, and I'm *not* scared of you, even if you *could* slice me in to with a glance."

"It's fine. I'm not in battle mode."

"And now I'm old enough to be your mother, and I *am* a mother, too. Oh — Mikeh — you have to help us!"

And Mikkálu said, "Yes, Ellekeh, that's why I've come."

And she understood that his coming was no accident. It was *meúr.*

***

Gharém roared! The whip raised welts on dead flesh. Rivers of haemosimulant fountained and flowed. Naked corpses writhed and thrust against their chains.

A dark, tall servocorpse with many breasts and filed teeth gnawed at his gnarled manhood. Gharém yanked out hanks of dead hair, shrieking in an ecstasy that was pain's mirror-doppling.

At that moment, a message disk blinked.

He grunted, extracted his penis from the perilous orifice, and turned to look at it.

Delphinoid secure field in place, Lord Collector. Veznávikas primed and programmed. Thinkhives ready. Containment field floaters, long-range displacement devices activated. Preliminary surveys done and collection should net close to 100%. We await your signal, Lord Collector.

But the dead were dancing ...

"I'll give the signal," said Gharém, "as soon as I complete my exercise regimen."

Dead men, women, and children screamed in simulated pain. "I am your ruler!" Gharém cried. "Your owner! Your master! Confess your sins!"

***

Alone in the prison, Sajit thought only of his doppling. His doppling consumed everything. In the gloom, he smelled his own hands, sniffed at his elbows, his armpits, knowing it was his doppling's scent.

How could the Starry Highness have done this to his own flesh and blood? Sajit was shaking.

The gloom deepened and he felt as though he was careening into an abyss —

Yet the feeling of Tijas' presence kept intensifying. He was so close! The scent of Tijas wasn't just his own scent. There was something else in the air. The air was growing thicker — more solid — a shape wavering in the emptiness —

If he reached out to hug the darkness, he could almost —

And suddenly, Tijas was hugging him for real. He had materialized on the displacement plate. The *locked* displacement plate.

"I'm going —"

"Crazy, no you're not, I —"

"Yes, crazy, this yawning emptiness, only —"

"You understand —"

— *Enough of finishing each other's sentences,* Sajit thought.

And Tijas heard!

— *We don't have to talk anymore.*

— *This apartness — it's strengthened the way we can reach other — I can hear you —*

— *In my head, louder than —*

— *Ever before —*

"Stop," said Sajit. "It's too —"

"Overwhelming. I know."

Sajit and Tijas sat for a moment. The tips of their fingers touched. There was an electricity there. Sajit could hear the thoughts, pounding at him from every side, but he realized he could turn them down, if he concentrated.

"We have to ... talk to each other normally," Tijas said. "We are freaks as it is. Have you been in here long? I felt it ... so powerfully ... a day ago."

"Daro? The Professor?"

"They went off-world. They did it to save me. Us, really, but they all thought you'd been captured already. They couldn't —"

"Feel me, like we can."

"Orifec has done this to protect you," Tijas said. "He doesn't understand."

"We can't let anyone see us!"

"They've got these birds. *Veznávikas,* they call them. They're like birds of prey, each one locked on a single target."

"But there's two of us. We can confuse it."

"How can we get away?"

"I don't know. The displacement plate is locked. Orifec keyed it to his DNA."

"Isn't there something here we can use? An old article of clothing, a bloodstain?"

"No. This isn't a room he normally uses ... wait." Sajit reached inside the pocket of his tunic. Was it still there? "I fought him really hard. I think I pulled out some of his hair."

Triumphant, he found the handful of hair and showed it to his doppling.

"Maybe if we sprinkle it in the center of displacement plate —"

"But what command can we give it? I don't know where to go, I don't even really know where I am, or how exactly I got here, except somehow your voice inside my head was so strong it overrode a thinkhive that the Professor had personally hacked and jimmied and reprogrammed to send us to a moon —"

Sajit said, "Hold still. Together, we'll focus on a safe place."

Sajit and Tijas sat facing each other on the displacement plate, then Sajit took the hank of the Princeling's hair and place the strands carefully around them, encircling the two boys. "Closer," Sajit said. They squeezed together, locking legs and arms to take up as little room as they could.

They would have to stay inside the thin line.

They knew no special subvocalizations. They would have to focus on one thing: *safety, safety,* hoping the thinkhive would be programmed to —

Sajit saw his brother's shape start to shimmer a little. It wasn't working right! "Hold tight!" he said, thinking at least if they were going to become a cloud of particles somewhere in space, they would at least be together....

Another figure began to form in the same space as theirs — an unthinkable anomaly — they would be destroyed for sure! — and Sajit looked up, hugging his doppling even harder to himself, and saw —

Orifec! Glowering, looking down at the boys who were occupying his space, and his mouth was opening, he was about to speak when —

The room vanished and they were still alive, still together — but what was the place that the thinkhive had designated as *safety?*

***

Éluma deopaqued the Chamber of the Goddess and led Mikkálu through a small portal that displaced to her private quarters, and she found Orifec with his head buried in his hands.

"What happened?" she said.

He said, "He's gone."

"Gone? From a locked room?"

"A locked, sealed, keyed-to-my-DNA room."

"Who could have have done this to us?" She sat beside him, looked at his face, and once again felt that he was hiding something. "There's something else. You have to tell me. What have you done with him?"

Orifec said, "I can't speak of it!"

Mikkálu had followed her in. He spoke up now. "Starry Highness," he said.

"You!" Orifec said furiously. "The wild boy."

"Don't!" she said. "He hasn't done anything."

Éluma saw that boy felt awkward, intruding on his Princeling's grief.

"Mikeh came to see us. He's working for —"

"The Child Collector," Mikkálu said. "He brought me along as his equerry. Well, personal slave, really. He doesn't like to use servocorpses, likes the power of actually intimidating a living person — especially one who could decapitate him with a glance," he added, laughing.

"You haven't changed," Orifec said.

"It's only been a month for him," said Éluma. "Even so —"

"I've squirmed out of a year's worth of trouble," Mikkálu said. "Got out of a lot of boring training by flattering the commanders and their lieutenants. Caught a big one — His Arrogant Lordship, Kyar Gharém, Collector to the High Inquest."

Even Orifec smiled a little.

"But I've come to see you in a time of turmoil," Mikkálu said. "Can I help?"

"How could you help?" Éluma said. "You, a child still."

"A deadly child," Mikkálu said. "But I *can* help."

"Yes, you can," Orifec said bitterly. "Persuade the Collector to go home. This collection should be aborted anyway, considering that the High Inquest has muddled its *makrúgh* and mixed up two different games. And destroyed millions of lives."

"In the High Compassion," Mikkálu whispered by habit. The ritual formula rang hollow. "Starry Highness, you know I can't do that. But I can find your son. I'm the only person who can."

***

— whirling, a kaleidscoping whirlwind of thoughts, blending, meshing, interconnecting —

Tijas! Where are you?

I'm inside you! Inside-outside-around-among-within-surrounding-melding —

A space. A space without dimensions. A time outside time.

The space resolved, it seemed, into a room of sorts. It couldn't be a real room because it had no walls. It had no up and down. And Sajit felt himself resolving. He felt the part of himself that he could feel as *I* pull reluctantly from the blended vortex.

We're in the space between spaces, he said without speaking. Without, if one can imagine it, even thinking.

We're in the place we always go to, in the femtosecond between displacements, Tijas said, *but the place we go to is too brief to have a name. No human being could ever perceive this.*

Indeed, how could it be perceived when the snippet of spacetime one travelled through was too brief to transgress the limits of uncertainty?

It must be because we travelled together, Sajit said, *entwined, and with DNA that cannot be untangled —*

— and because we did not give a clear command to pin down coordinates.

The thinkhive that managed displacements was being forced to delve into its memories to piece together a credible set of coordinates. Perhaps it was examining all the places this DNA had been before, in the short time it had been alive ... and sometimes in more than one place at the same time. It was taking long enough in its calculations for a perceptible moment to be generated. It was in this tiny moment that the two were able to communicate.

It's amazing — I'm inside of you, everywhere inside of you —

I think this is what adults are feeling when they talking about "bursting their milkpods" —

Laughter, cascading like a meteor shower!

I want this moment to last forever —

Yes! Forever and ever!

But it was already over.

They were in a forest.

In a chill gray space.

A pool of light in a deep dark forest.

Sajit spoke first, with words, because even the thoughts that passed freely between them were nothing compared to the intimacy they had shared in the space between spaces.

"So this is how the planetary thinkhive parsed the word *safety,"* he said.

Tijas said, "I've never been here, but I know it well. I've seen it in your thoughts, sometimes."

"Walk a little further in, and we'll come to a wall. And the ruins of a temple. And in that direction ... my old house."

"We have to be very quiet," Tijas. "The moons will be singing soon."

In a few minutes they had reached the clearing that Sajit knew so well. The moons were rising all at once. Eríkion tumbled in a skein of cloud. Half-Káruval glowered behind full Arrisát. Kalíth and Ralíth circled each other, and the scent of *vanjéris* laced the air.

Soon the rosella petals would start to fall, moonlit dust-motes in the deep night.

And in a few minutes the moons sang. Oh, Sajit knew now that they did not sing, that the music was the song his heart heard, woven from loneliness and silence.

Above the wuthering and the sighing in the trees, the voices of the moons were his own voice. But so clear ...

Den táthes eyáh —
Den Sirana

but this was no inner voice. Sajit turned and saw that it was Tijas who was singing. It was as though he was watching himself, in that lost world, when Urna was Urna, and a song was just a song.

"You've seen this place," Sajit said.

"Yes. I've seen everything now. When we were in the space between spaces, and we were both everywhere and nowhere."

Tijas took Sajit's hand. With complete familiarity, sure of every step, every old stone and every tree trunk. "There's a temple ... a little further."

Sajit said, "Even I never went there. It is too far from home."

"Let's go there. Everything's too far from home now. Home doesn't exist."

Tijas found the displacement plate, buried under leaves. Hand in hand the hopped onto it and reemerged in another clearing. Sajit had hoped for another time-stretched moment of melding, but the displacement was barely a blink.

The temple had an entrance, but no roof save for a canopy intertwined branches. Here the trees were generations old and had linked to form a leafy roof, replacing the old dead plastiforms. A holosculpt stood, its arms long broken off, half-buried in a profusion of weeds. It was of stone, and its face was the face of Éluma. Centuries old, but still the face of the love-goddess.

"My mother," Sajit.

"But not mine," said Tijas.

"I want us to merge, like we did in the space between spaces."

"We can't."

"Then, the way grownups do." Sajit said, "I've been in the Temple of Aërat, Tijas. I've seen what they do. What Arbát wanted from us. What the suppliants get from the servocorpses."

Impulsively, he kissed his doppling. Not as a brother, but as he'd seen in darkened corners of the temple. Startled, Tijas pulled away. "Weird," he said, wiping his mouth. "What happens next?"

"I think we're supposed to take our clothes off."

"Why? It's chilly. Anyway ... my penis feels weird. It's got a mind of its own."

"I think we're supposed to try to meld. Not with our minds but with our ... our *selves.*"

"It sounds stupid," Tijas said, but he had already shed his tunic. Through gaps in the leaves above, a hundred little shafts of light pierced his slim body. *I'm looking at myself,* Sajit thought. He too stepped out of his thin clingfire. "So we just look at each other?" Tijas said.

"I don't know, but somehow, after a lot of grunting, it leads to the bursting of milkpods," Sajit said. "Doesn't make much sense."

They both started laughing, then, and presently they fell asleep in the moonlight, on the bed of weeds beneath the statue of the goddess Aërat, who was also Sajit's human mother, with their garments heaped up and tangled over their intertwined limbs. And the moons sang a lullaby.

Sajit dreamed of a time when Tijas was not. Of his sisters, his parents, his village home. Of standing alone in the clearing. Presently, he came awake; of all the moons, only Eríkion was left, circling above the treetops, shifting the dappling patterns on his doppling's pale skin.

His memories of the time before Tijas were gauzelike, faded. *Before he came,* he thought, *I wasn't really me yet.*

Mulling over this paradox, he slid back into sleep.

***

And dreamed again —

This time, the rock was being hurled straight at his head. And the woman cloaked in shadow had turned her back. And Tijas was laughing, and his eyes were slitty-yellow, feline.

He woke screaming, but his doppling wrapped himself more tightly around him, and again, Sajit slept ... deeply, dreamlessly.

***

In another temple, almost as ancient, Kyar Gharém was the principal in a ritual far less innocent. He was coming to climax, wading through a sea of blood and entrails. He kissed a corpulent corpse, biting and ripping out her tongue. A dead woman wrapped an extruded intestine about his loins. He was in an ecstasy of torment.

He never wanted it to end.

He was drunk on his savage appetites. Again and again he plunged into writhing flesh. Death-rattles came again and again, for the dead may rattle more than once.

Once more he climaxed in a torrent of blood.

He lay on a bed of corpses, heaving. Incongruously, a neatly dressed page brought in a beaker of fresh *zúl* on an iridium platter. The walls dissolved and the programming was replaced by a rustic scene of meadows and rosella groves.

The page was not dead; his class of clientele merited some living servitors. If he *was* a corpse, it must be a very fine model indeed.

"Is your name Mikkálu?" Gharém asked.

"No, my lord. Though many of us *are* named that. There was a Mikkálu here once who made a name for himself, ten years ago ... many of us took his name because of that. He became a childsoldier ... by choice. Everyone knows the story of how he defied the law — and how the Starry Highness changed the law for love of the goddess."

"And are you not afraid of the coming of the Child Collector?"

"If I am on the list," the boy said, "it is *meúr*. No one can resist."

"Such enchanting superstitions you people have! I could tell you that answer," Gharém said, "with a flick of my mind."

"If it *is* to be *meúr*," the boy said, "I'd be happier not knowing in advance."

"You wouldn't want to seduce me into granting a reprieve?"

"What good would it do? Everything in this temple is at your disposal, my lord. Should you wish to sate your pleasure on my person, the goddess would insist on my compliance."

"You are not to my taste. Just go instruct your whoremaster to run this scenario one more time. The task I am about to do is not entirely to my liking ... I would rather experience the love of the dead ... for they have no free will."

Gharém could not help noticing that the page sauntered off with a smirk. An inferior who could be crushed with a word, but he looked down on Gharém's dark fantasies.

Let them despise me! he thought. *It comes with the job. On any planet where a Child Collector has landed, he is always the most hated person in the world.*

***

Orifec did not know how this childsoldier could find his sons, let alone save them. He knew only that once, before Sajit was even born, this boy had boldly burst in among the acolytes and saved Éluma. There was something more than bluster in him.

"I need to be up high," Mikkálu said. "As high above the city as possible."

"Come, then," Orifec said. "Shirénzang's elevators are not all broken." For he still knew how to find what remained of his old palace.

The Princeling led them through a corkscrew hallway to a displacement shaft. Mikkálu gasped as the circle they stood on hurtled skyward, the varigravs not quite in alignment so it was not a smooth, quiet ride but a rattling, stomach-turning journey through a crystal tunnel which was now bent in places.

At times they stopped to navigate a corridor on foot. Orifec moved purposefully; he had made this journey a few times since the people bins had landed. When Éluma had been busy with the business of the goddess, he had wandered these clear tubular pathways that had once formed the elegant stem and stamens of the flower-palace. There had been the remnants of a planetary council; though his world was reduced to a square inside a new metropolis, yet it still counted as its own world with this own culture, its own governance.

Éluma gripped his hand. They did not speak.

Many petals of the crystal flower that formed the palace that once overlooked the city had been sheared off, and the topmost turret was broken and doubled downward against the stem. Orifec found the passageway he was looking for, leaning precariously over a wall of glass and emptying out into his former throneroom. He eased himself down and helped Éluma.

Mikkálu leaped onto the throneroom. The columns of intertwining servocorpose pythonoids still stood. There was a throne, too, though it had been open to the elements, and — in a most unroyal fashion — was covered in bird droppings.

"We have two sleeps at most, probably only one," said Mikkálu, before the old lecher tires of his bloody fantasies. We will have to find him quickly."

Orifec said, "Are we high enough yet?"

The throneroom's walls were shattered. Here and there, forcefields were still in place; through gaps, a cold wind blasted them. Going to the very edge of the throneroom, which teetered as they walked across, the boy looked over the edge. Orifec said, "The parts of my world that are still standing ... a few temple, some deserted squares, beneath them all a network of tunnels that predates the displacement system ... over there, the bridge and the lake where the luminous loons gather. And sprouting from the wreckage, another planet ... bustling, mercantile, kaleidoscopic ... nothing like our simple world. It will soon swallow all that remains of Urna."

Over the lake, something ominous: a ship, as wide, it seemed, as the lake itself, blotting out an entire quadrant of the sky. The ship was ovoid and featureless.

There were none of the lights, fins, spirals and jags that a pleasure ship would have; it was plain and functional ... a ship for warriors. Its only surface feature was a silvery-black whirling nebula.

"That is the delphinoid that will take your son," Mikkálu said. "But we can get to him first."

The equerry took a message disk from his tunic and held it to his forehead, along it to interface with his thoughts.

"I'm getting us a finding-bird," the boy said. "A *veznávik.*"

"You can't!" Orifec said.

"What's a finding-bird?" asked Éluma.

"It's what will find him," said Mikkálu, "a devilishly clever thing, its sensors honed to a single DNA-signature. It can look around corners, through opaqued windows, below the ground and in the sky. It can outfly any floater, any speeder. One childsoldier, one finding-bird. It's relentless. It'll find your boy, dead or alive."

"And bring him to the Inquest! We're trying to stop that!" Éluma said.

"Look!" the boy said, pointing.

From the whirling nebula on the belly of the starship, a single point of light was detaching itself, then soaring up, a comet against the starship's shadow, a streak more bright than daylight, hurting his eyes, hurtling downward now, towards them as they stood on the unsteady parapet. The dot grew larger and Orifec saw now that it swooped on silver wings. Abruptly its shadow was overhead. An aquiline beak and broad wingspan, and a bloodcurdling shriek as it touched down now on the parapet and Orifec saw the talons, sharp and wide enough to skewer a human child. It shrieked again, a cry at once animal-like and metallic.

"This finding-bird has been programmed with your boy's identity."

"— but it will bring him straight to the Inquestors! —" Éluma said. "It's taking him straight to his death!"

Mikkálu closed his eyes and when he opened them he had armed his irises. His eyes turned citrine. He leaped up, whirled, shouted “Ishá ha!” the childsoldiers’ warcry and as he somersaulted twin rays of laser light sliced through one of the serpent columns. The parapet shuddered. The *veznávik* flapped its wings, each flap a peal of thunder.

“Not at all,” said the childsoldier. “Once the bird finds the boy, I will slice him to ribbons. No bird, no childsoldier.”

“Thank you,” Éluma said.

“Now, does this throneroom fly?” said the equerry.

“I’ll tell it to follow the bird,” said Orifec. He subvocalized a few commands and the floor began to hum.

Slowly, it uncoupled itself from its force-moorings and headed out. The finding bird flapped its wings again and hovered over their heads, its large compound eyes rotating.

“You’ll save my son,” Éluma said. “I know you will. I always thought somehow you would come back.”

The throneroom lifted off now, thrumming, and Orifec threw a reflecting mask over them so they could not be seen.

His heart was heavy. Events were spiraling out of control ... and he had still not dared to tell the goddess that there were two sons to be saved, not one.

Thirteen
Safety

Paradise lasted only a sleep or two; in the temple in the forest, Tijas and Sajit soon became hungry. There was a *gruyesh* tree, so by the second sleep they had picked all the fruit and sucked the juices dry and picked up a case of diarrhea besides.

Wandering further, they found another tree, but there is such a thing as too much sweetness.

"We should go to the house," Sajit said.

"House?"

"*Our* house."

"Except that I never lived there."

"You did. But you were in a box."

"I'm not *attached* to that place. I mean, I don't feel that it's *home.*"

"It doesn't matter. It's got food. At least, it still had food when we left home for the city."

Indeed, Sajit had been thinking of home since they arrived at the ruined temple. He wanted Tijas to love *home* as well, but perhaps it was true that he couldn't feel connected to it in the same way. But he know how to get them there. First, to the clearing, then a brief walk through the wood. Tijas was reluctant, but even he knew they couldn't live on *gruyesh* forever.

The village of Attembris was no more than the journey of a sleep. Sajit could tell the way easily, not so much by the trees and the twisted pathway, but by the scent of the rosellas, becoming more intense as they neared the ring of stones where he used to come in the night to be alone with the moons and with his music.

The petals whirled and churned. The moons danced.

And presently, they were at the edge of the village. They stood in front of the wall to Sajit's room, which abutted the forest, was indeed almost indistinguishable from the forest, as it was cloaked in a mirroring filter that reflected and re-reflected the trees. But the bedroom window was still keyed to Sajit's DNA; he touched a low-hanging branch and they climbed inside easily enough, though inside seemed at first to be just a continuation of outside; the holosculpt of the forest was still running.

Most would not hear it, but Sajit's fine-tuned hearing sensed the threshold thrum of a holosculptor, and he wondered why the house was still connected the the planetary thinkhive's power.

The boys were both standing in Sajit's old room now. For a moment it seemed that the last year had been a dream. Only ... there were two of him now.

Sajit tapped the wall to see if there was any food. It wheezed a bit and extruded a loaf of something vaguely protein, vaguely bread. "The kitchen is sort of working," he said. They shared the loaf; doubtless it was an admixture of all the right nutrients, but there was a staleness, as though the domestic thinkhive had become unused to cooking.

Thinkhives. They could be as cranky as people.

Tijas said, "At least it's not another gruyesh."

"Let's go to the family area," said Sajit, "perhaps there's a deactivated servocorpse we left behind, and we can kickstart it and make it turn the house into something livable."

He took his doppling's hand and they entered the breakfast circle where the family usually gathered. For the first time in months Sajit missed Vimla and Chanika. The sisters, the parents — or the people who he had thought to be his parents and his siblings — their chatter was so much a part of this room.

But yes, it had a scent of home. Perhaps a hint of a fragrance Ina sometimes wore. Perhaps the sour odor of a fermenting bowl of *zul.* Perhaps the sound of a whisperlyre —

No! "Tijas, we're not imagining this."

The first tones of an *alap,* the introduction to a song ... a love song. The choice of raga was anterior-retrograde, each tone nudged toward the flat side by a single *shrut* in the descent, as if to speak of regret, of love lost.

"Where is it coming from?" said Tijas.

And then came words:

bhasháur hyemádhen chítarans

Ga eyáh jariti
midhiá bhashandut

The boys knew that song well.

Some say that the homeworld of the heart
Is legendary Earth; though that's just a story.

They sang the next lines, coming in an improvised canon, adding florid melismata to the song's sustained tones:

z chítarans hyemádhen bhasháur
Uran s'Vareken, hokhkeliassá

but others say the heart's homeworld
is the High Eye of Heaven,
where the High Compassion dwells —

As they sang, the front door of the house irised open, and they could see a hooded, bent figure in the garden. He was looking away from them, but they knew who it was. They knew that they should be quiet, that they should not reveal themselves — not *both* of them. But they were caught up in the magic of the song.

bhasháurke ma u ejéndut
ma kens savra bhasháh
mori, hesti, darlukti
kal flúh em flúta

still others that it's the planet of our birth

the world whose fragrance speaks of
mother, the hearth, the light of a star
that flows like a river

It was the final stanza that made transformed these musings into a love song. But whether it was the love of lovers, of brothers, or of a master and student or even a human being and a world, a god, a cosmos ... that was ambiguous.

The boys sang, blending with an old man singing to himself in a light-drenched garden in a house in an abandoned village.

má bhashávo sarnang
hokhté chitres-hyémadh
midhiá em ga
em enguesta keliásek
melít em matésavra

but I say you *are the heart's homeworld,*
as mythical as Earth,
as compassionate as the High Inquest,
as sweet as the scent of a mother.

The music died away and it was Arbát who stood and turned to see them, the old teacher in a white robe in the entryway. The sunlight in the garden was bright and Arbát was a shadow.

Arbát said, "Don't be afraid. I hoped against hope there would be two Sajits."

The boys looked at each other, and back to their teacher.

"You're a gift to the world, to the whole Dispersal

of Man, Sajit. I knew my purpose in life was to take you, the rough-edged genius, to polish, to purify, to refine ... and then to give you up, because you belong to all the cosmos. Your words, your music. I am only a servant of the Art, Sajit, and I knew you were not mine to keep. But I always dreamed there would be a second Sajit, and that he could belong to me."

Sajit said, "We don't belong to you, Master Arbát."

Their teacher sighed. "Yes, that, also, I know." He set down the whisperlyre on the floor of the dwelling and walked over to where the boys were standing. He laid one hand on each boy's cheek. "You see, I am not horrified at the abomination. I'm not superstitious. How could I be, when I have digested the great songs of so many cultures, so many worlds?"

"But why are you in Attembris?" Tijas said.

"I thought you would come here. The city is a mess, imperfectly matched with an alien city, its sense of direction all topsy turvy. Combing through the city's grid can lead to many wrong turns; the cities are still intertwining as they begin to coexist. But Attembris may as well not exist at all."

"But what will we do?" Tijas said.

"You'll be safe here, Sajit."

"I'm not Sajit. I'm Tijas."

This comment seemed to pass unnoticed. Sajit could not fail to see how Tijas felt about it. Tijas was not another Sajit. Tijas was Tijas and Sajit, chronologically older, felt it was up to him to insist on it. "Master Arbát," he said, "you have to understand. You've been teaching us both, but you never knew which was which."

"Why does it matter? The spirit of music has granted my heart's desire. I can keep you with me always, *and* I can let you go."

"No, we're *not* the same person."

So Sajit understood that much as Arbát may have wanted to protect him, there was also something not quite right about this relationship. There was an obsessiveness. Something that made him queasy. Why else would the old man come to Attembris? Why would he *stalk* them?

Arbát said, "I've filled the house with supplies ... got them from other houses in the village. The place is almost completely deserted."

"Almost?" Tijas said.

"There are a few families ... families so uninvolved in the world that they hardly even understand that our planet has *fallen beyond.* Some of them are living in the school. You remember it, Sajit."

"Tijas."

Sajit thought, *Why does he always look at Tijas and say* Sajit? *Why, when he can't even tell us apart?*

Tijas looked at him as if Sajit had spoken aloud. He must have divined his thoughts. He whispered in Sajit's ear, "It's because I was the one who ... caught him with the pleasure corpse. He senses that."

People who can't tell us apart, Sajit thought, *don't truly understand us; we are not each other ... and yet we are.*

***

Gharém emerged, at last, from his dungeon. He assumed that his equerry of the blue flames would be waiting around in an antechamber, but there was no one. Only an attendant, dozing on a cushion of force.

Enraged, Gharém shook the man.

"You've finished, my Lord," he said. "I hope our service was satisfactory."

"Where is my equerry?"

"He went to pray to the goddess, my Lord."

"Tell him we are going back to work."

"Oh ... no, my Lord. We never disturb the goddess."

"What do you mean? This whorehouse is infested with two-gipfer goddesses. Surely my servant may be pulled away from whatever depraved thing he's doing."

"Oh ... your equerry is not engaged in any recreational activities, sir. He's not just with one of our priestesses who assumes the role of Aërat. He is with Aërat herself. They were friends, you know, before he joined the childsoldiers. Friends as children."

"That means nothing. A childsoldier has no past."

"And yet, Lord, if you are in no hurry ... perhaps another visit to our dungeons?"

Gharém was sated. He had tormented the dead for many sleeps. He had drenched himself in blood, semen, piss, and every foul fluid that could ooze from a corpse. "Another episode will deplete me permanently," he said.

He touched his temple with an index finger, awakening an embedded thinkhive, and subvoked a few terse commands. He saw then that Mikkálu had summoned a finding bird.

"Sneaky little squirt!" he murmured as the internal thinkhive showed him the identity of the one Mikkálu was going after. The child was going to net him the greatest prize of this haul, a childsoldier of royal blood. It was right to bring him to this world The boy *knew* things.

A childsoldier has no past, and yet ...

The Dispersal of Man is built on a foundation of equality. The Inquestors are like gods, but the humblest childsoldier could be raised to the High Inquest. And childsoldiery was the great leveller, for it was the destiny of every perfect child, lowly or noble, to serve the High Inquest and the dark game called *makrúgh.*

Mikkálu was clearly aiming to go far. He had wangled himself into Gharém's inner circle, knew Gharém's secret desires, and was, indeed, trusted by Gharém, insofar as he believed anyone could be trusted.

I will loosen the leash, Gharém thought. *Mikkálu will bring me the heir of Urna. He'll turn him over to me for ... what? a position, a commandership, something that doesn't bring death-risk with every assignment. And I will turn the child in for something big. Perhaps I shall be made a Princeling myself.*

Although then again, the High Inquest was too exalted to pay heed to the distinction between a princeling and a pauper. It was Gharém's own little game — exalting the lowly, humbling the high. *I should have been an Inquestor,* he thought. I *could* have been! If only I hadn't failed the compassion test.

Gharém pulled a message disk from his robe and tapped it to send a command.

Release more birds, he subvocalized, *and ready the transport. We're ready to collect the children of Urna.*

***

Orifec said, "There's something you must know about our child."

Éluma said, "I already know far more than you about our child."

"Yes. I've been distracted. But what I meant to tell you...."

The floater that had been a veranda of the princely palace moved through the night. Above them, the finding-bird wheeled, emitting its metallic-banshee screech. Mikkálu stood at the floater's edge, his slight form striated by the light from three moons, steering them, communicating with the finding bird.

But Éluma did not respond. She was always troubled now, and Orifec found her more remote. The knowledge of the dopplings was a hard, knotty thing in the back of his mind, always present. Only a member of the royal family could understand that this abomination was no abomination at all, but a different way to be human.

Orifec went to where the young equerry was steering the floater. He was flying with his eyes closed, seeing with the *veznávik's* attenuated senses. The Princeling touched the childsoldier's bare shoulder. It was steel-hard, belying its baby-soft complexion. Orifec was startled.

Mikkálu moved his head; slowly the sapphire flamestrands spun, following his movement. "Starry Highness," he murmured.

"You saved her once," he said. "You love her, don't you?"

"You would say, I love as a child loves. And I would

say to you, but you love as a princeling loves. And that can never be as deep as how a child loves."

Orifec wanted to tell him how untrue that was, how unfair ... but he doubted himself.

***

It did not feel right for the two of them to go down the school at the same time. "But," Tijas said, "we can get away with it ... if we're very sneaky."

"If some families are living there," said Sajit, "they'll have some food that's less boring than what Arbát has stashed in our walls."

And so it was that, making sure they wore an identical color of clingfire held together by the same synthserpentine belt, they made their way separately to the building where some of the families were living.

"You must not be seen together," Arbát had told them. "These are the most hidebound of all, these people. They seem rational until something cries *abomination* to them."

So that morning, Sajit entered the school and Tijas lingered outside. And Arbát sat by the door, working on a curvy new melisma for an old folk song.

Sajit only vaguely remembered these people — Tijas did not know them at all, of course. Sajit was inside, sharing a grilled heptopus and a loaf of fresh winebread with two old women. Tijas was outside and playing with other children.

Tijas had indeed not experienced a time so normal-seeming, so domestic. There was a boy named Bardelár, perhaps his age, who knew nothing about music at all, and not one word of the highspeech. But he knew all about hitting a grav-ball with a curved stick. He made the ball whir as he twirled the stick, sent it flying, swerving, almost crashing against the wall. A girl named Sávezh, his sister perhaps, was playing with a homunculus. An old dead lady, their nanny, watched them from afar.

Further away, towards the area's only displacement plate, three older children were giggling as they indulged in a three-way wrestling match.

"Want to try?" said Bardelár, throwing the stick at Tijas who caught it deftly, tried waving it a few times — it was a primitive kind of control with simple monosyllabic subvokes — *dha, dho, gha* —

The grav-ball danced in the air for a moment, defying the pull of the world —

And crashed!

Bardelár laughed as he snatched back the stick and with a wrist-flick reversed its polarity. The grav-ball swung upward.

"Stop showing off, Bardi," said his sister, before returning to snuggling with the homunculus, who bleated in a strange parody of a baby's cry.

Then it came —

A high-pitched, metallic keening first, a shriek from above, earsplitting long before its source could be seen ... it was a bird. No, not a bird. It grew closer. Bigger. Shinier, with wings that could lock position in a swooping straight streak of iridium. And when they flapped it was a sound of thunder.

Already! Tijas thought. *It only took this long to find us!*

The other children did not seem to realize there was danger. They all clustered together now, pointing, laughing, imitating the shrieking. As the bird drew closer they could see it was huge. Tijas was transfixed. *This is it, this is the end.* He reached out with his mind, trying to reach Sajit inside the school.

Adults were coming out now, but not Sajit. Tijas did not dare go inside for fear of causing an abomination panic, did not dare stay for fear of being swooped down upon, so he just stood, staring at the sky as the *veznávik* circled ever closer.

It plummeted now, diving down towards him. He screamed and —

The bird had seized the other boy.

Sávezh was shrieking. The bird's talons linked an locked to form a seat, scooping up Bardelár, knocking the grav-stick to the flagstones. The grav-ball ricocheted against the bird's skin with a clang. The linked talons extruded a restraining belt and held the terrified boy down.

"What's happening to him?" the servocorpse nanny muttered, its programming not anticipating the situation and making it walk in circles.

Then the bird flew up to the roof above the school building and spoke, it's voice chiming yet threatening, soothing yet a metallic rasp:

Glory to the High Compassion!

This child has been preordained since birth to serve the High Inquest as a childsoldier, the most glorious of all occupations. For childsoldiery is the straightest path toward receiving a clan-name and becoming more than an earthbound person. It is the path to the stars.

Parents, rejoice!

If your child survives, he will doubtless be someone of quality, someone with a true profession, someone whose clan will nurture and support for the rest of his life.

If your child falls, it is in the name of the High Compassion, which holds together the balance of the Dispersal of Man and on which all your lives depend.

Your child is a hero!

It did not seem that way to the parents, who had emerged from the building and were weeping, or to the sister who had cast the homunculus on the ground in a passion, breaking it in two, so that it squealed and begged to be glued back together, its torso walking on its arms and chasing its legs.

"Bardi! Bardi!" the parents cried. Others did too, relatives, perhaps, or friends. And Bardelár was whimpering. He had not been taught what an honour it was to have been chosen.

But presently the bird covered the boy's face with one wing, and pointed the other skyward. With a final screech it launched itself in the direction of the lowering sun.

***

At the house, Tijas said to Arbát, "You were wrong, Master Arbát. It is not safe here."

Sajit said, "We were told of the finding-birds. Each one is keyed to one child's DNA. There is one looking for us now."

"So there is nowhere on this planet you can flee to," Arbát said.

"On another planet, perhaps," Tijas said, thinking of how he had refused to go with the theater troupe.

"Urna is a backworld," Arbát said. "Now it is not even a world, because it has been folded into Alykh. Beyond this continent, there are oceans, there is another continent, we don't even know it. All we know is the star traffic."

"It will not work," said Sajit.

"We'll sleep on it," Tijas said. "Tomorrow we'll decide what to do."

***

But they did not sleep, not right away. They went to Sajit's room, opaqued the walls and the windows, made a hideaway, sealed themselves into a world.

Sajit said, "I wish —"

And Tijas knew what it was he wished for.

"There's no displacement plate here. And we can never reproduce ... the conditions."

"That place in the space between spaces," Sajit said, "that place that was a nothing expanded into realtime ... we were happy. We were inside each other's souls, completely."

No sooner had he said it than they were there again.

What? We can do this without *the displacement? How?*

They could not tell which of them was speaking.

Such a melding! Such a flooding of unknown memories! Such smells, such colors, their shared experiences made more intense by redoubled senses, overwhelming, ineffable ...

Sajittijas!!

And it was over. It had lasted ... no time at all. And like the addiction of dreamstuff, it left behind a longing, an unfulfillable need.

And they were in the room, in the darkness. Hugging one another close, in a desperate attempt to recapture the oneness.

"We can't stay," Sajit said. "And we don't have anywhere to go."

"Don't worry," Tijas said.

And he thought, *No, you shouldn't worry. I was created to worry for you. I was made to go where you should not go. I'm the spare.*

"You're *not!*" Sajit said.

And Tijas realized he had to shield his thoughts better. This connection could not be controlled. The barrier between them was weak, and not predictable.

Tijas tried to force himself to stay awake. Surely if Sajit slept, he would be free to think some of the thoughts Sajit should not hear.

Such as what he would have to do ... to save Sajit from being found.

"Don't even think about it," Sajit said, and drifted into slumber.

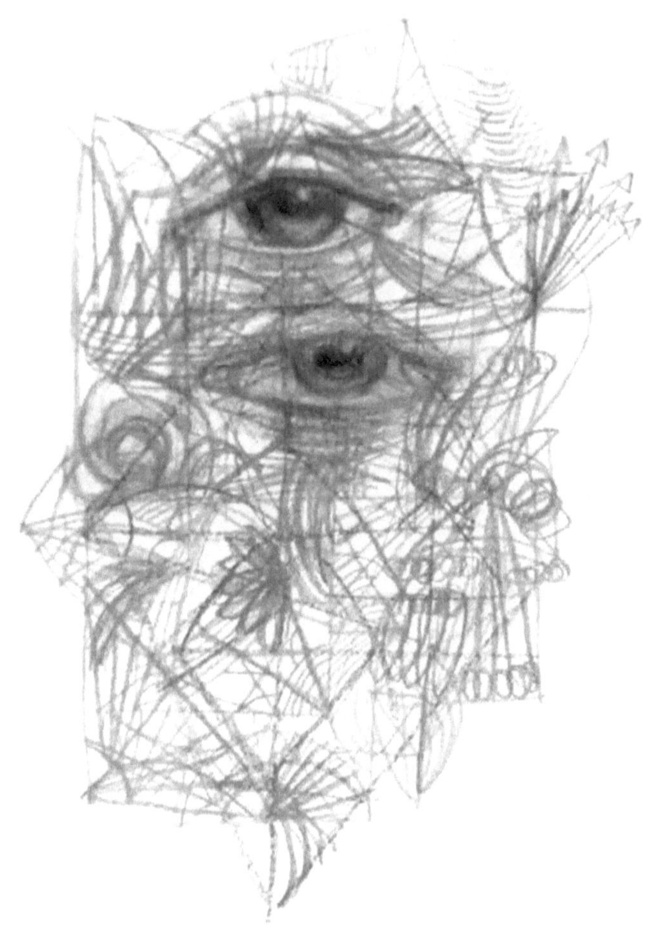

Fourteen
Running Away

When Sajit awoke, Tijas was gone.

He felt the emptiness before he was even fully conscious. It was the same emptiness he'd felt in the city, when they were apart.

The intagliate ring was gone from his finger. Sajit knew that Tijas would try to use it to identify himself as the *real* Sajit ... the one whose *meúr* would send him to die in the sky.

The Star of Urna had not even risen. Sajit deopaqued his wall and saw into the forest ... saw flattened grass patches that were perhaps footprints.

When he went to the living area he saw that Arbát was up, sitting, quite still. Sajit said, "You helped him, didn't you? You probably even advised him to take the ring — he wouldn't have thought of that."

Arbát said, "If you are separated, and you stay concealed, the finding-bird will be unable to follow you. It can't see through everything or penetrate past walls of force ... can it? And it isn't programmed to seek out ... *twins.*"

He could hardly bring himself to say the word. Even he, who seemed to have accepted the duality, the reasons behind it. *The idea of a doppling nauseates him, deep down.* Sajit sensed it, and it made him queasy.

"Where did you send him?"

"How should I know?"

"But you let him go. You've got to know where he went."

"Far. Far."

"What kind of an answer is that?"

"It is good, Sajitteh. You stay here. He'll use the ring and prove he is you — and that will save your life. After a few sleeps the abomination will be caught. Your life can start afresh."

"I've had two fresh starts already — my life being upended to go to Nevéqilas — my planet being merged with another planet by some bureaucratic error — I don't want a third fresh start, Master Arbát."

"But what can you do?"

Sajit saw the despair in the old man's face. Arbát's life, somehow, had become invested in Sajit's. But that was not his problem. His problem was the chasm that was opening up because his doppling was not there. "I don't belong to you," he said. "And Tijas is *not* an abomination."

"The Princeling must have given your family a doppling kit, knowing this day would come. It was a wrongful thing to do, against all nature, unless you possessed the bloodline of Orifec —"

Which I do, Sajit thought. He wondered how much Arbát really knew.

"Don't go, boy. Don't leave me. I'm old, can't you see that. I don't have much to live for these days." Arbát gripped Sajit's shoulders so tightly that he yelped. "No, no, I didn't mean to hurt you. I could *never* hurt you," he choked. "I merely —"

"I have to find him."

"Don't you see, this is *why* doppling is such abomination. We are born to turn to others for love, for our deep needs. Not to an empty copy of our self. There's a reason for the prohibition. Look at you. A small child, obsessed within your self, unable to look outside your own identity —"

"That's madness, Arbát. You can't ever know what it's like to be a doppling."

"But I need you!" the old man cried.

"Goodbye, Master, Thank you for all you taught me." And Sajit kissed the old man's hand.

At this, Arbát began to weep, as though someone had died. Sajit had never seen the man so unable to control himself. There were dark issues in the man's obsession with his student, but Sajit knew that the love was real and that it ran deep.

"Don't think of us anymore, Arbát. It is *meúr.*"

"That which is inescapable is no less unbearable," said Arbát.

Sajit pitied Arbát, but the emptiness of Tijas's absence was more powerful than an old man's obsessions.

Sajit returned to his sleeping room and went back through the window toward the forest, taking nothing with him, not even a loaf.

***

Gharém returned to his ship without his equerry. His time in the Temple of Aërat had enervated him, but the task ahead was swiftly bringing him back to life.

His ship, blackening a third of the sky even in the relentless daylight of Urna, had plunged much of Airang into winter. The park and the lake, in shadow, were bitterly cold; ice-flakes were forming, and the foliage was turning blue-red; dead loons floated.

Alone in his floater, ascending to dock with the belly of his great delphinoid, Gharém contemplated what was to come.

Only a few flocks of finding-birds had been released. Soon would come tens of thousands — soon they would black out what brightness remained in the sky.

Gharém slid past the irising airlock and entered an observation chamber in which all walls and floors had been deopaqued and were receiving images from outside; it seemed thus that he was standing on the air itself, looking at the world beneath, watching the crowd swarm in. The park itself had been cordoned off with forcewires.

Presently there came to him Kail Kruspar, the captain, and a dodecagon of childsoldiers that would serve as an honor-guard, four of them holding up sigils of Bellares, the military planet. The childsoldiers' eyes, like polished citrines, glowed soft, yellow, deadly light. They wore white tunics and belts of flame and stood on their hoverdisks, leaping, whirling, criss-crossing the air with streaks of eyelight.

And they cried out, in unison, the terrifying war-cry of the childsoldiers:

Ishá ha, ha, ha!
Ishá ha ha hey ha!

Lethal, the laser-lines arrowed the air, flinging up spiderwebs of death. No sound more elemental, more terrifying, more liberating than the prepubescent chorus of pure, focused destruction. Gharém loved the childsoldiers, children who burst into being like fireworks, who sizzled like the phosphorflies of Ont that live for but seconds, lived but to mate and die.

Gharém gazed down at the field below; they had cleared the park and in only a sleep or two they had built a pyramidal structure with a plateau on top, five-sided, and up each side a ramp with a slow-moving sliding stairway. The children would come to the ship from the world's five corners: lakeward, heartward, seaward, sunward, and nightward. Each side of the pyramid was painted in the colors of one of the five directions. In the park, children were already being herded in, processed, and allotted the stairway by which they would ascend to their destiny.

The five escalators, like silvery tentacles of a monstrous pentapus, met at the apex and the five-sized pyramid was crowned with a bulbous glazed quadrangular pavilion, the plateau forming a quincunx; atop the pavilion a quincuncial funnel hovered, and around it writhing, tubes that could suck the prospective childsoldiers, one by one, into the very belly of the delphinoid that hovered in the sky above.

"Ill take a floater down to the selection platform," he declared. No sooner had he sad this than the dodecagon of deadly children dissipated and reformed as two rows of five behind him, and two in front, holding aloft the inquestral sigils.

And together they shrieked, *Ishá há!*

Two servocorpse unrolled a displacement carpet and Gharém and his honor guard stepped through —

***

"Tijas!" he shouted with his mind, knowing that to shout with the voice could bring death. In the forest, he tried to follow the echo in the back of his mind. But the echo was faint. Tijas had done something to block him. He was sure of it. But what? *Nothing can keep me out!* he thought.

It grew dark.

Darker.

So many times he had been in the forest alone. So many times he had listened to the singing moons. So many times he had sung to himself or chanted to the strains of a crude whisperlyre.

Now he was alone again, but it was a different aloneness.

It was an aloneness that ached for the other half of the self. Not an aloneness that yearned for an unknowable other, but an aloneness born of the absence of an inalienable. Without Tijas, he was only partly Sajit.

Sajit trudged through tall weeds, thorns scratching through the worn clingfire of his tunic.

"Tijas!" his mind screamed again and again.

Then he tried shrieking out the name of his doppling. *Crying out in the wildness, he heard no echo.*

Walking and weeping. He went on. Beyond exhaustion. He must have been going in circles, for the trees became first unfamiliar then familiar again. And there was a kind of music in the air ... music that came with the darkness ... music in the air itself. Music not made by nature, but in his mind.

The singing moons.

At last he came to the ruined temple, near where the displacement plate had taken them the time they had melded.

He spent the night in the roofless portico, under the moons. They sang, but their music gave no joy.

***

Veznávikas were blacking out the moons. Only Kalíth and Ralíth remained visible. The finding birds were swooping and wheeling. Each clutched a child in its claws.

Gharém stepped out onto the parapet atop the pyramidal quincunx.

Nineteen whisperlyres, one for each pillar of the High Compassion, began to sound, each played by a masked bard astride a pteratyger, arranged in ascending flights of seven, five, three, two, and two more that encircled each other like mismatched twins, one a giant, one a pup, the pattern called *denónikas,* the Nineteen Worlds.

The music twanged and reechoed as Gharém spread out his arms and legs in a cruciform pose, his head and limbs forming the Great Pentacle of Longing.

At his gesture the music was answered by nineteen cloud bugles, played by angelic servocorpses, their lips welded permanently to the srinjid mouthpieces of their instruments, who floated under the flocculent canopy of the sky, who represented the *denoshtálkas,* the nineteen starships that once came from the nineteen worlds to seed the Dispersal of Man.

Another motion of his hands and from the ground below came the stridulant harmonies of nineteen times nineteen automated shimmerviols. On the lake below came the boom of nineteen water-organs. From the treetops nineteen flocks of phantasmagoric pseudornithons.

The sky, the earth, the lake — chaos of unsynchronized sound — yet underlying it, a certain grim order. For chaos was Gharém's objective. From darkness and chaos came the High Inquest; from the Inquest came a kind of order, the fragile order that balanced chaos with chaos. All other forms of order were heresy. That was why the childsoldiers existed — to nudge the human universe back to the perfect imperfection that was the High Compassion.

The children came from every world — collecting children was the only tax the High Inquest imposed on the million worlds of the Dispersal. It was Gharém's supreme honour to serve the collection of this taxation. He had collected children of every hue — from the golden-skinned sylphs of Ákkathorn to the blue-hued angels of Ájumma.

Here on this backworld, the children were curiously nondescript — average in height, eye color, without extraordinary variances in skin tone — from a long isolation, perhaps, they had bred to a dull uniformity.

Armies were converging on the five escalators now, shoving, confused, babbling. From the parapet they seemed to swarm like insects, but when the reached the lowest rung of the escalator they were forced into single file.

Gharém sidled over to the nearest moving stair. There were hundreds of steps, and on each step stood a child. Far below, their faces were a kaleidoscope of emotion: trepidation, anger, sorrow, unease, a few faces of fanatical courage or stoicism.

Did they cry for their mothers? But the journey up the escalator would soon transform these faces. The stairs moved slowly and the constrained cacophony of many orchestras had a hypnotic effect; by the time they reached the parapet, each child would be numbed, just as if he had been passed through a servocorpse factory and was now but a shell of a human.

"Welcome, my children," Gharém said, stretching open his arms as though to embrace. They streamed toward him. But before they could reach him, they would reach the sucking tubes, and with a whoosh of air they were carried into the sky, into the tubes which fed into the quincunx of collection. He could imagine the children, snapping from the trance of the music, flying around inside in a jumble. This was the beginning of the process. Disorient, confuse, erase the warmth of family, make them into empty vessels ready to receive the inerrant mastery of the High Compassion.

Since Man began it had always been children who had the fastest reflexes, the most pitiless instincts; for they grown into ambiguity. They were the Inquest's naked will.

And all around they came to him from the five-fold stairway to the gateway to glory. Gharém shrieked with joy. "My children!" he cried again and again. Finding-birds wheeled and the music rose to engulf all other sounds.

***

The cry of the finding-bird is a rasp, metal screeching on unlubricated metal. It is a screech that could come from no living creature. And now, as they threaded the deep night of the dancing moons, the screech came over and over. "Something's wrong," Mikkálu said. "The bird is flying in circles."

He and Éluma were watching. Orifec was not with them. The Son of the Starlight sat slumped against a far railing of the floater.

"Ori," she called to him. He did not look at her.

"Don't worry about him," Mikkálu said. "Things were better anyway. Before, when it was just you and me."

Éluma said, "He's hiding something. He knows something we don't know. I can tell."

Mikkálu did not know what it was. He tried to comfort her. She held him on her lap. Nuzzling against her chest, he found the curve of her breasts startling. "Not so innocent," she said softly. And kissed the top of his head.

"I'm still a kid," he said, "and you're not."

Time dilation had placed between them an unbridgeable gulf.

"But you still love me," she said. "As if it were yesterday."

"And you've seen so many things, staying pinned to a single spot in time, seen so much upheaval."

She held him.

"You'd still do anything I asked," she said.

"Without question," said Mikkálu, "even defy my oath as the living word of the High Compassion."

"You're a childsoldier," she said. "You can slice me with a glance."

"Do you find that exciting?" He laughed with bitterness beyond his years.

"It's all exciting to me," Éluma said, "because I am Love Itself. Every incarnation of love — from the infernal depths to the most exalted."

"Can I kiss you?" he said.

"Anyone can," she said. "I am Aërat."

But before he could, the screeching came, louder and more grating. The bird was swooping, diving, flying in circles. Bucking between the moons. On the ground below, it careening skeins of reflected moonlight.

Orifec had come up to them now. He too was gazing at the bird as it darted and spun. Its movements were erratic, crazed.

"The bird is crazy," Mikkálu said. "It's defective."

Éluma said, "Isn't its sole objective to zero in on someone's DNA?"

"There's no way it could be confused."

"But there is," Orifec said. "There is."

Fifteen
Planet of Dopplings

Sajit could not sleep. He felt *displaced.*

He was somewhere else.

He got up and paced in the portico, beneath the singing moons. But his mind was somewhere else.

Where would Tijas have gone?

Earlier, in the room, they had even been able to do a kind of merging with no displacement plate at all, just by thinking. But then there had been proximity. There had to be a clear system to how this could work ... not just an accidental interconnection of disparate selves.

Perhaps the displacement plate itself might yield a clue. In the moonlight he found his way there. It was a glint in the unkempt weeds. How to make it find Tijas? Somewhere in its memory, tied as it was to the planetary thinkhive, surely it had his coordinates.

Subvoking is a subtle thing, children learn it more slowly that audible speech. Until they learn it, they are tethered to their caretakers, for they cannot go far except by non-displacement means; a klomet is far to walk, a hundred klomets in a floater is barely anywhere.

You must say something without saying it, yet still activate the vocal cords and the muscles of the throat and lips. You must articulate without a sound, yet as clearly as though the air had passed through your lungs and was being expelled from your lips. That is subvocalising. There were, from time to time, people unable to do it at all. They were doomed to lives of isolation. As children they sat in shadows, corners; as adults they were invisible.

Sajit felt like one of those people now. As though he was in a place whose language he did not know. Yet once, he had been able to access the melding-place. What was the key?

Tijas....

He reached out, Over what distance could their connection be felt? When they wandered the city, they had felt each other's pain, sometimes with terrifying immediacy, sometimes like an itch that couldn't be scratched; but inside the displacement they had not just felt what the other felt, they had *become* each other.

But what if one did not subvocalize with words, but with *song?*

Sajit carefully wiped away the weeds that obscured the center of the displacement plate. Shards of the gleaming could be seen, reflecting the moons' light through gaps in the undergrowth. Sajit sat down, eased himself into the *savezhatá* position where his mind would be at its most open, most receptive to the underlying heartbeat of the cosmos.

Even person is like a musical tone, he thought. Each person has a certain pitch, a certain range of overtones. Even when people are similar, they still can be told apart, just as two notes can be only a *shrut* away from each other yet have each one a differing personality, a different color.

Tijas is trying to get away from me, Sajit thought. *But he can't stop thinking about me.*

Sajit settled into *savezhatá,* closed his eyes, thought of a tone, thought of *himself,* of the tone that most sounded like who he was.

He imagined himself a human whisperlyre, with all his cells like sympathetic strings, vibrating to the overtones of the fundamental tone. He imagined his own breath stirring the strings, one finger plucking a single note, letting it die away, squeezing it back to life, in the rhythm of his own heart.

A flash —

Tijas.

Running.

Let me find you!

There's nothing between you and me, Sajit thought. Not even a *shrut* within a *shrut.* We are the same string. We thrum together.

Tijas!

And suddenly, he was inside the great nothing....

***

Corridor.

Running.

No time to see the corridor, only to know it as a tube of pure force with walls of darkness. A corridor without end, and far far ahead a point of light, a flash that was Tijas.

You can't catch me!

Not true. The corridor accordioned shut with a shrill screech and now they were neck and neck and Sajit leaped into his doppling's shadow, and they were together again.

As they had lain together in the doppling kit, deep in amniosis.

The corridor telescoped open again.

"Where is this?" Sajit cried out.

It is everywhere. It is nowhere. He had answered himself.

The corridor closed in on itself. It twisted. It writhed, it coiled, it bent backward and always they were together, the still center of chaos.

***

"What do you mean," Mikkálu said, "there is? I've been with the Child Collector for sleeps of sleeps. These finding birds are not supposed to get confused. The only time I ever saw this —"

But Mikkálu didn't even want to think of it.

"It's something he has been hiding," said Éluma. "He's always been hiding it."

The *veznávik* flew in circles, its cries rending the air. Now it spoke in a metallic voice:

Glory to the High Compassion!

You are found, O child, lost, found, lost by the finding-bird!

But the bird had found nothing. It was going mad.

It had encountered something it was not programmed for.

You are found! You are lost!

You are lost! You are found!

And the bird swooped and soared, chased its tail, screeched as the floater followed it, above the canopy of forest.

Mikkálu said to Éluma, “It could only happen if —”

The memory came to him, as disturbing as it had been then —

***

The planet was called Karkárak. It was a backworld, like Urna ... perhaps even more remote. There was only one inhabited landmass and it was dotted with spiky outcroppings, so that there was no area large enough to accommodate a formal Quincunx of Collection.

So the platform was built in the air, and droves of finding-birds sent out. It was Mikkálu’s first outing as Kyar Gharém’s equerry.

It was a much leaner production than the spectacle in the park at Urna. Yet there was enough grandeur to inspire any childsoldier. First came five phalanxes of crack troops, shooting like a five-petaled firework into the sky, and as always the air resounding with the shrill cries of *Ishá ha!* Below them the surface was like the taut-stretched skin of an ankylosaur; on the spikes rested villages and tiny terraced farms; travel from village to village was effected by gliding between spikes on rickety boats hanging from strands of silky metal.

The music, too, was far more subdued than he

would later be used to; there was only a mixed consort of shimmerviols and a pair of kalophonons bleating plaintively, and five nude servocorpses puffing away on iridium shofars.

But it was not the relative paucity of the music or even the weirdness of the spiny terrain that made the impression.

It was the finding-birds. Thousands upon thousands launched from the culling platforms, diving down towards the villages in the glow of two red setting suns; and suddenly —

All of them going insane! All of them flying in circles, crashing into each other, some dropping out of the sky into the crevices between the spikes of rock. And then, the ones that survived, descending with outstretched metal talons on the villages —

"What's happening, Kyar Gharém?" he blurted out, ignoring his duty which was to be utterly silent unless commanded to speak. Gharém was so startled he did not even slap the boy for his cheek — Mikkálu had already flinched instinctively.

"I don't know *everything*, you inquisitive monkey!" Gharém said.

Now the finding-birds were flocking together and reversing direction. They moved in orderly lines towards the platform. As they came closer Mikkálu saw the unthinkable; each *veznávik* clutched *two* children. And each pair of children looked identical.

It was nauseating. Each pair was even dressed alike, as if no attempt had been made to even conceal the horror that was doppling.

Mikkálu lost control. He ran to the edge of the floating pavilion and vomited over the railing. This was abomination! It was a violation of nature — *twins!* he could barely think the word. He clutched the railing and heaved.

And suddenly he felt Gharém's big hands on his shoulder. He felt a curious vibration and after a moment, he suddenly realized that the Child Collector was laughing.

"Inquisitive," said Gharém, "yet also ignorant."

"Thank you, my Lord," Mikkálu said, forgetting his customary cheekiness in his confusion.

"You come from a planet with the twin taboo," Gharém said. "You think twins are some kind of horrific aberration. Do you know that in some of the planets with this taboo, one is always killed at birth? So barbaric. Is yours like that?"

"My Lord, I've never even seen one. I just know that it's ... disgusting."

"For me, too, for a different reason. It messes up my quota. Come inside, boy, so you don't have to look at these 'abominations.'" Not unkindly, Gharém led the equerry into an inner room and deopaqued the walls. An astrogator, Kail Esmána, and an assistant worked over some thinkhives. A star map spread itself across the room. Gharém set the boy down on a chairfloat, and then sat down himself, across from him.

"Before I decide what to do," Gharém said, "I need to know why. Mikkálu-without-a-Clan!"

"Yes, my Lord."

"Awaken the planetary thinkhive."

Grateful to be given a job, Mikkálu subvocalized a command and an eidolon appeared. The thinkhive assumed the avatar of a wizened, simian creature with bluish fur.

"I am the High Inquest's lawfully ordained Collector of Children," Gharém said. "I command you to give me appropriate explanations. There seems to be an unusual number of twins here."

Mikkálu winced when he heard the word, and was amazed that Gharém could utter it without any kind of negative coloring.

The thinkhive laughed and said, in its clipped amd archaic thinkhive-like speech pattern, "High Inquest very very big! Our world very very far. Things happen here, not seen, not seen." A panorama of the world's history played out in holosculpt animation.

"A thousand thousand sleeps ago, plague. No help. Whole planet almost die. Compulsory twinning made law. Now whole culture change, everyone always paired, birth, sexual coupling, even death."

The thinkhive's eidolon popped out of being.

"What will you do, my Lord?"

"Stick to my mission," Gharém said. "What kind of backworld witchdoctory is this, with some kind of crude automatic doppling made compulsory? We have clear instructions from the High Inquest. One of each DNA imprint. Come, boy. Now you will see a vision of the awesome power of the High Inquest."

He grabbed the boy's hand and pulled him from the inner chamber. Once more they stood on the parapet. The air was thick with finding-birds, each with a child in each talon. Again Mikkálu's gorge rose, but now he tried to stifle it. This was a different culture. It had different taboos. Why, back in training in Bellares he'd met a boy on whose planet they routinely bludgeoned to death men who loved other men. He remembered how horrified that boy had been when Mikkálu told him of an average day in the Temple of Aërat.

"I've got to stop being so provincial," he told himself. But the sight of so many twins was still unnerving.

Yet the next thing he saw was infinitely worse.

Gharém raised both hands, balled into fists, high above his head. He closed his eyes, perhaps communicating with their own starship's central thinkhive. The birds became very still, hovering;

Gharém opened his left fist.

All at once each bird raised its left wing with a resounding *thwack* that made the very air snap and released its left talon. A thousand children were released. A thousand children tumbled, to be impaled on the rocky spikes below. Mikkálu heard the collective scream, more like a howling wind than the sound of a thousand children. The scream followed by a wail from the survivors, a keening that pierced his soul, beyond sorrow.

"There," Gharém said. "We were only ordered to bring back one of each."

"But you just killed a thousand people!" Of course, one the rare occasions when twins were born, one was always killed — so Mikkálu had heard, although he'd never *seen* a doppling. But compassionately, and generally pre-partum. What kind of society would let abominations live, even base itself on them?

"I am sure they will be recycled by some servocorpse factory," Gharém said. "Pretty little dead children are always in demand as servants."

And now the birds flew one by one onto the

floating pavilion, each dropping its remaining child before folding itself back up into a compact silvery egg and rolling back into the storage area.

The platform was filling up with the Karkárak children. They stood, bewildered, disoriented from the flight and from having seen their brothers and sisters tumble to their deaths. Gharém's childsoldier attendants barked at them, moving them into lines, creating some semblance of military order. Yet they broke ranks, huddled, whispered, clutched at one another, and always came the keening.

One *veznávik* remained. It spread its wings wide, casting a ravenlike shadow over the crowd of children.

And spoke in ringing, optimistic tones:

Glory to the High Compassion!

These children have been preordained since birth to serve the High Inquest as childsoldiers, the most glorious of all occupations. For childsoldiery is the straightest path toward receiving a clan-name and becoming more than an earthbound person. It is the path to the stars.

Citizens of Karkárak, rejoice!

If your child survives, he will doubtless be someone of quality, someone with a true profession, someone whose clan will nurture and support for the rest of his life.

If your child falls, it is in the name of the High Compassion, which holds together the balance of the Dispersal of Man and on which all your lives depend.

Your children are heroes!

All over the world, in village after village, these gilded words were raining from the sky ... along with the redundant children.

Mikkálu was looking up at the silvery bird with its outstretched wings blacking out the setting suns. He heard a thud behind him, then another.

Whipping round, he saw —

The new-minted childsoldiers were dropping, one by one, to the floor of the parapet. Crumpling up like dolls, falling down lifeless, each time hitting the pavement with the sound of a hollow skin drum.

"What's going on?" Gharém shrieked. "I forbid you to die!"

Mikkálu cried out, "My Lord, didn't you hear the thinkhive? It told us this would happen! *Everyone always paired, birth, sexual coupling, even death.* It told us they would die! They can't be apart!"

The kids kept toppling. Gharém did not even scold his equerry for impertinence, but seized his arm again and dragged him to the inner room. So furious was his demeanor that the pilot and the attendants scurried away. Gharém did not even remember to opaque the walls. As his master raged, Mikkálu saw the children's corpses pile up outside.

"My Lord —"

"You impertinent pipsqueak!" Gharém slapped the boy so hard that he reeled. And slapped him again, again, again, again —

"My Lord, I'm not a servocorpse," the equerry said, summoning up a shred of assertiveness.

Gharém stopped, looked at his hand, deep red from slapping the child. "Oh. I forgot," he said distractedly.

Then he added, "If you ever say a word about how I, Kyar Gharém, could not control myself, I shall have your laser-eyes gouged out."

"Of course not, Lord Gharém," Mikkálu said. "You

know I keep all your secrets."

"Clean up my mess, then. Have the children placed in stasis; they are good, unblemished stock and will fetch a premium when recycled as servocorpses."

"Yes, Lord."

"And pick out a nice, voluptuous pleasure corpse from the cabinet, any gender. Make that one of each. And a phial of the finest dreamstuff. I need a thorough emotional draining before I report to the High Inquest. Remember, boy, I may beat you from time to time, but I too have a master."

It was the day that cemented the connection between Child Collector and equerry, the day Mikkálu found himself relieved of the routine of training on Bellares and found himself chosen more and more as this man's ... slave? jester? confidante? ... it was, in a way, a mutually vampiric relationship.

***

"Yes," Mikkálu said, "I *have* seen this before, once."

***

Get out of my mind! Tijas spoke without speaking. *Don't you know what will happen if we are both intertwined like this? I need you to get away from me.*

They tussled in the darkness.

— *But I can never get away from you.*

— *You must. Sajit, I was made for only one thing, and now the time has come and I have to do what I was made for. I was made to live an alternate life for you, to die an alternate death.*

— *No* —

Both materialized on a displacement plate in the

middle of an open field. It was dawn.

"I told you not to follow!" Tijas said.

In that moment the shadow of the finding-bird fell across them. The air was all talons now. They were caught up. There was a rush of wind, thundering in their ears. Each was grasped firmly in a claw of the finding-bird. The boys reached out, clasped hands.

Together, they both said with their minds, *no matter what.*

The bird flew straight at the rising sun. And presently Sajit heard a sound above the wind.

It was a woman, screaming in terror.

A woman screaming as if she had seen some nameless nightmare, some unimaginable horror.

It was his mother.

Sixteen
I am not a Thing

Suddenly, the bird was descending, landing, and Orifec saw that the thing he most dreaded had happened. The find-bird had plucked *both* children away.

Éluma was screaming. The revulsion felt by an Urna native on seeing the order of nature negated — Orifec understood it, even though he himself was a doppling. She had not been prepared for this. He blamed himself.

And the two boys stood, their hair ragged from the whipping of the wind, two shadow-slim lads with the eyes of Aërat, who is Love personified.

"Mother —" they both said.

"How? How? One of you isn't mine. One of you is a demon, a thing of the dark."

And Mikkálu said, "I *knew* it. And so did you, Starry Highness."

"Yes," Orifec said heavily, "I knew."

"How could you hide this from me? How can I tell which one is my true son?" Éluma cried.

Orifec answered, "They are both as truly your sons as they are each other. Both were born from our love, even though one of them was nourished in an artificial womb."

"How can you stand there and tell me this?"

One of the boys spoke. "I am Tijas," he said. "I was birthed from a doppling kit. Sajit and I are one flesh."

Orifec said to Éluma, "How can you cry *abomination* over a human being we made together? Don't you remember the clouds and the rain? Don't you remember how I loved you? And you know very well that *I* am a doppling."

"That's different. You're a Princeling. You are not bound to the laws of nature. You renew yourself eternally, passing your memories on through the generations. That's not for mortals. It's blasphemy."

"But you yourself are a goddess, Éllekeh." Orifec reached out but she flinched. "You *earned* your divinity."

"Get rid of it," she said.

Tijas said, "That's all I ever wanted, mother. To be got rid of."

She shuddered; Orifec was moved. "When the palace sent the doppling kit to the village, it was so that when the Child Collector came, I would be the one to go, to fight, to die in glory, and Sajit would remain, would grow up to be the greatest bard in the Dispersal of Man. My death is part of the plan. It is *meúr*."

"No!" Sajit cried out. "You are part of me as no one else can ever be. I won't let you —"

"— lift the shadow from your life," Tijas said, and Orifec saw that Éluma marveled, how they finished each other's sentences. "Sajitteh, I was *born* for this, brother —"

"You weren't *born* at all. You sprang full grown from the box because I awakened you —"

"— when you shouldn't have. When the Inquest came calling, that was the time to quicken me and hand me over and forget that there was once a mysterious box lying in your breakfast circle."

"But I *had* to quicken you. Or I would never have been complete."

"I've heard enough," said their mother. "You break down the boundaries between person and person. Your existence is a blight on nature —"

Then Mikkálu said, "No, no, Ellekeh. I've been to other worlds. I've seen places where twins are not *harám.* I was on a world where there were *only* twins. The first time I saw them, I vomited. I know better now."

"Are you mad, Mikkeh?" Éluma said. "I am Love Herself. I am all the values of this world. I *can't* accept this. I wouldn't be the goddess anymore."

But Orifec saw the boys and knew that he loved them both. They stood, frightened, close to each other, as the floater drifted — aimlessly for the moment — the ruddy star of Urna glistening in their windswept hair. And the eyes. Éluma's eyes. The love he felt was beyond logic, beyond rhetoric. He knew that he could not take back this love.

"I sent the doppling kit ... as protection, Sajit. I didn't think ... there was *another* Sajit inside it. Another *you*. Another son whom I must love equally. I've seen you together so many times ... I cannot say one is real and one is false ... I was the only one who knew ... and I understand you. I understand the loneliness of being cut off from myself. For I too am a doppling."

But Éluma was unmoved. Her face was all anger and revulsion. Orifec could not answer her. He knew he should have told her, knew also that telling would not have helped. The laws of culture were far more rigid even than the laws of nature.

And the one who said he was Tijas cowered, unable to meet Éluma's gaze.

He said softly, "I'll go to the collecting place, Starry Highness."

"No," said Orifec.

"Yes, father," Tijas said. "This is what you made me for. You always knew that Sajit might be Collected. You broke the sacred law. You had the doppling kit sent to the house of Areon Dar-Sajit. You caused Arbát to be our tutor. You had us brought to the citadel of Nevéqilas. This is the destiny you made for me, Starry Highness. You are a Princeling. If you made me for a reason, who am I to go against your plan?"

The finding-bird flapped its wings.

"I don't care about any plan," Sajit cried. "Tijas is my brother, more than my brother, he's me! The plan went haywire the moment I activated the doppling kit."

"And because you are my brother, more than my brother, because you're *me,* because I only exist for you," Tijas said, "I will become what I was made to become."

Orifec said, "No, no. Do you remember when I first knew there were two of you? Do you remember when I called you from your hiding place? What did you say to me, Sajit?"

"I said, *His* name *is Tijas.*"

Orifec said, "That is where you broke the natural order, Sajitteh. You gave him a name. Do you know how doppling kits were first invented?"

"No, father," Sajit said.

Orifec saw that Éluma was still half collapsed in rage and revulsion. How could he help her understand, when the sight of twins was a trigger for people of this world, evoking millennia of ingrained hatred? "Éluma," he said gently, "I'm telling you, as one who has learned a lot about other worlds, that your terror of dopplings is as illogical as any other taboo. In the ancient world, twins were feared as monstrosities. As were those who were left-handed, or palely pigmented, or who enjoyed sexual congress with unacceptable partners, or enjoyed the fruit of some tree or another. Urna's taboo is as illogical as any of these.

"But doppling kits were invented in a world where people did not fill their brains with consciousness. Their contents were simply sources of replacement organs, no more sentient than the kits themselves. Yet there were those who wanted a copy of themselves, a living copy they could love, who would understand them. Thus the technology came to be abused in some worlds."

"Ori, this is abomination. I don't care what learned explanation there is for it. The phantom child must die! It *must!*"

"But Sajit *named* him."

"Father is right," Sajit said. "*Things* do not have names. Tijas is not a thing."

"No, I'm not," Tijas said. "And because I am a person, I choose this for myself. I choose to die for my brother, my friend, my lover, my other self."

Orifec watched as Tijas embraced his brother. They kissed. Neither as lovers, nor as brothers, but as something other; something to be envied, not loathed. They were beautiful as a song is beautiful. He had an overpowering urge to protect them.

"Revolting!" Éluma cried. "This wounds me. I am Love. Love can't be mocked. Mikkálu — *kill the doppling.*"

Tijas turned his back on them all. He called out to the finding-bird, the ritual formula of submission to the High Inquest: "*Jãtái evéndek hokhkeliassá* — May I live forever in the High Compassion."

The bird spread its wings wide, perched by the rim of the floater, poised to envelop the boy, claws, wings, and all.

"Mikkálu, laser him!" Éluma cried out "If you love me, kill him!"

"If you love me, Éluma," Orifec said, "don't say that."

The bird's claws stretched out like a stepladder. Tijas approached, was about to step, and the wings were about to enfold him —

Orifec saw that Sajit, too, was walking resolutely toward the *veznávik.* He could not bear it. He ran to shield them and —

"Laser him, Mikkálu!:

— Leaped up throw his arms around his sons and —

"Laser him!"

"I have to obey you, goddess!" Mikkálu cried out. He had sworn. In a timeline too recent for the oath to have been softened.

Mikkálu swooped up on his hover disk, spun, his eyes dilated and turned bright yellow —

— and missed! —

Orifec felt blinding pain. He blacked out.

***

Sajit fell to the floor of the floater and the finding bird, gripping Tijas tight, soared skyward, wheeled overhead.

"No! I cannot miss! I am a childsoldier! I cannot fail!" Mikkálu felt tears spurting, felt self-loathing well up inside him ... tears of yellow light bursting in air, showering prinprick pinholes in the metal railings of the floater.

The slice of laser eyes cauterizes as well as cutting clean through flesh. Sajit saw half-Orifec, just above the thighs, and the other half lying inert. The upper half of his father was still alive. Sajit knelt beside him. The pain must be unbearable. Éluma knelt too. They did not meet each other's gaze.

Mikkálu whispered, "I'm sorry."

"Sorry?" Tijas screamed. "You've killed our father, our mother's lover, the man who loves the goddess you worship!"

Sajit and his mother glared at each other. He had known her most as a woman cloaked in shadow. Could this woman really have given him life, was it this that gave her the right to his life away? Now, Sajit realized, he knew her not at all.

Mikkálu kept talking, talking too fast, trying to fill in the awful silence. "I didn't mean to kill him. I didn't mean to kill anyone. You said *if you love me* — Éluma, you know I've always loved you, I'd cross the universe for you —"

"Be quiet, Mikkeh. I know you didn't mean this," Élumeh said. "But now he's dying. Orifec, our Starry Highness, is dying. And he has no successor."

"*You* killed him, mother," Sajit said, pitiless. "This man loved me. He gave everything to protect me. He's always known about Tijas, and he loved both of us. You can't understand. You'll say you love me, too, but you tried to kill me. Tijas *is* me. We're more than biological twins, we're dopplings."

"I'm not dead yet," Orifec gasped. "Sajitteh ... summon the thinkhive of my palace."

"How?" Sajit said. "We're not even *in* the palace."

But they were; the floating parapet was still an extension of Orifec's domain ... but Orifec was weakening fast. There was no blood, only the smell of burnt flesh and a pair of dead legs severed just above the thighs. Sajit subvoked and the palace's regenerative mechanisms began to activate. Fleshy tendrils snaked up from the floor and attached themselves to the princeling. A fine mesh of flesh simulant wrapped itself around the wound. Injectors pumped analgesics and and poured a fuming mélange of anti-devivement reagents over his face.

"You won't die, Starry Highness," Sajit pleaded. "Tell me you won't die." For Orifec seemed revived.

"I will, my son," Orifec said. "Your doppling will take your place among the childsoldiers. And you will rule Urna as its first true artist-prince."

"I won't become you," Sajit said softly.

"I daresay not," Orifec said. "I became all my other selves. But ... you needn't."

Sajit cried, "What Urna anyway? Urna will soon be completely sucked into Alykh. Even if I *could* be a Princeling, I'd be Princeling of a room in a ruin."

Why was he even speaking to them? He could feel Tijas being carried on the wind, speeding away. He could feel Tijas' terror. And the love that had made him willing to throw away his very identity.

"Mikkálu!" Sajit said. "Where is the finding-bird going?"

"To the collecting grounds, Sajit. In the old days, it was a park by the Lake of Luminous Loons."

"Do you know how to fly this thing?"

"No, but ... I think you can."

"Yes ..." Orifec said faintly. "You subvoked and got the regenerators to activate. Years ago ... I keyed the palace thinkhives with your bio-signature. I wanted you to have ... all this." Orifec actually smiled. "Ironic, no? But I want to see a little more ... I'll ... cling to life a while."

"Not a while," Sajit said. "We'll get you plugged into a proper iatromaton when we get back. And I'm going to go and save Tijas."

The goddess of love wailed ... it was the cry of a dying loon ... the death-screech of a deactivating thinkhive. Mikkálu stared at her, at Sajit, at the half-man he had created.

"I'm sorry, I'm sorry," he kept repeating. "I never ever did that before ... I never misused my killing gaze. I was confused ... because ... how much I love Éluma."

Sajit wanted to pummel him with his fists. But the boy had laser eyes.

"Poor Mikkeh," Orifec said, growing fainter. "You don't even know what love is."

Sajit squeezed his father's hand. "I can't forgive him," he said. "And I'll *never* forgive *her.*"

Éluma said softly, "My son, my son." She had ceased her keening and now sat whimpering.

"I *had* a mother," Sajit said. "She perished when the people bins came. I had a father too, and siblings. They're all gone down and now there's only you and a dying father and my other self ripped out of me. My life has been sliced in two."

It all came flooding back. Attembris. Circles of starlight. A life without a doppling, without a goddess for a mother and a princeling for a father. Chanika, Vimla ... why had he not thought of them since all this happened? So many feelings, so many images — guilt. Grief. Self-hatred.

Éluma stood up now. She spoke tonelessly, beyond emotion. "Urna is undone," she said. "The laws of nature aren't working anymore. *Things* are people. Abominations are my children. I've given the man I love a death-blow."

"No, Ellekeh," Mikkálu said. "The world is a different world. We have to change."

"I can't change," Éluma. "I am eternal. I am the Unchangeable Truth of Urna. I am Love."

And with great deliberation she walked to the edge of the parapet.

And leaped.

***

Mikkálu ran to the railing. He saw her fall. She did not flail. She had a sereneness to her. Her garment flapped about and hid her face.

"Ellekeh!" he cried out and began to weep, not caring that the flooding tears could warp the alignment of his laser-irises. A random spark flew from his left eye, slicing an upper railing. The wind whistled.

He had to save her. He summoned his hoverdisk and hopped on, sending it spinning, adjusting its trajectory with quick subvocalizings so the disk would swoop down fast enough to catch up with gravity. Wind whipped his face and dried his tears.

She plummeted. He sped. They were above a forest. He overtook her, swept upward, seized her by an arm. "Let go!" she screamed, the wind drowning her out.

Mikkálu took control. His training made it easy. He folded an arm around her waist, held her face up. Instinctively, she clung to him — though she may have wanted to die, her body couldn't help holding on —

He braked hard. The wind slapped at them. Mikkálu headed for a treetop — a maneuver he'd done many times in battle, to gain the high ground.

He decelerated quickly, tried to find the softest spot in the thicket. It was a cottonsilk tree; balancing himself on a branch and clutching Éluma's waist, he carved some criss-cross scratches in the bark with his eyes, and a misty white sap came spewing out, solidifying as it hit the air and weaving itself into a cushiony, bed-like mass.

Mikkálu moved Éluma into the densest part of the sap; it wove itself around her, keeping her from falling.

"You can't fall anymore," he told her, "not until I cut you free."

"I won't go back to Orifec."

"No. They are long gone. I'm sure they didn't wait around to see if you'd survive the fall. And I'm sure they are not waiting for *me*. They must hate me."

"Mikkeh, don't do this! I *have* to die! It's the only right thing to do."

"Calm down. I'll take you to the temple."

"Temple?" she cried. "You know I can't go there anymore. I've birthed an abomination. I'll never be clean again."

Mikkálu said, "I am still a child, Éllekeh, but I have loved you all my life. Soon I'll be too old to be a childsoldier. When I reach puberty I'll lose these lightning reflexes. I'll grow awkward. But then I'll be old enough. And I'll come for you."

Éluma even managed to smile. "I'll be an old woman on your next trip. Time dilation is the killer."

"If we're doomed never to be the perfect age for each other," he said, "I don't care. You are Love."

"Don't you understand? I *was* Love. Now I'm no one. Love is dead on our world now."

"If you're not a goddess, what are you?"

"A whore," she said.

"Never," he said.

She kissed him, a comfortless, cold kiss.

Yet he still loved her for it.

***

Sajit said, "Now there's only you and me."

"Don't be angry at your mother," Orifec said. "She's panicking because she's lost her anchor — her whole belief system. And she's a goddess, a guardian of that system."

"I'll try not to hate her. Or Mikkálu. He was torn, too."

"Where will we go now?" Orifec said. Sajit could see that he was visibly weakening. Orifec's breathing was irregular. The regenerators were only of moderate strength, cut off from the main thinkhives of the palace and without access to the rarest of medications.

"We'll go to the palace. We will save your life."

"But that's not what you're thinking, Sajitteh. You want to go to the Lake of Luminous Loons. You want to save your brother."

"Can he be saved?"

"I don't know," Orifec said. "You have gone far beyond the rulebook already."

"Can *you* be saved, father?"

"I also don't know. Perhaps. The life is draining from me. I'm not in pain. Enough analgesics are being pumped into me to numb an army. But it means that when I die, I will just turn off. Like an opaquing wall."

"What will I *do?*"

Orifec said, "You'll do what your heart tells you. And I will agree with you, because, Sajitteh, I *made* your heart."

The floater flew northwards, toward Nevéqilas. They did not speak for a long time.

Sajit knew where he must go. His heart had spoken. And he that Orifec, too knew.

So in silence they flew, as night began to fall. One by one, the moons rose.

Eríkion danced in the lowering sky. Kalíth and Ralíth began their stately figure-eight.

Half-Harikozmá hung low, misshapen, blue-green.

Slowly, the stars were coming out.

Here, in the emotional extremity between the inconsolable and the unattainable, between grief and revelation, between love and disillusion, he heard something he had never heard in any other place but the clearing in the woods in Attembris.

He heard the moons singing.

JiRARØS
2019

Seventeen
Ina and Areon

Tash Toléon said, "Hokh'Ton, I must tell you now of Sajit's other family, and what happened to them the day the world ended...."

***

On the day the sky fell, Areon and Ina and the daughters had been in their apartments, and the day had gone normally at first.

Until they had told Sajit the truth about the box. And about his parents.

Then Sajit left. They had not thought anything of it. Sajit often wandered off. He was an independent spirit, Ina reflected, and now that he realized he was not even related to them ...

The boy had never belonged to them.

Ina had tried. There was something — aloofness, perhaps — or *otheworldliness* — he often did not even seem to be present.

When he hugged her, he would seem even more remote, as though slipping right through her.

Ina had tried to be a mother to him. Eventually she did not try that hard.

It was almost a relief to tell him the truth, though she did not want to admit it to herself.

When he walked away, of course, she assumed he would be back after one his moody walks.

And then people started raining from the sky.

***

Their apartment was in the shadow of the crystal stem of Nevéqilas. Their rooms had no physical windows — they were not *that* highly placed in the hierarchy — but all the walls could change to afford views over many parts of the city. And the girls had been watching the Lake of Luminous Loons —

Criss-crossing the lake in zebra lines of light —

And their cries, carried electromagnetically across the city, close as though they were positioned at the lake's edge —

Vimla looked up and the vista followed her gaze. And she cried out, "Mother, mother, its raining people!"

Quickly Ina deopaqued all the walls all around so they could see what was happening. They were really falling out of the sky. Like a shower of dark meteors. People in stasis, in every possible position, curled up, stretched out, scrunched, unfurled, frozen in a moment that could have been a century or more ago.

And above them, people bins, disgorging their contents. People were pelting down like multicolored hail.

Ina had heard of these things. She never expected it to happen here. People bins were always emptied out on empty worlds. This was a mistake.

And the High Inquest *never* made mistakes.

She said to Vimla — Chanika was huddled in a corner, whimpering — "Sit tight. We're trapped ... all we can do is watch."

Then she heard — distant but persistent — a shrill, terrifying chorus —

> *Ishá há! Ishá há!*
> *Ishá ha ha héy ha!*

and knew it was the sound of childsoldiers. So faint yet so relentless. And it was getting louder.

She subvoked a quick command to the windows and the view changed to just outside Nevéqilas. That's when she saw they were coming.

It was a swarm. They were like bees, like birds, but in a precise formation, the space between them exactly the same. On their hoverdisks, they spun, cartwheeled, figure-eighted in tight formations.

The chant grew louder —

The images on the walls began to fracture —

The walls split open —

And then the earth shook, and their home fell on top of them.

***

They would not be able to perform their children's

death ceremonies. They had not even been able to retrieve their bodies. Ina and Areon had survived the initial wave by a miracle — two walls collapsing inward to form a tent that led to an opening and a corridor and a balcony that swung precariously, attached to the crystal stamen by a few metallic strands.

Areon had succumbed a day later, in the street, with no way to treat his injuries. Servcorposes took him away, perhaps to a factory where the body could be refurbished and made of use to someone, though Ina did not know what services remained in the broken city of Shirensang.

Servocorpses had cleared some rubble and Ina found that she had a little cave that had once been a spacious apartment. The doppling kit and a few random decorations remained. And the old whisperlyre which had accompanied Sajit when he entered their loves — that was lying on the floor, for the holosculpt tree it hung on had disintegrated. She sat, in a corner. One of the walls, a jagged fragment could still project some images of the outside world. She subvoked a few commands and she could see the metal spiders throwing up an alien city.

She sat by herself most days, eating little — in what was left of the plaza outside, they were distributing what they called the *Princeling's Bounty,* though no one had seen the ruler of Urna at all. The bounty was sometimes a bunch of *gruyesh,* sometimes a parcel of flatcakes or a jar of darkberry jam. They came from the royal stores, so there was still some kind of system in place, a government, even. She saw no one.

She was unable to grieve ... it had all been so

sudden, and now it was all locked away in some other world, a world that had had some order to it.

Once she found her way to the Temple of Aërat. She saw supplicants coming and going, but they looked alien — they even smelled alien. And they acted not like worshippers, but more like customers.

Sajit could not be located.

Perhaps he was dead.

But ... what if he wasn't? Could she even find him?

She thought of crossing over to the new city ... but no, surely, that was too alien, too disturbing to think of. And so she drifted in and out of the ruined apartment, eating little, just waiting for something ... waiting to join the rest of her family ... waiting for some kind of ending.

***

And one day, unanounced, a childsoldier appeared at the door. He was slim. He carried his hoverdisk slung around his waist. His skin was an unusual brown she had not seen in the city, his cheeks bore tattoos of firephoenixes that seemed to flap their wings. His expression was pitiless, but he spoke gently.

"Greetings, mother," he said. "I am Tarash-without-a-Clan and I am tasked by the Inquestral Child Collector to find a boy named Sajit-wthout-a-Clan, patronymic darAreon. Is he here?"

"Your friends killed all my children," she said bitterly, "and we don't even know why."

"Not Sajit," the boy said, his eyes gleaming citrine. "Our thinkhives don't show any erasure of his DNA signature."

Something stirred in Ina's deadened soul. Sajit was not dead. "He's alive?"

"Don't be worried, Ina desAreon. Yours will be a glorious motherhood," said Tarash. "If Sajit lives he will receive a clan-name and become one of those who travel freely between worlds, with a true vocation and a meaningful future. You will be proud. And if does not live, he will become one with the High Compassion."

"You're telling me he isn't dead. You're telling me that even though he's alive, you're planning to take him away and ... almost certainly ... kill him."

"Death is but a doorway into the High Compassion, blessed mother Ina," he said, giving her the title properly due to a mother of one who might become a martyr in the name of the High Inquest. "I'll come calling again," he said. "Or else, my commander will release a finding-bird. Wherever he may be, it'll manage to bring him to us. My commander is Lord Gharém, whose collection rate is known to be perfect."

"If you find him, where will you take him?"

"To the Lake, where we have built our collecting station. Your son will ascend the quincuncial escalator and be pulled into the belly of a great warship. And then he will ride the overcosm to Bellares, the warrior world. If you would care to see him, to say goodbye to him ... you could try waiting there. He'll come, eventually."

***

When the boy had gone, she tried to open the doppling-kit, even knowing that an abomination lay inside it. Surely to see a not-Sajit in the box would make her go mad.

Yet if a monster lurked inside it, that monster could go off to Bellares and die and her son would still be alive, somewhere in this world. He could still be found.

But nothing she could do would force it open, and when she pounded her fists against it, it rang hollow. Perhaps it had been a hoax from the beginning.

***

And so it was that she found herself in the park. The five-sided pyramid had sprung up right in the center, with the lake to one side, the woods to the other, and in the distance an alien city, thrumming and flashing and pounding as new buildings were being put up, new edifices arriving in a blink or two, the skyline clattering as new pre-formed city pieces were bolted into face by spiderlike robots.

And behind them the ruins. Urna was still a world, but it was a world rapidly being subsumed. It had already, in fact, ceased to be; what was happening now was just a bit of cleanup.

In the park were children and their relatives. Weeping, saying goodbye, exchanging last embraces. Five cordoned pathways led to the five escalators. Childsoldiers held back the throng, clearing the pathways. Ethereal music played from the sky, the water, the trees. Above was the delphinoid warship, blotting out many of the moons. It was the circling loons that lit the park, and the soft were-light suffusing the musical ensembles that played from every direction.

Ina made her way aimlessly at first. Seeing all the

goodbyes made her feel even emptier; she had not been able to say goodbye to anyone.

Taking advantage of the crowd, food vendors had set up portable stalls. There was even an open air theater with dancing servocorpses and a magician pulling hats out of lizards. Nearby, another pulled lizards out of hats.

The festival atmosphere blended incongruously with the general grief. But as she pushed her way through to the barricade, the sense of loss was more powerful, radiating from everyone as they pressed against the barrier built from cones of glittering metal linked with strands of force.

The forceropes were invisible but strong. You could feel your way to the gaps, slide your arms through a little way. Many of the families were doing that. Little siblings, grandparents, all trying to touch their children for the last time. For even if they lived, there was time dilation; a year could pass in the life of the soldiers, and this past would already be unreachable. It was goodbye beyond the parsecs that would soon separate them.

Children filed past, solemn, staring straight ahead, transfixed by their own role in the spectacle.

She did not see Sajit.

A hand brushed her shoulder and softly whispered her name.

Shocked, she turned. "Master Arbát!"

***

He had been coming to the collecting field for many days now, with some vague notion of snatching Sajit away ... Sajit or Tijas. Or both. Arbát had no clear idea of what he would do, what he *could* do. But he was drawn to the collecting field.

"You think he's alive, too, don't you?" said Ina desAreon.

Arbát did not answer. He was trying to figure out how much she should know.

"You've *seen* him," Ina said.

Arbát said, "I have."

At that moment, there came a raucous blast from the five-sided pyramid. The elevators reversed; children began to descend. From the platform there came five iridium shofars, each held aloft by three servocorpses, and they blared a terrifying music above which sounded a thunderous voice:

"The collection will now pause for one sleep and resume after a revolution of your world, so that the collected may be processed and stored and room made for the as-yet-uncollected.

"Rejoice, O men and women who are subjects of the High Compassion! Listed children will be found and trained to serve the High Inquest. Every listed child will be collected. Do not hide your children, do not shield them from their glorious future. Find them, bring them, say your farewells."

And then, bursting from the heavens, came the high-pitched massed voices of a million childsoldiers, singing the Inquestral anthem:

Dhelyá sarang z tóraka z nishis
hokhtin verapo pa' jitaaren mi
pa' zérveras, pan qériah dídeas mi...

I, a slave, a chattel, a nothing

throw before you all my heart
my thoughts, the works of my hands....

It was transcendent, overwhelming: the fervent, full-throated keening of a million young voices — utterly beautiful, utterly pitiless — the awesome, unchallengeable power of the High Inquest that had held the balance of the cosmos for twenty millennia. A sound of consummate beauty and terror.

The anthem rang out and many dropped down in genuflection. Some sobbed. The song reached its climax with the words

Eih auraín aiunaín
min yverprendéis práxein
suvitek, chom nikans ebrenden

Yrshíltraor — Urázbedar —
Eih eih hohk'kelassiaísti mun
dheyáin z tóraken z níshien

At the final hour
you will take me up into your arms
suddenly, as in a planet's destruction

Protector — Skyfather —
bless me with the High Compassion
I, a slave, a chattel, a nothing.

And all at once fell darkness; with a single movement the entire army had turned and displaced itself onto the ship, for each hoverdisk contained a homing displacement plate.

And the sky blackened with a single thunderclap.

"We have some time," Arbát whispered. We need not watch here.

"Come, Master Arbát," Ina said. "I've had no one to talk to for so long. Tell me how you came to see my son. Tell me how you know he is alive."

"I'll tell you everything," Arbát said, though that was not his intention. There was, however, a reason to cultivate Sajit's mother. The reason had been forming in his mind ever since the boys fled from Attembris. It was the reason he had come to the collecting field, after looking in vain for Sajit's family amid the disintegrating palace of Nevéqilas.

Gingerly, he took her hand — she clutched it, making him nervous, for no one had clung to him in this way for many decades — and they threaded their way through the crowd; a few displacement plates still worked and they could back to the ruined palace in a few jumps, with a detour or two.

When he saw how she was living he wondered how she had survived at all. The family's generously appointed rooms had been reduced to half a chamber, half filled with rubble. But when Arbát saw what he had been looking for, it was hard for him to contain his excitement.

The memory of his ecstatic, pained relationship with his two pupils who were one came flooding back — the shameful moments as much as the joyful ones — the moments when he knew he nurtured a talent far greater than his own, the moments when he wanted to be more than a teacher and tried to assuage his desire with servocorpses and fantasy ... all of it came back when he saw the box lying in the corner.

"Is that —" he asked her.

"If only I had never seen the cursed thing!" Ina said. "But it can't save us now. I can't even get it to open. And it's very light. It's empty. Somehow it must have aborted — as it should have — I should never have accepted to spawn an abomination in my home."

Arbát told her that his own rooms were less damaged — in fact practically intact, though he embroidered a little; the amount of living space remaining to him was as small as this, but he had not started off with a residence for a family of five and servocorpses and under the special favor of the Starry Highness. "Perhaps I could store a few of your things," he added. He was thinking of the whisperlyre.

Thus it was that not by lying, but more by omission, Arbát came to be in possession of the doppling kit.

Eighteen
The Collecting Field

Where once a crystal needle had threaded the sky, there were now shards, pylons, balconies leaning at impossible angles.

When the flying veranda docked, Sajit's father whispered, "Why did you bring me here? You can only save me, or Tijas."

"No, Starry Highness and Father. I can do both."

Sajit knew that if he could bring himself to the requisite state of mind, there was a way to find Tijas quickly. He would need to enter the space between spaces. Then he could find Tijas immediately — even *before* immediately, because the place he sought was outside spacetime. He knew he could do it. He *had* to do it.

As the veranda slid into place, servocorpses came now, erecting a healing tent around the Princeling.

"Go now," said Orifec weakly, "find your doppling."

Stepped from the balcony into a twisted corridor, and found a displacement plate. He sat down, emptying his thoughts, crossing his legs and entering *savézhata.*

Tijas! he cried out with his mind.

***

She had not been able to resist coming back. Each day, in the park, there was the same procession. The finding-birds landing and depositing their children, frightened or resigned, excited or placid as servocorpses.

What else did she have to live for? The children of her womb were dead. Her husband was dead. Her planet was dying as it was slowly being ingested by another.

Each day she waited at by the pathway to the quincunx. The crowd thinned each day. They must have found most of the children. What did not diminish was the pomp, the spectacle, the music pouring out of the sky, the Inquestral anthem shrilling from the heavens.

Above it all, a delphinoid filled half the sky, making the world both day and night at the same time.

***

Cloaked in shadow, another woman came to the the field. She had made her way back to the city easily enough; there were still displacement plates that worked, here and there, and she knew many secret subvocalizations that were taught only to the highest initiates in the temple. She moved among the throng, pulling as much shadow about her as her robes could generate, though they had not been recharged since the temple.

As she was cloaked in shadow, few noticed her, certainly none of the new denizens of the world that was no longer Urna.

But the people of Shirenzang could tell when she approached. Something fluttering. Something shimmering. A tree's shadow, darker than it should be. Though they saw only shadows, they moved out of her way. Instinctively, you knows when a god is present, you know to keep a certain distance. She would be seen, when she so chose.

And now, she did so choose. There was someone she needed to speak to.

***

Ina desAreon felt only the woman's breath at first; when she turned there was no one there.

Look harder, said a voice within. *I am near.*

And then another voice — not in her mind. "Ina desAreon. We have met, in another world."

"You are ... the woman cloaked in shadow," Ina said. "The real mother. The mother and the goddess."

Ina squinted and could make out very little. A shimmering, a flutter, a flitting shadow.

"Ina desAreon," came the voice that was right beside her, "our world is fading. Why have you come here?"

"I want to catch a glimpse of Sajit."

"How do you know he'll come here?"

"The same way you know, goddess."

The music was beginning again. The crowd leaned forward against the barrier. Ahead, the five-sided pyramid loomed; they were all in its shadow as Urna's red sun started to set. The loons were silent.

"It isn't really him, you know," Éluma said.

"Does it matter anymore?" said Ina. "I know that the doppling kit was activated. I don't know if I'll see Sajit or —"

"That obscene *thing,"* said the goddess.

"And I don't think we'll really be able to tell them apart. Really. Goddess — I lost my husband. I lost my two daughters. I lost the world I lived in. A shadow of my Sajit would be better than nothing."

"It's not what we believe in."

"I don't think anyone cares what we believe in, anymore," Ina said. "I don't think anyone cares if we even exist."

"But what if *everyone* made copies of the people they loved? Wouldn't life have no more meaning? Wouldn't you just be able to replace one child with another that was exactly the same? Would you shed tears if he died? If you could just open a box and bring put another one out? What about the sanctity of life?"

"Everyone *hasn't* made copies of everybody else," said Ina. "We are just talking about one person. And it's a person we both love."

"But *a* person Not two."

"Goddess, I know that if I see my boy again, I won't care if he's only a shadow's shadow of my son."

Now the crowd surged. Ina found herself pushed against the barrier. For a moment she thought she could see the woman's face.

But the goddess folded herself back in shadow.

***

The spectacle was beginning. A squadron of childsoldiers led the way, beating back the throng. On a hoverfloat came drummers, pounding on man-tall drums covered in human skin, their flayed faces flopping down their edges.

Breaching the clouds, a flock of finding-birds swooped down, each deposit a child in the middle of the walkway. The children stumbled forward, urged on by childsoldiers.

Mikkálu was there too. But he had not expected to see Éluma in the crowd. He tried not to see her, but, pushing against the barrier, her face emerged out of the darkweave that she wore.

"I said goodbye already," Mikkálu said. "I said I'd come for you one day." Why couldn't this have ended cleanly, like a servocorpse drama, in neat little segments?

The woman who was standing next to Éluma said, "Who is this boy? Do you know him? How do you know a childsoldier?"

Mikkálu could see that there were stories within stories here — doorways that should not be opened. He needed to slam them shut. The Child Collector would be waiting for his equerry.

The woman reached through the barricade, gripped Mikkálu's arm. "You know the woman cloaked in shadow," she whispered. "You know *something.* Do you know my son? Do you know Sajit?"

"Your *son?*" But before Mikkálu had time to react, another finding-bird plummeted down and disgorged

Tijas. Bewildered, unkempt, his clingfire ripped, the boy had landed right in the middle of the procession.

He held aloft a ring with an intagliate pattern of serpents and he shouted "It's me, it's me, I'm the real one, take *me!*"

The strange woman beat at the barricade with her fists. "Sajit, Sajit," she screamed, "let me through to him!"

Mikkálu grasped Tijas's arm. His fist was a boy's but his training was a soldier's.

"You killed my father," Tijas shrieked, "let go!"

"Your father —" said the woman Mikkálu did not know, "Your father was crushed to death when the people bins fell from the sky!"

"Ina, I'm not your son, I am Tijas."

"I don't care who you are! You belong with me!"

And then Sajit was there too, materializing out of nowhere, falling out of nothing into Tijas's arms.

The sight of twins — abomination, in broad daylight, was a shock. People around them were making signs of aversion or reciting mantras. A man bent down to find a rock to hurl. Another was already throwing a stone but in an instant Mikkálu looked up and pulverised it with a laser glance. The crowd was screaming, back away.

"No stone throwing!" Childsoldiers were in crowd control mode, barking at the the crowd and quirting them.

***

"I knew that I could save you," Sajit said. "I knew I could leap through the space between spaces and find you."

Ina said, "You've come back to me."

"No, mother. I've come to take my doppling's place. Take him. Love him. You never really loved me anyway — I wasn't really yours. But you can atone for that. You can love Tijas."

"I think I can," Ina said.

And once more Éluma was shrieking — *"Abomination! Abomination!"* ripping the darkweave that girded her, baring the bosom of the goddess to the crowd. She was flinging herself against the barrier. Ina was trying to hold her back —

"How could you reject him?" Ina screamed. "From a womb or from a box, *your* DNA!"

Éluma rent the darkweave. Her breasts emerged from the fabric of darkness. As she raved, darkness billowed about her, showing that which humans may not see, except when celebrating the most sacred of all mysteries.

"Aërat!" Some crowd members were crying out, some falling to their knees, some shielding the eyes of their children.

"I have birthed a living twin!" Éluma cried. "I'm forever defiled, no goddess — I'm a whore!"

Wailing, shrieking, she flung herself against the barrier. Ina caught her, took her in her arms. "You'll always be the goddess," she said.

***

Consternation was spreading. Sajit could see that he and Tijas were being pointed at, laughed at, reviled. He could see the two mothers, one raving, the other trying to comfort.

"One of us has to die," he said.

He turned away from his mothers.

"And it's going to be me," Tijas said.

The path to the quincunx, perhaps a half klomet, was lined with citizens of Urna and curiosity-seekers from Alykh. But those nearby, just across the barrier ,were already recoiling.

He remembered, from his childhood, the nightmare —

The ritual stoning of the twin —

Sajit ran.

But Tijas ran too.

Neck and neck, feeling each other's footfall, in perfect synchronicity, they ran. Past gaping children, chiding old women, stern childsoldiers.

Stoning the twin —

The memory came. Each time his feet pounded the paving, he saw a stone whistling and the crowd roaring out its deep, hungry mantra —

Life is sacred.

Life is one.

Life is not two.

Two is abomination.

Above them, Mikkálu wheeled on his hoverdisk. He somersaulted. He shrieked out the childsoldier's warcry, egging them on. They ran, their thoughts bouncing back and forth.

Sajit remembering —

Tijas whispering in his mind: *That is not my nightmare. That is* yours, *Sajit.*

Then I must remember for both of us, Sajit thought.

The rock smashing the baby's skull...

They ran.

At the foot of the escalator childsoldiers stepped out to block their path. "One at a time."

Sajit pushed his brother, tried to knee him off the upper step — the childsoldiers tried to separate them until Mikkálu spoke to them. The escalator moved up, slowly. The dopplings didn't speak. Each was trying to shove the other off the escalator. There was no railing and the the drop would be steep. As the escalator moved higher, they became more careful with each other.

Sajit did not want to kill his brother. But he had to get ahead.

They gripped each other tight. They were sweating, slippery, and the moving escalator precarious. They embraced in violence and love. They were deadlocked. They ascended. The plateau-like parapet hove into view, and at its top, the Child Collector waited, maniples of childsoldiers perched on their whirling hoverdisks, while above them, like the snakes that symbolized the royal house of Urna, twisting, writhing tubes that were sucking up children into the sky.

Mikkálu ran ahead, all the way to Gharém, who stood, impassive. Mikkálu did not know what to say, how to get out of the situation.

"My Lord!" Mikkálu cried out. "I'm sorry it took so long — but I've come back with your prize — twofold."

***

Kyar Gharém was not fond of surprises. The Collection was supposed not supposed to have hitches. Seeing the equerry disheveled and out of breath, he reacted by slapping him sharply.

"My Lord!" Mikkálu gasped. "Did you really need to do that? I'm not one of your servocorpse lovers."

Gharém resisted the impulse to strike him again. "I give you a *lot* of leeway," he said, "because your impertinence amuses me. But know your place."

"Kyar Gharém, I've brought you your prize trophy. But as you can see, he's been doppled."

"Well, what is that to me? Dispose of one. The count must be correct."

"You want me to randomly kill one?" Mikkálu said. Gharém, in this kind of mood, always felt a bit contrary. Perhaps, he thought, the equerry was playing him.

"No, of course not," Gharém said, "the Inquest is compassionate. Send one back."

"My brother will go back," the twins both said.

"Dopplings," Gharém said. "According to this world's traditions, one twin is always slain at birth. Only their royal family is allowed the privilege of doppling and therefore the twins would not be identical, but disparate in age. We have, it seems, an anomaly."

"Lord Gharém, they *are* of the royal family," Mikkalu said.

"Then let them show their humanity."

Gharém clapped his hands and space was cleared. The childiers formed a five-sided space. Above them, the suction tubes hovered, hissing as they twisted, the necks of a monstrous hydra.

"We'll have a little contest. Which of you loves the other more? Who will sacrifice himself? You shall fight — and the one who remains conscious — *he* will be adjudged the better childsoldier. The other will be thrown back to earth — a Princeling without a country — as worthless as dust."

***

Tijas whispered, "Go limp when I hit you. Then I'll run up to the tubes —"

He didn't finish his sentence. Sajit had already punched him. Tijas reeled, thinking, *How did you hide your intentions from me?* — and Sajit was running toward the center of the pentagon.

Childsoldiers began a rhythmic chanting —

shashashasha há há! shashashasha há há!

shrill, elemental, terrifying. They rattled their hoverdisks against their sides, the slap of metal on hard young flesh sounding *chaka chaka chaka* against the keening of their warcry.

No! Tijas leaped, tackled his twin — Sajit's forehead thudded on the flagstones and Tijas tasted blood, he knew he was feeling what his brother felt, the pain radiating our from above his eyes —

Tijas ran toward the center of the parapet, where the quincuncial archway waited.

The childsoldiers moved in formation, metal boots clanging against the stones. Narrowing the area, step by step, they chanted —

shashash sha há há! shashashasha há há!
shashash sha há há! shashashasha há há!

Tijas cried out into Sajit's mind: *I'm stronger than you because this is my* meúr. *You can't stop me. I was made to take your place.*

Sajit pulled himself together. He sprang, tripped his twin; they both fell, feeling each other's pain as they grazed the pavement, feeling the feedback loop of the pain as it echoed back and forth — pain in waves, bounding and rebounding. Sajit pushed himself up. Tijas was nearing the center of the quincunx, and the tubes from the sky were coming together, ready to draw their prey into the sky.

Sajit leaped. He tripped Tijas and sent him sprawling. "Powers of powers, Sajitteh! Just let me do what I'm here to do!" But now Sajit had Tijas in a wrestling hold. The pain they felt, each other's pain, tinged with love and heartbreak — it was unbearable. They were both weeping. And the childsoldiers were moving in, chanting and banging their hoverdisks. The suction tube was closing in. He could feel the air emptying around him. For a moment he wavered —

And suddenly it was Tijas who had him pinned down.

And the childsoldiers were laughing. Tijas saw mockery. He saw the Child Collector, self-satisfied, whisper in Mikkálu's ear.

He felt his brother's pain — his regret — and the terrible love his brother felt which amplified itself over and over as it bounced back and forth through their echo chamber minds —

One of us has to let go, he said in his mind. *Or the pain will kill us both.*

At that moment, the childsoldier barrier split open. Two women pushed their way through, and the childsoldiers did not stop them.

One was Ina, the not-mother who had not even known of Tijas's existence before today.

The other, with only a few strips of shadow clinging to her perfect divine body, was the goddess — the mother who could not accept him.

They were weeping. They had fought. Somehow, they had achieved a kind of concord. "Come home, Sajit," said Ina. "Come home, Sajit," said the goddess of love.

But they're not saying my *name,* Tijas thought.

A wave of desolation, of aloneness, overwhelmed and his grip slipped.

I am *a monster,* Tijas thought.

"No!" Sajit cried aloud. "You're not a monster, you'll never be a monster — how could you be, when I'm willing to die for you?"

And Sajit stretched his head toward the sky and the writhing tubes caught him, and tendriled around him, and held him fast, jerking him up into the air and into the maw of the sucking tunnel that stretched all the way to the delphinoid in the sky —

In Tijas's mind — silence.

The connection was broken.

Tijas could not feel his doppling anymore.

The pain was ebbing, replaced by an still more terrible numbness.

***

There were no downward escalators from the Quincunx of Collection. It was designed as a one-way journey. Thus it was that while the childsoldiers and the Child Collector immediately turned their attention toward the new line of recruits advancing up the escalator — a line that was beginning to stabilize now that the scuffle was over — Tijas found himself face to face with the two women — not knowing whether he should embrace them or fear them.

"You say you love me," he said. "But neither of you

would say my name."

Ina tried to reach out. But Éluma turned her back ... in a way that Tijas had seen before....

In Sajit's nightmare. The stoning, and the Woman Cloaked in Shadow turning her back....

Tijas looked away from the two women.

Only Mikkálu paid heed to them, and he did so with one eye on his master, who might summon him to his side at any moment.

How could he look at Éluma, when he'd killed the father of her child ... while trying to kill her child? ... Nothing could ever be the same again.

And Ina ... what was she to the child he almost killed?

A childsoldier is pitiless.

Tijas tried to reach out to Sajit but it was if a wall had sprung up between their minds. Something inside the tubes ... or perhaps some force radiating from the delphinoid shipmind that hung overhead.

Never, since he first came out of the box, had Tijas felt so desolate. Behind him, children moved in five sets of single file towards the center, and one by one they were being sucked into the star whale's belly.

The Child Collector motioned Mikkálu over and said, "Send them away. They're a blot on the beauty of this ritual."

Mikkálu subvoked a quick command and a mobile displacement plate pushed its way up through the floor of the pentagon. A floater materialized in the space ... a maniple-sized floater, military issue, used in the ambushing of cities.

"Go where you want to go," he said. "The High Inquest doesn't need you anymore."

And they went.

***

Mikkálu watched the goddess stumble toward the displacement plate, helped by the village woman who had raised her child. The displacement plate vanished in a halo of blue light.

Mikkálu did not want to weep again; excessive tears could misalign the laser-irises in his eyes. The railing of the palace parapet was peppered with holes from his tears. He could not have his eyes go out of alignment. Better to pluck them out. Childsoldiers do not make such errors.

He had already misfired once. There could never be another.

He was glad Kyar Gharém did not yet know....

"As for you, my impertinent little equerry," Gharém said, "I seem to have cut you a lot of slack. You have been my favorite equerry, precisely because you are hard to cow, you're unorthodox. But this time you've gone too far."

"I'm sorry, my Lord."

"Get out of my sight," said the Child Collector. "I'll chastise you in my own good time."

Mikkálu clenched back a terrible anger.

Nineteen
Princelings and Goddesses

The floater had brought them to the lowest level of Nevéqilas. They had not said a word to one another. When the reached the base of the crystal flower, the boy who so resembled Sajit strode purposefully away, and Ina did not know where he was going.

The floater left them, standing amid the rubble and the shattered crystal that had been their world. Urna's star hung dim behind violent-fringed clouds. There were two pale moons.

"He's going to his father," said Éluma.

"His father is dead," said Ina desAreon. But it rang false; she knew her son and his doppling had had another life as well, other parents.

"I mean the Princeling," said Éluma.

"Should I follow?" Ina said.

"How could you?" said the goddess. "You are just some villager. And his father is a Starry Highness."

"But you do not follow? His father may be a princeling, but you are a goddess."

"Not any more."

Ina said, "There are so few of us left. Surely we've got to find a way to ... find some kind of peace."

"Peace?" Éluma cried. "I caused Orifec's death! I turned my back on my child!"

"But there was abomination. You had no choice."

"Oh, I was blind," Éluma said, and she wept bitterly.

***

When Tijas reached the palace, a speaking boy-corpse had been waiting; he was led to a room that could be reached only through displacement ... a garden of glass, a field of clear crystal pebbles. He found the Princeling surrounded by servocorpses — functioning as medics, orderlies, and courtiers. Orifec lay under a canopy of a a glass tree that grew in the center of the chamber — a chamber that seemed infinite because its walls reflected each other infinitely.

"Where am I?" he asked the corpse.

"This is called Véravur," the corpse said. "It's the Princeling's chamber of dying and remembrance." The boy said, "Let the Rememberers enter now."

Tijas went to Orifec's bedside. Half his body was submerged in an amniosis balm, but his head and part of his torso could be seen. The iatromaton mad cooing sounds as its tentacles touched the Princeling and read vital signs. He had been shaved.

"Ah, Tijas," Orifec said.

"How can you tell us apart?" Tijas said.

Orifex said, "Perhaps a lucky guess. Or perhaps, as possessor of half your DNA, I'm just better at guessing than other people." A frown, briefly. "Tijas, you must not be afraid I am in pain. I know you're thinking that. In fact I am buoyed up by so many opiates that though I'm severed in two, and my functions are all grinding to a halt, I ... still speak, cogently, even volubly."

Tijas smiled. "The goddess, my real mother, has gone mad because of me. And as for my foster-mother — I don't know what she thinks."

"She'll come round." Orifec said. "They both will. Our ancient civilization is no more — there's no need to cling to superstitions."

"Honestly, Starry Highness — did you *really* know it was me?"

"I guess," said Orifec. "But I guessed with good logic."

"Why?"

The glass fronds tinkled. A soft breeze came; servocorpses were fanning them with the feathers of firephoenixes. Above, the moons danced. Holosculpts-views to be sure. The room was a womb.

"I know you would both to anything to save the other. But Sajit is the elder. I know that the elder will always sacrifice to preserve the younger — I know this because I am myself a doppling, and I have the memories of generations of dopplings."

"I understand, father." He did not really understand how any emotion of Sajit's could be more powerful than his own. But he tried to listen to every world Orifec said. He knew already that this would be their last time together. He sat down on the soft meniscus of the amniofluid.

"I would have welcomed either of you," Orifec said. "But one of you *had* to come. I could not wait for ever. I'm barely holding on — you cannot tell, because I am in no pain. But I must anoint the next Princeling. And I must give you all my — *our* memories."

Rememberers were materializing around them, all in the white robes that signified their calling. They were all ancient, wizened men and women, their brains stuffed, no doubt, with generational histories.

"Do I have to listen to them *all?*" Tijas said, bewildered.

Orifec managed a wry smile. "That would take lifetimes," he said softly. "They are just here as part of the ritual. Do you know why you have to be here, Tijas?"

"I think so," Tijas said, but he didn't like the answer.

Orifec wants me to succeed him.

"I'm not your doppling," Tijas said, "and I don't have a planet to rule over."

"That is true," Orifec said, "but I can't die until I pass on all these remembrances. Or they, too, will die."

The chief Rememberer held a glass dish in his hands, on which there writhed a little green worm ...

"Tash Tonadár," Orifec whispered. The Rememberer's name and clan-name.

And Tijas knew that the worm would be the conduit, boring into Orifec's skull to extract his memories ... and to transfer them to his own....

The Rememberer picked the work from the dish and it started to lengthen, its segments multiplying until it coiled again and again around the Rememberer's wrist....

Tijas cried out, "I don't want memories ... I want to *forget!*"

"I know you do," said the Rememberer whom Orifec had called Tonadár. "And yet ... you are empty now. And your mind needs filling."

Tijas said, "How can I explain this emptiness? Sajit was with me every second of my life. We *were* each other."

Tonadár said, "Those delphinoid shipminds ... they cast a psychic interference field that blocks a lot what goes on in a human mind. It was not aimed at you specifically. It is because when humans travel in the light-mad overcosm, they can be driven insane unless their thoughts are a little dulled."

"Will I sense him again, then?"

"That I don't know. The connection between dopplings is not well understood."

But we reached out to each other even in the space between spaces! Tijas thought.

"Perhaps, when the shipmind has reached its destination, you will feel him again."

"I'll have to hope," Tijas said.

Thus it was that he did not resist when the servocorpses started to shave his head and when the worm of remembrance was placed on his scalp and began to burrow....

***

And Ina made her way back to the ruins of her home. Now there was truly nothing to live for. She sat in a corner for a day, perhaps many days, not eating ...

around her, the holosculpt projector played landscapes on shuffle, switching from cityscapes to ice deserts to spiralling mountains and scarlet snows, the views fading from one to another. At length, their repertoire played out, the walls blanked; still she sat.

She did not remember eating, though she must have. She only sat, remembering moments from before, shards of moments.

After a measureless time, a young dead page displaced into the room. He wore a tunic of shimmerfur, knotted with a belt of mating serpents; she knew that he came from the palace.

He handed her a message disk, which said to her, in a soft, childlike voice, *The Starry Highness requests the presence of Ina desAreon.*

Confused, numb, she followed him.

***

She was a shell. Weeping had drained her of all feeling.

She did not know how long she walked, how many times she crossed the same street to find it different every time. Her feet had lost their covering and only pieces of the darkness that cloaked her remained.

But in the end, she found herself at the entrance to the Temple of Aërat. And the corpses who guarded the gate still knew her, though she was naked, filthy, even bloodstained.

And they called her "Goddess."

They took her to her quarters, cleansed her, perfumed her, and gave her a new cloak of shadow. They painted her face and lined her eyes, and reddened her lips and rouged her nipples.

The temple was full of tourists; there were few real worshippers now. When she left her dressing chamber, some tourists recognized her from the holosculpt images that were everywhere. Some did a mocking obeisance — oh, they did not know they mocked, but thought they were participating in some quaint, picturesque ritual.

In a courtyard, goddesses in training danced to the twang of an untuned kítharon. Their finger-cymbals clicked in time to the batting of eyelashes, and they pointed their feet daintily.

An acolyte held up a reflector and she saw herself and she thought ... *I look almost like myself.*

A dead page met her in one of the gardens and told her that the Starry Highness was asking for her presence.

"But isn't he —"

"You'll see, Goddess."

***

There was a garden all of glass, a garden without doors, accessible only by displacement.

One by one, important guests were materializing on the plates the rimmed the chamber. Éluma had never heard of this room, did not even know where it was; at its center there was a tree, all glass, with tinkling leaves, branching all the way to infinity, though she did not know if the reflective crystal of the ceiling was a holosculpt.

The people in the room were dressed in their palatial best — incongruously perhaps, since they were the elite of a civilization that was barely clinging to existence. Éluma saw a few other divinities — though

Love was the most venerated on Urna, there were lesser deities, all represented in the world by their human embodiments. The Death God was there, his hair aflame and his nude body painted completely white, his four arms undulating, with a servocorpse on a leash. The God of War was present too, a mechanical in the shape of a childsoldier, whose joints clanked, metal on metal.

Then there were nobles ... Éluma recognized them from their visits to the temple ... she knew some of them quite intimately, knew their arcane requirements when celebrating the rituals of love.

Beneath the glassy canopy, on a crystal throne, sat ... the abomination that was like her son.

In front of him, in a crystal sarcophagus, afloat in an opiate bath, was the torso of the Princeling who had once been her lover. The two were connected, shaved head to shaved head, by a tendriling, twisting annelid that had burrowed into both their skulls. The worm quivered and undulated.

Behind them stood a row of Rememberers, in the white robes of the Clan of Ton.

A few servocorpses moved about the chamber, trayfloats at their fingertips, serving chasers of concentrated *zul* and canapés made from chocolate and flowers. But no one was eating or drinking.

Éluma knew the ceremony ... knew it from the tellers of history, for she could not have been present at the last one. It was an accession ceremony. And *Tijas,* the Abomination, was going to be Princeling.

The woman Ina desAreon was beside her suddenly. Éluma had not noticed her before. The woman was not dressed for the occasion but wore a shapeless stola fastened with crystal brooch. She seemed to have come straight from the invitation without having stopped to make herself look presentable; either she did not know the protocol for a princeling's invitation, or she had nothing to wear.

Éluma did not wish to speak to her, even to acknowledge her. The emotions that had passed between them in the Collecting Quincunx were too painful to relive. But Ina came closer, refusing to melt into the crowd.

"Please," she said. "I don't know anyone here. Please ... goddess."

"Not any more," Éluma said bitterly. "You've seen what I am."

Ina reached out to her. She found herself clasping Ina's hand. With a strange desperation. And then the voice came.

It was the voice of Orifec, yet not his voice. *I am the Son of the Starlight, the High Princeling Orifec z'Urnasi Tath, hereditary Lord of Nevéqilas, Commander of the World Entire, He Who Answers Only to the High Inquest.*

The voice did not come from where Orifec lay, but was broadcasting from the walls, the floor, the ceiling itself, a sound both human and brittle, like glass itself.

To me alone is vouchsafed the forbidden. I have died and returned many times over. In me is the wisdom of my previous selves. It is our tradition.

But our world is ending, and our civilization must evolve now. Urna is falling beyond. *And thus it is that we shall break tradition. My memories will not go to a doppling but to a changeling.*

He is young, but inside him will be the voices of Starry Highnesses going all the way back to the first. Obey him as you would me; for I live again in him.

Now you will witness this child, born from the union of Goddess and Princeling, as he slays his father and becomes the new Son of the Starlight, the High Princeling Tijassah darOrifec z'Urnasi Tath, Who Answers Only to the High Inquest.

A gasp. This was inconceivable.

But in a moment, Tijas had yanked the worm from Orifec's forehead. A strangled cry escaped the princeling's throat ... and then a death-rattle ... amplified by the crystals of the chamber, so that the branches shook and the crystals tinkled and the whole chamber seemed to howl.

The crystal coffin containing the dead princeling wavered a little, blinking in and out of existence. Then it vanished, displacing to the secret, orbiting mnemothanasion that was the burial place of all Starry Highnesses.

A chill came over the chamber. The Rememberers, the guests, even the servocorpses fell to the ground in prostration. Even the gods inclined their heads.

And so it was that Éluma found herself still standing amid a sea of backs.

And it seemed that the only other person standing was Ina desAreon.

Tijas said, "Mothers, come to me."

Éluma threaded her way through the still-prostrate throng. The suppliants shifted, parted, making a pathway. A few steps behind, Ina too was approaching.

Tijas came down from the glazen throne. The two women stood in front of him. He said, "I didn't choose this. It should have been Sajit."

Ina said, "I know, Starry Highness. This is why the doppling kit was brought to our home. We always knew that there would be a culling of childsoldiers. We didn't dream there would be a *falling beyond.*"

Éluma said, "But I didn't know. Nobody warned me. Nobody prepared me."

"And how could they have, mother," said Tijas, "knowing that you are the living goddess, the emblem of all that this world stands for, the guardian of all its traditions?"

"We made Sajit out of our love," Éluma said. "I had no rôle in making you at all. Orifec planned to defy tradition. I never really understood."

Tijas said, "But now, only one of you can be my mother. And I can't be the one to choose."

Twenty
The Goddess in the Ruins

Tijas dimissed the throng. One by one they filed to displacement plates and blinked out. Now only the three remained. Tijas returned to the throne and sat down again. He deopaqued the walls and ceiling and now it seemed as though the were on a sea of glass, beneath the clear night sky of Urna, under the singing moons. Only the crystal tree and throne remained from the garden of glass.

Tijas was alone with the two women who were not his mother.

Two women who could never understand his bereavement, his emptiness.

He sat, the worm wound round his shaved head. It was shrinking now, and soon it would be completely absorbed into his brain.

Already there were alien memories and thoughts — whispers, contradictions. He was beginning to know the weight that rested on Orifec's mind all the time.

Memories of murders and lovers and disappointments ... memories of being both the traitor and the betrayed.

He was his father, holding the child Sajit, feeling his father's dream of breaking away from the past.

He was Orifec in the forest, hearing Sajit's voice for the first time, swelling with pride and sadness ... already foreseeing the coming of the Child Collector....

He was Orifec again in the Room of the Clouds and Rain ... making love to the Goddess ... he was the pinprick consciousness of a single sperm cell swimming upstream ... the moment of Sajit's conception — he was there, he was inside his own mother....

I'll go mad! he was thinking.

He pulled at the worm with his hand, staying its progress. The voices grew quieter.

He looked at the Goddess and felt what Orifec felt when he first saw her. He could see her conflicted feelings — her love for Sajit, her gut loathing of Abomination — and most of all her guilt. He saw the Goddess in a thousand ways, for behind this goddess there were other goddesses seen by other Orifecs as well, all the way to the beginning.

He looked at Ina, who had lost everything. Her face was weathered and aged not by time but by suffering. But in her eyes, he saw, there was the dawning of a kind of love.

Again he tugged at the worm. Its loose end writhed and spiralled against his skin. A greenish rheum dripped from the tail end which had been plugged into his father's skull.

"Oh, mothers who are not my mothers," he said. "What future is there for us?"

***

"*I* killed him," Éluma said. "*I* killed the Starry Highness." Once again, as she before in the quincunx, she was weeping uncontrollably, lashing out with her arms. Ina tried to hold her still.

"But you were trying to kill *me,*" Tijas said.

"And I broke Mikkálu's heart."

"Yes, you did. You gave him an impossible choice." Tijas was implacable.

"I killed Sajit, too. I killed my child."

"You don't know that."

"Yes I do. There's an emptiness. You know it. You feel it."

"You don't know it, Éluma. He may survive being a childsoldier. You know the ancient ditty."

"Yes. *A million young boys dreamed of the stars ... one hundred thousand became childsoldiers ... ninety-nine thousand died ... one became an Inquestor.*"

... a song that children sing when passing the time on long journeys.

"I'm all you have left. Yet you rejected me. But then again, we never had a connection. Do you know how many times I joined the family for breakfast — and Sajit was watching from concealment, laughing? You never knew, never guessed. There was nothing to reject." She felt his sadness, far more hurtful than anger would have been.

Éluma said, "I can't solve this. I'm broken, and nothing can put me together again."

"Then go where you wish. It was my thought to reestablish the long-forgotten position of Valydé, the Princeling's Mother, but I see you will not accepted it."

Tijas summoned a servocorpse with a wave of his hand. He told it to lead the Goddess wherever she wished to go.

***

Ina was the only guest left in the room, save for servocorpses.

"I'll be your mother, Tijas," she said at last.

"I know," Tijas said.

"How?"

"I know everything Orifec knew. I know why this family was chosen, this village. And you knew about the doppling kit all along, and you didn't ... abhor it."

"I can tell you things about yourself ... your other self ... that even you don't know," Ina said. "Come down from that throne."

"I've got a worm trying to burrow itself into me."

"Hold on to it ... pull at it, slow it down. Once it's in there, you really will be the Starry Highness. You will be my Lord. And you will be every Princeling of Urna before you. But for now ... you're still ... the shadow of my son."

"Tell me one of these things I don't know," Tijas said.

The boy was no Princeling, not yet. Ina saw a frail, frightened child. She thought of Sajit, in the hold of the delphinoid shipmind, perhaps in stasis, about to travel for who knows how long. But she could still see her son in Tijas's eyes.

"He used to wake up from a nightmare," she said. "I used to think it was fantasy, but now I know it was premonition ... foreshadowing."

This is the story she told Tijas....

***

He would come to me in the night, in a cold sweat, and he would say ... they're stoning me. And I would say Who? Who?

And he said, Everyone we know. They're in a circle. They're throwing stones. Smashing my face, my skull, oh, mother, it hurts, hurts. *And I said it's just a dream. But I knew better.*

When Sajit was a toddler there was a doppling-stoning in the village. And he witnessed it....

I should have let him sleep. I didn't know. I took him from his bed and held him in my arms at first but he was getting heavy now. I let him walk. He let go my hand. He toddled ahead.

These ceremonies have long been outlawed. Devivement is supposed to be painless. But this child's family was religious. They needed to see the death for themselves, to make sure the abomination was truly rooted out.

He saw me cast the stone. He picked one up himself and thrust it at the child, though it fell short. They stamped their feet and chanted age-old curses.

When he threw the rock I threw my arms around him and took him back inside.

From time to time, he would dream of it ... but I told him it was only a nightmare.

He was four years old.

***

Tijas said, "He never showed me this."

He started to cry. Ina took him in her arms. “It will be all right,” she told him. “Whatever you do, I’ll stand with you.”

“I know,” said Tijas.

“Will you renounce the kingdom?”

“Kingdom? It’s only a memory of a kingdom ... yet I’m told we still have the rights to some tiny patches of this planet.”

He let go of the memory worm. It slithered inside him. More memories came, crowding, all demanding his attention. But they would never be his own memories. He would never really be Orifec. That was the gift his father had given his kingdom, though the gift had come too late, only in the kingdom’s last days: he had moved it from stifling repetition into a time of change. After all these centuries, Urna would be ruled by *someone else* — someone who yet held the memories of the past but could use a new viewpoint to discover fresh truths, fresh paths to travel.

“No, I won’t,” said Tijas, “not just yet.”

***

Éluma reentered the temple, and she summoned all those beneath her: all the gods and goddesses in training, all the stewards, all the pages, even such servocorpses as had been endowed with the capacity for thought and speech.

“I’ve been here all my life,” she said, “and yet I’ve never seen this temple for what it is.”

And she commanded her minions to deopaque all the walls, to shut of the holosculpt generators, to silence the music that had never been silenced. And all of them stood there, gaping at the reality of Aërat's domain.

There were broken columns. Flagstones veined with ancient weeds. A chipped planter with a wilted rosella-tree. There were walls with patches of bright murals — scenes of lovemaking — images so ancient that they did not even move.

"Our world is being subsumed into Alykh," Éluma said. "On Urna what we do is sacred. In Aírang, which they call the City of Love, we are whores. Let us embrace this."

She watched the faces of her acolytes — those that had faces, for the dead only have the simulacrum of a face, without true feeling, and many of the humans had already abandoned the temple. Dead or alive, they wore little expression. She understood — their lives had been divested of all meaning without warning, without reason.

"I want to tell you that I am the last incarnation of the goddess. The goddess is no more. Look around you. It is illusion. It's *always* been illusion."

"But even if it's illusion," said one the stewards, "should we not at least cling to it?"

"Worlds die," Éluma said. "Civilizations collapse. Even the High Inquest itself may fall one day."

That caused a gasp.

"All my life I've known as a fact that the sanctity of the human soul means that we are unique — that to be double is abomination. When ... *twins* ... occur in our lives, we know what must we done. We do it, the act itself is abhorrent, but we *have* to do it. Just like we have to have children, to die, to make love. Only the Princeling may reproduce by doppling — because state of Princehood is itself unique. Then I learned that my own child was a doppling."

More gasps. The steward said, "I heard a rumor, goddess — some kind of scandal at the Collecting Field."

"No rumor. *Nothing* we knew as fact is true now. Urna is ended."

Éluma had never spoken so many words at one time. Her very godhead depended on mystery. Her sexual power was so refined she could control the very pheromones she exuded. She did not need to speak except in riddles. Her addressing the acolytes, like the proprietress of a bakery or a corpse factory regaling her staff, was a novel thing to do and yet she found herself, in a strange way, enjoying it. They were listening to her, and not because she was repeating a millennia mantra ... because she was struggling to find a pathway that they all must follow.

"This is another world and we must adapt," she said. "We were adapting a little bit, allowing them to enter out sacred halls and gawk at our quaint rituals. But we have to go further."

"How, goddess?" said the steward, pursing her lips.

"These people are merchants. And we have skills they can't even dream of. How many of them can name number the erogenous punctilia of a man's penis? Even a seven-year-old among you acolytes knows how to prolong the suppliant's sweet anguish beyond the point of explosion, to a transcendental union with infinity. Can they do that? Will they not pay for it? We too have something we can sell. After the people bins came, a man named Lang viHurek came here and offered us a contract ... an, to his mind, an entertainment deal. I slapped his face."

The temple, decaying; the walls half crumbled, the holosculpts fragmented and pixellated ... on the unmoving murals, the ancient technology, remained fresh. Thousand-year-old young lovers, in contorted positions, frozen ecstasy ... speaking from the past.

"Follow me," said the goddess. "We are going to find viHurek and make that deal."

The gates of the temple were not gates at all. They had always been an illusion. The temple's roof had caved in since the coming of the people bins.

Éluma stepped through the gates that were not gates.

A pathway led towards what had once been the city center. Beyond it, the new city, Aírang, was still expanding visibly; its skyscrapers were still inching toward the sky, its spider-architects still frantically piling more units on top of units.

"Follow me to the city of pleasure," Éluma said. "In our new existence, we are not deities. We are whores. Embrace that. We have skills that will blindside their imaginations. We'll dazzle their *dorezdas.* We'll remake their world. They call themselves a city of pleasure! We'll show them pleasure! We'll become the thing they are most know for!"

She laughed — a laughter in which each silvery peal was modulated to arouse.

As she said this she began to tear great strips of shadow from her body. Such was her art that the more she revealed, the more she seemed to conceal. The acolytes followed suit, flinging their vestments into the street. Threads of darkness crisscrossed, twirled.

I've lost everything, she thought, *so I might as well be free of everything.*

She began to sing. So this motley parade of naked beauty made its chaotic way down the street, with the corpses hardly less lively than the living, for they were well programmed, to catch exactly the mood of those they were with.

***

Meanwhile, in what had once been the private throneroom of the Princeling of Urna, or more properly the High Princeling Tijassah darOrifec z'Urnasi Tath held court, such as it was.

The governance of Urna had not changed since even before the world had become absorbed into the Dispersal of Man. It had always been a sparsely populated world with but a single land mass, a single major city, and a network of villages. The court of Urna had been mostly ceremonial for generations. Yes, the Princeling wielded absolute power; but custom decreed that the real power was held by deputies and, ultimately, by thinkhives.

The Starry Highness held authority in the name of the High Compassion of the Inquest.

The throneroom was not as it was when Sajit and Tijas had spied on it ... which had not been that long ago. Holosculpt generators were out of sync. But the twined serpent columns were still there — they were real, just giving the illusion of marmáreon.

The court comprised only a few people: a Rememberer whose white robe seemed soiled, as though he had dressed in haste to come to this assembly; the Princely Vizier, a barechested old man in a pointed hat and curly-tipped slippers — someone Tijas had not even known existed; and the usual corpses and scribes.

On his right hand they had set up a seat for Ina, who by default had assumed the millennially obsolete title of Valydé, the mother of the ruler.

Tijas knew what to do, from the memories he had absorbed. But what he had to do seemed so irrelevant.

The Vizier had begun his daily recitation of the kingdom's assets. "Of land, there remains for your use ... one square klomet."

"That's my whole kingdom?"

"By rules of Inquestral *makrúgh,* when a planet *falls beyond* one square klomet may remain as a living mnemothanasion, Starry Highness. The world Alykh has encroached on everything else ... in law if not in fact ... and within your reserved territory, often in fact though not in law."

"And you don't care, that our whole civilization has been reduced to one square klomet?"

"Should I, Starry Highness? Truth to tell, I've never left the palace. I was born and raised in your service."

"My service?"

"There is but one Starry Highness, ever and always."

"I don't have a world to rule," Tijas said, wondering why he had allowed the worm of memory to slither into his brain at all. He rubbed the pinhole where it had gone in. "What *do* I have? Wealth? Assets?"

"You have immediate liquidity of seven trillion iridas, and some investments off-world. Personal funds, Starry Highness."

"So ... I could, for example, take passage on a delphinoid. I could go off-world, anywhere."

"Indeed."

"And the thinkhives can rule in my name and no one would be the wiser."

"It has generally been so, Starry Highness."

Tijas said, "Then ... soon ... I should go."

Ina said, "Where, my son?"

"I don't know," he said.

Sajit! Still unreachable. Cut off. The aloneness could not be described, not even in music.

Then he started thinking of Daro. And the Professor with the rainbow eyelids. And the tales they told of the lives of wandering actors, the hair-raising escapades, the alien cities, the amazing creatures, the light of other suns....

And, to the Vizier: "Do I own a whisperlyre?"

Twenty-One
The Soldier, the Bard, and the Whore

... the dream ...

... rock striking child's head ... crying, crying ... but the child ... is it me? ... or am I watching?

His eyes were trying to open now but he didn't want them to. He tried to squeeze them tighter. But something was forcing them.

... rock striking ...

He was numb. He couldn't move his limbs at all. But his eyes ... they blinked. They were crusted, but he couldn't move his hand to rub his eyelids. No. Now he could. Slowly, slowly, as though emerging from —

"Stasis."

A familiar voice.

"Mikkálu!" Rage shook his mind, but his body would not rage along with it. Instead the rage went inward. Like bottling up a hurricane.

"You'll come to soon," Mikkálu said. The boy was standing in front of him.

Standing in a corridor, with frozen children on either side, stretching into darkness as far as the eye could see. The children in single file. The corridor — a little curved — like a tunnel — a cavern. The walls, segmented, as though they were inside a metallic annelid.

The only light came from Mikkálu himself. His eyes were projecting a pool of cold blue light.

"Not something the planetbound get to see that often," Mikkálu said. "They think — a childsoldier's eyes, they only spit out killing lines of laser light. But there are other settings. They are a marvel of the thinkhives' inventiveness. My eyes can give off light ... I can even cook a piece of meat with them. And make it precisely medium rare. In a millisecond."

"You killed my father! You snatched away my brother!"

Sajit could not feel Tijas at all; the bond had been cut off as soon as he was sucked into the belly of the delphinoid.

... rock striking ...

"You more than took him away. I can't even feel him."

"Ah. The notorious doppling psychic link. Studied by scientists, explained by no one. *Abomination!*"

Sajit winced.

"I know. I don't know how much it hurts. It's not in my worldview to have a psychic link with anyone. But then ... I grew up in that whorehouse you call a temple, and I was in love with the goddess."

"Not any more?" Sajit said.

"The next time we see this world again — if we live through a war or two — a long time will have passed. This is time dilation. See all those other kids? They'll wake up, a second after they were sucked up the shaft, and only the powers of powers will now how much realtime has gone by. Forget Urna. Forget Alykh. Forget it all, Sajitteh."

"Don't call me by my child-name."

"Oh ... Sajitteh ... you don't know it yet, but I am your only friend on this ship. I'm the only one who understands even a scintilla of what's in your brain."

"Why would you be my friend? Why am I not in stasis anyway?"

"I didn't mean to kill him," Mikkálu said. "You know that." For a moment he seemed strangely vulnerable. "And you have done something bad to me, too, though you don't realize it. Because of the ruckus you and your twin created, I'm no longer the Child Collector's favorite equerry. I'm off the roster. And guess what my last order was? To fetch *you.*"

"Me?"

"You're the new favorite now. I think it really excites him, you know, *down there,* to think he has all this power over someone of royal blood. Someone they went through *such* trouble to conceal. Well, I wish you all joy of your newfound status."

"But what do I have to do?"

"Anything he tells you. And don't think your blue blood can fend off a beating. Or even a rape."

"Rape?"

"You seem very ignorant, Sajitteh, or else you've lived a sheltered life. Rape is like making love, except you do it with hate. Sound familiar? Maybe you've experimented with your twin? Another perquisite of the psychic link?"

But Sajit was thinking of the space between spaces. How he and Tijas had melded into one attenuated entity, in a place without dimensions. He ached. "I don't care what becomes of me now," he said.

"I daresay you will avoid ill treatment," Mikkálu said, "as I always do. With my attitude. He likes attitude. His corpse lovers never give him any."

It was then than Sajit saw a bruise on Mikkálu's arm, and he knew there was pain behind his bluster. *My mother loved him — believed he'd do anything for her, including killing one of* me, he thought.

"I won't be having so many privileges anymore," Mikkálu said. "I might need your help."

Sajit put out his hand and the boys touched fingertips. "All right," he said. "Take me to see him."

***

A room in Alykh: candied, rosy light, lush, cushiony music of shimmerviols, a bedfloat. The woman who was once a goddess was not cloaked in shadow. She wore an extravagant kaleidofur loosely wrapped, like a blanket, which blinked in and out with her heartbeat. She wore a hairpiece fashioned from arachnid silk, a living spiderweb that wove and unwove itself in the air around her.

Lang viHurek had made a deal after all. The tourist board would reconstruct the temple as a sensuality theme park, and the goddess would be chair of the advisory board.

In a tennight she and her former acolytes had taken over a row of shophouses in the whores' district of Aírang. The word was already getting out that the practitioners of this establishment had skilled that were, literally, of mythic proportions. Sex rituals of a dead planet. The temple would be for fooling *dorezdas;* this alley would be the real thing.

The door sang out, "A client."

"Come!" she said, with a cunningly modulated half-laugh in her voice.

There was an old man in the doorway, dressed in the manner of Urna — this, already, was beginning to seem quaint. The old man had a baby in his arms, and a battered whisperlyre hung about his waist.

"I am —"

"Arbát," said Éluma. "I try to remember all our former congregation."

Arbát said, "I've done many terrible things, goddess. And so have you."

"Who is the child?" But she knew already.

"Look at him. Do you feel *abomination?* Does your blood curdle, do you want to hurl stones?"

Éluma said, "Yes. I do feel ... a twinge of horror." *Harám, harám,* her mind cried out, *and yet* —

"I took the doppling kit from the ruined home of Ina desAreon. There was enough of a charge left, enough DNA left on this old whisperlyre to unlock it, to seed it. There may be more than one charge left, in fact. The copy may be imperfect. I cannot tell. They were only designed to function once. Yet I could not resist, goddess."

"I've failed as a goddess, and I've failed as a mother," Éluma said.

"But now there's a chance to start over. Hold him. Look into his eyes."

The old musician placed the child in the crook of her arm. The child's eyes opened and he gurgled. His eyes ... *my eyes,* she thought.

"Don't you see, Éluma-without-a-Clan? This is a new world. We are other people now, though we wear the same flesh and blood. We can begin again. And why not begin by naming him?"

"Jatis," she said without hesitation.

"Look! Is the baby smiling?"

***

There were no displacement plates in the tunnels and it was a long trudge — perhaps two klomets — to get to an antique door that opened by applying physical pressure to a lever, and which swung open like the lid of a box.

On the other side, there were the normal cabins, displacement plates, holosculpt environments. But no virtual windows.

Looking on the overcosm drives men mad ... Sajit knew this well ... it was something every child knows.

"Quick, come," Mikkálu said. He took Sajit's hand and lead him through more plates —

More cabins of frozen people — childsoldiers, accountants, chefs, jugglers, carelessly stacked like toys, on shelves, waiting to come to life —

And finally the Child Collector's chamber.

It was a kind of inferno. The floor was strewn with servocorpses, maimed, decapitated, tortured, some simulating death (though they were dead anyway), others groaning, clawing their way around the room. And there was Gharém, whom Sajit had last seen decked in a ceremonial uniform. Now he was naked and in the throes of —

Sajit remembered what Tijas had said about spying on Arbát.

Bursting the milkpod.

"My Lord," Mikkálu said, ignoring the ghastly spectacle, "I've brought you Sajit-without-a-Clan, as you ordered."

The Child Collector stood, sweaty and disheveled, and and turned a beady gaze on Sajit. Meanwhile, Mikkálu was setting the chamber to order, switching off the corpses and putting them away in a closet that irised open in the wall, restoring the room to a more formal environment, with a starscape and dragon-shaped nebulae.

"So you're my new equerry," said Kyar Garém.

"I don't even know what an equerry is, sir," Sajit said.

"It's an Old Earth position. Something to do with horses."

"Horses?"

"They look like hippopters, but without wings. Before there were starships, people rode them. How they rode horses to the stars then, I know not. It is a myth — like the homeworld of the heart itself."

Gharém summoned a chairfloat and sat cross-legged in the air.

"Master Gharém," Mikkálu said, "shall I leave you to torment your new plaything?"

Gharém made to slap the boy's face, and Mikkálu had genuine terror in his eyes, for just a second, before reverting to his cocky self.

"You'd never, Lord." he said. "Why, you know I could slice off your hand with a single glance."

"As well you could, Mikkálu. But you won't. You've been well programmed. You couldn't resist my authority no matter how hard you tried. This other one, on the other hand...."

"Don't harm him," Mikkálu said. "This one, the Inquestors themselves are looking out for."

"Indeed. You have, perhaps, a great destiny, Sajit-without-a-Clan. But to reach it, you must first pass through the fire. It is as they say in the song — the one about the million boys who dream."

"Yes, Lord Gharém," Sajit said.

"But first, a gift."

Even Mikkálu gasped. The Child Collector, it seemed, did not *give* anyone anything.

He hopped off the chairfloat and waddled over to the closet which parted a little at his subvoked command; he reached in a pulled out a whisperlyre. "It is a rustic thing," he said, "which I acquired on ... some world we wiped out. The tree it was carved from is of a species that is no more. Its whispers are the sighs of worlds *fallen beyond* forever."

He tossed the whisperlyre over. When Sajit's fingers touched the dead wood he could feel it living. It had a soul. It had been waiting since its world's destruction for the touch that would give life to all it remembered. Already it had started to whisper, sussuration of sympathetic strings tuning itself to the vibrations of his hands, his heart.

The Child Collector climbed back on the chairfloat. "Now, Mikkálu," he said, "I've demoted you to a common dogsbody. And for the mess you made of my collection, I should probably have beaten you, although we are far too refined to *actually* beat people, are we not?"

"The threat is bad enough, Master Gharém," said Mikkálu with a mock groan. Yet Sajit could tell that the threat was not entirely empty.

"So you shall not have the privilege of attending me when I rest," said Gharém. "Instead, I shall have ... *Sajit* ... sing me to sleep. I have been told that the whole universe will know his songs one day. Well, *I'm* going to be the first. And if his songs do not please me, perhaps ... the universe will *not* know them."

And he laughed — the laughter of evil villains — from which Sajit realized that this was a vulnerable and insecure old man after all. Like Arbát. And not as evil as he himself would have wanted to appear.

"Well now, my Princeling-without-a-Planet, let me hear about loss, about desire, and about longing for that which can never come," said the Child Collector, "so that my own pain can be stilled a little. And you, Mikállu, you miscreant — don't come back unless you are summoned."

All right, Sajit told himself. "Since you spoke of it, Lord Gharém, I'll sing the song called *Asheveraín,* a song about the Homeworld of the Heart.

He thought of his two mothers and his two fathers. Dead, perhaps. Or stranded in a world they could never return to. His sisters. He didn't even know if they had survived the people bins' planetfall. Guilt and sadness came all at once. He clenched back his tears.

Tijas! If I could only summon you ... even a shadow's shadow ... for though we inhabit separate flesh, we are one person.

He began to weep, and as his tears dripped on the strings of the whisperlyre their whispering became a shimmering, fluctuating harmony ...

***

... and Tijas went to the forest beside the village with the clearing of singing moons, because he knew it would remind him of Sajit.

He went alone. As Sajit had.

But it was not the same, because when Sajit used to go there, there was no Tijas. And when Tijas came it was not as some village boy dreaming of stars and moons, but as Princeling able to buy them.

And though he walked into the clearing alone, a small group of attendants stood just out of reach and out of sight. And after a moment in the clearing, he told himself, he would go back to his courtiers. And plan his voyage.

That was how it had been when the last Princeling of Urna came to the clearing, hoping to catch a glimpse of his son.

Three of the moons were full. It was a clear night, and chill; the perfect time to imagine the singing of the moons.

Tijas had a whisperlyre with him; they had found one somewhere in the palace, in the museum collections which had somehow remained intact.

It was a pristine instrument. He did not know what others remained in the museum, but he would restore them all one day. And create an army of bards.

He tuned the whisperlyre beneath a tree.

What did the moons say?

You are not who you think you are.

That was what they had told Sajit ... a memory whose edge he had touched, in the space between spaces.

He sounded a note, the note that is called *dha,* which sometimes called *thunder.* On this whisperlyre *dha* was the fundamental tone and when he touched it, the tree itself trembled and he felt the sympathetic vibration deep inside himself.

He sang:

Pu eyáh chítarans hyemadh?
Where is the homeworld of the heart?

A question asked a million times by a million poets of the Dispersal of Man.

Sajit! he cried out in his mind. *Up there, somewhere, perhaps in stasis, silenced by the space between spaces.*

Shenom na chítarans hyemadhá
We yearn for the heart's homeworld ...

It was an ancient song that children know. A melody so simple a beginner can strum it, yet so subtle that only a great artist can do it justice.

***

Sajit sang:

am plánzhet ka dhand-erúden

We wept for the dead Earth ...

and saw that Gharém was already asleep on his chairfloat, and snoring a little. The room, cleared of corpses, was no longer a brothel of the dead.

But he was not singing for anyone who claimed to own him.

He was singing to Tijas.

Or rather, *with* Tijas.

For though time and space are relative, there is synchronicity in souls, and in the spaces between spaces all points in spacetime are adjacent.

And so, for a second that seemed to last forever — he felt his twin, and knew his twin felt *him.*

Tijas! he cried out. And heard his doppling's answer even as he cried out: *Sajit!*

It lasted only a moment after all.

But the moment had been long enough for him to realize ...

Tijas! There's another —

***

—one in here with us, Tijas answered.

***

"Look! Is the baby smiling?"

— Bangkok, Korat, New York, Munich, Berlin, Olomouc, Vienna, Bratislava, Bangkok 2015-2020

Afterword
Forty Years On

In 1985, the last Inquestor novel was published by Bantam. It was, in some ways, an ill-fated series. My first professional sale, *The Thirteenth Utopia,* published in the April 1979 issue of *Analog,* had introduced the world of the High Inquestors, and the story made quite a splash, missing a Hugo nomination by only two votes, I'm told; the series itself came into being in spurts, a short story here, a novelette there, mostly in the pages of *Asimov's Science Fiction Magazine,* thanks to the energy and encouragement of George Scithers.

In 1982 came *Light on the Sound,* a full length novel in this universe, followed swiftly by its sequel, *The Throne of Madness.* I was young. The stories were getting a lot of attention. People I admired greatly were praising them: Orson Scott Card, Theodore

Sturgeon, Robert Bloch ... and there were those reviews: the Washington *Post, Publishers Weekly,* the L.A. *Times.* In 1983, I was a rising star of science fiction, but a few years later, everything changed. It looked as if this trilogy was going to be the first step in a slew of trilogies and I'd have a series as popular as any of the others at the time to which it was being compared ... but it was not to be.

First, my publisher, *Timescape,* went through a bit of a reorganization and basically downsized, leaving the third volume of my trilogy in limbo. In other words, there were two volumes of a trilogy in print, but they were sorting cutting off the *Timescape* brand and therefore not going to publish the third book.

Then, the publisher who took me up next, Bantam, wanted to do the whole trilogy, but since the first two books had gone out of print and were from a different publisher, they wanted a new approach, so I suggested taking all the Inquestor novelettes and short stories that were in print, and weaving them together with a framing story that could be a different way of introducing the final volume of the trilogy. And so *Utopia Hunters* came about.

Utopia Hunters introduced characters from different timelines who had never appeared in the first two volumes of the trilogy, and so *The Darkling Wind* became *both* the third volume of a trilogy with the first two books from *Timescape,* and the second volume of a two-book series beginning with *Utopia Hunters* and carrying on the story of the characters who first appeared there as well. *The Darkling Wind* was therefore a *fat* book, because it was the third volume of one series *and* the second volume of another, all merged together.

These four books are, as far as I know, the *only* example of a *five-book trilogy in four volumes.* It was a level of mathematical complexity beyond my publishers, who as soon as they reprinted the first two books in the series, put the second two out of print.

During their heyday as it were — at no time was the entire series ever all available at the same time — and never from the same publisher.

These decisions made by executives in New York were based on big picture issues — the lives and deaths of entire lines of books, not the survival of a single midlist author. But effectively, the decisions reduced the books to a special-interest commodity, sought after only by true believers. And I rather despaired of science fiction and as my readers know, I drifted towards other fields ... and in the early 21st century, I found myself doing more and more music (my first profession) so that my writing career of 50 plus novels and books seemed more and more like a side trip on the convoluted journey of my artistic career.

***

So ... time goes by. Three decades in fact. Once in a while, I would get letters. They are of the "Whatever happened to..." variety mostly. I discover that there's a small number of people with battered, wornout copies of these books. In the words of one of them, "I've lent them out so many times that they've fallen apart ... I wish I could get new copies."

I had all the rights back by then, so a couple of years ago I entered the brave new world of print on demand, turned myself into a my own publishing company, and quietly slipped everything I ever wrote back into print. For the first time, all four the books were available at the same time, and all from the same publisher. What's more, there was no middle man between author and reader. I was like a bard singing for my supper at the dinner table of a mediaeval lord. The history of publishing had cycled back to its beginnings.

It didn't matter than only one or two copies sold each month; it was like free money. Those people trying to replace their wornout copies were keeping the series alive.

At some point, these same people started asking for more.

***

There is a lot more to say in this world. I realized that after it lay to one side for three decades. For each doorway I opened, I left a dozen more still sealed.

My first thought was to get back into the series via some "juveniles" as they used be called, with young protagonists — shorter novels like Anne McCaffrey's *Harper Hall* books which develop alongside the heftier Pern books. This is why I started looking at the character of Sajit, who we first meet in the short story *The Rainbow King* which is reprinted in this first issue of *Inquestor Tales*. My first thought was to write a simple, brief story of Sajit's childhood — a childhood talked about briefly in the existing canon — a dirt poor street kid, neglected, abused, clinging to music and finally pulled into the Inquestor world through an accidental encounter with the young Inquestor Elloran.

But as I thought about telling his story, which would have been an easy story to tell, because nothing could be simpler for me than to weave the same tapestry I've woven before to the same pattern; the pleasure city of Alykh in a way is sort of a mega-Bangkok, so all I'd have to do is sit where I am and close my eyes and start imagining just a little bit. But then a different character began speaking to me, and I had to find a way of reconciling the two, somehow. So, without spoiling it for you, I'll just say that the pathway led in a more convoluted direction than I originally thought it would.

Taboos and Sexualities in the Dispersal of Man

The stories in the Inquestor series first appeared in *Analog* and in *Isaac Asimov's Science Fiction* magazine. The time was the 70s, and through the first half of the 80s. Emerging from the "free love" era, science fiction was still a little constrained, because most of its authors were still very white, very male, mostly straight, and somewhat suburban; diversities were only just emerging. Indeed, I was at one time pretty much the only Asian science fiction writer to penetrate this exclusive world, and the few women who were there were often quite ... unorthodox. They were known by the extraordinary sobriquet of *femmefans.* When I entered the community, it was still very much a male-dominated one, and the great science fiction of the Golden Age which preceded my advent was also male dominated. For a long time after I entered the field, many of the most powerful works had few women in them, or had women who existed only to serve tea to the important scientists who were often the protagonists.

Writing mostly in *Asimov's* which at the time was a bit retro in some ways, one didn't really break too many sexual taboos, but the novels began to sneak away from this.

I was on a panel with, among others, David Gerrold, well known writer of the *Star Trek* episode "The Trouble with Tribbles" and I casually mentioned a brief scene in *The Throne of Madness* "where two boys make love in a desert of powdered chocolate."

To my surprise, David became very interested in this and demanded to know the page number. I suddenly realized that despite science fiction's staid reputation, it was actually one of the only genres in which one could explore things that were not talked about in whitebread American society. I was rather embarrassed to tell him that the entire sex scene was over in a single sentence.

Books and stories that really blasted holes in these taboos were often written by women — I'm thinking of Ursula le Guin's *The Left Hand of Darkness* or Joanna Russ's *When It Changed.* I'll never forget that in one of Vonda McIntyre's future civilizations, asking a stranger "Is there anything I can do?" meaning "Do you want sex?" was a matter of normal politeness, and refusing anyone of any gender was viewed as a bit rude.

As the Inquestor series gradually left the magazines and grew into novels, I started to evolve a picture of the sexuality of that universe, which follows completely different assumptions from most modern cultures. The Inquestors themselves, rather like Imperial Romans, have no inhibitions. On some planets, servocorpses perform menial tasks and are also freely used for the satisfaction of any sexual urge however "perverted" — much as slaves were during the Roman period. But the fact that they are corpses, and presumably lacking in real feelings, gives this institutionalized necrophilia a kind of macabre justification.

It is fair then to say that in Inquestral societies, apart from extremely isolated worlds or worlds deliberately keeping themselves apart from mainstream culture, there really are no sexual taboos as such, especially when such acts are performed with corpses. Between humans, there is a hierachy of constraint; from no constraint at all for the highest, the Inquestors, down to a more hidebound sexuality for the lower orders (who are still permitted anything they want as long as it is with the dead.)

In *Homeworld of the Heart,* the Inquestor universe toys with autoeroticism of a kind that can't be found in our world — a powerful love for a manufactured clone of oneself — even though Sajit and Tijas are perhaps too immature to really understand these urges. They are really somewhat inchoate; whether the urges are finally acted upon is a matter that isn't answered in this book.

It's not only sexual mores that are different in this universe; the casual assumption that children are the only possible soldiers because they have the best reflexes, the implicit caste system dictated by clan-names (caste by Inquestral fiat rather than by birth), and the basic premise of Inquestral philosophy — that utopias must be eliminated because they will lead to stagnation.

Which brings us to a a widespread taboo on Urna and many nearby worlds, one that was found in Stone Age societies (even to this day) on earth, but which most civilized people find absurd — the taboo against twins and by extension dopplings. It seems as ridiculous as a taboo against left-handedness, but both taboos were once commonplace in early societies.

When interviewed by Darrell Schweitzer a very long time ago, I said that I wanted to create a universe of incredible beauty *and* brutality in the Inquestor series. One of the ways of doing this is to extrapolate from primitive earth societies, supposing that they had powerful future technologies. The amount of brutality possible increases exponentially.

Beauty is another matter. It is in the eye of the beholder.

Speeding Towards the End of ... What?

This book looks increasingly like part one of a trilogy. Or at the very least, a "dilogy". Sounds a bit filthy, eh? Bilogy? "Duology" is a word I've seen sometimes, but etymologically it's a bit uncomfortable. It's clear, anyway, that Sajit's side story will end up being told in more than one book.

Could the Inquestors series, three decades later, suddenly spawn a whole new spinoff trilogy? I had thought, perhaps one book about the childhood of

Sajit, and one book about how the High Inquest came to be, centering on the Lady Varuneh.

In other words, I was thinking of doing two more books, one because so many mysteries are hinted at in the series already about the origins of the High Inquest — but I did not myself know the answers — the other because the character of Sajit, the perpertual outsider who watches history unfold with clear-eyed *gravitas,* has always been one I felt deeply sympathetic to.

More sympathetic than normal, even. Perhaps, on some level, I see myself in this character. Someone so conflicted in identity as to sometimes fracture into two (or more) individuals. Someone who has moved from civilization to civilization during a curious, eventful childhood.

I noticed that I have something in common with one of my childhood idols, Chip Delany (Samuel R., that is) — which is that when I started publishing, my protagonists tended to be about ten years younger than me, but as I aged, they did, too. In writing about Sajit I seem to have returned to my own beginnings, though I seem to be looking at them from a old man's viewpoint. It's strange.

I never dreamed that Sajit would split into two. It happened when the character took on a life of its own, much different from the flashbacks and brief descriptions mentioned in the 1980s tales of the High Inquest.

In those stories, Sajit was a child of a slum: today he would be sniffing glue or fleecing tourists in some huge, vaguely oriental-bazaar-like city. But when I started writing this novel, there was a Sajit with a completely different background, and a completely unconnected childhood, yet I recognized that this childhood was a true as the random snippets that have existed for forty years (the Inquestor Universe first surfaced in *Analog* in 1979, so that's really how old it is).

Not only did I have to write about this childhood while not rendering the previous stories un-canon — I had to reconcile the more than one past — find out how they became one *person's* past.

And that, you see, is why this story while take longer than one novel. Because it has to happen without time travel or alternate histories. I can't cheat.

Okay I can, but only when making the rules; once the rules are in place, there's no more cheating....

And it looks like there's *another* Sajit as well.

A Schism with Rome

In *Inquestor Tales,* I reprinted the story that began the whole series — and it's the original version that became non-canonical by the inclusion of a single Latin phrase:

pater noster qui es in inferno

You see, the story that set all this in motion was a one-off. Indeed, it had something to do with a big rollercoaster somewhere near Richmond, Virginia, in an amusement part called King's Dominion. It was about a 90 minute drive from Alexandria, Virginia-not-Egypt, and I would often go there to let off steam. The rollercoaster was called *Rebel Yell* and I was younger then, I used to love rollercoasters, indeed I collected them.

I wasn't sure whether I would even call them *Inquestors.* My first thought was that there would be a clear line of succession from the inquistion and thus they would have to be inquisitors. Since this was a 12,000 word novelette, not a five-book series with thousands of pages of backstory and language notes, and since science fiction is supposed to be *show, don't tell,* dropping a misquote from the Lord's Prayer was the fastest way to provide a few millennia of speculative backstory to the character of Ton Davaryush.

So, the original story, *The Thirteenth Utopia,* was at first tethered to the history of the Roman Catholic Church, with the reader's images of the Inquisition providing context to its events.

However, the tale, as Tolkien would put it, "grew in the telling." It didn't just grow in one direction. *The Thirteenth Utopia* was not the beginning, nor even the middle, or the end. It was a snapshot from somewhere in a massive continuum that was slowly coming into focus, a piece here, a piece there. Even now, forty years after the *The Thirteenth Utopia* came out, more fragments are emerging. Like the fact that there was more than one Sajit.

(Sajit — the poetic voice of a million worlds and twenty millennia — well, how could he be *other* than a multi-body person? But that is a different essay.)

As the Inquestor universe grew into its past as well as its future, it became clear that it needed to be unmoored from Earth.

My choice to deviate from the term *inquisitor* and to invent a new word proved to be liberating. (And odd therefore that in some translations, like the French version, the High Inquest has been rendered as the Inquisition after all.)

The root word *inquest,* in any case, adds the implication of a *coroner's inquest* to the word. That the rich, lush, brilliantly colored universe laced with savagery that I created and which the Inquestors scrutinize with such ruthlessness is not only vibrantly alive, but also already dead.

And in the end Catholicism didn't seem to be the right coloration for the Inquestors. Certainly, they have *guilt* — but not in the same way. The Inquestors have the ostentation, self-righteousness and intellectual gymnastics characteristic of a certain segment of the Catholic Church especially during the periods in history when people really believed in a physical heaven — and even more in a physical hell. But the Inquestors don't have a God. Or do they? That is something that may be revealed in a later novel in this endless "trilogy".

So please, allow me to thank all those who have continued on this journey with me. It is amazing to revisit the beginnings of my science fiction career, and more amazing still to discover that my youthful self has more stories to tell me.

It's like a time-loop story when you meet an older version of yourself who tells you things you need to know in order to grow to become that older self.

Except in this case, it's the other way round.

— Somtow

An Appeal to My Readers

This novel was made possible because a few dozen people became my supporters by joining this website: www.patreon.com/spsomtow.

I'm no longer doing these books with the backing of a vast New York publishing conglomerate. It's pretty much do-it-yourself, with all the labor-intensiveness, snatching time away from money-making activities, and sloppy trying to proofread one's own copy implies.

If a few dozen more people would sign up — or a few hundred — my ability to resume my science fiction career would be much enhanced. So, please consider it.

Supporters get to read all my books chapter by chapter — in their unenhanced, inaccurately proofred and yet-to-be refined incarnations — right as they come out of my head. They get Christmas presents (though I am habitually late with them). You can join for as little a $2 a month — though hopefully you will be able to do a higher level.

About the Author

The most well-known expatriate Thai in the world
— *International Herald Tribune*

Once referred to by the International Herald Tribune as "the most well-known expatriate Thai in the world," Somtow Sucharitkul is no longer an expatriate, since he has returned to Thailand after five decades of wandering the world. He is best known as an award winning novelist and a composer of operas.

Born in Bangkok, Somtow grew up in Europe and was educated at Eton and Cambridge. His first career was in music and in the 1970s he acquired a reputation as a revolutionary composer, the first to combine Thai and Western instruments in radical new sonorities. Conditions in the arts in the region at the time proved so traumatic for the young composer that he suffered a major burnout, emigrated to the United States, and reinvented himself as a novelist.

His earliest novels were in the science fiction field but he soon began to cross into other genres. In his 1984 novel Vampire Junction, he injected a new literary inventiveness into the horror genre, in the words of Robert Bloch, author of *Psycho*, "skillfully combining the styles of Stephen King, William Burroughs, and the author of the Revelation to John." *Vampire Junction* was voted one of the forty all-time greatest horror books by the Horror Writers' Association, joining established classics like *Frankenstein* and *Dracula*.

In the 1990s Somtow became increasingly identified as a uniquely Asian writer with novels such as the semi-autobiographical *Jasmine Nights*. He won the World Fantasy Award, the highest accolade given in the world of fantastic literature, for his novella *The Bird Catcher*. His seventy-seven books have sold about two million copies world-wide.

After becoming a Buddhist monk for a period in 2001, Somtow decided to refocus his attention on the country of his birth, founding Bangkok's first international opera company and returning to music, where he again reinvented himself, this time as a neo Asian neo-Romantic composer. The Norwegian govern-ment commissioned his song cycle Songs Before Dawn for the 100th Anniversary of the Nobel Peace Prize, and he composed at the request of the government of Thailand his *Requiem: In Memoriam 9/11* which was dedicated to the victims of the 9/11 tragedy.

According to London's Opera magazine, "in just five years, Somtow has made Bangkok into the operatic hub of Southeast Asia." His operas on Thai themes, *Madana, Mae Naak,* and *Ayodhya,* have been well received by international critics. His opera, *The Silent Prince,* was premiered in 2010 in Houston, and, *Dan no Ura,* premiered in Thailand in the 2013 season. Since then he has composed many more stage works including the acclaimed fantasy-based opera *The Snow Dragon* (premiered in Milwaukee in 2015) and seven operas in the *DasJati* sequence which aims to put all ten of the iconic *Ten Lives of the Buddha* into music drama form.

He is increasingly in demand as a conductor specializing in opera and in the late-romantic composers like Mahler. His repertoire runs the entire gamut from Monteverdi to Wagner. His work has been especially lauded for its stylistic authenticity and its lyricism. The orchestra he founded in Bangkok, the Siam Philhar-monic, has mounted the first complete Mahler cycle in the region.

He was the first recipient of Thailand's "Distinguished Silpathorn" award, given for an artist who has made and continues to make a major impact on the region's culture, from Thailand's Ministry of Culture.

In 2017 he was awarded the European Cultural Achievement Award by the Europa KulturForm, citing his building of bridges between Asian and Western cultures.

Books by S.P. Somtow

General Fiction
The Shattered Horse
Jasmine Nights
Forgetting Places
The Other City of Angels (aka *Bluebeard's Castle)*
The Stone Buddha's Tears

Dark Fantasy
The Timmy Valentine Series:
Vampire Junction
Valentine
Vanitas
Vampire Junction Special Edition
Moon Dance
Darker Angels
The Vampire's Beautiful Daughter

Science Fiction
Starship & Haiku
Mallworld
The Ultimate Mallworld
The Ultimate, Ultimate, Ultimate Mallworld
Chronicles of the High Inquest:
Light on the Sound
The Darkling Wind
The Throne of Madness
Utopia Hunters
Homeworld of the Heart
Chroniques de l'Inquisition - Volume 1 (omnibus)
Chroniques de l'Inquisition - Volume 2 (omnibus)
Inquestor Tales One: The Singing Moons

Inquestor Tales Two: A Woman Cloaked in Shadow
Inquestor Tales Three: The Child Collector
Inquestor Tales Four: The Space Between Spaces

The Aquiliad Series:
- *Aquila in the New World*
- *Aquila and the Iron Horse*
- *Aquila and the Sphinx*

Fantasy

The Riverrun Trilogy:
- *Riverrun*
- *Armorica*
- *Yestern*

The Riverrun Trilogy (omnibus)
The Fallen Country
Wizard's Apprentice
The Snow Dragon (omnibus)

Media Tie-in

The Alien Swordmaster
Symphony of Terror
The Crow - Temple of Night
Star Trek: Do Comets Dream?

Chapbooks

Fiddling for Waterbuffaloes
I Wake from a Dream of a Drowned Star City
A Lap Dance with the Lobster Lady
Compassion — Two Perspectives
The Bird Catcher

Libretti

Mae Naak
Ayodhya
Madana

Dan no Ura
Helena Citronova
The Snow Dragon
Dasjati:
- *Temiya - The Silent Prince*
- *Sama - The Faithful Son*
- *Bhuridat - The Dragon Lord*
- *Mahosadha - Architect of Dreams*
- *Nemiraj - Chariot of Heaven*
- *Prince Vessantara*

Collections
My Cold Mad Father
Fire from the Wine Dark Sea
Chui Chai (Thai)
Nova (Thai)
The Pavilion of Frozen Women
Dragon's Fin Soup
Tagging the Moon
Face of Death (Thai)
Other Edens
S.P. Somtow's The Great Tales (Thai)
Terror Nova (in press)
Terror Antiqua (in press)
Alien Heresies (in press)

Essays, Poetry and Miscellanies
Opus Fifty
A Certain Slant of "I" (in press)
Sonnets about Serial Killers
Opera East
Victory in Vienna (ed.)
Three Continents (ed.)
Nirvana Express
Caravaggio x 2
The Maestro's Noctuary

www.ingramcontent.com/pod-product-compliance
Lightning Source LLC
Chambersburg PA
CBHW020530310726
48979CB00014B/2274/J

* 9 7 8 1 9 4 0 9 9 9 4 4 9 *